THE NINTH AVATAR

THE NINTH AVATAR

WHEN THE SLAIN MARCH, PROPHECY WILL BE FULFILLED.

TODD NEWTON

TRAPDOOR BOOKS ⊠ LYONS, COLORADO

Trapdoor Books is an imprint of Trapdoor Publishing.
First Edition

Discovered by Rowan Matney
Edited by Paul McCarthy
Cover & Book Design by Sue Campbell
Cover Illustration by Pete Thompson, Atomhawk Design Ltd.
Map by Katie MacGillivary Nichols
Author Photo by Stephanie Romine

Cataloging in Publication Data available.

ISBN-13: 978-0-9842070-3-9 (hardcover)
ISBN-10: 0-9842070-3-1 (hardcover)

ISBN-13: 978-0-9842070-4-6 (trade paperback)
ISBN-10: 0-9842070-4-x (trade paperback)

ISBN-13: 978-0-9842070-5-3 (e-book)
ISBN-10: 0-9842070-5-8 (e-book)

Post Office Box 1989
Lyons, CO 80540-1989
www.trapdoorbooks.com

Printed in United States of America

FOR MICAH
THE ONE WHO
NEVER STOPPED BELIEVING.

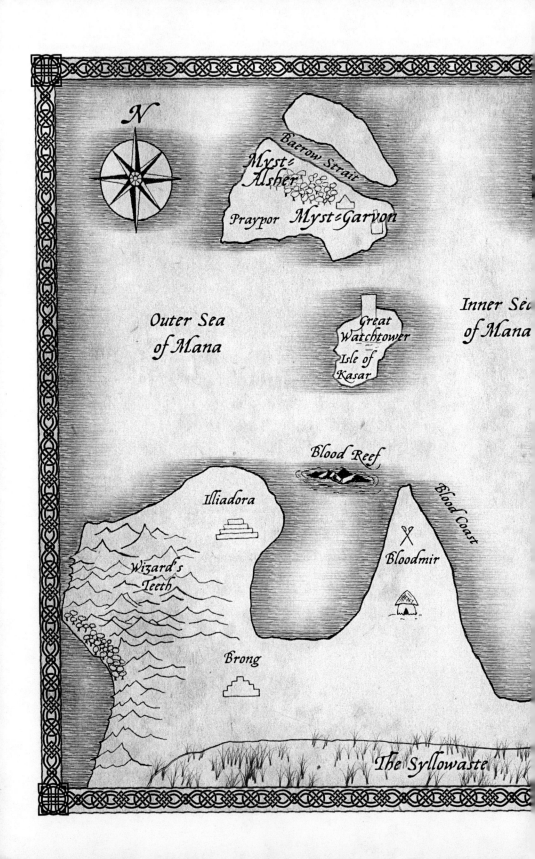

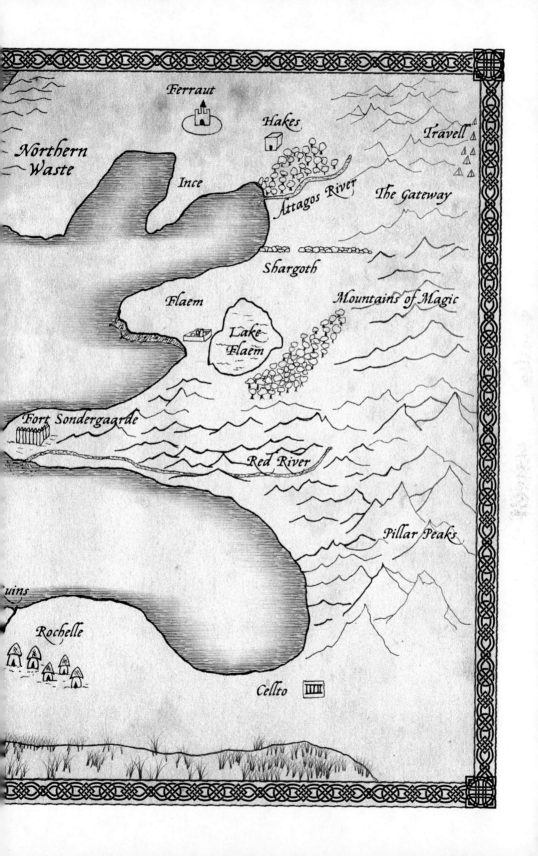

PROLOGUE

THE CARRION SOLDIERS WAITED, HIDDEN, FOR THE SIGNAL to advance while Zion surveyed the skirmish at Bloodmir from a hilltop. Neither Brong nor Rochelle could claim victory as momentum waned by turns for each army. Despite the raging pandemonium of battle, the noise failed to disturb the Commander or his mount.

A handful of officers surrounded Zion. The rhythmic breaths of their horses kept time while clangs of steel and cries from the nearby armies punctuated a sadistic harmony. He allowed the lethargic fray to continue, confident his army's patience would last a moment longer. One loose end remained before Zion announced his presence.

His gaze shifted to the beaten form a few feet away as the soldier struggled to his knees.

"Rise," said Zion. He did not allow his tone to waver, despite the subordinate's importance. All knew the price of betrayal. Shielding his torso with an arm, the soldier rose and halted within kicking distance from the Great Commander's stirrups. Zion barely recognized the broken face, covered with black Carrion blood and red sand. Familiarity no longer mattered.

Zion wrapped his hands around the horns implanted in the soldier's temples. "You will serve me no more," he said, then tore the horns out.

Screams erupted from the betrayer's mouth and his temples sprayed blood. The black liquid arced as if to chase the horns, but faltered as he collapsed. With both palms pressed to his temples, the soldier fought through his last moments of Carrion life. His wails, already loud enough to catch the attention of a few Brong troops, intensified as the Great Commander squeezed the horns. When they shattered, it brought a new description of misery from their previous owner.

"See what awaits those who turn their backs on the darkness," Zion whispered as the cries died down. He flicked his hands at the body to rid himself of the viscous mess, then raised an arm to signal the attack.

Messengers relayed the signal and, all around the battlefield, the Carrion army came alive. Beastly grunts and officers alike licked their blades and howled in the throes of their bloodlust. As the eager Carrion legions cleared cover and advanced, they surrounded the stalemate between Brong and Rochelle before the human soldiers could react.

The unlucky fringes — those already in retreat or wounded — died first, overcome by the speed of Zion's soldiers. It took little time for panic to spread through the field. Those who dropped their weapons met uncaring opponents. The Carrion army granted no quarter as they sealed off any hope of escape. Brong soldiers in red accepted an unspoken trust with those clad in the gray of Rochelle. They turned to the common enemy and fought together for survival rather than glory, something the Commander hadn't counted on. The late and fleeting effort entertained him.

Bloodmir's crimson sands, dyed from numerous battles between the old rivals, darkened a shade deeper as Zion's legions overcame the already weary combatants. As the dust settled and the Carrion grunts culled the wounded, less than a hundred from each side remained alive to surrender.

Zion's smile spread behind his visor as he ordered capture of the survivors. They would wish for death before the end, and then they would be his to command. He delighted in the carnage, but would not stay for the transformations — that tedious work he left to the officers.

Victory over the weak armies Brong and Rochelle proved the Carrion's true potential. As Zion's elation died away, a runner came near and dropped to its knees.

"Great Commander, the wizards of Illiadora have observed your victory," said the messenger, its eyes averted in respect. "They ask now if their involvement is still required."

Zion gazed at the scout with disinterest. The wizards, too squeamish to fly the short distance and watch, forced his army to waste time with relayed messages from the oracle stones. Zion digested the message, angered by the word *required*. Did these men honestly think he needed their assistance?

"If they delay any further," Zion replied, "their fate shall be the same as this rabble."

Part of him wished the wizards would attempt to break faith; not much would please him more than an excuse to rip the still-beating heart from a mage who called himself "The Invincible."

"Yes, Great Commander." The scout bent forward to press its small horns to the ground, then dashed back down the hill. Zion watched the messenger race away with a swell of pride for his creation. No human in the known world could run as fast or far as his Carrion scouts — he'd made sure of it.

"Great One," said an officer, "we should move further east for a better view of Rochelle."

Zion nodded his assent and took up his reins. With one final glance at the betrayer's corpse, he kicked the flanks of his mount to depart.

∂ℓ℘

ACROSS THE CHANNEL, THE CITY OF ROCHELLE STILL SLEPT. WITH the men away at war, the women and children had no reason to rise early. Morning light brought a glow to the grass rooftops of buildings large and small. The rudimentary structures betrayed a scorn of masonry and looked only a rainstorm away from destruction. Many stood either half-built or half-destroyed already; Zion could not tell which from such a distance.

Like Brong, Rochelle kept to old ways and simple beliefs. Refined metals remained their latest achievement, and its purpose only emboldened the conflict with Brong. Zion laughed at their petty rivalry, proud to be the one to finally quash what hollow words on dozens of treaties never could.

Zion searched the sky for a sign of the magical assault. To the northwest, he spotted a cluster of gold flame. At first it resembled a second sun, but as the spell approached, it spread out and hovered above the city like a rainstorm.

Hundreds of meteors, some the size of a man's head, fell from the swarm. Each missile exploded on impact, showering the city in fiery debris. The ground shook, even across the channel, and the tremors added a third threat to the fire and chaos.

Huts fell in on themselves, engulfed in flames, to trap their panicked occupants. Fleeing mothers disintegrated seconds before the fire consumed their trailing children. Choruses of shrieks rose and fell even as the swarthy people dove into the boiling sea. The golden fireballs continued to assail Rochelle while fissures split the land. Water flooded into the divides and a massive cloud of steam hissed forth to obscure the view.

All at once, the fire storm ceased. The survivors found momentary respite, though the sand around them still burned so hot it would turn to glass as it cooled.

Zion smelled the ashes of the dead carried on the winds and wondered what power it took to wreak this much decimation. When the steam dissipated, he looked across the channel to see a singed and dead Rochelle. Few huts stood, the majority of them still ablaze. He listened to the wounded, so loud they could still be heard from across the channel. The screams echoed through him and further fueled his passion for slaughter.

With a shake of its head, his mount blew a snort to clear ash from its nostrils. Noise and movement broke Zion from his trance just as the runner returned.

"Another plea from the wizards, I assume?" the Commander asked.

The scout nodded, but kept its gazed lowered as before. "Rochelle has been destroyed. The wizards wish to confirm dissolution of the alliance, Great One."

A subordinate knows his place, he thought, unlike those Illiadora wretches. The tentative partnership showed Zion's authority, but if the wizards sided against him later, their potential to bring so much power to bear would threaten his conquest. He would have to preempt their betrayal. Besides, thought the Commander, who needs allies with no stomach for war?

His thirst for carnage still unquenched, Zion turned to give one final command before he retired for the day.

"Kill the wizards."

CHAPTER 1 – *Starka*

THE FIT CAME SUDDENLY UPON STARKA AS SHE KNELT FOR morning devotions. At first it manifested as an uncontrollable shaking of her hands. When the pain began, the girl's eyes shot open. Her throat constricted; all air choked out in gasps. Every muscle tensed as she fought for breath and clawed at the bedcovers in a desperate effort to contain it. Concentration eluded her and the vision pressed its way into Starka's mind.

Waves of pain and spasms wracked her body like no prophecy had before. An Eight-Horned Beast, a massive bulk of flesh and bone knotted together, rose above the land. With its presence came darkness enough to blanket the world.

Naked on a barren field, Starka could only watch as the Beast approached. Its many eyes studied her hungrily. Frozen in place, unable to flee or scream, the girl felt each chomp of its jaws like sword thrusts through the gut. Starka's skin burned where the Beast licked her, then went ice cold as it drew away. It left her half-consumed, yet Starka did not bleed from her wounds.

Images came quickly as she passed through the Beast's clouded wake. Soldiers fought on a red battlefield. Many died; some surrendered. A man brandished glowing weapons in defiance. Cities burned at the hands of smaller beasts with similar horns. She saw the Beast's rise to power begin and end in the span of a moment. Then all went black.

With the trance ended, Starka's body dropped to the floor. The fall jarred her bones and forced the last of her breath out. She panted, unable to muster the will to move for a time.

Starka blinked to clear the images from her vision, but they persisted as if she had stared into the sun. After feeling returned to her limbs, the girl rolled over and pushed herself up. With her muscles — so alive mere moments before, now heavy as lead — she had to lean against the bed frame to stand. A breeze drifted through the window and chilled her cold sweat even further. She forced her arms up to close the shutters, but continued to shiver.

She stumbled across the room and collapsed in front of her shelf as the desperate search began. The sum of her possessions was tossed aside to find what she needed: a pen, an ink bottle, and parchment. She swept the remnants of breakfast from the table and scrawled the details of her revelation while the images remained fresh.

With trembling hands, Starka fought for enough control to write about the Beast. After she tore and discarded the first two attempts as illegible,

Starka took a deep breath to settle her nerves. The words came easily, but the pen shook again every time she tried to phrase the Beast's touch. To distract herself, Starka tried to create a mental list of items she would need before she left to present the prophecy. She wondered if they would even let her in the Great Cathedral.

She paused in mid-sentence at the thought that they may not even take her, the former prodigy to Seeress Elestia, seriously. Ostracized by the Order after the disappearance of her twin brother, Fandur, Starka remembered their curses well. She mourned his loss even deeper in spite of their accusations. Entire days still passed when she did nothing but cry behind the safety of her door, lost without her only great love in the world.

Incest remained akin to murder in the eyes of the Divine, and even the suspicion could damage a person's standing in the Order. Starka would have rather given up her vows, her faith, even her life before her brother. She told them so in her grief and the priests added blasphemy to the charges.

They couldn't fathom her attachment and assumed the worst. Destroyed inside, Starka still struggled with studies and her routine chores.

She revealed the secrets of their relationship soon after Fandur vanished, though she couldn't bring herself to tell them everything. Honesty might have been valued in cases of innocence, but the priests had cursed her very name after the confession of a single kiss.

Her attention on her hands continued to wane as Starka's gaze returned to the shelf. Keepsakes sat overturned or upset by her frantic hunt for pen and parchment. The few pieces of jewelry her brother left behind caught her eye. Starka choked back a sob of guilt as one hand came up instinctively to feel for the matching necklace.

The only trace found of her brother was his faith symbol, a square cross made of steel that acolytes carried at all times. *Its weight shall remind you of your burden,* the Order decreed. Nothing more had been found after an entire year.

Oh, Alsher, has it been a year already?

Starka gritted her teeth and tried to turn her attention back to the parchment. To pass the gate guards, she would need a veil. At one time they would have fallen on their faces across puddles for her, regardless of any detriment to their person or armor. Starka's name formerly topped the list of priestesses with enough potential to succeed Elestia. Only one or two would achieve the status of Seeress in their lifetime.

Since Fandur's disappearance she cared little for the rhetoric of Myst-Garvon's Priesthood. Orphaned while still in the crib, the Order had wrapped its great arms around Starka and Fandur. They trained in the separate arts of divination and worship from the time each could speak. With the ousting, the cathedrals took away her only reason to live. Her keepsakes, scattered on the shelf, and a meager inheritance to cover her food and the one-room hovel were all she had left.

Starka survived the days through prayer for the mercy of the Divine Female, Alsher. She refused to give up on her beliefs; faith would see her through anything. Perhaps this explained the prophecy, she thought, as her visions had been empty for months. Her devotions also went to Garvon, the Divine Male, for the safety of her brother. Lately, however, she prayed more for the strength to survive without him.

Breathing and eating remained the only easy parts.

She wiped a tear away with her free hand and, again, forced back the admission of his death. Fandur might still be found, stranded somewhere in the world; anything was possible in the places she had never seen. The small allowance she lived on could not provide enough means to search for him. *Not to mention*, she lamented, *I have nowhere to start*.

Months before, she made one earnest attempt. Praypor, the vagrant city only twenty miles away, awakened her to what the real world looked like. She'd given up without even leaving the continent.

After Starka finished writing, she fanned the parchment back and forth to dry the ink. Satisfied, she rolled it up and placed the page inside a protective wooden tube. It would look like an innocuous message to any curious eyes.

The young girl peeled off her moist sleeping gown and stepped out of the garment. She left it on the floor and drew a towel across her skin, then donned clean underclothes. A rough brown robe hung from the bedpost, the last of her clean laundry, and Starka hoped it would be enough to protect her against the chill morning.

She ruled out her priestess robe, an article which the Cathedral never thought to reclaim, as it would bring too much attention. The pristine garment still hung idle beside the mirror and Starka struggled to remember why. Regardless of her outfit, the priests were just as likely to dismiss her prophecy as useless.

With the veil fastened across her nose and mouth, she lifted the hood of the robe to hide her hair. Starka turned to give her home a last glance and took a few deep breaths to steel her resolve.

"Why does it feel like this is the last time I will see this place?" she whispered. Starka checked her disguise one last time in the mirror before she opened the door and stepped outside.

A CRISP BREEZE BLEW OVER THE DEW AND CHILLED HER TO THE bone. So much for protection, she thought. Starka couched the prophecy in the crook of her arms and breathed into her hands. A light mist hung in the air between her home and the Great Cathedral of Myst-Alsher. Despite the cold, she paused a moment to gape in awe as sunlight flashed against its golden rooftop. Then, after averting her eyes from the majesty of her former home, Starka began to walk toward it.

She passed through the gates into the courtyard of the Cathedral without incident, hiding among the other worshippers. As she approached the sanctuary, Starka heard the sweet sound of hymns from the open entrance.

The tide of the crowd carried her through the immense doorway accompanied by a din of hushed tones that drowned out the songs. Though it seemed odd so many people were headed her same direction this early in the morning, Starka ignored it. When she found the same inside the Great Hall, however, her heart began to beat faster. The contents of her prophecy would hardly set the people at ease. She hid it within the folds of her robe and pushed deeper into the sanctuary.

Hundreds of nervous worshippers packed the pews and aisles. Shouts went up as people shoved each other aside and the clergy worked to calm them.

Starka ducked her head and threaded her way through. When she saw Great Priest Wadam at the pulpit, the girl had to stop herself from cursing aloud. A portly and temperamental priest of the Order of Myst-Garvon, Wadam always delivered the worst news. Always emphatic and outspoken, Wadam believed in returning to the fundamentals of Myst-Garvon: strength, resolve, bravery. He likewise scorned the facets of the Divine Female: mercy, forgiveness, love.

Wadam's memory had always been poor for everything else, even to the point of forgetting her name in the middle of Starka's trial. Her eyes narrowed as she noticed the man had a larger hat than last time. *Cardinal* Wadam, she thought.

The large man cleared his throat and spoke to the assembly. "Everyone! Please calm yourselves. Let us recite the Divine Charge."

Starka joined the unison chant on reflex; the words would always remain in her memory. The Charge began as a cacophony of mumbling, but eventually flowed into a single voice.

"We believe in our Holy Trinity: Myst, our beloved and wonderful creator; Garvon, our mighty Divine Male; and Alsher, our beautiful Divine Female."

The crowd paused after each line as they repeated the familiar verses. "We believe that we have been set apart for a purpose. We believe that we are blessed and watched over and that our creator will guide us through all shadows, large and small.

"We believe that all others, those who do not believe in this and those who cannot believe in this will answer to the Creator as we take our seats beside him."

A moment of silence permeated the huge cathedral, as if the people of the crowd all waited to exhale.

"May Myst watch over you," the Cardinal said.

"And bless our breath and faith," answered the crowd.

Wadam passed his hands over the mass to bless them and any chatter ceased. The Cardinal allowed the quiet to hang a moment longer before he spoke again.

"We know many of you are worried for your sisters and daughters, but you need not be afraid. The protection of Myst is upon us."

Starka almost rolled her eyes at the words; they were obviously meant to dismiss the fear rather than address it. If others received her same prophecy and it inspired the same kind of torture she endured then there would, indeed, be reason to worry. She fought back a shudder at the memory of the Beast's touch.

"Now," Wadam continued, "if you know of any more girls who have received ..."

"I have!" Starka blurted the words out before she could think about them. She lifted and brandished the wooden cylinder as if it were the result of a crucial election. The assembled crowd, formerly pressed in close, edged away with frightened stares. Wadam cleared his throat again and for a second time that morning Starka felt naked beneath a piercing gaze.

For a moment Wadam merely stared, nonplussed, from his elevated position. "Come forward, then, dear one, so we may retire to examine you — and your prophecy — properly."

The crowd parted between Starka and the pulpit to allow the hooded and veiled girl to approach. She averted her gaze, as she held the cylinder out ahead.

"Look at me, child," Wadam said.

Starka peered up, taking in the all-too-familiar sight of Brother Wadam at his podium. His accusations nagged at the back of her mind, but Starka kept her gaze locked.

Past Wadam, light filtered through the most famous of all the stained glass reliefs inside the Cathedrals: the Divine First Female reclined, her hand outstretched to the Divine First Male, who knelt just beside. The picture illustrated the love between the first beings of Creation and symbolized the Almighty's undying love for them.

For a moment Starka wondered whether the love extended enough to help the Order accept her message, or if they would usher her right back out the door when her veil was removed.

The sun shone through the glass window to illuminate its magnificent colors. Tears welled up in her eyes as a page boy grasped her hand and led her toward the recesses of the cathedral's antechambers.

⁂

STARKA WIPED HER SWEATY PALMS AGAINST HER ROBE AND clutched ever tighter to the wooden cylinder. With each step, she second-guessed her decision to come here. It would have been so easy to forget the prophecy, to go on with her daily tasks as if it hadn't happened at all, but she had not. She committed to her fate when she wrote the prophecy down — her actions gave it permanence.

No, she decided, I must do my duty to the people whether the Cardinal wants me here or not.

They came to a stop in a small but well-lit room and the page boy retreated backwards. Beyond the threshold, he dashed away to his next task. He had kept his eyes on Starka the entire time and held her arm rather than walking in front of her.

"Never trust a stranger," she repeated from the Holy Book. To prevent any confusion, Starka loosened her veil and lifted her hood. As she waited, Starka casually examined a tapestry with another familiar scene. This one represented a story she heard — and told — so often as a priestess acolyte.

The Divine Male battles a beast called Evil, having many heads and limbs. The Divine Female stands aside, astonished and in utter awe of the strength exhibited by her counterpart. Evil, in all of its many forms combined, is torn apart by Garvon, and Myst the Creator uses its entrails to create the rest of the world. This explains the presence of evil deeds and thoughts everywhere but the Mystian Land, birthplace of the faith. Set apart on their own northwestern continent, they were cut off from the world's influence.

She frowned, again unsure of the last part. It never sat right with her that people who did not live on the proper land contained a taint, especially since those who did remained far from perfect.

The imagery of the Beast from her vision made Starka shiver again. She hugged her chest tightly and forced back the memories. Just as she turned away from the depicted reminder, footsteps echoed from the hall.

Wadam strode into the room with his usual air of authority, but stopped short when he saw her face. "You look familiar, my child," he said, "What is your name?"

"Starka," she replied, her chin held high. "Of Starka and Fandur."

"Starka?" he repeated, incredulous. "Sweet Alsher, what are you doing here?"

She avoided a direct answer in an effort to figure out the situation. "It appears I'm not the only one who received the vision. What does it mean?"

"A girl of your meager years is quick to jump to conclusions and easily reads too far into things," he accused. "What could you, of all people, have to offer the greatness that dwells within these walls?"

Without a word, Starka opened the cylinder and presented the parchment to him. Wadam read through the document, front and back, no less than three times as she waited in silence.

Starka refused to allow his dismissive nature to intimidate her this time. The vision came to her for a reason, she knew, and all of the years she trained to remember and properly channel prophecy could not be thrown away simply because of his demeanor.

"This ... I ..." He stammered and looked up, dumbfounded.

"Take me to Elestia."

CHAPTER 2 – *Cairos*

OR CAIROS, THE ORACLE STONES PROVIDED INVALUABLE foresight on days like this. The assault began before he could exit the divining chamber and find his way to a defensive position, but the wizard rushed through the halls to help. Cairos leapt up a flight of stairs and reached the long meditation hall. It remained empty and silent, just as he left it the night before.

He broke into a run and shoved open the large wooden doors at the end of the chamber. Sunlight flooded into the hall and wind extinguished dozens of candles. The door slammed into a Carrion soldier and sent it spinning to the ground, horns first. When a second grunt turned and growled, Cairos realized how far the sneak attack had infiltrated. He dodged a swipe of the beast's blade, but it didn't give up so easily. The soldier chased Cairos down another set of steps and straight into the practice yard.

The trampled grass hosted a miniature battlefield. Pairs and threesomes of Carrion grunts dispatched his wizard brethren left and right. Some fought back with staves or spells but could not match the ferocity of the humanoid beasts. Up close, the Carrion looked like men save for their leathery skin, similar to shoes left too long in the sun. Cairos knew the soldier still gave chase and ran right through the middle of the fray. He dodged aside to avoid wayward swipes of blades and claws, still aware of his pursuer.

He gritted his teeth as the memories of the yard were stomped by the invaders. So many times, Cairos had stood here with a row of his peers to practice spells or hear lectures on staff shaping. He fought for control of his emotions and did his best to avoid looking at the faces he passed.

More than once, a spell manifested too close to him. While they were intended to char or freeze an assailant, Cairos was forced to evade those as well. He balled a fist harder around his weapon and leapt into the air, landing on the back of a hunched grunt with one foot and propelling himself forward with the other. With this aided leap, he rushed forward and reached the other side of the courtyard unscathed. Cairos paused when he came to the immense stone columns, unsure whether to assist or escape. He needed to see the rest of the city to decide, and that took time and safety.

The wizard planted his left foot and staff and hurled himself to one side, falling to the ground behind one of the columns. He heard a gasp as his pursuer's momentum carried it off the high platform and hurtled to the street below.

From the platform's vantage, at the rear of the school and high above, Cairos observed the single-minded brutality of the Carrion army. Rusted swords slashed and ripped through anything within range. Teeth and claws found any exposed flesh they could. Those who fled were stabbed in the back.

We should have known better than to ally with them.

The sorcerer fought down bile as he watched the Carrion butcher everyone in the city below. Systematic and calculated, the grunts searched every house and dragged the occupants out onto the flagstones to be executed. Most living in Illiadora knew Cairos, many he called friends, but not all could wield the powers of magic in their defense with his skill. The city embraced and encouraged magicians of any caliber with no regard for chaotic or troubled pasts.

Yet the wizards, good or poor, were not targeted in the attack. Every visible man, woman and child met the blade whether they fought or fled.

The ascending layout of Illiadora worked against its people in this type of assault. As the Carrion invaded from four directions at once, the concentric streets flooded with soldiers one level at a time. From the school at the apex, Cairos watched his people struggle to find holes in the organized lines.

Though Illiadora was his second choice, Cairos had grown to love the place over the years. The University of Flaem, across the sea, held higher favor because of its history and temples, not for its design. If he decided to escape, Flaem might be his best option.

From his temporarily hidden perch, Cairos could only marvel for a moment at the durability and resilience of the Carrion soldiers. Even with missing limbs — or sets of missing limbs — the beasts still came on. Their glossy black horns led the way. He stood and began to come to terms with the hopelessness of the situation. If he couldn't decisively turn the tide of the invasion back, his only choice would be flight.

Cairos gripped his battlestaff in one hand and his *terasont*, or life-stone, in the other. The azure rock acted as a magic capacitor, a source of compressed energy he could draw upon as necessary. Its creation took him years to master, and still the *terasont* had limitations. Cairos refused to consider his odds without one — the evidence screamed and died all around him.

As he tapped the stone against his staff, an old adage of his melee instructor echoed through Cairos' head. *Regardless of how much magic power one has, he can't get a spell out if his throat is cut. Most learn this the hard way.*

Even so, few sorcerers carried a weapon after a certain age. Cairos proudly named himself one of them, though many Elders openly scoffed at carrying objects to focus one's magic power. Crutch it may be, Cairos would never sacrifice his staff. Today, he thought, it would become less a matter of preference.

At thirty-four years, he remained less than half as old as the youngest Elder on the Council. While he appreciated their endless wisdom, Cairos scorned their stubbornness. He couldn't warn them before the attack began, but, he realized now, they should have seen it coming. With Illiadora's participation in the destruction of Rochelle, Cairos would have been surprised if an army hadn't come knocking at their door.

This army, however, did not come to seek revenge. All coercion aside, they were allied with the Carrion. The Elders fell back on the typical excuse of having no choice if they wanted to stay out of the war. A poor rationale for the number of lives they'd ruined, maybe, but the pragmatic Elders wouldn't change course with their own lives at stake.

Somewhere inside, Cairos knew a war with the Carrion was inevitable. Though it pained him to think, even for a moment, his city deserved this attack. Illiadora had tipped the scales for the Carrion and Vexen, the Pillar of Justice, would never bless vengeance for this. Death would balance out death, but Cairos refused to lie down with the fallen just yet.

The Carrion betrayed them. To allow these beasts to continue was as much an affront to justice as destroying Rochelle in the first place.

Cairos readied to leap down into the fight, but stopped short as a wave of force barreled through the crowd below. Bodies of Carrion soldiers, sorcerers, and commoners alike were tossed in all directions as the wave swept through the wide thoroughfare. Cairos gazed back towards its source and swelled with pride.

Vortalus the Invincible, a legend in the flesh, had arrived.

Dressed in his usual golden cape with crimson lining, the Invincible did not wield a staff. Even from a distance, Cairos could see the talismans of his station around Vortalus' neck and wrists. These trinkets also imbued the man with much of his additional magical strength similar to Cairos' *terasont*. From his turban-wrapped head to the well-shined boots, Vortalus glowed with power.

His curriculum always proved too advanced for any student, even Cairos, to grasp, but it always gave them something to aspire to. Though he didn't command the Council outright, Vortalus spoke with the loudest voice.

The street just beneath Cairos went silent as the air blast died away. Stunned Carrion regained their feet and charged at Vortalus. Their weapons led the way as the beasts hopped over corpses and debris. Vortalus stood still as the grunts closed in, then cast again. Each assailant stopped mid-stride, held in place by some invisible force shield. Cairos couldn't hear the wizard cast, but he had a feeling what would come next.

White bolts shot from Vortalus' fingertips, chaining from one body to the next and leaving each incinerated to ash. The soldiers struggled against the shield, but could not so much as touch him. Arrows and other projectiles — a few of the Carrion threw their swords — bounced harmlessly away from the shield as well. After wiping out two score of the beasts, Vortalus bellowed out a laugh.

"Is this the best the Carrion army can do?" he called.

Wave upon wave of enemies rushed toward the challenger, unfazed by his confidence. Vortalus held his ground and hurled explosive fireballs to consume dozens of the grotesque soldiers. Cairos counted one hundred fallen or incapacitated before the rush halted. He nearly celebrated, but rather than abandon the attack they moved aside to clear a path for Invincible. A vaguely familiar figure appeared at the opposite end of the street, accompanied by a burst of rainbow color.

In a high-pitched whine, the newcomer called down the street. "General Circulosa of the Carrion Army challenges you, Vortalus! Let us see how invincible you truly are!"

Before Vortalus could react, a sphere of wispy black screamed toward him. The dart's undertow collected the debris it passed and collected a spiraling trail of limbs and dust. Vortalus held his hands forward to reinforce the shield spell, but the dark sphere crashed through it like a pebble into a pond.

The bolt hit Vortalus' chest with the force of a catapulted boulder and buried his body beneath its accumulated refuse. Cairos staggered as a surge of magical current washed over him, and his stomach dropped when it passed. The magic seemed altered, tainted somehow, and then the feeling disappeared. Cairos recovered after a moment, but had to step back from the ledge. The rupture in the currents split Cairos' attention, but he had to set it aside.

He waited in hopes that Vortalus would rise from the pile, dust himself off, and retaliate. The Carrion grunts returned to their butchery, but Cairos saw no sign of movement from where the Invincible fell. Still, he refused to believe the greatest mage in Illiadora could be bested by a single attack.

Cairos gripped his staff tighter and aimed it toward the figure at the end of the street. Circulosa, the skinny, short emissary he'd met once — and only in passing — wore a globe-shaped helmet. He noticed no horns protruded from it; an odd omission for a Carrion officer. The General lowered a curved weapon and bounced his shoulders in a scoff. From the way the short man held it, Cairos would have mistaken the weapon for a bow, but its ammunition suggested otherwise. Before Cairos could utter a syllable to attack, Circulosa disappeared in the same colorful manner he'd arrived.

As Cairos looked back toward the Invincible's corpse, his gut wrenched a second time. If Vortalus could be felled so easily, what chance would there be for the rest?

HAVING LONG SINCE ABANDONED HIS QUEST TO REACH VORTALUS' body, Cairos made himself useful where he could. The strange magical tide continued to wax and wane, but he still didn't know what it meant. Cairos used an ice spell to freeze and shatter an oncoming Carrion soldier with no ill effects. His magic remained functional, but fears of how long that remained the case plagued the back of his mind.

The magical currents never shifted in such an immediate or noticeable way, at least not in his lifetime. Cairos had no idea what to expect, only that he did not wish to meet Circulosa alone while uncertain of his own strength.

Cairos vaulted over a pair of grunts and landed on a stairway to climb Illiadora's great southern wall. He raced up the steps two at a time, knowing his chances of survival would increase proportionately with his mobility. Cairos began the short chant he needed to satisfy Valesh, the Pillar of Change, but his words trailed off when he reached top. Legions more of the hideous soldiers swarmed toward the gate.

"By the Nine," he cursed, "I've got to …"

An angry cry from behind forced Cairos to dodge quickly from the swipe of a rusty scimitar aimed to split him in half. He dealt two jabs with his staff against the chest of his attacker to halt the beast's momentum. A third blow pushed it backward into a snarling companion and off the stairs entirely. The pair plunged into the tumult below and landed atop a crowd of their comrades. Cairos stifled a grin as he finished his flight spell and launched himself into the air. He turned again to view the southern gate.

Cairos recited an elementary-level spell and augmented it with the power of his *terasont*. He called again upon Valesh, this time to transform the earth around the gate. The power responded and a large patch of ground erupted into a huge column of dirt and stone. It surged forth to gain a common height with its caster. The displaced rock effectively blocked the gate, but the power of the spell did not die as it should have.

The altered magical currents tugged again at his consciousness, like a fly buzzing past his ear. Cairos felt his spell shift just as he saw a section of the pillar crack and crumble. The assembled stone and dirt dropped like a giant tree — much faster than the Carrion soldiers could react. It flattened nearly half on impact and sent a dust cloud high on either side to confuse the rest. Cairos fought the urge to smile with satisfaction; his spell had been tampered with. Still, the plan to waylay the Carrion worked, however temporary it was.

Cairos forced all thoughts of escape from his mind. He poured all grief and outrage into bolts of lightning and cast them at whatever groups of Carrion soldiers he saw. Undaunted by his efforts, more spilled into the city from all sides and the slaughter continued. Survivors of the initial blockade dumbly hacked at the earthen barrier he had summoned.

Though the city was lost, Cairos refused to give up.

While he hurled explosive fireballs, Cairos effortlessly dodged back and forth to avoid arrows and spears. Before long, it became obvious the stalled Carrion were not aiming for him, but merely lobbing pointed objects high over the wall to dispatch anything on the other side. Attrition seemed their only strategy, as the missiles hit Carrion grunts more often than not.

Governed by his pragmatism, the wizard sailed to a corner battlement and surveyed the losing battle one last time. Cairos knew underground passages existed to escape Illiadora; he could only hope some of his friends found them.

Though he struggled with the admission, Cairos knew he could do no more good for the city. If he could not destroy all of the Carrion soldiers, or at least prevent the entry of more, then he would have to live and fight another day. Avenge the fallen, he thought. But with the loss of so many, the words meant little.

The gross impossibility of the carnage just below mandated the final conclusion; he had no choice but to flee. Circulosa and his Carrion army betrayed and slaughtered them, and Cairos would make them pay. The wizard said a quick prayer to Urrel for the sake of his friends before he turned east and flew toward the horizon.

CHAPTER 3 – *Starka*

HE DARKNESS COMES AND SWALLOWS ALL OF MY PEOPLE," Starka began, "A beast with eight horns and four mouths rises from the highest tower to survey. One mouth speaks with fire and entire cities burn by its word. Another mouth speaks with plague and the people fall dead in mid-stride. The third mouth has a sword for a tongue and cuts down the walls of even the mightiest fortresses. The fourth mouth is the largest and from its maw comes forth horns of its like to remake the people in the beast's image.

"Those who stand before the beast are destroyed, save one who can resist its power. This one is marked and in one sweep turns the battlefield red with anger and in another turns it pale as snow. Death follows closely behind him."

"We've heard this before," Wadam interrupted.

The Seeress waved away his protests and spoke with the authority of all her predecessors. "Come closer, Starka. Please continue."

Starka couldn't help but be awed in the presence of the taller, older woman. Though Elestia had seen over sixty winters, she didn't betray a hint of her age. Starka remembered the great pains of the Sisterhood to prepare and maintain the Seeress' appearance; the mixing of dyes was as arduous a task as full-day devotions. Elestia's straight, black hair and pale skin presented a contrast similar to Starka's own complexion, though the elder woman's hair hung much longer.

The older woman sat dwarfed by the size of Alsher's Seat, also referred to as "the throne"; a playful nickname, perhaps, but one that bordered on disrespect. The Seat, a mystical conduit, allowed the Seeress to receive and interpret prophecy on behalf of the Divine Female.

Like the Seat, the bare stone of the chamber's walls and floor emanated cold. The long room had no windows and only one exit at the rear. Starka's heart ached, feeling unwelcome in the holy place she had missed so much.

As she looked up at Elestia's color-changing eyes, the girl realized her former mentor had asked the reading to continue.

"Why do we need her present to read the prophecy aloud?" Wadam asked.

The young girl's mere presence seemed to unsettle Wadam, and Starka found it odd despite their history. Elestia simply glared in his direction, content to outrank the Cardinal in the hierarchy of the Cathedrals of Myst, though not by much.

Females could only hope to attain a level of power equal to Seeress; the one chosen to be the messenger to and from the Divine Female, Alsher, and to represent the people's compassion and beauty. Starka used to pray for the difficult calling every night. Males, on the other hand, held extremely high positions inside their own cathedral. They made the majority of logistical decisions revolving around life, interpretation of doctrine, and politics.

In response to Elestia's glare, Wadam retreated a few steps and bowed in obeisance. The priest turned a baleful eye to Starka, though, as if she had somehow made him lose face. She frowned, saddened by his resignation to make this even harder on her.

Did he think she wanted to receive this prophecy? Did Wadam believe special privileges accompanied this prophecy? She wanted to scream, to berate him with the truth of it. Shoved back into the world she had been so violently forced out of, granted responsibility she had already mourned the loss of; these things were more than the young girl wanted to bear. Not to mention everywhere she looked, Starka was reminded of her brother's absence.

The Seeress cleared her throat politely and Starka snapped out of her thoughts. She looked again to the words on the page and let the memory of the dream flood back into her mind. Tears welled up in her eyes as she mouthed the words, struggling to keep her emotions in check. The words hurt to read, and Starka's muscles tensed up all over again.

"Behold, I see the fields covered with the bodies of dead soldiers. The catalyst stands alone among them with his red sword raised, calling out to the darkness, daring it to envelop him. His white sword is broken, but it does not stop him. Spirits flow around this man and assail him, but he cannot be hurt by their cries for blood and mercy. An unnatural darkness begins to cover the world and blanket everything in shadow and death.

"Light shall be replaced with Darkness on the world's altars. The Ninth Symbol is branded and encircled, and the Temple of Man falls in upon itself. Take heed, my people: the catalyst is a lever — he can be pushed or pulled."

A delicate silence settled on the chamber as Elestia, Great Seeress of the Cathedral of Myst-Alsher, began her most sacred duty. The older woman's eyes rolled back and her body stiffened before slumping forward in the Seat. Only after a deep breath did she begin her interpretation.

"By Alsher," the Seeress rasped, "It is the ascension of the Ninth Pillar. Someone, or something, is being heralded as the Avatar of Darsch. Thank the Divine that you did not dismiss her, Wadam. There is no mention of this catalyst man in any of the other ninety-nine accounts."

"Then I am the hundredth," said Starka, her voice trembling even at a whisper.

"Why would acolytes of Myst receive a prophecy about the Nine Pillars?" Wadam asked, fidgeting with the belt of his robe.

"The Nine Pillars? Aren't those the gods worshipped by mages in Illiadora and Flaem?" Starka felt a little embarrassed to ask and hoped it would not incur a scolding — or a history lesson.

"Indeed, young one," answered Elestia, "they are representations used by sorcerers from those two regions as well as other locations around the world. But the Nine Pillars are not looked upon as gods, nor are they worshipped as such."

Starka could barely listen to what the Seeress said, her mind already occupied attempting to fathom why she — a girl no longer in the Order — had received such a prophecy. Wadam seemed to struggle with it as well, by the expression on his wide face.

The priest stood and took a step back. "I must inform my superiors at Myst-Garvon of this. I shall return shortly."

Silence continued to reign after he left. The only sound came from a scribe's steady scratches against parchment as she documented the Seeress' interpretation.

Starka looked directly into the chameleon eyes of Elestia and could say nothing. Her shame came rushing back from when the Seeress refused to communicate at all despite the young girl's former favor. Starka wiped away a tear as she recalled the twisting of the knife.

"Seeress, after all that has happened, why did I receive this prophecy?" Starka asked.

For a moment, the older woman's gaze softened. The scratching of the scribe paused and the attendant looked up, unsure whether this conversation should be documented. The Seeress waved her off and added, "File it with the rest."

Only when they were alone did she answer Starka's question. "Child, what you did or did not do is irrelevant now. Alsher forgives, but not easily, and this world is cold and cruel all the while."

Elestia sat back in the Seat, her eyes a verdant green. "Forces move outside of our knowledge and control, but we know things happen for a reason. I believe you will be a deciding factor in regard to this catalyst."

"But I know nothing of the Nine Pillars," Starka protested.

"They are not so complicated to explain. According to the texts of their faith, such as it can be called, followers believe the Nine Pillars represent specific traits and needs of humanity as a whole. They do not, however, represent a concept of right and wrong or, more importantly, good and evil.

"The closest relations are Life and Darkness, the Pillars Tera and Darsch. Remember, though, the wizards' pragmatism usually allows them to ignore any consequences of their actions that do not affect them. Sorcerers cannot be trusted; they are nothing like us, just as the people of Brong and Rochelle have their own faiths."

Starka struggled to keep up with the older woman's words, who looked toward the ceiling as she spoke.

"The teachings of *Serené* are more about peace and harmony with the natural world, freeing the people from perceived fetters of right and wrong. Those from Rochelle have their own methods — tribal dances and herbal remedies — and these are aside from the point."

Elestia let out a long sigh before she spoke again. "It is obvious to me that, though we do not believe in the Nine Pillars, we were given this prophecy so that it would not be fulfilled. Though they do not believe in evil, believing that the world has entered into a period where it is ruled by Darkness will be a dangerous thing."

Starka's mind staggered from the amount of information the Seeress relayed. Again, she realized the world was much bigger than she thought.

"It's important to remember that the wizards do not pray to the figures as deities but to the concepts the Pillars represent. Representative figures in the mythology of the Nine Pillars are referred to as Avatars.

"Our prophecy is the fulfillment of the Ninth Avatar. Alsher is not abandoning us, child; one-hundred is the divine number of our cycle. She knows we model more things in our world after this number than any other. Alsher is warning us of this ascension. She wants us to prevent it."

Afraid, but compelled to know, Starka asked, "What if we can't?"

Before the Seeress could provide an answer, the door at the rear of the chamber opened and Wadam slipped back inside with wide eyes. "Great Seeress, there is grave news from the south."

The pious woman nodded slowly, her voice rising to a terrible volume that echoed through the large room. "I have seen the dawn of the darkness this very day. Through the great stone I bore witness to a clash of two armies on the battlefield of Bloodmir. They were cut down not by each other, but by a common enemy; a beastly army from some unknown source. The soldiers of Rochelle and Brong were completely decimated."

Starka gasped and Wadam did not move to comfort her. She could not tell if the Seeress, already aware of his news upset the Cardinal, or if the news itself did.

"I'm afraid it does not stop there." Elestia paused for only a moment to wipe a tear from the corner of her own eye. Her tone returned to one of saddened reverence. "Both cities have been destroyed, as well."

"I was not made aware of this," Wadam stated flatly.

"Spirit of Myst, it cannot be true." Starka's heart turned to a lump of stone and her breath caught in her throat. The cities were far away, but she knew of their size and had read about their peoples. World population was one of the main subjects taught before missionaries traveled to foreign lands; they needed to know where they could avoid persecution. "How is it possible?"

Her question hung in the air. No one seemed willing to decipher whether it was rhetorical or whether the young girl really wanted to know how the people died.

"Young Starka, the details are too horrific to relay. But you may yet see the havoc that has been wrought."

"Who would ... who could do such a thing?" Wadam stammered.

"A new force has risen in the world carrying darkness as their flag," answered Elestia. "All I could see of the leader were his horns, yet he was fearsome to look upon."

The priest clutched his hands. "The prophecy ..."

"Indeed, the events are in motion. Soon, this army of darkness shall sweep across every land. I fear no army now exists to stand against such a ruthless power. They are truly inhuman." Elestia's final word spewed out as if the Seeress was glad to be rid of it.

"We have already increased the patrols to the south and west," Wadam stated, "though if an entire army comes I doubt it will help much. We are weak, and our trained zealots are few."

Wrapped in her thoughts, Starka barely heard him. Like her understanding of the world, the situation had grown larger than she thought. Her prophecy not only encompassed the fates of two cities already destroyed, but threatened many more if someone did not defeat the Beast. Starka wondered what would happen to her people after the darkness consumed the rest of the world, for the prophecy had not been specific.

"We must also keep in mind that if magic was employed it would seem the wizards of Illiadora are allied with this dark force," the priest continued with a sour expression. "The Pillar worshippers will always be a danger to us."

Elestia's countenance again reverted to sadness and her eyes flashed a cool blue. "No, Wadam. Illiadora saw a measure of justice as the same soldiers that laid waste at Bloodmir poured into the city hours later and put many to the blade. The city itself remains, but at a great cost. The wizards of Illiadora will be no danger or aid to anyone for quite some time."

Wadam let out a heavy sigh. "Who does that leave, then? Our forces can barely maintain the borders, much less open war. Myst, they can't do much more than the sea already does." He began to pinch a finger as he counted down, "Flaem has ever been a city of neutral chaos and even more staunch in their neutrality than Illiadora. Rochelle and Brong are already beaten, and we have no idea of the allegiance of the other southern cities. Ferraut's knights protect only their own kingdom. We are doomed!"

"Peace, Wadam. We cannot change what has already come to pass. We must be of one mind in this. Divided, we cannot hope to save this world." Elestia's calm exterior and forceful tone did little to quell the priest's panic. He resumed rubbing his sweaty palms together.

"But the prophecy," cried Starka. "There must be a way to stop all of this!"

"If there is then the two of you must find it," Elestia concluded. "Find this catalyst man, whoever he is, and persuade him."

"Me?" Starka could barely contain her surprise, but Wadam swayed as if ready to faint.

"*Her?*"

Elestia did not waver, but pointed a finger at each of them to drive her sentiment home. "Starka is the hundredth to receive the prophecy. You, Wadam, have a history with the girl and can watch over her. The fact that both of you stand before me now is not a coincidence."

The Seeress rose from her Seat and spoke again with inherited authority. "My decree is that none of us shall perish waiting for a wizard or diplomat to protect us. Myst will guide and keep us, but we must be the ones who act."

"But we don't even know where to start or what to do, Seeress!"

Wadam ignored the girl's comment and spoke right over her. "How can you ask me to travel with the likes of ..."

Elestia's glare halted his words. It turned a few degrees colder as she concentrated on the priest, as if looking deep into his heart.

"I am not asking."

CHAPTER 4 – *Xymon*

LONE IN THE SMALL ROOM, GENERAL XYMON REFLECTED upon the frozen faces of the people of Brong. So many had died — with so little effort — and the General took great pride in his clandestine work. The black armor and smooth mask facilitated his ability to step into a shadow, even in daytime, and become invisible. Zion said once that his General was blessed by both Darsch and Hooden, Pillars of Darkness and Secrets.

The creaking door interrupted his thoughts as Drakkaram, the most brutal of the three Generals, stomped through. Even crouching, his monumental frame barely fit, and Xymon heard the General curse the builder. Xymon raised a fist against his chest in salute, tilting his head forward. Sometimes referred to as the "Son of Zion," though not within earshot, Drakkaram also bore three horns.

The General wore no helmet, preferring to show his horrid visage to his enemies. Pointed teeth accentuated bony, hollow cheeks the pallor of dead flesh. His boots slammed against the floor, causing so much noise it could alert anyone nearby. Xymon addressed that hours before, of course.

With a final effort, Drakkaram sank into a chair across from Xymon. The large Carrion General laid his weapon across the table, an immense black broadsword similar to the one Xymon carried, but much wider and heavier. *Perfect for beheadings,* Drakkaram always said. Both could easily cleave through steel, but Drakkaram's would cut through half a dozen men, armor and all. At least one of every ten Carrion in his third of the army made use of a similar blade.

In a flash of color Circulosa, the General who most favored magic, entered the small room. His arrival warped the nearest wall, upsetting a shelf and spilling its contents across the floor. The round General removed his helmet and placed it on the table. With a sour face at their surroundings, he whined, "What a hovel."

"Lucky for you we had the meeting here in Illiadora," Drakkaram nudged, noting the General's colorful entrance. Xymon also used the magical currents as a teleportation method. It had become much easier since the occupation, but whether the change was due to the Carrion presence or the absence of its former occupants, he could not say.

"Lucky for us that you were already here," Xymon whispered.

The dark General turned to the newcomer and remembered the frequent and appropriate nickname, "the round man." Far from derisive, the description encapsulated Circulosa's presence as being adorned by many round symbols. The shape of his helmet more resembled a child's fishbowl than an actual piece of armor. Circulosa spoke with a high-pitched tone and was only modestly tall — in every way the polar opposite of Drakkaram. His long staff glowed in Xymon's vision with an intense inner power. It could, allegedly, become magically bent into the form of a bow with which to assail enemies from afar.

Xymon wondered if he'd used it to dispatch Vortalus the Invincible.

He saluted Circulosa differently, with less respect in the gesture. The round General had no horns at all, and Xymon thought any man who remained merely a human was a waste of potential in the Carrion army. So few lingered, particularly after the raid at Bloodmir. As the newest member of the elite triumvirate Circulosa's purpose remained unclear, but Zion must have placed him in command for a reason.

Xymon mused about the improbability of the three greatest mobile powers in the world assembled in the same room. Meetings would continue to challenge them, but their greatest strength remained autonomy. Zion granted the Generals enough control to make decisions without consulting the Great Commander before every move or skirmish, something Xymon knew to be rare.

Xymon joined the other two Generals at the table to start the meeting. Each sat equidistant apart — another sign of pride in their own authority.

"A prophecy is not something to underestimate," began Xymon, his voice a dark hiss that practically dripped from his mouth.

"What, are we supposed to fear ninety-nine women?" asked Drakkaram, his roaring tone eager to dispel any questions about his security. "You saw how easily we destroyed the armies of Brong and Rochelle!"

"Don't be so fast to assume, O Barbaric One." Circulosa's sarcastic reply cut the air between them. "One must assume there was a reason you were present and, as such, one must discount the ability of the southern armies. Besides, our Great Master was also there to aid and guide you."

Unperturbed, Drakkaram fired back, "This from the one who let dozens of Illiadora wizards slip through his grasp? Enlighten us, O Wise One!"

"I would like to see you last five minutes against a sorcerer without those protective wards you wear." Circulosa chuckled, folded his arms, and leaned back in his seat. "They would tear you to shreds within two."

Incensed, Xymon cut in, "This is pointless. If you two insist on squabbling, our meeting should be adjourned until you can focus. We have much more important matters than your egos."

The others scowled, but ultimately assented. Despite any jokes of son-hood, they knew Xymon dominated the Commander's ear if it came down to one against the other.

"What is the report from the south?" Xymon asked, looking to Drakkaram.

"None have survived the assault at Bloodmir. I would laugh at any cowards who were able to escape from it. Three thousand additions to the cause." Drakkaram paused to stretch his mouth into a grotesque, lipless grin at his handiwork. "Rochelle is nothing but an island chain now, with only a few burnt huts to decorate it — those run by women."

"Thanks to me," Circulosa added.

"Brong is silent, as well." Xymon continued the conversation, ignoring the sorcerer.

Circulosa's voice rose. "Is that so? I was curious what orders you were given that would destroy a city without the help of my magic."

The dark General attempted to retort, but Drakkaram interjected first. "Your help isn't required to do a job properly. Don't become boastful just because you killed one wizard."

Xymon slammed his fist against the table, raising a small dust cloud. "Enough," he hissed. The other Generals shifted in their seats. Xymon smiled behind his smooth black mask and, after a moment of uncomfortable silence, continued.

"A rare black orchid grows around the shrine of Shinjou, their 'dark dragon,' which is toxic to humans in any form. It was quite a challenge to infuse their water supply with this toxin and even more difficult to ensure that everyone in the city would die, simultaneously, at the hands of it.

"We fed them to a few local beasts and dropped them upriver from the wells. The poison is benign without a catalyst to invoke it, but since their primary food is rice, that ingredient was already present."

"Fascinating," commented Circulosa, pursing his lips. "And the infants?"

Again, Xymon's smile spread behind his mask. "Rice milk."

"Ha! Genius! Not even their precious *Serene* could save them!" Drakkaram's purposeful mispronunciation brought a wince from Xymon.

"You ridicule their worship yet you find respite in your own. I tell you again: prophecy is not something to be trifled with. Remember, our Master seeks to become the Ninth based on prophecy."

"Ah, yes, the wisdom of the words of the Mystian fools in the northwest. It is high time that their light be extinguished."

"Simple though it may sound, Drakkaram, I must be the one to silence the zealots of Myst. So speaks Zion himself."

"I have received similar orders to march upon the eastern cities, starting with Flaem," Circulosa stated matter-of-factly, in an effort to sound as important. He turned to the much larger General and questioned, "What, exactly, will you be doing with your newfound glory of exterminating the weak links of the world?"

Drakkaram let out a haunting laugh. "I am to join our Master atop the Great Watchtower and keep our experiments in line."

"The Tower of Kasar," said Circulosa dreamily, "He could not have picked a better place."

The brutal General looked about the room for a moment, weighing his options. "I think while you take Flaem, Round One, I will lay waste to the eyesore Fort Sondergaarde. It would make a nice addition for field experiments.

"Besides," he continued, "I have not been sated just yet."

"Do what you must, Angry One, but know that wizards will be there to greet you when you arrive," warned Circulosa.

"Then they shall join our ranks just as all the rest have — either before or after their death." The grotesque grin returned to his face and he rose to leave the table.

"I will be curious to hear of your progress against the fortress," said Xymon.

"As will I," claimed Circulosa, though his face betrayed otherwise. "Perhaps you can join my ranks to regroup in Flaem after you're routed."

Drakkaram exited the chamber portraying good humor at the round General's final words to him, though he wanted nothing more than to tear the throat out of the impetuous human, mostly because he felt the same, but Zion did not tolerate infighting. Any attempt on a fellow officer's life would be considered the ultimate betrayal.

Information had been incredibly scarce as to the quick rise of Circulosa. His predecessor remained famously preferred over the wizard. Xymon thought it a shame when Terrant chose to abandon the cause, but he couldn't deny the punishment had been well-deserved. The dark General assumed Circulosa's promotion was tied to foiling the conniving betrayer, but had no evidence. Zion foresaw the entire plot, making the mystical power of Darsch all the more numinous.

With a salute, the round General exited the chamber and left Xymon alone with his thoughts, orders, and a little less confidence in the other Generals. He decided to evaluate their success before considering an assault on the Cathedrals of Myst. Convincing Zion of the plan would not be difficult, once Xymon relayed their spiteful words.

CHAPTER 5 – *Wan Du*

EVERYONE WAS DEAD.

Everyone.

Wan Du stood inside a silent Brong and lamented the greatest loss of his many lifetimes. His usual stoicism deepened and twisted into a grimace with each step he took. When the large man reached the well that marked the center of the city, his legs could carry him no further. He collapsed with grief and spoke aloud, though he knew no one could hear.

"Why? Is this the fruit of all our labor? The death of our army, the death of our city, the death of us all? What has this child done, or that one, to deserve such a fate? What have we soldiers done to receive this punishment from you, Most High?"

He prostrated himself on the ground and sobbed. Wan Du wanted nothing more than to submit to the willpower of the Higher Being, having proved so much of a failure on his own.

"Shall I add myself to this giant gravesite? What is your will, Master of Winds and Waves, that it should be done? What must your servant do to rid himself of this yoke of sorrow?"

Wan Du's words echoed back from the empty buildings. The intersection he collapsed in usually bustled with people about their daily routines. It had amassed a collection of corpses. The vacancy, more loathsome to his ears than the cries of his slain brothers hours before, tortured Wan Du. He looked up and saw the Thousand Steps to the Temple of the Winds.

The army had only been gone a few days, he thought; how could the population of so great a city be expunged so quickly?

His escape from the battlefield of Bloodmir brought dishonor on Wan Du, as he remained the only one to make it back. A horde of inhuman creatures had exterminated the entire Brong army, save for him. The people needed to know what happened to their men — every single one of their officers and warriors. Everyone but him. Wan Du fought past his shame as the sole survivor; even as his mind attempted to tally the dead, he wished to be back on the battlefield.

A mile away from the eastern entrance of Brong he had sensed something wrong. No children played and no maids fetched water for laundry; he saw no sign of life at all.

He wandered through the city and called out the names of every person he knew. After Wan Du found the bodies of his wife and children, all collapsed around the table, his tears flowed freely.

Some of the corpses appeared to have fallen in mid-task the large man noticed as he wandered through the entire city. Across the street a basket of groceries spilled from the collapse of an old woman. Next to her, a young boy lay on the ground with candy still in his mouth. Further down the street, the remains of a deserted smith's furnace still smoldered. Animal tracks appeared throughout the city, but he found no living beasts. Not even crows wished to investigate.

Aside from the lack of scavengers, what bothered him most was that none of the dead were wounded. Wan Du saw no broken bones or missing limbs; no blood had been spilled at all. What silent killer stole the lives of his people? Had some poison succeeded where years of conflict with Rochelle failed?

Rochelle; the name remained a thorn his mind. Though he had only been there once, Wan Du remembered the straw roof huts and swarthy people. Their dark skin showed just how different one race could be from another.

After so many years of conflict, could they have decided to end it in one cruel stroke? Wan Du balked at his own question, for the men of Rochelle had been massacred at Bloodmir as well. They would not have sacrificed their army to destroy Brong. No, the nightmarish creatures were responsible for this, and probably something similar to Rochelle.

Wan Du leaned into the city's main well and nearly vomited as the stench of poisonous vapor invaded his nose. The entire water supply of Brong had been contaminated. As he lifted the bucket, Wan Du looked at the stagnant water and tried not to breathe. Murky, almost brackish, the water smelled like fried ginger. None of his people would have consciously consumed water so foul.

After a long moment of contemplation Wan Du cast the bucket aside. Tears streamed from his eyes as he shifted to a familiar meditation position. He tried to calm his emotions and began to speak again.

"Great and Powerful *Serené*, Master of the Winds and the Waves, Lover of the World and Creator of Man, I vow to you this very day that I shall not move from this spot unless you move me. I am your instrument to command. I am your clay to shape to your Divine will. I await your order, whether it is for me to die here and join my departed brethren or to seek vengeance against those who have murdered them."

By the time the sun rose on the second day, lonely silence and thirst drove Wan Du to delirium. His muscles had gone numb, but still he stayed. So much time passed since he wailed through the streets and looked for survivors yet the corpses remained untouched — even by flies. His head swayed forward and back and his eyes fluttered open and closed. As he felt death's chill creep up his spine, Wan Du let out what he thought would be his last breath.

Rather than embracing him, however, the chill died away. The strange tingle of waking limbs spread through his frame. It relaxed his shoulders and abdomen and, when it reached his ears, Wan Du began to hear a sound on the wind. In between light chimes, he heard a soft voice — little more than a whisper.

"I, Master of the Divine and Mortal, have chosen you, Wan Du. You will avenge the deaths of those whom I have blessed at the hands of these Carrion. The Darkness shall not touch you nor suffer to be touched by you. Though you will not see the end, I am here with you in the beginning. Fear nothing; seek and find your revenge."

The voice faded and Wan Du's awareness returned with a snap, along with his hunger and thirst. His throat felt like sand from shouting and his eyes were so swollen from tears he could barely see through them. Light from the mid-morning sun assaulted his already-reddened shoulders. The large man lifted himself from the ground, but only after a few unsuccessful attempts. When the feeling returned to his limbs and joints, he stumbled to the well and raised another bucket of foul liquid.

Wan Du, unafraid, drank the poisoned water and swallowed. His throat rejected whatever dark poison came with it, but the water quenched his thirst. He grabbed a loaf of bread from the discarded groceries and began the long trek to the top of the Thousand Steps.

He gnawed on the bread absently while he stared at the immense Temple of the Winds — the symbol of Brong's history. The temple rose in a pyramid of stairs, built so a man could climb it from any of the four directions. Older than even the walls, its recesses housed the remains of the city's greatest leaders. Wan Du remembered all of these things as he climbed, drawn to the top.

When he reached it, Wan Du came upon a kneeling monk. Though obviously dead, the old man's arms were raised high as if he offered something to the sky. Wan Du crested the top of the steps and saw a halberd rested on the monk's upturned palms.

The weapon's long shaft of bleached wood and blade both glistened white in the sunlight. Wan Du took the weapon and lifted it high as he said a quick prayer of thanks to *Serené*. He would use it to rid the world of this Carrion scourge. Even from atop the temple, the large man heard only his own breath. As he turned in each direction, a vow formed on the man's lips.

He faced east and let out a battle shout so great it echoed through all of the halls and corridors of Brong. Only then, having declared his mighty presence, did Wan Du descend the Thousand Steps to return to the battlefield of Bloodmir.

CHAPTER 6 – *Wan Du*

HE RETURN TRIP TO BLOODMIR WENT BY MUCH FASTER than his escape, spurred on by rage and confidence. With intent to approach from a different angle than he fled from, Wan Du piloted his small craft northeast from Brong instead of straight east. After carefully navigating the Blood Reef, he reached a relatively hidden edge of the battlefield and abandoned the long canoe. Wan Du picked his way through the rocks, staying in the surf to avoid being spotted.

His large frame, though not ideal for stalking and hiding, allowed Wan Du to climb only a few feet of the cliff to peer over it. From far away he saw two distinct types of Carrion; some wore the brown leathery skin he remembered, but others had a sickly gray pallor like old corpses. From his concealed position, the layout of the encampment looked more like a poorly assembled field hospital.

Hundreds of fallen soldiers, both the dark-skinned of Rochelle and pale of Brong, lay on cots while emaciated Carrion pawed at them with long, slim fingers. The beasts, already covered in blood, inspected human limbs, sewed up wounds, and removed all clothing and jewelry. Heads were inspected before being given an impromptu and difficult shave. They had to be dead, thought Wan Du, as the clumsy cuts would have woken the soldiers otherwise.

The hurried scene reminded him of a banquet being prepared, and the thought turned his stomach. This sensation doubled as he watched a Carrion stab a pair of smooth black horns into the head of a dead man, and Wan Du realized the incomplete shaves were to prepare the insertion points.

A transformation began immediately after horns met flesh. Lifeless convulsions racked the body, as when a chicken's head is cut off, and the Carrion soldiers backed away. The body expunged all blood and bodily fluids through any available orifice and the process created a cacophony of wet choking.

The corpse's skin wrinkled, distorted, and finally turned to the familiar Carrion gray. As the spasms stopped, the eyes shot open and the newly-created Carrion soldier came to a sitting position. Its eyes turned black and looked more like holes. The beast stood and shambled away from the cot, its mouth hung open and drooling.

Halberd in hand, Wan Du made ready to leap over the cliff edge and attack. A human scream halted him, and words in his native tongue followed. Though hoarse and nigh unintelligible, the man's voice echoed across the encampment, strained from hours of pleading for his life.

Wan Du frowned as he recalled an inscription on the Temple of the Wind. *The Spirit of Death has no ears to hear cowardly souls beg for their lives. All shall come to meet their end, whether boisterously or peacefully.* He repeated the words silently to himself as a reminder.

The man's screams were silenced by a hand over his mouth and Wan Du heard a kind of speech even more confusing than the eastern language. Long, intense and guttural noises filled the air between two thin Carrion standing over the captive soldier. Eyes wide with fright, the man trembled while the creatures seemed to argue. Finally, one of the beasts swiftly knocked the man unconscious with a wooden club and let out a whistle. Two more misshapen attendants appeared, one for the hasty shave and the other with a pair of horns for insertion.

Before Wan Du could move or protest, the violent transformation began. The skin of the man darkened and dried to resemble old leather. His fingers extended into curved black claws that shined like dark steel. As the new soldier awoke, it flexed its claws and growled, repeating similar tones of speech to the others, and the Carrion released its limbs. With black eyes staring out of a now-empty skull, the new grunt hurried to assist the rest.

The large man again fought the urge to charge and attack; someone would need to be told that the Carrion were made from men. He scanned beyond the camp of toiling Carrion to take in the true breadth of their actions. Past the bloodied dirt and piles of discarded armor, Wan Du saw thousands of gray Carrion soldiers — poorly outfitted, but ready for the fight.

A cry of alarm erupted nearby, and Wan Du felt, rather than heard, a spearhead bounce off the cliff face. With no time to deliberate, the large man leapt from the small cliff and let out as fierce a battle cry as he could.

"Come and die, foul creatures! I shall send you headlong into the abyss!"

The initial response to his challenge seemed to be confusion. A few Carrion soldiers nearest him looked around as if waiting for a command. They clicked and grunted in their odd language until a taller and more prominent soldier — an officer, by its look — shouted what must have been an order to attack. All at once, the humanoid creatures returned Wan Du's battle cry and charged.

Wan Du brought his gleaming halberd to bear. With a wide swing, his first blow removed dozens of legs and heads. As they encircled him, Wan Du found it took more effort to avoid connecting an attack.

No matter how many he dispatched, more took their place. The Carrion soldiers climbed over each other to get at him, showing no fear of death. But as each creature touched his blade, it began to decay and turn to ash, and the continued trampling of the carcasses created a massive cloud.

The gentle southern breeze swept the ash all around him, obscuring the creatures he attempted to destroy. Wan Du's rational mind thought it somewhat better that way; he wouldn't have to see the hideous creatures or their distorted expressions as he decapitated them — Wan Du feared he might recognize his friends.

Hundreds of the mindless beasts fell in the first few minutes. Wan Du fought through the haze, screaming curses and killing as many as he could. Even those touched by the wood of his halberd received fatal wounds; they would not stand to be touched by him, just as *Serené* said. The wind intensified, sweeping the ashes away to reveal the faces of his adversaries.

Tears streamed down his cheeks as he recognized the features of his former comrades, contorted and corrupted by the Carrion horns. The gray ones were thrust forth first, it seemed; mere fodder to tire him out. After watching how they had been created from his fallen comrades, Wan Du could not quiet his rage. He showed no mercy, and now was not the time to mourn their loss.

After Wan Du noticed a swipe of his blade knocked free one of the horns embedded in a grunt's skull, its reaction made him reconsider his aim. Those he struck this way died slowly; they howled and clutched the wounds until the end came.

Wave after wave of the mottled Carrion came on until his swings began to slow. The weapon became heavier with each swipe, sapping Wan Du's immense strength with victory a long way off. His opponents caught onto his fatigue with relish and redoubled their efforts. Their attacks poked through his defenses, scoring shallow cuts across his arms and legs.

Some Carrion held simple swords or rudimentary axes, but the majority attempted to slash at him with their long fingernail-like claws. Wan Du noted the brown Carrion carried true weapons, most likely taken from the corpses that became their gray counterparts. The smell and taste of the blood flying with each swipe of his great arms only served to encourage the monsters further.

Though he struggled with the admission, escape had become his only option. The beasts did not stop coming and their numbers would overwhelm him eventually. Yet, even as Wan Du's arms went completely numb, he fought on until an opening presented itself.

With a final swing he dispatched the closest of his adversaries and gained enough space to take off at a run away from the encampment. The beasts pursued, but Wan Du's long strides outmatched theirs. When he could take no more, Wan Du slowed to a walk and dared to look back. Nothing pursued, so he stopped and leaned against the pole of the halberd to rest. He had not killed them all, but his aching muscles reassured Wan Du it was enough — for now.

THE TOWN OF BLOODMIR LAY JUST SOUTH FROM THE RED SAND battlefield region of the same name. People from Brong were always loath to go there, for the city earned its reputation and wealth from raiding corpses after the skirmishes with Rochelle.

Merchants of Bloodmir modified and repaired equipment only to sell it back to both armies at a higher price. A place of cutthroats, citizens of Bloodmir ignored any sense of conscience and cared only for money. Unfortunately, it remained the only nearby place where Wan Du could find a day's rest. He crossed a narrow bridge, slicing the cords that held it to land to waylay any pursuit.

It wouldn't stop them forever, he knew, but he could at least make it to the city. Wan Du turned and continued walking, his eyes on Bloodmir's muddy buildings across a flat plane.

As he trudged along the dirt path, Wan Du's mind began to process the atrocities he witnessed and what they might mean. If, indeed, the Carrion could replenish their ranks from the armies they defeated then they truly were an unstoppable enemy.

He remained curious about the differences in appearance and mannerisms between the revived and the ones doing the reviving. The latter were brown, almost reptilian, but these new creatures looked gray, like corpses left in the rain. Based on his attack, the gray ones seemed more like shock troops; foot soldiers to crash against the enemy like a wave with no concern for attrition. The brown Carrion seemed more intelligent, though he hated having to use that word.

Wan Du stopped in his tracks as he realized the horrible truth. The large number of Carrion indicated some submitted to the horn implantation willingly. His stomach suddenly sank at the thought. He stepped from the road and dropped to his knees, wiping the black blood and bits of flesh from his loincloth and chest. With a heavy heart, he fell forward onto his palms in supplication.

"O *Serené*," Wan Du called out, "Creator of Light and Banisher of Dark, please grant your humble servant your mighty wisdom."

For the second time, Wan Du heard the sound of chimes on the breeze and a whisper followed, "I have the answers you seek."

"What are these things I fight?" he asked. "How can the dead stand against me?"

"The Darkness, itself, stands against you," came the cryptic reply.

The large man shivered as exhaustion caught up to him. "And I destroy it, as you have bid me. But am I to fight it alone?" he asked.

"I, *Serené*, Creator of all things great and small, am with you. You must have patience." The last word faded as the voice died away.

Wan Du closed his eyes as his body collapsed to the ground.

A GENTLE, COOL BREEZE AWOKE HIM FROM HIS REST. NIGHT SKY stretched out overhead and on the horizon he saw the twinkling fires of Bloodmir. By the silence around him the large man surmised the Carrion had not caught up with his trail. He wondered if the creatures abandoned pursuit before or after they tallied their losses.

Wan Du released more than a few groans as he pulled himself to a standing position and again surveyed south toward the city. With a final massive stretch, he set off again with large strides toward the distant lights.

No matter how many Carrion foot soldiers he killed, it would not abate his sadness. He hated them for destroying his people's legacy, but knew his rage and anger paled in comparison to the rage and anger of his deity.

Twice now, he had heard the voice of his god and trembled, though both times it spoke with calm sadness. His own drive for revenge paled in comparison to the deity's loss. With each step Wan Du's purpose became clearer, repeated like a mantra. *Serené* charged him with making the Carrion pay for all of the deaths they wrought — Wan Du would be the instrument of their destruction. His grip tightened around the anointed halberd, reaffirming the promise to his god.

Men could inhabit a place, but they could never claim to be the place's chosen people. Brong would live again, but only once the Carrion were dead.

From his first conversation with *Serené*, the large man knew he might not see it happen, but his sacrifice would make it so.

Wan Du stopped suddenly as he came to the edge of Bloodmir. Torches burned on simple posts illuminating signs in three languages. He could only read one set of characters, since only Rochelle had adopted the ways of the northerners and sacrificed their heritage for convenience.

Most of the signs read as advertisements for merchants; he saw no warnings or rules regarding city laws or ordinances. Wan Du looked past the signs to see Bloodmir lacked even a gate. A squat wall separated the territory inside the city from that outside, barely high enough to keep animals out of gardens. He found this a deceptive portrayal of the city's hospitality.

In Bloodmir, domiciles sat roughly and unceremoniously next to other buildings, sometimes even sharing walls. The structures looked poorly constructed, made from the most easily moved and abundant resources available. Seeing these made Wan Du long for his home and its reassuring stone walls. Even the metalworking shops, made obvious by their inordinately large chimneys and open storefronts, looked like they could be torn down at a moment's notice. Speed and ease seemed their path to wealth, and the scavengers did not hide their lifestyle.

Wan Du walked tall as he entered the city, momentarily forgetting his agenda. No shops conducted business due to the late hour, but locals ran clandestine errands or stood idle on street corners. A glint of steel caught his eye in the moonlight and he turned to get a better look at it. In front of a store stood a post with a crossbeam, the equivalent of a practice dummy, for display purposes. On its makeshift shoulders sat a well-shined breastplate hued bright red — the armor of Brong.

Upon closer inspection, Wan Du hoped to find it a mere replica or cheap fabrication, but the thickness of the metal confirmed its authenticity. The large man shut his eyes tightly to fight off the tears; he knew what happened to the owner of this armor.

With his mind wrapped up in how fast the vultures of Bloodmir worked, Wan Du barely noticed when his hand grasped the crossbeam and began to pull the armor off of it. Because of the wedged placement of the wood, the armor resisted, so he began to get more forceful. Soon he shattered the wood in his rage and held the armor in front of him like a trophy.

It was too small for him to wear, of course, but he couldn't stand it being in the hands of anyone who would sell or buy the armor of one of his friends.

None deserved to wear the armor of Brong any longer, and no man would be allowed to so long as Wan Du could stop them.

A shout of alarm from behind echoed into the quiet night and the city came to life. Similar cries went up from all around, and Wan Du heard the sound of boots on well-trodden dirt pound their way closer. Still holding the reclaimed armor, Wan Du tried to run, but found himself locked firmly in place beside the mangled post. His feet refused to move, as if turned to stone.

Men poured into his vicinity, all shouting a language he didn't understand. One guardsman brought a torch close and shook his head, obviously certain of Wan Du's origin. The shouting stopped, but weapons were not sheathed.

Wan Du stood, petrified in body and in mind, unable to even speak to defend himself. But what would he say: the armor rightfully belonged to him as the last of his people? Bloodmir would need to be allied with the Carrion to reap the looting benefits so quickly, especially with the battlefield so close. The thought of the humanoid soldiers brought another level of panic to his heart. Would these men turn him over to the Carrion army?

Finally, a man approached Wan Du in a more ornate garb than those who held spears and swords at him. The newcomer picked up Wan Du's halberd and inspected it, testing its immense weight in his hands. His mustache curved in a smile and he pulled the weapon upright to prop it on the ground like a staff.

"What a lucky thing we are on our way to Cellto, thief," he said in Wan Du's native tongue. "A big man like you might be worth something extra."

CHAPTER 7 – *Cairos*

CAIROS' MOUTH TASTED OF ASH SINCE HE LEFT ILLIADORA. Death screams of his friends and fellow students plagued his mind, mingled with the horrid faces of Carrion soldiers. Their rage-twisted visages and hollow black eyes haunted him even after five mugs of the same dark ale before him. He vowed inwardly to never consume meat from an animal that bore horns again.

He repeated the same routine for nearly two days: curse, sigh, and berate himself for escaping rather than fighting to the end.

His flight spell failed just as the walls of Flaem came into view. Even from a distance, they shimmered like gold in the setting sun's rays. Laid out in a square, hemmed in by thick walls, the older city of sorcerers remained as rigid and resistant as ever. The bricks themselves were held together and strengthened by ancient magical wards that produced their twilight glow. A modification of an old word for "beacon" gave the city its original name.

The corners where the walls intersected extended even higher in the form of huge towers. These provided visibility as far as Fort Sondergaarde to the south, and in the other direction, the ruins of Shargoth and the Great Northern Wall.

With his spell failing and his destination in sight, Cairos drifted to the ground and plodded the rest of the way. All the while, he punished himself for abandoning Illiadora. The long flight nearly exhausted his magic, even with the aid of his *terasont*, but the wizard continued to fight off sleep.

"I should have stayed," he muttered under his breath. The words held less conviction each time he uttered them.

The tavern patrons ignored the anonymous wizard at the corner table as he brooded over his mug. Even the barkeep only appeared interested when the empty mug made its telltale sound against the wooden tabletop. Similar to Illiadora, magic users were more than a commonality in Flaem, though the latter housed the more prominent and less accepting *Magna Scholae Magicus*.

Illiadora trained anyone with the will to learn; from time to time this brought about a clumsy or ambitious sorcerer who caused — or became the center of — conflict and scrutiny. Though this education would be sufficient to train a wizard, Flaem could go many steps further than what the Elders in Illiadora could offer. They focused on control most of all, especially after the advanced tactics had been learned. Cairos never studied in Flaem, but his lust for knowledge had forced him to garner various texts of their curriculum. All of which were lost now, he lamented.

After years of control discipline, Flaem's sorcerers were by nature calm and slow to action. This made them popular as excellent strategists as well as advisors for their impartiality to conflicts of all kinds. The city's population increased exponentially at the end of the Sorcerer's War, just as Illiadora's had, but with Flaem's impartiality came a stigma. The world saw Flaem as centered only on self-preservation and survival. Its people held little concern about what went on outside, aside from commerce, and this recalcitrant pragmatism only bred mistrust from other nations.

Hence, why the Carrion army chose us instead, Cairos reflected. None followed him east, since the soldiers could not fly. The army seemed to have it in for Illiadora, but not Flaem. As he eyed his ale, his intoxicated mind envisioned some dark deal the Flaem Elders made with Circulosa and his ilk to protect their own interests.

Just as they had during the Sorcerer's War, rumors proliferated about the Avatar of Darkness. Even in Flaem, people spoke of the ascension with fear in their voices, as if it might happen the next day. Over a century passed since the last ascension, and the world had not broken then either.

Still, if the Flaem Elders allied themselves with the Carrion, what would it mean? Darsch possessed no Avatar, and Cairos did not understand how the concept commanded so much fear. He lifted the tankard and drank deeply, dismissing thoughts of fear and darkness and enjoying the indulgence. Wizards rarely touched alcohol as it hampered control of spells and lowered inhibitions of casting them. At the moment, he couldn't care less.

The taste of the ale brought Cairos back to younger days, sneaking a sip or two from the barrel despite parental scolding. New to the art of magic, he started applying to the *Scholae Magicus* long before the acceptable age. Each year, Cairos and his father turned out for the ceremonial festival regardless of the far trek to Flaem. His mother would stay behind and chide them both, opting to miss out on the exotic food and fiery displays. One year there had even been a dragon, but she dismissed his excitement entirely.

Would-be apprentice wizards from all over came to participate in the festival, to test their strengths against each other in an attempt to gain acceptance to the University. Even alumni came to assist in the trials, treating it as quite an honor to see the up-and-coming applicants before they got accepted and trained. Wizards could not help but be curious about their future competition.

For the first few years, Cairos failed in the early rounds of tests. Unschooled mages always did, he heard, unable to prepare for things they could not yet understand. Cairos never gave up, though; the talent for casting would not let him. It nagged at the back of his mind until he could set the power free and learned to master it.

This remained his method to explain the call of the Pillars, but the untouched never understood — Mystians from the northwest least of all. Many simply nodded and assumed him adept at fabricating elaborate lies or sleight of hand. Cairos loathed their disbelief in magic. It reminded him too much of his mother.

Perhaps the presence of creatures created by Darkness will change their minds, he thought.

When Cairos hit puberty his magical power increased a hundredfold, but even with so much power Urrel's Luck evaded him and the University continued to turn him away. For five years straight, he successfully passed all fifteen trials, yet the Elders refused to admit him. Their process, if it could be called such, relied more on heritage and wealth than strength or will.

To transcend his humble beginnings, Cairos tried to prove himself stronger than any of the other potential students to make it in. Nothing less would do.

After ten years of excuses, Cairos resigned himself to a four-year set of courses in Illiadora with his goal of notoriety dead. He accepted an apprenticeship to learn specialization and, more importantly, the dangerous magic the professors refused to teach in classes. Though he still struggled with control, Cairos excelled under his mentor and became one of the most productive students in the city. His dreams and lust for knowledge, however, would not be sated. He continued to apply for advanced studies at the University, but they would not let him in.

Even after so long, the city made him feel ill. The place murdered his potential for greatness. Not even educated with years of experience under his belt would they accept him — not after being "tainted" by the less-selective hands of Illiadora.

His research ultimately revealed a deep rivalry between the two schools as to who could produce the best wizards. Illiadora chose raw talent and willpower and scorned the nepotism of Flaem. Both cities produced incredible sorcerers — that was half the reason the old war had gone on for so long — but the struggle to one-up each other continued long past the old conflict.

The Sorcerer's War taught both schools, however, that once a wizard stepped outside his structure he could no longer be restrained by the boundaries of neutrality; discipline could easily be forgotten and every man had his price.

"Scythor curse them all," he spat. "Not that it matters much now, anyway." Again, the boisterous crowd of regulars and merchants took no notice of the otherwise quiet man in the corner. So many people, wizards and otherwise, died in that old conflict. Cairos wondered if, with the destruction of Illiadora, there would be enough of a force to stand up to the Carrion. Either way, his future looked bleak.

While in flight toward the safety of Flaem, Cairos considered ending his own life. It would have been so easy to climb continually higher on the magic of Valesh and then let himself fall in a great splash into the Inner Sea of Mana to find a quiet watery grave. Likewise, it would have been no great task to summon a great ball of flame and let it consume him. Younger sorcerers fairly often did it accidentally. He might have achieved ultimate peace after a mere moment of discomfort, but something reassured him of a purpose for his escape. Perhaps the fortune of Urrel smiled on him, but fate was too cruel to count on.

Regardless, the feeling since disappeared and left him with an emptiness he tried to drown in ale.

He should have felt empowered to seek revenge upon the Carrion, but the circumstances still bothered him. Their betrayal was unprovoked, without a doubt, though the Elders had participated in the razing of Rochelle. He doubted the Pillar of Justice sanctioned Illiadora's fall, but the possibility turned his gut. It could just be the drink, he reflected.

The wizard envisioned his revenge over and over. Defending his home and friends; the way it should have been. In his mind, Cairos perched atop Illiadora's southern wall and hurled spell after spell at the onslaught of Carrion until he killed them all. Surviving Elders showered him with praise and honorary titles, and the war ended before it truly began. The scene looked so glorious in his head, probably because his fantasy omitted the death throes of his friends.

Dispelling the delusion, Cairos gave in to the admission that he was not powerful enough to stop the Carrion alone — not that it helped. Even with every reason for vengeance a rational man would have needed, Cairos sat quietly in the tavern, immobile as an island. He could never claim to be a rational man.

Harboring no delusions about his recklessness and complete disregard for the safety of others during the furies of his spell-casting, Cairos showed time and time again just what the Flaem Elders scorned: chaos. He lacked the natural control and they turned him away for it. Cairos surpassed each trial set before him, after years of practice and preparation, but he did such a thorough job that something or someone always suffered for it. His final attempt at the trials ended in complete and utter disaster. Cairos closed his eyes, recalling the fateful day.

Two young men squared off on an empty desert field. With nothing but their rudimentary spells, they were to battle until the surrender of the other. The final trial gauged power as well as control, but neither combatant knew it. *Fire is a magnificent force in the world*, a professor since told him, likening Cairos to the element, *it brings us light and heat, but when left to its own devices it will consume anything in its path*.

Spell after spell blasted across the plain. While the amateurs defended themselves well enough from the flashy displays, they would inevitably have bruises for the next few days. The attacks were more for show than causing any real damage, but should one have truly connected, it would have pointed out the carelessness of its target. At its heart, the final trial seemed to Cairos a mere test of endurance.

The pyrotechnics could not last forever. If a potential student attempted to execute spells nonstop, without rest, he would eventually collapse into unconsciousness and forfeit. It took both physical and mental constitution to call upon the magical energies for an extended time. Even if one held objects or artifacts to waylay the drain, it caught up to them by shortening their lifespan and inflicting severe headaches. A trained wizard knew to only do this in mortal danger, but many inexperienced became addicted to summoning the power. Those who succumbed to repeated drains fell into a comatose state that could not be cured.

Soon, tired of the game of weak spells, the young men began to fire stronger blasts with improved accuracy. The combatants dodged and deflected as best they could. Each spell continued to cost them, but each man tired at an equal rate. Their power waned until both reverted to their weakest spells, and even those missed. Too tired to stand, Cairos panted, but continued to glare at his opponent from a distance.

The Elders of Flaem used oracle stones to watch the action, he found later, and saw neither prospective student willing to give up. Based on this, and their potential, the Elders had decided to admit both men. They were en route to retrieve the men when something happened to revoke that decision.

With an unprecedented stalemate looming, Cairos' opponent held up his hands to parlay. He proposed a tie, since neither seemed able to best the other, and suggested to allow the Elders to pit them against different foes the next day. Elated, Cairos dropped his guard and agreed. His quick trust proved nearly fatal, for the opponent let fly a spell he hadn't yet used. A barrage of missiles slammed into Cairos from all sides and sent him reeling.

Beaten, but unwilling to accept an unfair defeat, Cairos struggled to keep his eyes open and trained on the traitorous and grinning youth. Anger reawakened what little strength he had left and Cairos channeled it into the formation of a spell.

"Born in the hearth of the underworld, tempered in the mouth of the sun, let the breath of Vexen be upon you ..."

His opponent couldn't hear the words, but a warm breeze began playing with the young man's hair. His grin turned into a chuckle and then a laugh as he continued to revel in his unearned victory. A faint aura shimmered in the air between them, like red smoke, as it traced the symbol Vexen. Even with his limited experience, Cairos knew what it meant: the blessing of vengeance.

"Disintegrate!" he screamed.

The breeze intensified into a gale as the spell took form. Natural winds would have carried even a person away with it, but the spell kept the youth's feet rooted to the ground. The heat increased and his flesh began to burn and flake away. He tried to scream, but the power pressed its way into his lungs and tore through his insides. Flesh and blood were blasted away, and with a blinding flash, the body shattered. The bones fell to the ground, still glowing red hot.

CAIROS RETURNED TO CONSCIOUSNESS WITH A SNAP, NEARLY knocking over his half-full tankard. The wizard uncrossed his sore arms and shifted in his seat, wondering how long he'd been asleep. He glanced around, but the patrons, engrossed in their own business, continued to ignore him. For a moment the crimson sigil of Vexen remained imprinted on his vision, but Cairos blinked it away and took a long swig of his now-flat ale.

Through the window he saw the stars twinkling against a ceiling of black. Night fell during his nightmare and still the wizard had not made a decision. Cairos heard the growl before he felt it and realized his own stomach was trying to send him a message. His avoidance of food seemed to be catching up with him.

Shrugging away the famished pit, Cairos stood and staggered toward the hallway at the other end of the tavern. He relieved himself and wondered how late the tavern served hot food. After a meal, he'd have to make up his next move as he went along — as always.

CHAPTER 8 – *Cairos*

CAIROS FLED DOWN A STONE CORRIDOR AS FAST AS HIS rapidly sobering legs could carry him. A raucous and insistent buzz pursued. Mundane or not, he should have known the chest held some kind of trap. He cursed his own impatience and added a few select epithets for thinking this "mission" would be so easy.

A flier promised a short quest with high rewards: slay the master of a cave fortress and return with a special tome they stole. The location laid an entire day's travel to the east of Flaem by foot. After a nominal rest, Cairos ventured into the higher elevations and found the honeycomb of passageways and old mines.

He accepted the job in hopes that some treasure inside could help him against the Carrion. His *terasont* and battlestaff would see him through any duel, but against an army he needed something considerably stronger. While the flier explained exactly where to go to find the cavern, it omitted any description of the place's defenses or other dangers. As he hurdled corpses, most not even starting to decay, their frozen screams punctuated the point that many had already tried and failed. Cairos had no time to linger and study them, but the familiarity was not lost on him.

More and more bodies littered the cave as he ran, most dressed in the restrictive metal armors of soldiers and treasure seekers — possibly unable to use magic. Their failures gave him a plan, however. Cairos clutched his stone even tighter and whispered an incantation to Hemur, the Pillar of Body, to harden his skin like steel. He whirled to face his enemy with staff raised, since the enchantment would make further flight impossible.

The tiny creatures flew all around him, but did not come close enough to touch him. None so much as brushed their wings against his metallic skin. Cairos fought to keep his eyes open and take note of their metal bodies as they swarmed past. Thankful they were not true insects, it still gave the wizard pause to think what else waited deeper in the cavern.

As the buzz died away to a dull roar, he let out a sigh and wondered how he would turn back around. He berated himself internally for not listening to his usually heightened sense of danger; he didn't want to end up like the men and women who littered the cave. A called challenge forced him to finish his turn abruptly and face his new adversary.

"Well met, wizard of Flaem! But you shall know my wrath for intruding upon my home!"

Before he could react to the melodramatic challenge, a bolt of energy blasted against his metallic chest. It burnt a hole through his tunic and sent him to the ground flat on his back. Cairos landed with a dull clang.

"Oh, was that too much?" his opponent bellowed. "Fine, then, your turn for a free shot!"

Cairos, head still fuzzy from the alcohol and the blast, knew he needed to act quickly. His own propensity for theatrics could hurt him in this enclosed space, but with more than one foe to think about he needed something big. He watched, immobile, as his opponent came into better view about twenty feet away.

Magical thorns poked from his skin at every visible spot and obscured the man's features. The answer to the situation came as quickly as Cairos' chant could. He let the spell fly while still lying on the ground; the steel skin enchantment made his body so heavy that he'd never be able to stand until he negated it.

His opponent braced for the impact of the spell and shrugged it off as if it had been nothing. He laughed to punctuate the point — fools always did — and ignored the receding of his thorns.

"You'll have to do better than that if you're looking to best me!"

Quickly, and with a vengeance, the roaring buzz returned to fill the chamber.

"Not really," said Cairos.

As thousands of the hornet-type creatures passed overhead, Cairos wished he could have covered his ears. The other wizard stood agape without even time to react before the stings began. The swarm became an opaque wall around him and before long he slumped to the ground, quite dead, pierced by so many tiny darts that his skin looked like the inversion of its previous thorny state. Cairos refused to breathe until the creatures disappeared back in the direction they had come. He blinked and struggled to calm his heartbeat.

The gamble paid off; the disenchantment of his opponent regained the attention of the seeking creatures who, having in their mind dealt with a non-enchanted intruder, returned to their chest to await being summoned again. A simple trap, Cairos noted, but an effective one.

Cairos waited a few extra moments before he dispelled the enchantment on his own body. Once again mobile, he stooped to raid the corpse of his opponent for the sought-after tome. The dead wizard carried a book, but it did not match the benefactor's description. As he flipped through, Cairos realized it was a spell journal, a record of the wizard's research of new incantations. Most books of this type were common, but some proved invaluable in his search for new spells.

Thumbing through the book, Cairos searched for the spell his opponent used to create the thorns. He examined the words carefully to avoid any accidents and pictured the result in his mind. With closed eyes, Cairos gritted his teeth before he recited the short chant ending with "thorn skin."

After the quick — and relatively painless — transformation, Cairos tested his dexterity. The presence of the thorns didn't seem to hinder him at all. He smiled at the now-dead wizard and tucked the spellbook away, a little annoyed at the shambles of his tunic.

Many uninspired spells failed simply because the combination of words was incompatible or because the chant had too many syllables. These took years of research to perfect, but another wizard's tome bypassed this tedium. These unpublished volumes proved the most valuable and least dangerous way of learning new spells, and always fetched a decent price in Illiadora's marketplace.

Cairos fought back a pang of guilt as he realized it would never be the same again. Returning to a safe Illiadora, with no more thoughts of his dead friends, became Cairos' motivation. He believed he could find peace by taking back the city and putting his people to rest in the ground. First, though, he would have to kill the Carrion soldiers.

All of them.

He examined the fallen wizard's tunic for a possible replacement, but found it useless and in shreds after being pierced by hundreds of stingers. For now his own damaged clothes would have to serve. As he tore the shirt away from the other man's chest, Cairos saw the symbol of Valesh burned into the exposed skin near his heart and scoffed at the useless gesture. For hundreds of years thieves and fools marked the symbols of Hooden or Darsch on themselves and hoped for some kind of reaction. They received nothing but ridicule for their superstitious nonsense.

The magic, as the Pillar of Acton clarified, remained in the spoken word. No spell could be enacted merely by writing or thinking it; all such wizards who carried this power of "innate invocation" had been dead for centuries.

His opponent carried nothing else of use, suggesting that he served a master. Cairos smiled at his fortune — at least he hadn't wasted any real effort. With a glance down both ends of the passage, Cairos decided the direction he had been fleeing would bring him closer to his goal. Since the dead wizard guarded the passage, Cairos assumed it the right way to go, especially with no desire to test his theory by tracking back to the chamber that housed the trapped chest.

He began to stalk deeper into the cave with one hand on the wall and all senses alert for other traps. The passage ended and the walls gave way to reveal an impossibly large chamber. The ceiling stretched so high that darkness cloaked its true limit. Throughout the expanse, Cairos saw pillars of rough stone placed sparsely. Most stood too tall to see whether they supported the roof of the cavern. A glow from jewels embedded in the rock helped to illuminate the chamber. The glow provided as much light as the moon, but in mixed colors. Even so, the soft light made the place seem all the more eerie and Cairos stayed near the outer wall as he explored.

The wizard's heart skipped a beat as he realized what an immense, hollowed cave usually meant. Though dragons remained incredibly rare, they did nest in just this type of place. Hundreds of feet below the surface, dens like these avoided the elements as well as constant challenges of would-be slayers. The beasts became scarce over the centuries as men who sought wealth nearly annihilated the race with their harvesting campaigns.

They failed to realize that the dragons they succeeded in killing were the weakest and the smallest. The survivors, Cairos read, should be avoided at all cost. Most men would rather die than stumble unprepared upon a dragon, but their rarity only added to the beasts' mythical mystique, and the Elders of Flaem eventually decreed a ban on any slaying.

Dragons were a passion of his for years, a fascination since childhood, yet Cairos could only recall some theory and history about them. Mastery of spells dominated his studies, to the avoidance of nearly all else. He did enjoy reading the legends of the Shinjou Dragon from the southwestern city of Brong. The serpentine black dragon's mythology, a beast so large it once encircled the world, was staggering to even imagine — let alone believe. In his youth Cairos tried to visit the shrine there, but couldn't find it because of the language barrier. Since then, he had devoted hours and days to Acton, the Pillar of Speech, to improve his speech capabilities. Cairos hoped he would survive long enough to attempt the visit again.

The likelihood of a dragon inhabiting the cave almost made Cairos laugh, but the body count in the tunnels made him think twice. A few traps and an inexperienced mage didn't take a genius to overcome.

It was too few bodies, Cairos suddenly realized, that would imply response to a flier in Flaem; there must have been a promise to this place worth more than some stolen trinket. A dragon's hide would be valued higher than treasure accumulated during a king's lifetime — not that he planned to slay one. Any thought of riches dissipated quickly, though, when a low growl echoed through the cavern.

CHAPTER 9 – *Cairos*

AIROS LAUNCHED EVERY ATTACK HE COULD THINK OF, BUT the dragon refused to be ensnared or damaged. Its golden, interlocking scales absorbed each fireball and iceshaft from his chants to Tera, the Pillar of Life. It even deflected the shadowblasts of Hooden, the Pillar of Secrets, and those rarely missed. The dragon advanced, undaunted by Cairos' magic.

Bolts of blue lightning shot from the beast's mouth, lighting up the cave as they struck stone. Cairos raised his staff to absorb the bolts, but they avoided it and found his limbs instead. Cairos cursed under his breath as he dodged the relentless assault, unable to so much as scratch the beast.

Dragons were notorious for their resistance to magic, another reason they had been hunted to near extinction, but his spells should not have been useless against it. A pet dragon made sense; the minion he fought in the tunnel and the chest trap implied more skill than that of a novice.

As the young wizard ran around the perimeter of the cave, he began to notice things seemed a bit irregular. The complete absence of droppings caught his attention; a creature this large routinely left piles as tall as a man. He should have been practically swimming in them since the cave had only one small exit.

He noted, also, the creature avoided striking with its jaws, claws, or tail — major weapons an animal would never hesitate to use. In fact, the only moves it made allowed the dragon to better aim at him. Cairos latched onto his instinct, his attack options exhausted.

With a chant similar to the one in the tunnel, he hurled a disenchanting spell at the dragon. The spell connected in a flash of green sparks and the dragon dissipated like steam in the wind. Cairos paused for a moment, shocked the spell even connected.

Cairos fought to catch his breath and surveyed the cavern for another threat, but the dark closed back in quickly after the dragon's bolts ceased. The light from the embedded jewels helped little, and the young wizard still had spots in his vision from the lightning.

Use of illusions marked the master of the cave as a follower of Hooden — figurehead of deception. The possibility struck Cairos as odd since sorcerers did not usually supplicate to that Pillar; they left it for thieves and assassins.

"Very good, young sorcerer," called a voice from the darkness. "You are the only one to have come this far. I know you seek the book and that you will not stop until you have procured it, but do you have any idea with whom you are trifling?"

When a shadow shifted, Cairos pointed his staff toward it and launched a twisting blast of yellow flame. The spell illuminated an aged man, but the fire passed through him and struck the stone on the other side.

The older wizard began to laugh aloud. "You cannot hope to best me! I am Gabumon, Master of Illusion!"

He had been more afraid of the dragon, but that sentiment disappeared quickly. The name sounded familiar and Cairos wracked his brain to figure out why. He took cover behind one of the stone columns and searched his memory, recalling the name being listed on a faculty sheet.

Gabumon taught illusory magic at the Academy in Illiadora — a course Cairos avoided. His tenure ended, and Gabumon stepped down to allow another to be elected in his place. Apparently he went to Flaem seeking work. Wizards of his caliber should have been in high demand since the Carrion attack, thought Cairos; why would this one steal a tome and hide in a cave? Perhaps the old man had not been told of Illiadora's fate.

Cairos broke cover to question the other wizard, but met a barrage of magical attacks first.

"What are you doing here?" shouted Cairos between deflecting spells. "Don't you know what's going on outside? Illiadora's been overrun by Carrion soldiers!"

"What, by the Nine, is a Carrion soldier?" asked the older wizard. "Some kind of animated corpse?"

"Humanoids with black horns that serve Darsch," Cairos answered, peeking around the stone.

"Ha! Making it up as you go along, are you? Don't try to distract me with your nonsense, boy!" Gabumon shot more blue lightning, this time from all ten fingertips, sending pebbles and dust flying as they connected with the rock around Cairos.

Ducking back behind the stone, Cairos tried to keep the other wizard talking. "I was there, you old fool," he said. "You think I give a damn about some book? I seek a means of vengeance!"

"Lies," yelled Gabumon, not letting up with his attacks. His denials and spells raised in equal strength. "No one serves a Pillar without an Avatar, and no army could ever take Illiadora!"

Cairos shielded himself from the spells as best he could, knowing words were his only weapon. "If you care at all about the fate of our home, then listen to the entire tale. You may not be able to hear it from anyone else."

The attacks paused and Cairos took the opportunity to add, "Kill me later, if you have to."

It seemed this assurance was enough. "Very well," said Gabumon, "Come out and we will talk."

Cairos moved to step out, but stopped himself short. The situation reminded him too much of the youth that betrayed him at the Flaem trials years before, and he wanted to be sure he didn't trust too quickly. He glanced around the rock column again to make sure the older wizard did not have another spell aimed his way.

Gabumon looked to be at least twice Cairos' age. About his body hung a metallic robe woven with dark gray patterns. Over each shoulder sat curved plates of a lighter shade, possibly silver, tapered and hooked on the man's belt. His hands extended from long and billowed sleeves, the edges tattered from the magical effects called forth during the short fight. Gabumon wore a modest goatee of the same salt-and-pepper color as his smooth hair, as if he saw no reason to be presentable. Cairos looked down to the dirtied hem of his robe, wondering how long he lived in the cave.

Seeing the older wizard's passive stance, Cairos stepped out with his hands raised. When Gabumon nodded, he began to recount the fall of Illiadora. He described the intrusion and demand of the Carrion soldiers the month prior, and how the round General Circulosa gave them the spellbook to utilize. It contained only one fire spell, sourced in Scythor, the Pillar of Death. Cairos would never forget the name.

Through the oracle stones, he witnessed the destructive power of "Meteor," made more deadly by the concert of nearly one hundred other wizards. Gabumon did not seem as impressed.

With effort, Cairos tried to include all of the names of those he saw die. At a few, the older sorcerer's eyes widened, but he stayed silent. Cairos finished with the last details of his escape and how he came to be in the cave.

"Do you really believe Vortalus the Invincible to be dead?" Gabumon asked.

Cairos nodded. "There was nothing I could do."

"Then this Circulosa must have a weapon of great power. Funny that I have never heard of him." Gabumon paced while he spoke, not speaking to Cairos directly.

"I have called to Vexen for assistance," the young wizard added, "but the power seems to have turned its back on me."

Enraged, Gabumon threw his hands up in response. "Of course! You brought this fate upon yourselves! You want Vexen to bless your vengeance against something you brought about?"

"Don't lecture me, old man. You weren't there! We had no choice, but to help the Carrion." Cairos faltered as he said the words, once again feeling an emptiness his excuses could not fill.

"No choice?" he replied. The very concept seemed to offend the older man. "A wizard always has a choice. Between dying and causing the deaths of countless innocent people, you take death."

Cairos stared at the floor and didn't respond.

"Of course, it ultimately came to that anyway, didn't it?" asked Gabumon. He shook his head and sighed, adding, "You were fools to trust them."

"I will speak of it no more," Cairos said, casting his gaze aside. "Will you help me or not?"

Gabumon turned and walked away from Cairos, deeper into the immense cavern.

"Where are you going?"

"Go away," answered Gabumon. "Leave me be."

"I can't do this alone," Cairos admitted, his voice barely above a whisper.

At this, Gabumon whirled to face him again, still shaking with anger. The younger sorcerer took a deep breath and worked to keep his tone neutral through the shame.

"If it is not valid to seek revenge because we were wrong for causing it, then all I have left is to avenge the death of my friends — of our friends."

Gabumon opened his mouth to interrupt, but Cairos pressed on. "I accept my responsibility in destroying Rochelle, but all of Illiadora has been hurt because of it. Many have suffered for the actions of a few — surely there can still be justice."

In the darkness between them a glyph appeared and hung in the air, glowing crimson. Light bathed both men's faces as they stared at each other through the symbol, and the surrounding embedded jewels all turned red. The aura reminded Cairos again of his Flaem trials — Vexen again blessed his vengeance.

After the light of the symbol faded, Gabumon gave a single nod. His face showed calm once again, all fury abated by Cairos' admission.

"Very well," said the older wizard. "You have been judged and found worthy, it seems. I will help you."

Cairos wanted to punch the air in triumph, but held his enthusiasm in check and merely smiled. Things were finally starting to look up.

"But two will still not be enough," Gabumon continued, "particularly with Circulosa's advantage and an army at his back. We'll need to return to Flaem and gauge the situation there."

"As neutral as ever, I'm sure," replied Cairos.

"If that is so, then perhaps the Carrion have underestimated us. Neither side may have won the Sorcerer's War," said Gabumon darkly, "but the world should have learned a hard lesson."

As the older wizard turned and led the way out of the cave, he added, "I will help you so long as Circulosa is our enemy, but that is all. The rest of this army is someone else's responsibility."

Cairos agreed, but knew the war would not end with Circulosa's death. The Carrion had a master, and a flamboyant wizard was not it.

CHAPTER 10 – *Starka*

STARKA TOOK LITTLE TIME TO DECIDE SHE HATED SAILING. After an initial fit of common seasickness, the girl's main source of discomfort came from the loneliness she felt on deck. Being alone she could deal with, but with land out of sight, it became easy to believe the world was a flat plane of nothing. As the miles of tumultuous water went by, she found her respect growing for the hardy crew.

Of course, their lecherous glances and invitations to "become more acquainted" still made Starka blush. She began to feel self-conscious on the second day after leaving the cathedral's port. No one alerted the girl when they passed Praypor, a milestone for her and the last chance to spot land before they reached the open sea.

They avoided other boats entirely because of Wadam's agenda. The Cardinal wanted to get the trip "taken care of" and get back to his "real work." He repeated these words to nearly every crew member, always within earshot of where Starka stood. Each of the sailors seemed to wear an unsure grimace whenever Wadam came around.

At first, she thought it odd the crewmen wore nothing more than a pair of tight-fitting short pants and no shoes. When the boat began to pitch and roll with the larger waves, the girl's unwieldy feet learned why. If she or Wadam slipped and fell into the salty waters dressed as they were, they would sink like stones.

Starka went barefoot after the discovery, but kept her dress modest. She feared the desperation of being on the ocean — and having nothing but other gruff men to look at — might tempt the crew to take advantage of her. Being the only female on the entire ship seemed strange, but Starka had no choice. She submitted to the will of Elestia to seek meaning in her prophecy, lecherous glances or not.

On the third day of the voyage, Starka decided it best to confine herself to the meager cabin she'd been assigned. Wadam still refused to speak to her. He always stood near the front of the boat, bantering with the Captain. Fishing trends, weather, shapes of ships; it seemed to Starka that if Wadam hadn't joined the Brotherhood of Garvon he would have become a Captain himself.

No, she mused, an *Admiral*.

The days remained uneventful and Starka stayed within her makeshift bedroom, deep in the bowels of the ship. She found if she closed her eyes the constant sway of the waves ceased to be a bother, but the sinking always returned when the girl looked out the small, round window at the distant horizon. There was never much to see.

Once, she caught a glance of something to the east. It resembled a vertical structure like the tower of Myst-Garvon from far off, but none of the sailors would speak of it. They ignored her questions or treated the girl like she hadn't actually seen anything. Soon, Starka gave up talking to the crew altogether.

According to Wadam, their route took the ship due south through the Outer Sea of Mana until they reached the edge of the Blood Reef. The Captain would have to maneuver around its perilous shallows until they reached the Blood Coast, then skirt the coastline east for less than a day to reach Rochelle. She'd heard Wadam warn the Captain not to even attempt to dock near Brong, insisting that they'd brought enough supplies to get to Rochelle and back.

The Seeress hadn't said why she chose Rochelle as their destination, and Starka did not ask. She remembered little about the customs of the southern city except they sent all missionaries promptly home with threats of harm should they ever return. The cathedrals sent envoys quite a few times over the years, but communication remained closed.

Rochelle seemed an introverted place that only allowed outsiders in for commerce. The residents mated only within their tribal atmosphere. Starka heard horrible stories of banishment for those who chose otherwise. Even before Fandur's disappearance, she gave little consideration to marriage or love. The position of Seeress was a lonely existence, confined to Myst-Alsher and surrounded only by fellow priestesses and celibate priests like Wadam. Starka learned not to hate solitude in the months after her ousting, and being on the ship gave her little else to think about.

She busied herself by perusing more books, though most failed to hold her interest for more than a few pages. To further alleviate her boredom, Starka looked through maps and tried to memorize the major cities. It kept her attention for less than a day. When the girl returned to the few books she had about folklore of the southwest, she found the text cryptic and the handwriting poor. Starka scorned all texts from the Mystian continent; if she had to expand her horizons she did not wish to read the same old books.

Upon borrowing three short books on legendary tales of Illiadora from the Captain, Starka read about a figure titled the Invincible. She wondered if his title proved true when the Carrion attacked the city. Regardless, the romantic style of tales caught her interest, and she went back for more.

One book told a legend of the Blue King who made his home in Fort Sondergaarde for one hundred years. Starka never heard of a man living so long aside from early men in the holy scriptures of her homeland. She quickly learned that long life and ridiculous amounts of embellishment were common in stories like the Blue King's which, she realized, reflected poorly on her own faith's tales. Starka tried not to think about it and moved on to something else. With a desire to learn about their destination she poked around for texts about Rochelle.

As she flipped through the last few pages of *Harnessing the Trade Winds*, a volume of local customs and trade routes, Starka yawned and placed the book down on a nearby table.

Sleep, sickness, and the constant rocking were her only companions on the ship. She couldn't help but be glad when the vision returned to invade her dreams, except for the painful sights. Brutal reenactments of her original prophecy plagued her mind when she shut her eyes to sleep — everything but the Beast.

The visions came in flashes just as before and were difficult to decipher. Starka saw the catalyst man fight scores of enemies in massive battles and watched hundreds of women and children endure torture at the hands of shadows. Once, she dreamed of a horrible three-horned creature that stood like a man and stared up at a large white statue. It remained a fleeting image among many and did not answer any questions about the prophecy. Her nightmares were dominated by the dark battlefield and the "lever," though she still could not make out his face.

For at least a week on the open sea, Starka endured the dreams alone. Finally, after days of constant murmurs and painful groans from her cabin, a hard knock made the girl jump.

"Who is it?" she called.

"Who do you think it is? Open the door this instant!" Cardinal Wadam's demanding voice, though muffled, was unmistakable.

The door swung open halfway before the man's stubbly arms forced it open the rest of the way. After he cleared the threshold, he slammed it shut behind him and locked it. Starka took a step back, but after the priest didn't move to strike her, she became confident enough to speak.

"Where are we?" Starka asked.

Wadam scowled and looked her appearance over before answering. "Still a few days from the Blood Coast. The crewmen tell me you've been prophesying down here by yourself for days. How could you not have told me? Have you written any of it down?"

"It's the same dream as before," she whispered, fighting back a shudder and the urge to berate him. *You are the one who's been ignoring me*, Starka wanted to say.

Wadam considered her words for a moment with a furrowed brow. "Not a detail changed?" he pressed. "Nothing additional?"

Starka shook her head. With Elestia she would have shared more, but she knew Wadam had no power to interpret. Things were tentative between them already, and the girl did not wish to anger him further.

"The only difference is …" she paused, struggling to form the right words. "It hurts this time."

"Hurts?" Wadam asked, his face screwed up in confusion. "What's that supposed to mean?"

"The dreams. I feel the pain and the screams — they're not just dreams anymore. I'm connected to them somehow, like my heart is being torn out of my body every time."

The large man paced to the other side of the small room as he hemmed and hawed. "The dream is the same, but your condition is different," Wadam stated, then turned to her. "Elestia mentioned something like this, said it may be related to your proximity to the battlefield."

And you're just telling me now? thought Starka, forcing a mask of concern on her face rather than rage.

"I know you weren't given all of the details before we left, so I might as well tell you. It may put you at ease enough to sleep and thereby give the rest of us some peace."

The girl nodded, already uncomfortable that Wadam wished to put her at ease. She hoped he might shed some light on her prophecy content, but that died quickly.

"Here, sit down," said Wadam. "You already know that Rochelle and Brong have been rivals for centuries. Usually their skirmishes end in a stalemate with the commanders on either side calling a withdrawal after a reasonable, yet small, amount of their troops lie wounded and dispatched."

"Yes," she replied, "but none of my books talk about how it started."

Wadam looked affronted at the interruption. "How it started makes no difference. The southern world is filled with fools who do not need a good reason to kill each other. All you need to know is they are dangerous places, especially for people like us. Bloodmir is even worse; they have been pillaging the dead for weapons and armors to sell since the feud began."

Starka sighed, wondering if anyone could count the amount of money Bloodmir collected from the spilt blood of others. For a moment she couldn't decide if that made her angry or merely sad.

Wadam continued, "If either side suffered the worse for the pillage and resale, they would have put a combined effort to stopping it. That, by itself, speaks volumes of their lack of character."

Starka's attention waned throughout the conversation with Wadam, particularly as he began to ramble further about his disdain for the southern nations. He seemed more interested in teaching a lesson than actually caring what she knew. For a moment, Starka wondered whether Wadam had come out of pity or boredom.

The details of Brong's poisoning and Rochelle's destruction by raining fire threatened to give the girl more nightmares, but she tried to listen to it all. Before long, the constant rocking of the ship began to take its toll on her eyelids.

"We can talk more tomorrow," he said. "Just make sure you document any new pieces of prophecy that signal danger ahead."

Wadam left shortly after noting her tiredness and Starka locked the door again behind him. The darkness outside the window meant she had no way to discern how close to the Blood Coast they were. As time continued to pass, she lay awake on the cot and tried to find patterns in the ceiling boards.

Though the girl fought hard, exhaustion ultimately won out and lulled her into unconsciousness.

♻

STARKA COULD NOT SLEEP MORE THAN AN HOUR AT A TIME SINCE Wadam visited. Her waking hours became filled with more lonely actions, and the priest did not return as promised. She felt much like the corpses in her dreams. Sleep deprivation eventually brought delusions of black-cloaked invaders who towered over her while she lay in the cot.

The girl closed her eyes to block one such vision, but blanched upon opening them again. She saw a flash of her brother's face; half-cloaked in darkness, but unmistakably Fandur's visage. When she sat up to look around the room, Starka saw nothing.

The cabin remained silent except for her panting and the lapping of the waves against the hull. She shut her eyes, tightly this time, to try to get the vision of Fandur's face out of her head.

When she opened them again, the face had returned.

She jumped to her feet on top of the bed and retreated from the disembodied apparition. Starka knew it could not be him, but tears poured down her face.

"Fandur?" she asked.

The floating face did not respond.

"It … it can't be you …" she choked out.

The specter rose to her level and began to advance. Starka backed herself to the corner and struggled to breathe. Her heart began to twist and pound inside her chest, just as with her prophetic dreams. Upon confirming she was awake, a surge of panic welled up and pulled at her for escape.

She wanted to scream, but nothing worked. Who would come to save her, anyway? Would Wadam break down the door and exorcise the ghost? Starka imagined him sound asleep with an expression of bovine contentment behind his own door locked.

A vision of her brother, ghost or not, snapped Starka's already fraying nerves. She dashed to the other end of the cabin and unbarred the door without another thought. The half-face chased her up the long flights of stairs without a sound. Starka clambered onto the deck and spun to face the ghost of her twin.

His features glowed in the full moon. The faced looked calm, but completely lifeless. Fandur's visible eye opened wide, as if in fright, but the shadowed half of his face seemed covered by a mask. The vision floated at eye level, surrounded by an iridescence that did not illuminate the nearby surfaces. It continued to advance, floating steadily toward her despite the ship's constant movement. The girl retreated until she bumped into the rail and heard the water rush against the ship.

With only one choice left to get away from the haunting face, Starka threw herself overboard.

CHAPTER 11 – *Starka*

ER EYES SHOT OPEN AS A WAVE WASHED OVER HER. FACE down against red sands, she spat mouthfuls of horrid saltwater and even choked up a piece of seaweed. When she could breathe again, Starka pushed herself up to her hands and knees to take a look around. Corpses stretched as far as the eye could see, up and over the red dunes, in every direction. Starka's first instinct was to scream, but her dry throat refused to respond. When she noticed things moved among the dead, fear froze her breath again. Whether the forms were people or scavenging beasts, she could not tell from a distance.

In a flash the corpses disappeared and left only a vast expanse of crimson sand. The bodies seemed so real, Starka realized, they must have been part of her prophecy. She shuddered to imagine where all of the corpses went.

But the figures had not disappeared with the corpses, and Starka did not dare move as they advanced on her. Two large brown men, so hideous she couldn't be sure until they came close, approached in a hunched-over, skulking manner.

As her vision cleared, Starka realized they were not men at all. The girl flattened herself against the ground and closed her eyes, praying to Alsher they would simply pass her by. She knew her prayers had been ignored when footsteps stopped immediately in front of her. Parting her eyelids, she saw a leathery foot right in front of her — so close she could smell the drying blood on its toes.

The creatures seemed to communicate in unintelligible growls that might have been words in some strange language. Much like animals, Starka thought. Rough hands grasped her limbs and rolled her onto her back. Her eyes flew open in response and she took in the entirety of three grotesque creatures surrounding her. A third, she realized from its position and proximity, must have come from the other direction.

Two of them looked like they might have been human, once. That is to say their faces were intact. The third had half a face — the rest smashed beyond all recognition. Its similarity to her brother's vision made Starka want to scream, but again, the sound would not come. In its place came a violent retching.

The third creature's exposed flesh crawled with maggots, though it seemed not to notice or care. Each of the beasts had long arms ending in claw-like protrusions and a pair of glossy black horns. As they howled with sadistic glee and raised their rusted weapons to strike, Starka finally found the ability to scream.

Their cries were all cut short by grunts, however, as a foreign body crashed into the trio and knocked them away. Starka removed her hands from her eyes to see a lightly armored, but very bloody man recover from tackling the creatures. He spun a dirtied longsword in each hand.

His hair, sheared short and worn unkempt, had bloody patches on both temples. Tall but not huge, the man looked strong without the abnormal thickness of muscle of a warrior. The gray chestplate he wore was obviously taken from a dead soldier, as it had gaping hole in the front revealing his unharmed skin. The mismatched red leggings he wore seemed hurriedly acquired as well, since they didn't quite fit.

"Fools," he growled. "She'll not belong to the likes of you."

As the stranger raised both mundane swords to strike, Starka felt almost deflated — neither weapon had a red or white tint. Her eyes were quickly drawn to his forearm when a patch of skin changed color before her eyes. A blood-red pattern appeared from beneath the skin and took a shape she remembered from one of the books. The symbol of Vexen glowed on his forearm like some kind of magical tattoo.

Much like his demeanor, the man's eyes held a serious and dark aura. Starka wondered why everything he possessed seemed to be picked off of the dead. He paused for a moment to regard her — to make sure she was alright, Starka hoped — before leaping toward the recovering creatures.

Starka watched as the strange man carved his way into his opponents and back out again. His limbs moved so fast the beasts barely had time to react. One lost a head before even Starka could blink, the stump spraying black fluid high in the air. The others rose to retaliate, howling in fits of rage. Steel rang on steel as the creatures parried and countered, but they stood no chance against his speed.

With a double thrust the man put both swords through one of the beasts. His momentum pushed it to the ground and carried him on top of it holding the hilts of both weapons. Only the half-faced one remained and it attempted to catch its opponent off guard. It shrieked and clumsily launched itself forward, a small dirk leading the attack.

The stranger let go of his swords and dodged sideways enough to create a hole between his torso and his arm. He closed the hole, wedged the wrists of the beast against his body and reached out with his free hand to grasp one of its horns. The man yanked, blood sprayed, and the beast howled so loud Starka covered her ears in defense. It fell to the ground in a heap and did not move again.

The man dropped the horn next to the corpse and moved to collect his two swords. He pressed a foot against the creature's ribcage for leverage, gave a sharp pull, and both came free with another squirt of viscous black.

After he sheathed his weapons, the man turned back to her. "Don't let me forget," he said. "That's twenty-seven."

"Twenty ... seven?" she repeated, unsure what the number meant. With a look toward the corpses, the girl realized it was to keep track of his felled foes.

Starka felt almost ready to faint. The man seemed to be a soldier, but she had never heard of anyone keeping track of how many enemies they killed.

"They're called Carrion," he said.

Nothing seemed familiar about the man and judging by the Pillar symbol on his arm, he could not be from Myst anyway. She tried to study the mysterious symbol as he moved, but it looked like a simple drawing in red ink. The skin seemed raised slightly, though almost irritated — as if the symbol was more than just a mark on the surface.

As she moved to stand, Starka realized she owed him gratitude for her life. "Thank you," she stammered, "for saving me."

The man chuckled. "Saving you? All I did was kept them from killing one more person, which helps me out in the long run." He knelt down near one of the soldiers and began to remove its armor.

"Besides," he continued, ripping the chestplate free and a part of the beast's skin with it, "They have things I need."

After a few moments of re-outfitting through various stages of undress right in front of her, the man spoke again. "What are you doing out here, anyway?"

Starka stood apprehensively and looked around. "I'm not even sure where here is. I know that I should be somewhere near the Blood Coast but ..."

"Get down!" The man hissed and pulled her into cover behind a small hill. A volley of black arrows sailed by a moment later, sticking in the sand and corpses.

Starka's survival skills were limited, but she knew her nightgown would not protect her from the arrows. The moist cloth clung to her body and she couldn't help feeling self-conscious — hoping he couldn't see much through the garment.

"Who are you?" she asked.

He ignored her and kept watching over the crest of the hill, all muscles tensed.

"Call me DaVille," he answered without looking at her. "And stay out of my way."

"I am Starka, representative of the Seeress Elestia of Myst."

A moment went by, but DaVille did not acknowledge what she said. His gaze did not stray, intent on the source of arrows past the hilltop.

"You have to help ..." Starka began, unable to keep the fear out of her voice.

DaVille shushed her with a waving hand. The man had only one purpose, it seemed, and it had nothing to do with her. His arms carried scratches and blood leaked from a few, but they were shallow compared to his visible scars. When he leapt up from the hill and charged against a dozen more Carrion soldiers, Starka realized why he carried so many old wounds.

While DaVille occupied the creatures, Starka knelt and took a close look at the discarded horn. She dared not touch it, but stared intently at it as if she could learn something about its origin. The girl considered wrapping it in a cloth to take with her, but decided it best to leave the horn alone. She wouldn't have known what to do with it, anyway.

As she turned back to watch the man fight, she once again marveled at his prowess, especially with the two mundane blades he wielded. DaVille stood in a fairly aggressive stance, considering he faced five of the beasts standing in formation. The Carrion looked human in form, but their mannerisms seemed completely animal.

He swatted away one sword and dodged another. DaVille dropped low, attempting to sweep the legs out from one beast, but it leapt back. After a moment of pause, all five came at him, yet even outnumbered, Starka saw a calm and focused expression on the man's face. His longswords worked well to keep the enemies at bay, but he made little progress toward killing them. Each time one left a hole in its defense DaVille became tied up evading the others.

Starka watched the fight with intense worry and wondered if she should try to help. Her fate now depended on this man — however temporarily, whether he knew it or not.

The man calmly parried and dodged as best he could, as the Carrion circled and danced at him from all angles. She saw his expression change, and in an instant, the fight intensified. A sword grazed his armored back and DaVille spun his grip on one sword to hold it like a dagger. He thrust behind, then pulled the weapon back in a sweeping arc across his body. The assailant to his rear fell with the side of its ribcage torn out, and the arc passed through another of the creature's throats.

DaVille grunted and leapt back from a wild swipe, blood dripping from a fresh wound across his arm. The limb hung, lifeless, at the side of his body, but the hand still gripped his weapon.

Suddenly, a strange fit began to possess him. DaVille shivered and cried out like a madman in a tone borne of pure fury. He dropped both swords and stretched his open palm toward the suddenly confused beasts. Starka watched as the red symbol on his arm began to glow. It got brighter until a blast of energy shot out to immolate his snarling adversaries. They shrieked and threw their weapons down in full retreat, but five steps away, they melted and collapsed to the sand.

DaVille panted and stumbled, his energy completely spent. He made his way back toward the girl, squinting and struggling for balance. Two steps away DaVille fell forward and she moved to catch his shoulders, settling him on his back gently. Before he completely lost consciousness, Starka heard him utter one last thing.

"Thirty … nine."

She tried to rouse him and even slapped his face a few times, but DaVille did not respond. Starka checked to be sure his chest rose and fell, but beyond that she knew of no way to help. As the morning wore on, she saw more moving figures among the sands and began to panic all over again. If he did not wake soon, the girl feared she would have to leave him.

"DaVille, wake up! Please wake up!" She pleaded, pounding her fists against his armored chest.

With a start, DaVille's eyes opened and he seemed more frightened than her for a moment. He pushed her off and tried to stand, shaking off the cobwebs of unconsciousness.

"What happened?" he asked.

"How am I supposed to know?" she stammered, unable to stop the tears. "You were fighting … and then there was a spell, or something … and then you just … you just passed out and I … I didn't …"

"Okay, okay, calm down. I have enough problems without you crying about them." DaVille retrieved his swords and climbed to the top of their hill.

Starka raised her hand toward him and caught herself before she spoke the words. Was she really about to ask him to stay with her?

After he looked into the distance and muttered under his breath, DaVille turned back to her. "Grab what you need and let's move."

"Move where?"

"Away from here. The dead ones smell worse than the live ones, and that's saying a lot. We need to be gone before another patrol comes through."

Thankful he assumed she would come along, Starka checked around for what she might need. Her mind tried to piece together what happened before DaVille's unconscious episode, but failed. Despite his coarse attitude, she assumed the man had no intention to harm her — otherwise he would have done so already.

Finding nothing useful, she joined him atop the hill and looked toward the sea for any sign of her ship. She saw three boats, all larger than the one she remembered, and each flying a black sail. The trio loomed just off the tip of the coast but they were the only ships.

"What are those?" Starka asked as she shielded her eyes from the sun and pointed.

DaVille, impatient, abandoned the hill and went about looting the twelve corpses he'd created. He threw a few items her way, most of them dirty pieces of clothing and armor he expected her to wear. When she didn't move, he stopped searching.

"Those are transport ships," he answered. "They'll hold about a thousand soldiers each, and they'll be here soon. That's why we have to move."

Starka wrapped up the items he tossed over into a bundle and nodded. DaVille pointed to her feet and she followed his gaze downward to a small dagger. Being a pacifistic — and a girl — Starka hadn't even thought to pick it up.

"I … I can't," she said.

DaVille scoffed, then shrugged. "If you don't want to defend yourself, that's fine. Just don't expect me to do it."

She hoped his words were a bluff.

"What's it like?" she asked. "To kill them, I mean."

DaVille seemed taken aback at first, but he merely shook his head and walked away.

"DaVille," she cried out, "I want to know."

"It's just like killing anything else," he responded. The answer amounted to about what she presumed from his brutish exterior. Starka wanted to know if there was more to him than a killer and until she did, she wouldn't feel safe. He stopped and turned to face her, waiting.

"Like killing another man?" she pressed.

His features softened a bit and he looked at her with what she thought might have been admiration. She expected his next words to be haunting or easy to remember, but instead they sounded like a poetic soldier's creed.

"A man should only kill another man when he has to," he said. "Carrion, I kill because I want to. That's all you need to know."

He turned and resumed walking, apparently done answering questions. Starka caught up quickly and they moved away from the large ships. As the pair reached the remains of an encampment, Starka saw DaVille tense up again and reach for his blades. She took it as a sign to avoid calling out for survivors.

From the gray cloth of the torn and burned tents, Starka surmised it a stop for the Rochelle army. DaVille gave her instructions to find a boat so they could travel east across the channel while he picked through the remains.

Starka knew, even with her limited geographical knowledge, they had to cross the channel east. It would put them somewhere near Rochelle itself; her original destination. After all that happened the night before, Starka hoped she might find some safety there.

One look at DaVille told her it was unlikely.

Throughout their crossing of the channel Starka could not take her eyes off the man. Beyond him she saw the towering black sails on the horizon, making it doubly important for her to keep her vision toward the rear of the craft. DaVille faced the rear as well and pumped the oars with all the strength he could muster. He relayed to Starka in no uncertain terms that if the ships caught up to them before they reached the shore there would be no way to survive. Their small canoe would be dashed to pieces, but only after it was filled with black arrows.

Even from afar the ships looked immense; each contained at least the thousand soldiers DaVille guessed. The girl began to wonder if they pursued him, or whether she was just unlucky. DaVille turned in his seat, cursed at the ships' proximity, and muttered again about "making landfall." Starka watched the beach of Bloodmir recede into the distance, but did not turn to see how far they had left. According to her companion, however, an eastward current of warmer water carried them much faster than the oars alone.

When Starka finally turned around she nearly cursed as well. From a distance it looked like smooth coastline, but the land had broken up into shallow channels their boat would have to navigate. It must be difficult for him to only watch backward, Starka thought, and to have such a useless navigator.

"Do you want me to help?" she asked.

"You? Help?" DaVille replied over his shoulder. "Sure, tell me which way to go so we don't get stuck or run aground before we hit the mainland."

Starka turned around to face the front of the boat and realized her directions were now reversed. "I've never really ... done this before," she said. "How will you know which direction I'm telling you to go?"

"Sit closer to me," he answered. "If you sit right behind me and lock your arms in mine you can pull on whichever arm is the direction we need to turn. That way if we have to make a quick turn you won't be scrambling."

She moved from the front of the boat to take a seat immediately behind him. After pumping the oars constantly for so long, DaVille's skin perspired heavily and the musky scent of his sweat hung thick in the air. Oddly enough, Starka didn't find it offensive at all.

Perhaps I'm just willing to ignore it because he's saving my life, she mused. With her arms locked inside of his, Starka directed him as best she could to find a route through the shallows.

"One good thing about these is that they can't follow us," he told her. "They'll have to find a way around."

Her hands stayed steady on his arms as he pumped them back and forth. The rhythm nearly lulled her to sleep despite the discomfort. Sitting upright on their shared seat, little more than half a wooden plank, kept her awake and the constant bounce of the boat still bothered her slightly. With a slip here and there, Starka would grip a handful of muscle instead of just the arm. She marveled at DaVille's strength and knew he would make short work of her if twelve soldiers could not slow him down.

Starka broke the unsettling silence. "How far are you going to … travel with me?"

The question made him pause in his rowing, but DaVille recovered quickly. "I'm not traveling with you. You're traveling with me."

She considered this concept, but could not understand the subtle distinction. When she didn't respond, Starka thought she heard DaVille chuckling to himself. Nothing he said or did put her at ease, but the girl appreciated his presence all the same.

The smell of death and view of the result of the Carrion army made Starka curse the ships' existence. The burned coastline looked diseased by being repeatedly washed in the tide. While it cleared most of the corpses from the small channels, Starka spotted the occasional floating body. Sometimes she waited for DaVille to push past them while she shut her eyes and prayed. After each one, Starka berated herself for it as she neglected her navigator duties.

Here and there the boat bumped against a jutting edge of land or coral and Starka jumped each time, but the boat moved slow enough to avoid damage. After an uneventful slalom, they reached the true mainland.

Not wanting to waste their head start, the pair leapt from the boat and ran across the beach toward the smoking ruins in the distance. Regardless of the state of Rochelle, they needed food and shelter as well as transportation. Starka felt stuck with DaVille until they evaded the pursuit, but resolved not to be afraid of him. Being unfamiliar with men of war, DaVille fascinated her.

She also knew nothing about those who used the powers of the Nine Pillars, but something was different about the way DaVille had done it. From her books, Starka remembered the use of chanting or other methods to invoke spells. The intense shout that came from DaVille and the blast of energy immediately afterward dumbfounded her. At the camp, she nearly left in the boat without him, but her curiosity got the better of her common sense. Also, she never wanted to feel as helpless as she did when the man first appeared.

In retrospect Starka thought she would rather have him around than any of the three thousand enemies getting closer by the minute. No matter how much he scoffed, she would never be able to defend herself with a knife — especially against those merciless beasts.

Something else nagged at Starka; it couldn't be just DaVille's strength that kept her from leaving him. Though his dismissive words made her feel inferior, she also perceived a strange connection to the man. At first she figured it might be recognition, some relation to her prophecy, but Starka since dismissed it. That she would abandon her ship and wash ashore just at the right place to be saved by this man seemed far too convenient. Starka couldn't fight the draw to him, to his importance, but she had no idea what it could be.

DaVille turned his head then and made eye contact with her, as if somehow reading her thoughts, but she ignored him and kept trudging forward. Her borrowed clothes remained still damp and got dirtier with each step, but she remained hopeful they would reach Rochelle before the black ships.

What remained of it, anyway.

Starka's heart broke for the city she read so much about. The texts gave her the expectation of a metropolis of straw huts and commerce; the source of an indomitable willpower and excellent family values. The swarthy folk may have been tough on outsiders, particularly of her faith, but Starka still valued and respected their culture.

What they found where the city used to be was not much more than an army encampment, similar to the one they left across the channel but larger. She assumed it to be the remainder of a suburb of Rochelle proper.

With each step, Starka tried to avoid mounds of sand and dirt. She noticed quickly each had a marker sticking up to designate it, usually a tree limb wrapped in cloth.

"By Alsher," she gasped, "are we walking through a graveyard?"

DaVille stopped short and looked around. Starka followed his gaze, realizing for the first time the markers went on as far as the eye could see.

"Looks like we don't have much of a choice," he answered, and continued walking. Starka whispered a short apology by way of prayer and hoped they would not be killed on sight.

As they neared the village remnants, she began to wonder what would become of her. Though not dressed like a Mystian priestess, Starka knew a few words out of her mouth would give away her origin. They were in an unfriendly place, chased here by the same enemy that devastated it. Starka held little hope she and DaVille would be labeled as friends.

They surveyed the streets, little more than trampled pathways between buildings, and saw only a few local folk out in the daylight. She realized if they were seen they would need an explanation for their presence and hoped Alsher would forgive the deception.

"We need some kind of story," Starka whispered, "in case someone finds us."

"If you'd keep quiet," the man responded, "then no one would find us. Let's just find some horses and food and get out of here."

He led the way, more than once having to pull Starka down and hide as dark-skinned women trod past. He covered her mouth the first few times, presumably to keep the girl from crying out in shock. Eventually, they came to a long building where horse heads stared out from closed stalls.

Starka leaned close to DaVille. "I don't see any guards."

"All the men are dead," he replied. "Who would stand guard?"

No sooner than he said the words did the quiet corner of the city erupt in shouts and action. Swords slid from sheaths and cries roused occupants of the nearby huts.

"Halt!"

"Identify yourselves!"

The voices broke with panic as a group of armored soldiers surrounded DaVille and Starka, all of them female. She tensed, afraid only bad things would come of this. It crept into her mind that DaVille might kill them all if he felt threatened. Starka looked to him, and by the look in his eye, the man felt it one of those "necessary" times. She wondered, briefly, if she should even try to stop him — or whether she could.

DaVille's swords cleared their sheaths and he stood over Starka in a defensive stance. Some of the women wore gray leather armors, most of them ill-fitting or too large, while the rest used anything they could find. One even wore the remains of some kind of trash receptacle with the obvious assumption that any metal would do. The majority held long spears parallel to the ground, but none stayed steady. DaVille's presence gave him the advantage in this situation.

As the spears began to inch closer, DaVille stated a venomous challenge to the nearest woman. "Take one more step and you'll lose a finger. Any more after that and I'll cease to be merciful."

The unblinking gazes of teenage girls and middle-aged mothers made Starka want to cry. She would never forget the sadness and anger mixed in their expressions, though none uttered a word after the initial alerts. These women were not the trained and tempered warriors DaVille usually fought, but their weapons would draw blood just the same. Their fearful glances to each other labeled them neophytes, probably not much more use than she.

"Who are you? What are you doing here?" a particularly large woman with a mace demanded. In contrast to the rest, she wore armor tailored to her thick body. Starka nearly mistook her for a man before she spoke.

DaVille raised an eyebrow and responded, "Simple refugees, passing through. Just need food and horses. Who are you?"

"Do not think you are the first spies to be merely passing through," she retorted. "Be aware that Bathilde, wielder of the mighty Bruwand, faces you, longswordsman!"

Cheers erupted from the nearby women as Bathilde advanced and pushed them aside. The mace looked heavy, but the woman seemed able to lift it with little effort.

"Spies of what?" Starka asked.

DaVille ignored her. "Are you the leader of this army?" he asked, the last word said with obvious disdain.

Bathilde paused and looked to the females beside her before she nodded. "I am."

DaVille scoffed. "A leader wouldn't have hesitated, mace-wielder. Who makes the decisions here?"

The women noticeably blanched at DaVille's taunting words, which confused Starka, but she had no time to ask him about it.

"Please," said Starka, "we're just … simple travelers …"

"What insolence," interrupted the large woman. "You'll not see the Lady Mayrah unless you go through me first!" Bathilde waved the other women back and squared her shoulders to DaVille.

DaVille turned only his head toward Starka. "Stay here," he said, taking a step away. Starka could only watch at spear point as the fight began.

DaVille advanced, but his blows were thwarted from both directions by the teeth of the mace. Despite the woman's size, she dodged his downward swipes and parried away each horizontal slash. DaVille only grinned all the wider, seeming to enjoy the challenge she presented. He fought differently than he had against the Carrion. Each blow seemed more precise, even planned, whereas the previous opponents required him to watch and attack all directions at once.

Bathilde tried to ensnare his blades by turning her weapon at each parry, but DaVille pulled the swords away too fast. A particularly sharp clang of metal made Starka gasp, but the fight continued. She noticed Bathilde start to tire, but the smile remained on DaVille's face.

"Is this all a mace-wielder can muster?" DaVille taunted further.

"Stop calling me that!" Bathilde returned with a growl.

She renewed her efforts, and went on the offensive. The huge weapon hummed as it split the air, sending dirt everywhere when it struck the ground. DaVille leapt back, spun his blades and watched for an opening.

Starka, engrossed in the fight, barely heard a woman's cry of "Enough!" The command went ignored by both of the combatants, as well. Even if Bathilde heard it, DaVille kept her too entangled in the fight to safely extricate herself.

Bathilde blocked a clumsy stab of his left sword, but Starka saw his body had not committed to the motion. The mace deflected the blade and sent it flying away.

"Ha!" Bathilde rejoiced that she disarmed him, but froze as the cold steel in DaVille's right hand pressed against her throat. In her excitement, she failed to notice the feint for what it was.

"Drop the mace," he commanded. A thud resounded as the head of the weapon hit the ground. Despite Bathilde's ease in swinging the weapon, Starka realized it was as heavy as it looked.

"You almost fought well," said DaVille. "For a woman."

He grinned when Bathilde's body tensed. Starka didn't know whether he meant it as a compliment or a jab, but from her experience with the man, she thought it most likely the latter.

"All we wanted to do was pass through, but you had to have your fight," he continued. "Well, this should be a lesson not to throw your challenges around so ..."

"Hold!" The commanding voice boomed. "Let her go."

Starka looked past her captors, recognizing the speaker to be the one who commanded the battle to stop before.

The newcomer also looked well-armored, with gray plate armor fitting together as three separate pieces. Her arms were fitted with bracers and on her head sat an open-faced helmet that looked much like a claw grasping her forehead. Golden hair leaked out the sides and down the back of her neck, giving the helmet a hastily-donned look. With reins in one hand and a curved sword in the other, her eyes bored holes in DaVille from her mounted position. Rider and horse both seemed calm, but the weapon glowed with an intense azure, like the sky on a cloudless day.

"You must be Mayrah," said DaVille.

"Lady Mayrah to you, swine!" Bathilde growled, ready to die for indignation rather than incompetence. An increase of pressure from the blade at her neck reminded the woman to be silent, as did Lady Mayrah.

"Quiet, Bathilde! Enough of this," said Lady Mayrah as she sheathed her sword. "What do you want?"

DaVille laughed. "Food and horses, for a start. We were perfectly content to leave silently and let the Carrion troops trample your little camp, till your 'soldiers' ambushed us."

Again, his words brought gasps from the surrounding females, but Mayrah did not flinch.

"You hold a sword to one of my dearest friends, stranger. How am I supposed to trust you?"

DaVille's eyes narrowed. "When you wake up with a sword through your body, make sure to take a close look at the creature at the other end. Then perhaps you'll believe me."

"He's right," Starka added, "there are three-thousand of them headed this direction!"

"Silence!" Mayrah boomed. "We will cast a spell to determine the truth of this matter."

"Fine," said DaVille, "but try anything funny and she loses the ability to breathe."

Starka heard a soft chant from nearby, but kept her eyes on Mayrah. A green glimmer washed over DaVille and he turned toward the source of the glow. Starka didn't even have time to warn him before Bathilde, with a quickness that belied her size, spun out of the man's grasp and landed a meaty fist across his jaw. DaVille collapsed to the ground, unconscious again.

"Shackle his hands behind his back. We'll take these ones to Cellto and let them figure it out. If there truly are Carrion to the west, we'll need to head there anyway." Mayrah trotted a bit closer to examine DaVille's fallen form.

"The spell didn't affect him at all, My Lady," said the chanter.

Bathilde bent down to examine DaVille more closely. "It distracted him, that's all I care about."

Women pulled Starka's hands roughly behind her back as Mayrah approached. The mounted woman turned to regard the dirty and stained girl, opposites to Mayrah's swarthy skin and battle-hardened demeanor.

After a moment, Mayrah's eyes narrowed in suspicion. "Tell me, girl," she asked, "what is an Alsher priestess doing in Rochelle?"

CHAPTER 12 − *Xymon*

YMON DONNED HIS SMOOTH, BLACK MASK IN THE RELAtively safe confines of the cave. It covered his head like a cowl, a tight-fitting satin barrier to keep out the light. To the unknowing observer, he knew it looked as if he could not see through the mask. A sword through their chest usually proved otherwise.

As his troops prepared, Xymon exited the small cave to survey their target. From his vantage point, the General could see both the cathedrals of Myst-Alsher and Myst-Garvon. The latter of the two stood tall; its large, phallic towers stretched high from the tip of a generous peninsula. Its counterpart, modest and lackluster in comparison, sat further inland. Both structures shined in the dusk light, representing the faith of Myst.

Neither of the other two Generals could be successful here, Xymon thought. Drakkaram would butcher the zealots, making martyrs and solidifying their belief. Circulosa would have the same trouble, even with his talents, because magic would be viewed even more fervently as evil. No, he mused, defeating these people required stealth and precision; possibly even subtlety. The dark General considered it at length, but still had not come to a conclusion of how best to do it. A contingent of Carrion, likewise trained in the clandestine arts, waited at his command for days now, but Xymon still had no plan.

Each night he watched, Xymon felt a certain familiarity toward the place. It brought strange whispers into his thoughts, but they were drowned out by the desires emanating from his horns.

He could raze both cathedrals to the ground, but it would not defeat the people. The Mystian nation remained too spread-out and cautious for a plan like poison to work, as it had in Brong. Patrols continued to increase since Xymon arrived, and they were solid fighters with little fear of death. Even the Carrion corpses he created from them went berserk. They tore at their horns in rejection of the new cause and died screaming. If his ranks did not swell with the light-tainted Myst-followers as originally planned, the dark General thought, then so be it.

From a distance, he spotted an advancing band of cavalry. Mounted Mystian zealots carried pikes, but they did not worry Xymon. He alerted the troops, and they set out to ambush the latest patrol and scout a new place to hide.

Drakkaram had utterly decimated Fort Sondergaarde and with that, on top of his victory in Bloodmir, the dark General felt even more pressure against delaying the capture of his assigned territory. Action would need to come soon, as they made no progress dispatching small patrols.

As the cavalry entered the pass where his troops waited, Xymon slowly drew his fearsome black sword. Aptly named "Nightwind," the weapon was forged with the same experimental process as the Carrion horns. After a dozen similar blades turned on their masters, all but the General's had been taken away and replaced with mundane steel. Nightwind remained loyal, though he perceived its sentience each time the blade cleared its sheath.

Quiet as a wraith, Xymon barely touched the surface of each stone he leapt across as he circled to the cavalry's rear. When the leader drew up his horse at the mouth of the pass, Xymon flattened himself against the rocks. Night had not fallen in full, but the long shadows of dusk hid his troops well. Before long, the patrol's mounts began to protest and grow unruly. With a wave of his hand, the patrol leader motioned them forward.

Xymon smiled behind his mask and gathered the folds of his cloak in an empty hand to avoid catching it in the fall. With a leap over the rock, he dropped to the bottom of the pass and caught the trailing soldier unaware. The man had no time to shout before his severed head hit the ground, but his horse whinnied and bolted. Chaos and confusion appeared in the beast's wake.

A hail of arrows whistled from the cliffs and one by one the cavaliers died. One of the zealots raised his faith symbol, a cross of molded metal, and a burst of light shot from it. The beam sailed through the air and Xymon brought his cloak up to block and absorb it. As he cast the cloth back, he noticed a faint burned smell.

"So," he whispered, "you think you have a little power?"

The General drew the blade of his longsword across one hand, hard enough to draw a bit of black fluid out of his palm. A sting alerted him of the sword's acceptance as it drank in his blood and Nightwind responded immediately. The blade split into ten pieces that spun in midair before they sought out warm flesh. When their work finished, he recalled the shards and put the sword back to rest.

While his troops cleaned up the mess and disposed of the bodies, Xymon climbed back up the cliff. He looked southwest to observe the city of Praypor; a community of Myst-worshippers with too little money to live nearer the great cathedrals. Past the tent city of vagrants and dirt-people — hardly worth the effort to conquer or destroy — flowed the great river that split the island continent. Again he considered poison, but decided it would be a wasted effort. The cathedrals remained the only prize here.

XYMON'S HEAD CHIMED AND SHOOK FOR A MOMENT AS ZION'S projection coalesced. The pain from his small horns quieted as he employed the technique to cope with the long distance contact.

"Yes, Great Zion," Xymon hissed.

"You must immediately abandon your assault on the Mystians," said the Master. The voice echoed as if it came from the other end of a tunnel, yet still retained its original strength.

Xymon could not respond to the command, unsure of its implications. Had he not acted quickly enough? Was he not effectively scouting and probing the zealots? With effort, Xymon quieted his instincts and submitted to the will of Zion, refusing to let his ego betray any hint of concern.

"I go where I am placed," the dark General responded.

Silence reigned for a moment, and he began to feel Zion had tested him. Undying and unquestioning loyalty to one's superior were Xymon's most treasured attributes in his soldiers, and he made sure they learned through his example.

"I have seen in the oracle stones," boomed Zion's voice, "that Circulosa will fail me."

Xymon cursed the human General aloud, placing his hand back on Nightwind's hilt.

"Good, yes," said the Master. "I feel your anger toward him. He is inferior to you in every way, scorning our horns even while he swears loyalty to our cause. I have sensed something awry in him since the attack on Illiadora."

Of course, thought Xymon, the Great Zion would never have promoted the human to General status by mistake — there must be some flaw in Circulosa that would cause him to fail. His mind immediately went to the round General's ego during his banter with Drakkaram. The brutal General might talk highly but his reputation could never be called into question. Circulosa, on the other hand …

"I will do anything you ask," said Xymon.

A light sparked in front of the General's face and an image appeared inside of it. He perceived a mass of crystal he knew well; a rare substance that required an extreme amount of time, power, and preparation to create.

"When he fails, make sure he does not survive," Zion commanded. The image faded away with the Master's instruction. "Destroy any cowards who flee with him — they will be replaced."

CHAPTER 13 − *Wan Du*

NONE OF WAN DU'S LIMBS FIT THROUGH THE BARS OF HIS cell for they were too close together. He couldn't even grab and shake the guards as they walked by. It would not have done much good, anyway, as none spoke his language.

Imprisoned on arrival, Wan Du received no trial or attempt at justice. Cellto did not ask questions when prisoners were delivered, it seemed, by their trusted patrons. In his hungered, weakened, and beaten condition he could do little to stop them from goading him into a cell too small for his frame. An inadequate meal came soon after, but the guard who carried it didn't respond to any of his attempts to speak. Wan Du hoped his captivity would only last until they could find a translator.

He looked out across the bleakness of Cellto. Nestled in the crux of a large bay, the city was famous for its prison. Criminals and prisoners of war from all over came to Cellto as an extra punishment. Coincidentally, the city remained the region's largest supplier of meat products. Each time Wan Du breathed in, he smelled human sweat and animal slaughter. Just as with Bloodmir, he never wanted to come here — especially not in bondage.

Wan Du's thoughts turned to the blackened remains of Rochelle the small sailboat passed on the way from Bloodmir. He saw little, locked in the cargo hold of the ship when his captors deemed Wan Du too large to fit inside a holding cell. They chained him to the larger crates like an animal, instead.

Rochelle no longer even vaguely resembled what he remembered. Wan Du mourned the years he faithfully fought against the swarthy folk; even a century of rivalry did not warrant so much destruction. He hoped some of the people survived to ask for their forgiveness.

"*Serené*, did our battle do this?" he lamented quietly. "Is this why have you forsaken me?"

Wan Du struggled to ignore his snoring cellmate. The man, dressed in layers of brown with tarnished brass buckles, occupied the cell's only cot. Based on his attire and ability to sleep through the constant moans and cries, Wan Du deduced the dirty man had occupied the cell for a long time already.

The large man began to worry he would never even be free again. His halberd, the weapon *Serené* entrusted to him, had been confiscated by his captors. The mustached man carried it and disappeared into the city while the rest led Wan Du roughly off the ship and in the opposite direction. No one understood his protests. They delivered a few shots from the butt end of a spear whenever he spoke up. Even now, Wan Du's hands clenched as he imagined choking the life from the man who stole his only possession.

Wan Du counted hundreds of his cellmate's snores, having no other way to mark time, before a translator finally arrived. The small man's features marked him as a native to the southern region, but most definitely not from Brong. After he bowed, the flimsy old gentleman adjusted a pair of spectacles and smiled with the dumb sincerity of a trained dog.

The escort, a Cellto guardsman, pointed to himself and spoke what had to be his name. "Makson," he said, stretching it out as if Wan Du were an idiot rather than a foreigner.

The translator likewise introduced himself as, "Fung."

Wan Du stood, silent, and waited for the men to come closer to the bars. The guard and the translator looked at each other and spoke a few words before turning back to him.

"What is your name?" asked the translator. Fung spoke in a dialect similar to Wan Du's language. Even so, the phrases took effort to understand.

At first, Wan Du shook his head and refused to answer. He knew the process of interrogation, having been a soldier, and alerting these men to how much he needed them would be a mistake. With a perplexed expression, Fung muttered something to Makson. Both turned to leave, when the man from Brong surrendered.

"Wait," said Wan Du.

The translator stopped and turned back to face the cell. Makson sighed and rolled his eyes. Wan Du took a long look at the guard to size him up. Makson removed his studded helmet and wiped his sweaty brow with a cloth. Everything the guards wore looked restrictive and useless. Their unkempt appearance signaled they weren't ready to fight, despite the nearby Carrion presence.

Wan Du took it as an ominous sign; Cellto had to be allied to the Carrion army just as Bloodmir was.

"I am Wan Du," he said, pausing before he added the honoraries, "chosen of Serené and last servant to the Temple of the Winds."

He watched as Fung translated his words, including his name and something about Brong. Makson responded with what seemed like harsh words. After a pause, Fung relayed them more gently.

"Makson says, 'thieves pay the harshest penalties, no matter where they are from'."

"I'm no thief," Wan Du growled.

"It's been reported otherwise," came the translated retort. "You were caught attempting to steal a suit of armor from a reputable merchant in Bloodmir, were you not?"

Wan Du knew he could not argue with these men. Not only were they allied to the Carrion, but they could not fathom the disgrace of seeing the scavenged armor on display. The use of the word "reputable" only fueled his silent rage. Fung might be able to understand, but the old man would not care.

"I had a weapon, a halberd," said Wan Du. "I demand to see it and I demand that it is returned to me when I am released."

After bantering Fung relayed, "He doesn't know what you're talking about, but says he will bring it up to your captor when he returns to the city."

Wan Du's massive hands grasped the two bars nearest him as his rage boiled over.

"*Serené* bestowed that weapon upon me," he pleaded. "I am charged with destroying the Darkness of the Carrion and I need that weapon to do it. They have killed all of my people! I demand that you let … me … out!"

He emphasized the last three words with pulls on the bars. Grit dropped from the ceiling but the bars did not loosen. For a moment all was silent, except for the uninterrupted snores of the other prisoner.

Fung's eyes widened before he turned to the soldier and translated. The words brought mirth to Makson and Wan Du realized his words were too angry to be coherent.

"You both must think I'm crazy," he whispered, "but I have seen the Carrion horns transform men into beasts. They have destroyed Brong and Rochelle, and if this place still stands it is because Cellto is allied with the Carrion."

The small man didn't translate, but returned a pitying stare. Makson nudged Fung and gestured, curious to know what Wan Du said. Without breaking eye contact, Fung muttered something that satisfied the guardsman.

"Your words seem to hold much weight for a common thief," Fung accused, "but they will not prove your innocence."

Wan Du struggled to stay calm and respond. "Can't you see what is going on? They will kill us all and turn us into them!"

Makson beckoned to his side and another man, this one bald and garbed in purple robes, came into view. With a few wild hand gestures, he spoke a command word and a shaft of smoky blue sped from his fingertips into Wan Du's forehead.

The large man collapsed flat onto his back, arms spread wide. He took up almost the entire floor of the cell. Before Wan Du fell completely unconscious, he repeated his claim of Brong being poisoned and the horns. He could only hope Fung heard and cared enough to help.

CHAPTER 14 – *Starka*

STARKA KNEW HER EXPLANATION SOUNDED WEAK IN THE eyes of Mayrah and Bathilde. Both elder women tapped their feet with arms crossed during Starka's short tale of travel and being marooned. They each raised an eyebrow at certain points, obvious holes where the young woman left out something of interest, but Starka held to her story throughout the interrogation.

Close to thirty women shared warmth and safety, most in meager straw beds spread around the chamber. Many stared at the girl with the same expression Wadam had used — impatience and brooding resentment. Starka tried to avoid meeting their glances.

"I'll only ask you this one more time, girl." The heavy thud of Bathilde's mace echoed throughout the long hut currently used as the barracks. "What are you doing here?"

Starka fidgeted and refused to respond. In truth, nerves kept her from answering the question again. She knew that, at any time, they could all be trampled by thousands of Carrion solders from the black-sailed ships.

More than anything, she didn't want to reveal information about the prophecy. Wadam strictly forbade it, and though it might help explain things, she did not feel honesty would be appreciated in this situation. People from Rochelle already distrusted her kind; admitting she came on a mission from her god might get her throat cut. She did the only thing a person, even a priestess, could do when confronted with such obstacles: she lied.

"I told you, I have traveled here to pray for the souls of the departed! That they may find peace in the gentle and everlasting arms of Myst and that Alsher and Garvon forgive them. I was attacked by ghastly creatures and DaVille saved my life. We were running from thousands more of them when you captured us."

The girl contented herself in the fact that it wasn't a complete lie — she had prayed for the souls of thousands who died in Rochelle since walking near, and over, their numerous graves.

"Ridiculous!" A swing of the huge club smashed the table in front of Starka. Its pieces fell to the floor, mere matchsticks. Bathilde pointed her stubby finger in the girl's face. "You waste your time thinking any of us need your northerner blessings, and if I'd caught you desecrating our dead in the name of your faith you would have joined them!"

Silence fell on the room like the tremendous pause after a thunderclap. Starka looked at Bathilde, then to Mayrah. The slimmer woman calmly placed her hands on her hips. When she leaned her weight to one side Starka could see the curves of her athletic body. Mayrah's shoulders looked too broad to be feminine at first glance, but without the armor her womanhood became more apparent.

The only possible male voice cut the silence in half. "Don't fear her, girl. She's still mad about being born a woman."

A rampaging Bathilde almost brought the roof down on top of all their heads in response. She marched to the cot where DaVille laid, face down with all limbs tied behind him. The man actually laughed when she raised her club for another blow, but Mayrah halted it. Though not as upset as her counterpart by the comment, Mayrah did not seem much impressed, either.

"We had every right to kill the two of you as spies simply for the way we came upon you," accused Mayrah.

"Ha! You think we're going to openly march through settlements with three thousand Carrion right behind us?" asked DaVille, his ability to intimidate stifled by his bonds. "Lady, have you even fought one of them?"

"Oh, yes," she responded, "your *assailants*." She turned toward DaVille with pure indifference. "And why have we seen neither hide nor hair of them?"

"Probably because they haven't wanted you to," DaVille muttered, somewhat under his breath.

Unfazed, or perhaps simply because she didn't hear him, Mayrah continued. "The simple truth is that you attacked us without provocation and you were defeated and captured."

"So you're going to march us into the Syllowaste to die," he said. "Might as well kill the girl now."

Starka blanched at this, but the dark-skinned woman spun on her heels to face DaVille.

"That is no longer done," Mayrah said, a hard edge to her tone. "You will be taken to Cellto as prisoners."

"But we are not spies and certainly not criminals," Starka pleaded. "We're innocent!"

Bathilde laughed from across the room. "That is what they all say, girl. I can count on one hand the captives who have admitted to their guilt."

"The only thing I'm guilty of is wounding your pride," DaVille retorted with a grin. Bathilde bristled, but did not reply.

"This is your last chance to tell us the truth," said Mayrah, ignoring the man.

Starka brought her hands to her face and shook her head as she felt the tears begin to flow. How she longed for the comforts of home, where trust never became a life and death necessity. Even if she could separate herself somehow from DaVille, her chances of survival would still depend on these women. No, she thought, where he goes I go, even if that means to a prison — he got me into this, he can get me out of it.

"I've told you everything I know," the girl responded.

"Cellto knows how to deal with rogues like him," Bathilde said as she shouldered her weapon, "and liars like you."

AT FIRST LIGHT A COMPANY OF ROCHELLE FEMALES LEFT THEIR encampment with trading goods, supplies, and the two fugitives in tow. DaVille and Starka were shackled and lashed to the rear of a wagon to be dragged — if necessary — to Cellto. By midday it became so hot Starka could barely put one foot in front of the other. When she looked at DaVille, she saw the same determined expression on his face as when they left. Though sweat poured from his brow, he did not seem to notice much.

Even during the coolest season in the southern lands, crossing the desert would have been a difficult trip. Those days, however, were long gone. Starka thought she knew hot seasons, but the wind blowing north from the Syllowaste awakened her to worse. The few travelers who returned from the awful wasteland always told horrific stories, said her books. The legends seemed to either center around walking skeletons or large, hairy beasts that climbed up from tubes in the ground. Starka did not wish to find out which was truth.

Their trek crossed the mild desert region between the sea and the Syllowaste, but in her scavenged clothes Starka suffered for each step. Halfway into the afternoon, Mayrah called a rest and granted some water to her prisoners. Soon after the stop, a few of the rear scouts raised an alert; a cloud formed to their rear.

"Lady Mayrah!" The repeated summons came from the western end of the company as the speaker rode toward them. She frantically whipped her horse's flank and held on for dear life as it carried her as fast as it could. As the scout came closer, Starka saw the woman's leg and shoulder dripping blood — wounded by black arrows.

"My Lady, an army … a horde approaches! At least a thousand of those brown humanoids."

As she began to faint, another cry came from the opposite direction. "A scout coming from the east! She's wounded!"

DaVille tested his bonds and looked around. "Best start praying, girl," he whispered.

The pursuit turned her situation from bad to completely hopeless. So far away from home, Starka knew no one could help her. This is what it must be like to live in the outside world, she thought, to be completely alone and solely responsible for your safety. The truth of it saddened her as she stared at the man next to her.

Starka listened as Mayrah addressed all of the women at once. The eastern scout confirmed the enemy planned a pincer to entrap the group from both sides. It seemed a shipload of Carrion sailed past them while the rest made landfall and picked up their trail. This brought some worried cries from the assembled females, since some remained behind at the encampment.

Mayrah called to Bathilde and the women spoke briefly to formulate a plan. The two prisoners rested not far from the impromptu council, which sounded to Starka like both women cursing their rotten luck.

"We have only one direction to flee," came the leader's simple assessment.

"My club will take a few of them down with it!" Bathilde announced to cheers from the other women.

DaVille rolled his eyes at the predictable reply.

"What's your problem with her?" Starka whispered. "What was that all about when you called each other by the weapons you were wielding?"

DaVille ignored her again, intent only on the conversation of their captors. He didn't even make eye contact with her to confirm he heard her question.

"No, Bathilde," said Mayrah, "we need to head south before they have a chance to overtake us. It'll be dangerous, but we'll only go as far into the Syllowaste as absolutely necessary."

"I'm talking to you, DaVille."

He tried to wave her off again, but Starka grasped his hand and pulled hard, forcing him to look at her. She wanted answers now, sick of being at his mercy for them.

"Fine, fine," he said. "When you face someone in battle, in a duel especially, it's proper etiquette to address them by the weapon they carry only if you do not know their name. Of course, there are certain things to be expected when a person wields a certain type of weapon; a mace being one of the heaviest and clumsiest implements a person might carry. Basically, I inferred she was the equivalent of a pack animal; how's that?"

Bathilde shouted, "I don't know about you all, but I'd rather take on these Carrion than the things that come out of those caves, wretched as they are!"

Starka noticed the woman illustrated the very point DaVille made. Bathilde put on a brave face, but seemed to have an attitude that would eventually send her into a fight she could not win. The girl looked at DaVille and wondered how much of that trait he had in him. After all, he charged into groups of Carrion with no regard for his own safety. Though he came out victorious in the end, Starka understood enough about battle to know the ability to win did not equate to invincibility. Plus, with him tied up, even Bathilde stood a better chance against their pursuers.

Cheers in agreement went up after Bathilde's comment, but all of the women deferred to Mayrah for the decision. The females in charge of supplies began to discuss how much they could afford to leave behind to help them move faster through the desolate Syllowaste.

Over the din, DaVille challenged, "You're wasting your time."

One by one, the council of females turned toward the two prisoners. Starka began to feel awkwardly implicated in their stares and tried to inch away from DaVille as much as she could without being noticed.

"Oh, are we?" Bathilde scoffed. "And how did you come to that conclusion, O Bound One?"

To Starka, it seemed the two were only becoming more adept at their subtle insults.

"If you're planning to escape to the south, you might as well just fall on your swords now." DaVille raised his dry voice to speak to all of the women present.

They responded with outcries of, "Outrageous!" and, "What does this prisoner know, anyway?"

"Silence!" Mayrah bellowed. "They were right about the pursuit. Perhaps we should at least hear him out. Speak, prisoner."

"The fact that they divided their forces as they have suggests more than just intelligence; it suggests strategy," he replied. "Something much smarter than those creatures is controlling them. If you attempt the escape to the south, you'll run right into a third group. The flanking forces are smaller; they're only trying to herd you into thinking you have an escape."

Mayrah pondered it for a moment before replying. "How do you know all of this? How do you know any of it?"

The questions were the same on Starka's lips.

DaVille turned away and gritted his teeth. "We don't have time to play a game of 'who knows what.' If you believe me, you believe me. If not, cut us loose and head yourselves south."

"Cut you loose?" asked an exasperated Bathilde, ready to boil over. "So you can run back to the very army you're claiming to have information on? Report our position? Make that third force appear in the south?" Her breath came in short, ragged gasps and a vein could clearly be seen protruding from her forehead with every beat of her heart.

"He's right," said Mayrah. Bathilde turned to her in shock.

"My Lady, how can you trust the word of this ... this bloody vagabond?" she asked. "He was no soldier of ours, yet he wore our armor to infiltrate our very encampment and slay us after gaining our trust! You're doing his work for him, don't you see it?"

"No, my friend. Whether or not we go south, he is right that something much smarter is controlling these beasts," said Mayrah. "We need to make it to a city before we're all killed, particularly if either of those two have information that could bring the killers of our husbands and fathers to justice."

Bathilde seemed to tear up, the grimace twisting her dark and masculine features into something very foreign.

"What do you suggest, then?" one of the supply women asked.

"North," DaVille stated flatly, pointing back toward the sea. His bold word brought a huge response, mostly negative. For some reason, Starka noticed, Mayrah seemed to be his only supporter.

"Women of Rochelle," Mayrah spoke over the dissenters and their concerns quieted. "Even if there are those among you who would desert, it is likely you have nowhere to run. You have placed your faith in me as leader, and I say north is our only choice."

SANDY TERRAIN PROVIDED FEW PLACES TO HIDE THEMSELVES, much less the horses and wagons. Even their slow pace frightened Starka as she estimated their odds of survival. The group abandoned all non-essential supplies. DaVille deemed them a "sacrifice," and some were sent south pulled by pack animals who didn't complain as they approached their imminent demise. Starka watched the animals walk dumbly away, hoping they met a peaceful end when it came. The decoy would buy them some time, DaVille assured her, and the girl could only hope he proved right.

The planned route took them straight north for a measured amount of time and then, in a zigzag pattern, northeast to north as the land permitted. DaVille, not quite surprised, explained the delay between Carrion sightings as "enough time to formulate a plan of attack." Starka continued to wonder where he came from and who he truly was; he seemed a seasoned veteran of engagements when faced with a crisis, but otherwise singularly arrogant.

Mayrah discerned they were nearly to Cellto and relayed it would be less than a day more before they arrived at the city. Starka remained unsure of what would happen once they got there. Unshackled, the prisoners rode in one of the supply wagons near the front of the column and a tense readiness accompanied the uneventful plodding.

Bathilde looked all the more nervous as she rode next to the wagon. She didn't trust DaVille at all and refused to return his weapons after unbinding his hands. She seemed willing to leave him as vulnerable as possible, though unable to kill him outright.

UPON CRESTING A DUNE, THE LEAD SCOUT ANNOUNCED SIGHT OF the sea and the city. Once the wagon reached the hill, Starka could make out the lights of Cellto and caught a faint scent of dead animal. The party turned east, along the coastline, and increased their pace. As the first of the sun's rays glowed on the horizon, a cry of panic went up.

"Arrows!" Mayrah yelled. "Rear, bring it up! Everyone, make for the city!"

Stifled shouts and death cries of both horses and women went up though the young girl couldn't see much in the low light. A long, black arrow streaked past Starka's head and embedded itself into the wood mere inches away. She dropped to the floor and whispered prayers to Alsher and Garvon, begging for help to survive this.

"You go, My Lady!" Bathilde shouted, wheeling her mount toward the rear. "Anyone who is not wounded, go with her! Protect Lady Mayrah!"

Mayrah halted her horse and called back, "What do you think you are doing?"

"We won't be able to hold them off forever, but I'll make sure you can make it to the city." Bathilde dismounted and drew her great mace off her shoulder.

She held it in front of her with both hands and turned to the source of the arrows. Starka's wagon passed by the woman and she did not know what to say.

A small detachment of Carrion approached from the south, more than a little upset their prey eluded them. The large woman began a slow chant under her breath and her mace elongated to three times its height. A brown glow seemed to envelop it and Starka began to hear a slight hum.

"Go!" came Bathilde's womanly roar as she slammed the ground with her weapon. A great cloud of dirt erupted and a crevice in the earth began to burrow its way toward their adversaries, kicking up debris and stones as it went. She repeated this process again and again until the Carrion were too busy keeping their feet to launch their own missiles.

Mayrah kicked the flanks of her mount and steered the animal next to DaVille. She tossed him a bundle containing his longswords. Starka watched DaVille's face tighten as he nodded to the mounted female warrior, gripped the reins and whipped the leading animals forward.

Starka looked back and wondered if she would ever see Bathilde again. A prayer for the large woman came to her lips, but the girl caught herself when she remembered Bathilde's scornful remarks. She wished to die alone and meet an empty end, and Starka had no choice but to let her. All thoughts of Bathilde dissipated as the wagon reached the city gates of Cellto, closed tight in the early morning.

Carrion grunts howled and sprinted across the desert plain, threatening to overrun the fleeing party. DaVille pulled the reins to stop the animals and leapt down from the wagon to meet the threat. Starka climbed carefully down the other side and advanced on the iron doors as quickly as she could.

"Open the gate!" She screamed, impotent, as her fists slammed against the solid metal wall. Tears streamed down the girl's face and the heels of her hands would surely be bruised, but the gate, to her continued exasperation, held fast.

The few Carrion that dared approach DaVille or Mayrah were quickly cut to ribbons. Starka marveled at their tenacity, but knew if the gates didn't open the fighters would soon be overwhelmed. The larger portion of the Carrion army would catch up to this handful and, if that came before long, Starka feared she would die on the doorstep of their supposed saviors — or worse.

She assumed the gate would be open, especially once the sun came up. Again Starka found herself between an army of Carrion and an unattainable location, entrenched in desperation because of a comrade she could not depend on.

When a small viewing hole opened Starka barely paused to notice, but kept beating her fists against the gate.

"What?" a voice demanded. "We don't want any o' your fight!"

"Oh, praise Alsher!" She cried, no longer caring if anyone realized where she came from. "You must let us in!"

"Ha," came the response. "Don't think I let in just any Mystian at my doorstep, little lady."

Starka's heart dropped, suddenly drained from the brief hope it enjoyed. She considered asking DaVille for help, but knew what he would say. Faced with the possibilities of certain death and forcing this guard to open the gate, she chose the latter — even if it meant she had to lie again.

"I'll pray to whatever gods you want, just open the gate! It's not just me out here; Lady Mayrah from Rochelle is here as well as her people. You must let us in! We'll do anything!"

A few moments later, a small door inside the gate swung open. Starka rushed in just as she heard DaVille shout for a retreat and turned to watch him practically drag Mayrah from the defensive line. The woman yelled for Bathilde and the others and fought DaVille every step to make her words heard. When questioned, the delirious woman held firm the hope that, "Bathilde will survive. She's too tough to let any humanoid beast take her down. Have you seen the club she wields?"

Lady Mayrah seemed to cower without her large friend nearby, as if her absence dried up the woman's confidence. It reminded Starka of her own loss, and she sympathized with Mayrah's rejection of the certainty of her companion's death.

From the entire group that left the ruins of Rochelle, only eight now passed through the gate of Cellto. Mayrah collapsed against DaVille, spent from the fight. Starka nearly wanted to tear her off of him, but shook away the strange feeling. How could she be jealous of the woman who protected her escape? Besides, she did not feel anything romantic for DaVille — and she certainly did not own him.

Regardless, she did not suffer long, for DaVille practically flung the woman away. Even bloodied and tired, Mayrah looked quite beautiful, but it could be difficult to tell because of her manner. Only when her gaze directed at DaVille did her intensity abate a bit; the set of her jaw and furrowing of her brow usually hid her emotions and made her appear too masculine to be attractive.

After Starka's production at the door she expected no easy welcome. True to form, rather than calling a magistrate, the guards simply imprisoned the group until such time was acceptable for one to be summoned. Any inquiries as to how long that would be were ignored or met with a grunt.

Even after being repeatedly told that a huge detachment of Carrion forces approached their walls, the Cellto guards remained quite calm. They were a bit dismissive of the explanation for the party's haste. Starka even heard a chuckle or two when she became more emphatic about the danger. DaVille grabbed her by the arm and pulled her close to him. His gaze said without words to stay quiet and keep them out of more trouble than he already perceived them to be in.

Despite numerous protests, the guards herded them through a few dark hallways and locking gates. After the group ascended a tiring amount of stairs, they came to a precipice where the city proper could be viewed. DaVille and Starka looked out over what could only be a cell block; thousands upon thousands of vertical bars set into horizontal rectangles with shadowed interiors. Past that, they saw huge towering cylinders spewing unnatural amounts of smoke into the sky.

At spear point, the guards thrust the eight survivors into cells a handful at a time. DaVille, Starka, and a female soldier occupied one in a long line of cells along an immense corridor. Mayrah and the others were placed further away, presumably out of sight range to avoid escape plots and to generally discourage hope. DaVille gripped the bars tightly in both hands and gritted his teeth. He turned and leaned against the metal, looking unsure for the first time since she met him.

Starka retreated to the rear of the cell and kneeled to pray, desperately in need of guidance or comfort.

"Better get some rest," said DaVille. "Might need it for later."

She paused between sobs and stared at him. Before she could speak, the Rochelle female piped up, "Can't you do anything? My friends are still out there!"

He waved her off, similar to how he treated Starka, but the woman persisted. "You heartless bastard! My sister died to protect you and you don't even care!"

DaVille turned with narrowed eyes and stared the swarthy female down. His hands clenched and opened again, obviously wishing he held a weapon. "Speak to me like that again, and you won't make it out of here alive. It's your Lady's fault I'm here at all, and if it weren't for me you'd all be dead."

His words made the female from Rochelle reconsider her reproach, and she sank onto the cot with her head in her hands.

"Besides," DaVille added, "your people know a thing or two about heartlessness as well."

CHAPTER 15 – *Drakkaram*

HOUGH THE BRUTAL GENERAL HATED TO ADMIT IT, Circulosa was right. Drakkaram encountered a large magical resistance upon landing at the peninsula, even well north of Fort Sondergaarde. He briefly considered the possibility that the wizard somehow alerted them to his arrival, but dismissed it.

Not even Circulosa would be that stupid, he thought.

Regardless, no amount of impromptu magic could offset his pure numerical advantage. As he surveyed the scene from outside the southern gate of the fortress, he saw his expected results.

The main force occupied the defenders while his sneak troops traversed the tunnels and gained access to the inside of the fort. Once behind, the Carrion caught the resistance from both sides and tore through them easily. Fort Sondergaarde's gates were open long before the remaining people could organize another defensive, and the battle ended in minutes.

Drakkaram's long pointed teeth gnashed together in a mockery of a smile as he continued to hear the screams of women and children erupt into the night.

"Ha! Invincible Fortress!" He bellowed. "It might as well have been made of leaves and twine!"

In fact, the walls of Fort Sondergaarde were reinforced many times over with wards and spells to absorb and redirect magic. Its high walls of wooden posts stood for centuries, much longer than any structure on the continent — including Flaem. The fortress earned its reputation as an outpost at the southern end of the civilized territories during the Sorcerers War; it discouraged conflicts from finding their way north.

Situated at the root of the peninsula and guarded by massive cliffs, no army could land south of the fort and assail it from that angle. To sail too far north risked arriving somewhere near Flaem, and the high coast in between provided perfect vantage points. The fortress ultimately proved to be less than impregnable, Drakkaram reflected, since the walls had no defense against the Carrion strength.

Drakkaram cut short his celebration, feeling an attack break against his armor. A faint heat blast from a fire spell warmed his neck, but did little else. He spun his horse to face the attacker and nearly burst out laughing all over again. A single wizard in a coat of many colors stood against him, pointing his staff directly at the General.

"You killed my family. Now I will make you pay! Vexen, bless my revenge!" The human screamed while he trembled in fear of the heartless Drakkaram.

Without waiting for any further attacks or threats, the General spurred his mount into motion. He held his broadsword to his side and charged at the puny man, knowing one swift stroke would end his useless babble. As Drakkaram neared, the man cast a spell that made his horse draw up and kick the air. A wall of color appeared where the hooves should have touched nothing.

Annoyed, Drakkaram hacked at the wall with his sword and the colors shattered like stained glass. Once the spell dissipated, he found the wizard gone from his original spot.

Again, the challenge came from behind. "You shall know my wrath, for I am Warkardis, the greatest sorcerer in Fort Sondergaarde!"

Drakkaram sensed the fear in the man's voice and knew his appearance did most of the work to inspire it. His sharp teeth parted to respond as he again wheeled his horse to face the wizard.

"I shall eat your insides for that, human," he growled.

The wizard stood agape for a moment, as he assumedly tried to process that Drakkaram spoke to him. Many things of his former life had been forgotten, but the common language remained fresh in Drakkaram's mind. The General grinned and kicked his mount into motion to charge the confused man. After a few steps the sorcerer regained his wits and resumed casting.

A red ball of flame shot from the tip of the wizard's staff and blazed toward the General only to explode inches from his chest. Undaunted, the sorcerer spun and cried out a different incantation to summon sheets of ice. Drakkaram's mount reared again and kicked at the nearest one and the rest fell like dominos. As the beast leapt onto the pile of ice, Drakkaram saw bolts of lightning shy away and strike the ground nearby.

He halted his horse and stared down at the wizard, narrowing his eyes. No mere spell could impede him, and the look in the man's eyes only heralded Drakkaram's victory.

"Now you die," he said.

With a kick of his beast's flanks, Drakkaram surged forward. He easily spanned the last few yards of fallen ice to land directly in front of the wizard. The man, in a last moment of panicked defense, brought up his staff in both hands to block Drakkaram's slash. Steel split wood and bit deep into the man's flesh, rending him in two. The halves fell to the ground as Drakkaram turned back and began a light trot toward the fortress.

"Brute force always succeeds where magic fails," he said, mostly to himself.

Drakkaram laughed again at the thought, something he had wished many times he could show Circulosa personally. His three great horns gave the General strength, not a bunch of flamboyant chants. The importance of magic in their creation notwithstanding, Drakkaram saw no further use for it.

Magic was a hindrance; he'd never needed it to help him twist the heads off the impudent weaklings that stood in his way. To compensate for this, and to tempt his enemies, Drakkaram no longer wore a helmet.

From the gate rode Thistle, a Carrion Lieutenant, to deliver his report. Drakkaram knew well the unspoken hierarchy within his ranks; the officers quickly figured out which Lieutenants he favored over others.

Unique in his methods, Thistle earned a special place in the General's eyes. Two overly-spiked maces hung from his sides, ready to dole out a special kind of spiked punishment. While Drakkaram respected this, he originally scorned the Lieutenant's refusal to carry a broadsword — the common weapon of the troop. Thistle's armor consisted of plates with many small spines, barbs, and hooks that covered him from head to foot, no doubt much to the discomfort and detriment of his horse.

"The fortress has fallen, General. A mere three-thousand peasant troops will be added to our ranks. The rest ..." Thistle raised his parted hands in a shrug.

The phrase "peasant troops" referred to humans killed in battle, but with bodies still in good enough shape to be transformed into Carrion. Close to double the dispatched lay inside the fort in pieces, no longer recognizable as human beings.

"Get on with it, then, Lieutenant."

"As you wish, General, but," the Lieutenant hesitated before he added, "we don't have the means to transport them."

"By my horns, must I do all of the thinking here?" Drakkaram growled. "Why do I even appoint officers in the first place?"

Thistle shifted uncomfortably in his seat, but did not answer. His grip on the reins tightened a bit and he blinked his dead, black eyes.

"This pitiful excuse for a fortress is made out of wood, isn't it?" asked the General. "Build me a boat, Thistle. Build me two! Tear this eyesore to the ground, if you must!"

"It will be as you command. What should we do about the enchantments on the timbers?"

"Enchantments be damned. Let them swim for all I care," Drakkaram commanded. He saw the uses of the gray ones, but not their value. They moved and fought half as quickly as his regulars, the living converts to his army, and could fall in battle only once before they became empty husks. His regulars at least could be revived to fight once more.

"There is one more thing," said Thistle.

Drakkaram placed a hand on the pommel of his sheathed greatsword. "Be out with it and get on with your orders."

Thistle spoke quickly, made aware of how thin the General's patience stretched. "This is something you should see, General. A statue stands in the middle of the Fort made of something unbreakable. I have never seen the likes of it before. Blows with our mightiest hammers have only granted us broken hammers."

At this, Drakkaram raised an eyebrow. He paused for a moment to consider the possible implications of this statue. Could it be related to what made the fortress formerly impenetrable?

"I should like to see this," said Drakkaram. "If it is in the middle, as you say, then I shall find it myself. Get to work."

Thistle gave a quick nod of his helmeted head before he spun and galloped away. Drakkaram spurred his own horse into motion toward the ruins of Fort Sondergaarde's northern gate. As he passed the threshold, a voice pounded into his head and nearly threw him from his saddle.

"Tell the soldiers to leave the statue alone, Drakkaram."

All three of his horns seemed ready to vibrate their way out of his skull. The General reined in and brought a hand to his forehead; a gesture to invoke his inner speech. Even as the link with Zion solidified, his head continued to ache.

"Why, Master?" asked the General. "Should we not smash the icons of these puny humans to show them our power?"

In response, the pain inside Drakkaram's head increased tenfold. "Do not question my orders! Your job is to do, not to ask why. Tell them its horns mark it as a friend and to leave it be. Send your peasant troops north to aid Circulosa and return to me at the Watchtower."

The throbbing of his horns subsided and Drakkaram allowed himself a moment to recover. "By your will, Zion," he whispered, and spurred his mount again.

⊘

THE GARGOYLE STATUE TOWERED OVER TWENTY FEET TALL, A MAS-sive feat since in its kneeling position. Long bat-like wings lifted high and parallel, and the beast's eyes glowed like two fist-sized rubies. Every inch of the white statue looked solid and thick, from its horned head to the humanoid torso. Its mouth hung open in a roar pointed toward the ground in front of it, as if something smaller made the beast angry before it turned to stone. Even mounted, Drakkaram's horns only reached to its chin.

He wondered at its origins, whether the red eyes held some glimmer of life or if it had been carved by human hands. In either case, the gargoyle struck an imposing figure and remained the only piece of the fortress unmolested. Just as Thistle reported, the statue's stone skin remained smooth and unscathed, though numerous discarded weapons lay broken and twisted at its feet.

The General announced Zion's decree to the soldiers and they fell back from it to work on the ships. The gray Carrion shuffled away as if their legs were already full of sand and seawater. His gaze followed a few and Drakkaram nearly struck a pair down as they passed by, dripping saliva.

"Useless trash," he said.

Drakkaram regarded the statue from his mounted position before shaking his head in disgust. Even upon close inspection, the stone remained unaffected by the combined efforts of his soldiers. He did not like defeat, but he liked even less the prospect of a force to challenge his authority. Drakkaram had to find a way to denounce the power of the statue without disobeying Zion.

He lifted a foot from the stirrup and swung to the ground, landing with a thud. Drakkaram's plate armor adjusted to his motion and shifted back as he stood straight. As he drew the greatsword from its sheath, the facets of the black blade glowed with reflected light.

Drakkaram would show both his master and his soldiers that he was not afraid of some carved rock.

The General faced the gargoyle and brought his head near its open jaws. He held the sword out to his side as he spoke his challenge.

"Mark my words, pebble-creature, and mark them well. Drakkaram fears neither man nor mountain in this world. Upon completion of my Master's tasks I shall return to this place. If I find you are still here, I will carve a new form out of you — a statue to display Drakkaram's triumph over this puny fortress."

The General pointed his blade into the gargoyle's mouth and added, "Just as I have destroyed this puny fortress, I will destroy you. This, I swear."

Though the stone figure did not respond, Drakkaram thought he saw a flicker of light move across its ruby eyes. He turned away, sheathed his blade, and went to oversee the shipbuilding.

CHAPTER 16 – *Circulosa*

THE ROUND GENERAL SURVEYED THE CITY OF FLAEM FROM his vantage point high in the air. Floating above everything, he felt almost regal. Circulosa waved his staff absently back and forth in deep thought. Hovering casually above the killing ground, he pondered the so-far formidable defenses of the great eastern city.

He lifted his free arm forward and the gesture signaled the troops below. The catapults launched another volley and a half-dozen stones sailed through the air. Each magically-enhanced rock — an addition to the original plan — crashed into the impenetrable warded walls and burst into nothingness. The General let out an exasperated shout and slammed his staff against his open palm. Even his best efforts at amplifying the stones' power failed; the city's warding magic remained as strong as ever.

Early in the siege he discovered that however aerodynamic the creatures looked, Carrion grunts met the same fate as a stone when catapulted toward a wall. Both would eventually run out, of course, but the rocks were easier to replace and, in most cases, smarter.

Circulosa lingered in the air a bit longer to assess the situation. The siege had succeeded so far, insomuch as the citizens of Flaem remained captives inside their walls. Of course, he thought, it would have been better to avoid the entire mess and capture Flaem. The Elders saw the attack coming, however, and sealed the city against him. Circulosa wondered if he had Drakkaram to thank for that, but shrugged the thought away.

The Elders refused all attempts from Circulosa to speak, scorning a peaceful resolution through surrender. Yet despite their recalcitrant behavior, Flaem stayed dormant and refused to counterattack.

Zion would not be pleased with his progress, and Circulosa knew it. A scout reported Drakkaram's successful razing of Fort Sondergaarde, despite magical defenses, though the round General saw the smoke rise from his elevated position hours earlier.

How was he, Circulosa, the General of obviously superior intellect and bolstered by magical force, foiled where Drakkaram's brute strength succeeded? Even without the element of surprise, his Carrion troops should have been able to storm the city and take it within hours. The beasts were usually unstoppable — how could they falter now?

Circulosa wondered if the Flaem elders negated his attempts to cloak the army's progress and intentions. The oracle stones became powerful objects in the proper hands; he used them to see events in the past, present, and future. His memory of foiling the betrayer's ridiculous plot made Circulosa grin. How he relished the means and the end of becoming a General of the Carrion army!

A waving pair of arms from the area beyond the catapults caught his attention. He turned toward the southern foothills and descended, ready for an update on his latest plan. With the success of the tunnels, his victory would be guaranteed. The bombardment could keep Flaem's magic and attention occupied in the meantime.

The only flaw in his plan, Circulosa reflected, was that he had to depend on grunts to implement it. They took far too long, and he had no choice but to stay visible to avoid arousing the city's suspicion.

"Fire at will," Circulosa called as he passed by the Carrion that operated the siege weapons. The dumb creatures hefted boulders, and anything else they could find, and carried on with the bombardment.

He sailed through the air and landed next to one of the open tunnel passages. The creatures that made the hole were sloppy and obviously cared nothing for aesthetics. Circulosa knew this haphazard execution of his plan could negate all of his effort and knew exactly who to blame for it. If he had not selected a spot so far away to begin digging, the city would have caught on already.

Impatient, he demanded a progress report from the soldier that flagged him down. The grunt merely shrugged, grunted, and ducked back into the cave. Circulosa brought in a long breath and blew it out quickly. He had no more patience for nonsense.

"Lieutenant Rot!" He shouted into the gaping hole. No response. Circulosa counted to nine, ready to shout again when the hideous horned creature emerged into the sunlight. Covered in boils and sores, Rot stepped out of the shadows carving a path in the dirt with the heavy sword behind it. The blade swallowed up all light around it creating a black spot in the General's vision.

Circulosa turned sideways so he didn't have to look directly at his sickening officer. "I don't have time for games, Lieutenant. Why did you flag me over if you weren't even waiting?"

Rot shielded its eyes and looked toward the city for a moment before speaking. The words came between hisses, as its tongue and throat carried the same weeping wounds as the rest of its body. Circulosa shivered just thinking about it.

"We are close to halfway, General."

Circulosa folded his arms and waited for more. When no information came, he asked, "Halfway? *Only* halfway?"

"There are many passageways already running underneath the ground here. I lost half of my diggers for most of the day because of a cave in," said Rot. After a pause, the Lieutenant added, "We could move faster with some magic."

Circulosa waved his hand to silence Rot, then forced himself to turn and face the creature. "My patience is running thin on your excuses. When will the tunnels be complete?"

Rot clicked his thumb claw against the rest before answering. "We expect to be past the wall by mid-morning tomorrow."

"Tomorrow?" Circulosa screamed, his voice breaking. "That is not nearly good enough! Can't you animals work any faster?"

Circulosa regretted the words immediately after speaking them. Had more than one of his subordinates been nearby during the exchange, it could have been a complete mutiny. As it was, Rot's one undamaged eye narrowed and a curl came to its already-misshapen upper lip. Both scarred hands went to the hilt of the huge sword, but before Rot brought an inch of the weapon to bear, Circulosa's short battlestaff came within an inch of its face.

The General knew, even this close to the magic-swallowing blade, his spell would be effective.

"Don't test me, Lieutenant. I am in control here, and no one would search for your corpse." After Rot's muscles relaxed and one hand dropped away from the hilt, Circulosa added, "Now get your carcass back down there and get me under that wall!"

After a noticeable moment of consideration, Rot turned and stomped away into the darkness. Circulosa wrung the staff in his hands, indeed wishing Rot had tried something so he could be rid of one more useless Carrion officer.

Circulosa remained one of the only willing followers "untainted," as he liked to call it, and certainly the only pure human to aspire to such a rank in the Carrion army. Though his lack of horns granted him less respect than the other two Generals, Circulosa decided to keep his options open — always looking toward the future. He commanded one third of the unbreakable Carrion army, surely with time he could do even better.

He worked twice as hard, and the way he saw it, needed to kill twice as many of his subordinates to keep the troops in line. The General had not attained his position in the army by being soft or forgiving, but by seizing opportunity when it came. If the siege failed, Circulosa would simply name Rot as the scapegoat. In the meantime, however, he still depended upon the Lieutenant's detachment completing its quarter of the plan.

As Circulosa made it back to inspect the siege weapons, frustration continued to gnaw at his insides. Flaem proved to be an obstacle, but he would not fail. The General kept his wits about him and concentrated on patience. After all, it was only a matter of time until he brought the walls down and added the most powerful soldiers to the Carrion army yet. Or, perhaps, his own army.

Just for good measure, he extended blue energy from his staff and decapitated two grunts. The General made sure the army knew the soldiers died because their catapult failed to breach the wall. As a pair moved the corpses and took their place, Circulosa's brutal display coaxed a renewed vigor from the Carrion. They worked faster and harder to reload and fire the catapults, but their stones continued to disintegrate against Flaem's magical barriers.

CHAPTER 17 – *Wan Du*

WAN DU WEPT TO HIMSELF. HE CRIED FOR THE DECEASED and recalled the faces of his wife and children. His mind called out for the presence of *Serené*, but the voice did not return. The hairs on the back of his neck rose as his mind came to a halt on a single thought.

His purpose was not to mourn, that he had done already. Wan Du had become a tool, an instrument — a weapon.

Setting his jaw, Wan Du cast all sadness aside. He wiped the tears from his eyes and focused on his anger. As he imagined the mustached man touching and admiring his halberd, the large man's rage burned. He should have forced them to pry it from his bloody fingers after they ran him through.

Were the words just excuses for being afraid? While kneeling in front of the well in Brong surrounded by corpses, he longed for death. Shouldn't he want to see his family and friends again? Shouldn't he want to see the face of *Serené* and take his place floating in the River of Eternal Wind?

Wan Du shut his eyes tightly to block out his fear. Perhaps what he saw at the Carrion encampment — what the soldiers had done to the dead — continued to haunt him. Death would be better than a mindless and mottled existence, merely an extension of the darkness that tightened its grip on the world.

The large man could not stand the confinement for much longer, each minute a painful reminder that his task went unfinished.

"O *Serené*," he prayed, "I have done everything you have asked, but I sit here now, impotent, while the Darkness thrives all around me. What can I do? I implore you, allow me to die or fling wide these prison gates and allow me to continue your work!"

Wan Du listened, but heard no response. Hours passed and he refused to move. The muscles in his lower back and legs began to go numb. Ultimately, he collapsed to the floor and the world went dark. Before he lost consciousness, a single word echoed through his mind.

"Patience."

✑

WAN DU'S EYES FLUTTERED OPEN AS HE HEARD AN ODD METALLIC noise. From the floor, he watched as a small disc rolled across the cell toward him. The glint caught his eye from a few inches away and Wan Du reached out to pick it up. It seemed a common piece of silver currency used in the southern realms, but the coin emitted a small vibration in his hand. Both sides held an embossed symbol, and though Wan Du did not recognize it, he knew the glyph meant magic.

He nearly dropped it in disgust before a whisper came through the bars. "It will help you escape."

The large man recognized the voice immediately as Fung, the translator he talked to earlier. Wan Du turned the coin over in his palm and looked at it closely.

"Help me?" he asked. "How?"

"I know you do not like magic, but the coin is imbued with power from the Pillar of Acton. All it does is allow you to speak and to hear languages other than ones you know," Fung replied, his tone still hushed. "Use it to speak to people here and get them to help you, or at least warn them of what is coming."

After a pause, the translator added, "No one will listen to me, but I have seen it in the oracle stones."

"Seen what?"

"I have seen the Carrion ..."

A shout came, and a sudden rustle outside the cell ended the conversation. He saw Fung shake his head emphatically and the translator hurried away.

"Halt," barked a voice. Wan Du could no longer see Fung, but he recognized the sound of a sword being drawn. The translator's panicked voice babbled, then stopped suddenly. Wan Du saw a splash of blood fall across the floor outside, and a gasping cry told him Fung had been killed.

Makson appeared again at the bars and drew a cloth across his sword to remove the blood. "What did he tell you?" the guardsman demanded. "Did he give you anything?"

Wan Du struggled to hide his surprise at understanding the man's words. He balled a fist around the enchanted coin and shrugged, playing dumb as best he could. The guard scowled, but left without another word.

As he opened his fist, Wan Du began to believe perhaps *Serené* had not abandoned him after all.

Hours passed by slowly in the prison while Wan Du pondered his escape. The coin allowed him to understand the gibberish spoken by the gangly folk who came to clean up the blood and drop off trays of food, but their conversation held no value to him. Wan Du tried to speak to them himself, but they ignored the man.

From Fung's quick dispatching, Wan Du figured any conversation held with a prisoner required a guard's authorization. Cellto deserved its reputation; it justified how many criminals and prisoners were sent there. Wan Du sighed, knowing he could not escape through any means of his own. He retreated to the rear of the cell and decided to get some more rest.

WAN DU JERKED AWAKE TO THE SOUND OF REPEATED SPITTING from his nearby cellmate. In between coughs, he heard, "You expect me to drink this?"

He opened his eyes in time to see a cup dashed against the floor in protest, the liquid splashing on the feet of the guard outside.

"Shut your trap!" The armored man shouted. He kicked the bars of the cell and walked away as he muttered, "Ungrateful twops."

Though only a curse and barely audible enough to hear, Wan Du mouthed a quick prayer to thank the passed spirit of Fung for being able to understand the words.

"Bah! This is worse than drinkin' me own piss!" His cellmate cursed, more to himself than to anyone else. Wan Du wondered how much truth there was to the statement. "Ah, yer awake. Big man, ye sleep more'n I do."

Though Wan Du found this hard to believe, his expression did not change. The man reached into his coat to reveal a metal flask and shook the vessel to indicate a lack of contents.

"Ye wouldn't happen to have any..."

Wan Du shook his head slowly.

"No, 'course not. Ye wouldn't be havin' a place to keep it." He gestured to Wan Du, indicating the larger man did not even have a pocket. "Least ye can understand me, eh?"

"What is your name?" Wan Du asked.

"Captain Satok, I be," said the man, puffing himself up and placing both hands on his hips.

"I am Wan Du of Brong."

"Thought so, hmm. Me sorrows to ye, then. Me crew tried to put in there but ..." His words trailed off, obviously remembering the massacre.

Wan Du gestured to the bars, "I must get out of here."

"Ye will, ye will. Ye think I never been in before? Ha!" The captain pointed to the wall to indicate dozens of parallel vertical marks. "An' that's just in this cell," he said with a dirty-toothed grin.

He had thought the Captain young until his mouth opened; his stained smile made the man seem much older. Wan Du ignored his bravado and reiterated, "You must help me escape this place."

"Fine, fine," the Captain replied. "Show me a quicker way out than waitin' and I'll sail ye wherever ye want to go." Satok emphasized his sarcasm by alternating his tone. He sank back down to the cot and picked his teeth with a fingernail. Despite his initial misgivings, Wan Du decided the Captain was not such a bad man to share a cell with. His antics made the man from Brong want to smile and, under different circumstances, he might have.

Wan Du walked to the front of the cell and stared outside. *Serené* had given him another gift, and sarcasm or not, he would hold the man to his oath.

CHAPTER 18 – *Wadam*

ADAM FOUND IT HARD WORK TO PURSUE THE GIRL, AND even more difficult to care whether they caught her or not. Gone three days without so much as a note, her loss inspired clear and warm weather ever since. She could be dead by now, he thought, yet still able to waste my time.

The Cardinal spent the majority of the time in his quarters as they had no reason to dock. Their food storage remained more than enough to get them home, especially with the loss of a passenger.

He missed his congregation and their captivated stares, but longed for his priestly quarters even more. Being confined to a ship inhibited his creativity even while it gave him time to do little but work. Casting his homesickness aside, Wadam slammed his fist against the makeshift desk where his current project sat.

He went as far, this time, as to condemn those who did not live on the Mystian continent, "because they were being influenced, daily, by a world gone awry." Wadam believed they, "needed to extricate themselves from the distractions that would inevitably make their faith waver and keep them from achieving the ultimate goal."

His title, "The Sustaining Truth of Mystianity and the Clever Falsity of all Other Faiths," might raise some eyebrows, but he knew it wouldn't be enough. The Myst-Alsher females remained too forgiving — too tolerant. These traits had their place, but misused they continued to enable weak links in the Mystian chain.

Wadam sighed. Were the people of the larger world even worth saving? They started this war, just like all the rest. Why not let them fight it out and destroy each other?

His people would survive, untainted by evil that infected the rest of the world. The northwestern subcontinent, blessed by the constant and eternal presence of the Divine Male, enjoyed a safety the other nations could not provide. He heard many accounts, even from visitors, describing a noticeable sensation when they landed on the shores — something they did not receive elsewhere.

"Let the beacon of light attract them to it or blind them forever," he said aloud. Wadam wanted to write it in the essay, but could not bring himself to do it. The Seeress and her ilk would never allow something so exclusive to be said, though the True Way of the Divine Book spoke it clearly enough.

"All peoples shall believe," Wadam repeated from memory, "whether by kneel or steel."

Some always doubted the translation or context, challenging his passages with interpretations of their own. Flowery speech remained their best defense. They would twist his words to make them sound unmerciful and then censor him, just as they did before. He remembered the first time he tried to enforce the True Way; the ungrateful laymen nearly flogged him and threw him into the sea!

No matter how much he missed youth, the days of virile body and infinite possibility were long gone. The chronicles of the first few Mystian zealots still captivated him, though. He latched onto their staunch and unyielding attitudes, writing things like, "Why should we forgive the world, when it is because of them that evil remains a constant presence at our border? If they would not embrace truth, then they should die and be revealed, the ultimate proof in their disbelief."

He worked hard to make it through his studies and applied the same efforts to become a speaker at the pulpit. So many people took his words to heart and riots broke out in towns even outside the Mystian subcontinent. Groups of soldiers from three different countries came to Myst-Garvon to demand Wadam's head.

Still, Wadam toiled to make his words be heard — to have an impact by using the truth to tell people how incorrectly they lived. He wanted to free them from their horrible choices and show them how easy life could be if they would only trust and walk the True Way.

For thirty years, Elestia assumed the role of his most outspoken adversary with her own designs on how things should be run. The chief priests and other Cardinals cowered in fear of the charismatic Seeress; the mood of the Divine Female could never be outright discounted, and all that.

Pandering hogwash, thought Wadam. He no longer cared whether this work would be allowed or not — he had things to say. Elestia's time would end before his, and Wadam believed with war on their doorstep he could influence the populace in the proper direction. Moreover, it behooved him to do so.

He pondered who the next Seeress would be. Having met so many "prophetic" young girls in the past few years, he could hardly keep any of them straight. Most proved useless; a farm girl or merchant's daughter had an interesting dream one night and sought out the Sisterhood. Their selection process remained the source of much skepticism on his part.

Wadam scoffed at their methods and tried to remind his peers men were selected on faith and intelligence — a much better gauge of divine choosing than mere imagination. Yet, the tradition of the previous Seeress naming a successor from her deathbed persevered for generations. Wadam hoped for a prettier girl this time — perhaps with fair hair.

Lifting the pen, the priest nearly laughed aloud when he realized he had been scribbling all of his musings onto the paper. Wadam picked the parchment up and pressed the words to his lips before he discarded it with the rest. He began to write again and resolved to choose stronger words, ones to influence the people of Myst against the evils of mercy and forgiveness toward unbelievers.

His heart swelled with pride as he imagined his cathedral still standing long after this conflict ended. The essay finished with, "War may be at our borders but the Divine protection of our faith shall keep us safe from all harm."

As he reread the words, Wadam decided his writing needed to make it back as quickly as possible. If the lost girl — whatever her name was — could not be found by sundown, the ship would return without her.

CHAPTER 19 – *Wan Du*

HE SOUNDS OF SOBBING ECHOED THROUGHOUT THE ENTIRE cell block. It was a common sound, more prevalent since the cell next to him had been filled. Though Satok seemed able to ignore it, Wan Du sympathized with his fellow captives, having shed many tears of his own in recent weeks. Each person in a cell had a story and some were undoubtedly similar to his own.

As a soldier, he learned innocence could not keep a man safe like armor would. In the Temple of the Wind he learned a man lives only by the favor of the Master of the Waves. Comfort and faith could only be found in the continuation of one's own life.

"O *Serené*," he whispered, "please guide me in this hour of my captivity. Guide me in your purpose and will, O Creator."

Wan Du reminded himself to be patient. He ignored the food placed inside the cell and touched his forehead to the floor again in supplication.

His eyes closed, Wan Du began to recite the prayer inscribed at the top of the Thousand Steps. Barely audible, he repeated the prayer over and over again.

"The sun shines upon me, the wind blows around me, the water flows through me, the spirit lives within me."

A melodic female voice broke his concentration using the one word his ears had been waiting for.

"I know how you can help us escape," she said; "use that same power you used at Bloodmir!"

A sardonic male replied, "Look, even if I knew how to make that happen, which I don't, what makes you think I want to spend hours unconscious again while you two escape and leave me here to die?"

"Two? No chance. I'm not leaving this city without Lady Mayrah." A deeper female voice responded.

"Let her find her own way out. She's caused nothing but problems for the two of us." Wan Du heard a small scuffle as he crouched near the front corner of his cell.

"Don't even try it, Mirrin. We're not friends." The male voice sounded angrier than before.

After a pause, the melodic voice began tentatively, "Please stop it, you two. We'll never get out of here if we can't work together."

Wan Du knew he had to do something. He leapt up and tapped on the cell wall with his knuckles to get the attention of the juxtaposed occupants. As their shuffling came close, the pretty female voice appeared again but quieter.

"Who's there? Lady Mayrah?"

He opened his mouth to speak, then paused. If they expected a woman to answer, he feared they wouldn't trust him enough to talk.

"No." Wan Du's mouth and throat formed the word in his own tongue, but somehow, the sound that came out was not in the language he intended.

"Who is that? Who are you?" the man demanded, his voice replacing the girl's.

"I am Wan Du of Brong," he answered.

"So what?"

"I must escape this place also," said Wan Du. "I will help you."

"Oh, yeah," challenged the voice, "how do you think you'll do that? Got a dragon in your pocket?"

"If you will help me out of the cell, I swear upon my life and oath in the name of *Serené* to carry you out of this city and to wherever you choose. Where I come from, saving a man's life binds you to him forever."

There was a pause as the man considered his proposal. Wan Du thought he heard a low whisper from one of the female voices about "trusting a follower" but the rest was too quiet.

"Do you have any idea how to get out of the city?" asked the man. "We're only three-strong in here."

Wan Du turned to look at Satok, asleep again.

"The other person in my cell is the captain of a ship. He has promised to take me wherever I want to go if I can help him escape."

"Convenient."

Another pause, this one much longer than the previous one, made the large man nervous. He wanted to wake the captain, but figured it best to wait. Wan Du heard the sound of a whisper here and there, but could not make out any of the conversation. He gripped the coin as tightly as he could until a response came.

"How do we know we can trust you?" the man asked.

"I could ask you the same question as you are in this prison, too. I do not care how or why you are here, but you have not even told me your name."

The man sighed, showing commitment even before conceding agreement. "I am DaVille."

"There is also a woman there, is there not?"

The melodious and baritone female voices chimed in simultaneously with, "Starka," and, "Mirrin," to the response of much shushing by DaVille.

"Are you a sorcerer, DaVille?" Wan Du asked. "Or have your gods granted you some way to unlock doors?"

"I'm not sure what it is, but I'll show you," he replied. "You and the captain will want to stand as far back as you can."

Wan Du retreated to the rear corner of the cell and crouched next to the cot that the captain snored on, so oblivious that it almost made the large man laugh.

DaVille gave one last warning. "By the way, I hope you're pretty good at fighting off guards."

The large, stoic man pictured Makson's face and did not respond.

CHAPTER 20 – *Mayrah*

LUTCHING AT HER PRISON BARS, MAYRAH STARED BLANKLY across the way. She was ready to completely give up and would have ended it all if she only had the means, but her weapons had been stripped from her for quite some time. Her hand unconsciously stroked her hip where the curved scimitar, "Windsong," used to wait at the ready. She missed its comforting glow, the same glow that infused her mate's similar blade on the day of their joining.

Mayrah's mind settled on all of those close to her she lost in this; merely the beginning of a war. Her composure almost disappeared entirely when she thought about the life formerly growing in her womb. Mayrah doubled over and clutched her stomach while she closed her eyes as hard as she could. There was nothing that could have been done. With her city destroyed and her mate dead, she was not willing to bring a child into the world with no one to care for it. She would not have been able to bear her son or daughter dying from starvation or something even more awful at the hands of the Carrion.

There would be more losses to come. Perhaps not for Mayrah — everything she could lose had been stripped away already — but the Carrion army would march across the world and separate or destroy all of the families that were inside of it. She sank to her knees with neither the willpower nor the strength to stand in their way. Empty, she realized life would be even harder without Bathilde to lean on. Oh, how she missed the large woman and her comforting mirth!

She remembered so many little things about their time together; how happy the larger woman had been when Mayrah found out she was with child, how she cried for hours in Bathilde's comforting arms after the massacre at Bloodmir. The large woman advised her not to choose a name for the child.

Mayrah held her breath after coming to the last thought and remembered the final words in her mind before the fatal blow came. Against everything she knew and heard, Mayrah had chosen a name.

As she pressed her fingernail against the third mourning mark on her arm, for Bathilde, a low sob escaped the woman's lips. She could find no solace now — no one could ever comfort her the way her mate had. Though their marriage was arranged since birth, they knew each other well before the time came. Mayrah remembered loving him even before she became old enough to understand her future. They would frolic along the beaches of Rochelle and play childish games where she would hide and wait for her betrothed to find her. She remembered the last great peace accord with Brong came and went while she was that young; another in the long line of farces and false promises following the Sorcerer's War.

"He's come back from dozens of battles before!" She remembered pleading with anyone who would listen while they rearranged the burnt debris of their once great city. For such a long time, she lived in denial. Mayrah alone kept up the hope that, even though their army had been decimated and her home was gone, he would return. She would look to the horizon and expect to see him walking toward her with a triumphant smile on his face and a collection of treasures in his hands. But the days passed and she slowly accepted that he was gone, forever. No matter how much blood she drew from herself in sacrifice, Mayrah could not bring him back.

The old ways — the blessings, the hexes, the dances — these produced no result and couldn't quiet her raging heart. Mayrah's grandmother taught her ways to communicate across great distances but death, it seemed, was the greatest distance of all. When a mate dies, the spirit lives on with what they were most attached to, but the person is gone, precisely why she would never be allowed to find another mate. Friendship carried her through the mourning periods, but now, with Bathilde gone, Mayrah would be alone for the rest of her life.

Soon after her arrival, Mayrah tried a few of her tribal remedies to help her escape the cell, but gave up quickly. Whether she could escape or not, she had nowhere to go. She had been to Cellto before, for trading and diplomatic purposes, but never graced the inside of a cell here. The cell block portion of the city was designed to be a veritable labyrinth, difficult to memorize because everything looked the same. This discouraged escapes, but did not completely prevent them. On the nearest wall to her she saw many vertical scratch marks placed parallel to each other. Mayrah wondered if the previous occupant ever saw free land again.

She looked out through the bars of the cell and despaired. Mayrah resigned herself to death at that moment, and began to hold the breath in her lungs. If this didn't work, she decided, then she would bite her tongue until she bled to death. Lady Mayrah was ready to meet her end.

Suddenly, she felt a warm hand on her shoulder. The feeling of comfort spread from there and she began to feel an encompassing warmth throughout her torso. It spread to her limbs and she let out her held breath in a long sigh. Her head tilted back as the feeling focused back to her center, her abdomen. It intensified for just a moment before disappearing entirely. Mayrah's eyes slid slowly closed as she passed into a trance state.

Swirls of color filled her vision and whispers filled her ears. Mayrah could not make out one voice from another and all of them seemed to be saying something different. Her conscious mind could have used a word to describe the place her mind tapped into, but her other mind merely floated along the currents of color and voice. Energy wrapped itself around her limbs and fed itself into her mouth.

She felt the widest range of human emotion possible in a single second. Something even began to arouse her, but mischievously sped away. Again, Mayrah let out a great sigh. The colors shaped themselves into an image before her eyes. Her mate stood in all his glory, brandishing his blade called "Wavesong." Mayrah reached out to touch the image and nearly did before something stopped her.

The floor shook violently, knocking her off balance, even from her knees. Mayrah pushed herself off of the cold cell floor and shook the stars free from her vision. She blinked to gain her bearings, not sure whether she had simply dozed off or worse. The vision of Wavesong remained clear in her mind, and it was all that she needed.

As she saw familiar faces approach, the woman stood with a strange new feeling of purpose.

CHAPTER 21 – *Starka*

HE POWER OF THE EXPLOSION SHOOK THE ENTIRE CELL block. When she recovered her senses, Starka gasped at the hole and mangled metal that formerly barred their escape.

DaVille began to sway just as the large man from the adjacent cell came through to catch him. He had to stoop just to clear the passage, but cradled DaVille as easily as a doll. Starka's eyes widened when she saw how large the man was, but she tried to hide her fear. He wore simple cloth armor from the waist-down and only a set of oversized threaded beads around his neck to guard his upper body.

She forced a smile as the man threw DaVille unceremoniously over his massive forearm. Without pause or salutation he climbed back into the other cell and dragged a resisting — and incredibly cranky — sailor out of bed.

"What the ... leave me alone! Eh? How? I be dreamin'!"

The dirty man continued to protest as he stumbled through the hole. He looked too young to be a ship captain; Starka always pictured them much older and hairier. Upon closer inspection, she noticed his eyes only made him seem young, but the accumulation of scars made him look much older. She wondered what the man would look like freshly showered and shaved.

The captain adjusted his hat to both her and Mirrin, in turn, and then practically leapt out from the hole made in the junction of both cells. He seemed to grasp the entirety of the escape with no explanation. Starka wondered if he had been listening to their conversation or if he had done this before, but his wrinkled clothing and groggy step said otherwise.

"Satok, I be. Me ship'll be at the dock," he said, lifting his hand and pointing down the corridor. "This way."

Starka hoped his clumsiness on dry land meant he would be more at home on the sea, but Mirrin completely ignored the captain's words and began a slow trot in the opposite direction. She searched each of the cells, and repeatedly called the names of her comrades — Lady Mayrah loudest and most frequently.

DaVille would have ignored Mirrin or, at the most, just left her there while he escaped. For once, Starka found herself glad to have him unconscious, though it put her in greater danger. She spoke directly to the large man, who seemed to have the most command of the situation.

"We've got to help her find Lady Mayrah," Starka said.

He stared at her with a solemn frown, but then nodded and began to follow Mirrin. Starka didn't have time to contemplate the politics between Brong and Rochelle; their rivalry seemed postponed or at least the man's stoicism didn't betray any ill will toward the other woman. She wondered if their feud could become an issue during their escape.

Starka turned to the captain who still stood with his thumb out.

"Wait! How will we get her out once we find her?" she asked. "How are we even going to get out of here?"

Satok smiled, showing two rows of stained teeth. "Both be easy questions and both be answered the same way. Come 'long."

AFTER CHECKING A DOZEN NEARBY CELLS THEY STILL HAD NOT found Mayrah. They came across two cells with Mirrin's comrades locked in them, but the women deferred to the group's quest to find their leader.

Much to Starka's relief, they found her only a few cells away. Attempts to pull the cell gate open failed and time continued to work against them. The large man dealt with two guards, but a third sounded an alarm which, Satok made clear, would soon cause dozens of soldiers to pour into the small cellblock walkways. Their phalanx would create an impenetrable wall of armored men to bar escape.

The captain pondered over the multitudinous levers against a wall at the end of the cellblock corridor as Mirrin relayed the events of their escape to Mayrah. Every time Starka looked at the large man she thought she noticed him searching for something. She looked into the cell where two Rochelle women stood, gripping the bars in the hope that they would soon escape.

A loud click and a lazy creak accompanied the door of Mayrah's cell swinging open. The swarthy woman lunged out of the cramped space and embraced Mirrin. At the far end of the corridor, a dozen armed men drew their swords.

"Captain?"

"Only one thing to be doin', girl. Grab our Lady and move!"

Starka heard the creaking and clicking as Satok's quick hands pulled more of the levers. Mayrah waited until the cell with her comrades opened before she joined the party. As the last two escapees arrived, nearly a hundred prisoners swarmed out of their cells and began to violently impede the small force of Cellto guards. Starka followed the rest as they made for the stairs.

SHOUTS OF "HALT!" ACCOMPANIED THE GROUP ALL THE WAY FROM the cells to the water's edge. With their belongings collected, they followed Satok through the winding corridors and onto the docks. As the prow of the Captain's ship came closer Starka's heart both leapt and sank. She couldn't forget what happened during her last time on a ship, but she knew what would happen if they remained in Cellto. Starka hurried to escape the stench and pursuit of the place she decided to be the antithesis of her home.

Soft groans to her side meant DaVille was beginning to stir. The large man, Wan Du, either didn't notice or didn't care, focused as he was on getting to the ship. From a distance, Starka saw sailors hauling a huge anchor and frantically chopping at the mooring lines.

The ship's timbers were actually a shade of incredibly dark red, much like blood mixed with the lightless depths of the ocean. On the front of the ship, a completely nude — and very well-endowed — carved female grasped a long wooden beam. Her eyes glowed like red jewels even in the low light of dawn and her feet dipped into the water each time the ship bounced with the waves.

Etched on the side of the ship, the name *Bloody Lady* showed the craft obviously titled for its imposing figurehead. The naked and lifelike visage of the wooden woman gave the vessel a mysterious and bold appearance. Her eyes always faced outward, forward, ready to seek a new destination.

Starka ran past Wan Du as he carried DaVille, searching for some semblance of shelter on deck. The large man waited on the dock as everyone jumped onto the deck via the long plank of wood linking the two. The captain gave quick orders to sever the remaining mooring lines and get underway, as their pursuers were adept at chasing escapees via boat. Starka was amazed at the large man's leap as he carried DaVille into the boat even after it drifted a few yards away from the dock. He landed solidly on his feet and lowered his charge to a seated position.

"Ever'one down!" cried the captain. "Drop the hard sail! Ready the rear cannon!"

A heavy layer of canvas unfurled right in front of Starka to separate her from a score of crossbows aimed directly at the ship. The men and women on deck took shelter where they could or dashed into a compartment to escape the impending barrage. The telltale twang of crossbows heralded a series of thumps and popping noises as the arrows embedded themselves in the ship and tore through the hard sail. Starka joined in the screams following the first volley and knew the arrows would pelt the ship until they were out of range.

She peeked around tentatively to see another line of bowmen join the first. Both sets of arrows were knocked and ready to loose, but before they did, she heard the distinct voice of Satok shout an order to *"Fire!"* and her world turned upside-down.

The ship lurched forward violently as a huge burst of energy erupted from the rear. The dock exploded and the *Bloody Lady* pitched under the water to send a huge wake outward in every direction. Wayward arrows splashed into the water as archers, residents, and debris went flying. A minor tidal wave leapt onto the remains of the dock to scatter anything not nailed down.

"Ready the oars, mates! Get us out o' here!"

Two dozen wooden poles with widened, flat ends extended from the sides of the ship and began to stroke the water in unison. Starka heard the repeat of "Stroke!" as she watched the city for pursuit. Satok came up behind her and paused until she turned around.

"Don't ye be worryin' about them. They know better'n to be chasin' me." He gestured toward the decimated dock. "Got me ten o' them ready at all times!"

HOURS LATER, STARKA SAT IDLE STARING OUT A WINDOW ACROSS a tranquil sea. Satok referred to it as the Inner Sea of Mana, an immense body of water separating all of the lands of the east. The most powerful coastal cities faced each other across it. Illiadora, Rochelle, Cellto, Fort Sondergaarde, Flaem, and even the cities of Ferraut faced into what he called the Inner Ring.

Starka did not know their destination, just that they headed north. The Inner Sea seemed far less choppy than the waters she sailed before arriving in Bloodmir. As she looked out the portal to the west she saw black clouds gathering on the horizon, and the gloom mirrored her lamentations. Though DaVille might laugh it off, she shuddered to think herself an escaped criminal. Starka wondered if agents from Cellto might be hunting for her even now.

When she came below deck, she saw Wan Du sitting between two large oars and tossing them back and forth as effectively as the rest of the wooden poles operated by two crewmen each. She wanted to speak with him a bit more, to get a better idea of who he was, but the scowl on his face deterred her. She retreated to Satok's cabin, designated for her for the duration of the trip, and collapsed from sheer exhaustion.

Once rested, Starka stood and examined the clothing laid out for her. The armors DaVille provided previously were moist, frayed, sweaty, and stained with blood. They seemed like so much trash in comparison to the fresh outfit.

Starka longed for a bath ever since the day she met DaVille, and couldn't remember the last time her hair had been washed. She could barely recall the last time she ate; a salted meat and hard, yet chewy bread provided by the crew shortly after their escape. So many more important things took precedence since Bloodmir, and her appearance and health suffered because of them.

Without another thought, she began to disrobe. She loosened the multiple sashes around her waist and slipped her leggings off completely. Once naked, Starka took a step toward the basin to wash her hair and body, but paused at her own sight in the mirror. The armors left aggravated impressions on her torso and she stroked them tenderly to work her skin smooth again.

As Starka regarded herself in the oval glass, she saw a dirty reflection of a girl she barely knew. It was a rare occasion to see herself nude; not even Fandur would recognize the gaunt, dark-haired girl in the mirror. The scratches on her arms nearly made her laugh in spite of herself. Battle scars, she chided.

Her condition could have been much worse. Had DaVille not appeared when he did, she would be lost to the evils of the Carrion. Something flashed in her mind, then, and she remembered his first words to her.

Fools, she'll not belong to the likes of you.

Starka pondered the words as she rinsed her cuts clean and dipped her hair into the basin. It felt both great and horrible to cleanse her hair again, she decided. As the comb blazed its trails, Starka winced every time she came across a knotted patch. Her eyes drifted to the dagger belt lying neatly on the bed. She knew she would continue to be helpless without it, but she still could not bring herself to even touch the thing. *There are reasons priestesses do not carry weapons,* she remembered learning at some point.

"Probably because we would be tempted to use them," she said aloud, wincing again at the comb's assault.

The words seemed meaningless now after having faced death — or worse — at the hands of the grotesque beasts. She slipped the dagger out of the sheath and balled a fist to hold it in front of her. The blade was about the length of her forearm and wider at the base than at the tip. DaVille mentioned something about it being called a "dirk," but she had been in too much of a hurry to retreat into a cabin to care. Common sense told her all she really needed to know: the pointed end went toward the enemy.

She fell to her knees next to the bed and prayed for the strength and courage she would need if the dagger ever came unsheathed. Suddenly, Starka burst out in a fit of giggling. To think that she could actually hold her hand steady enough to stab, wound, and possibly kill another creature seemed preposterous — particularly considering her actions when she met DaVille. As Starka slid the dagger back into the sheath she came to the hard realization that she would rather die herself than kill another person.

Others could do it, however. She wondered if this small group of warriors could make a difference against the Carrion. What was it Elestia had said to save the world? We must be of one mind, recalled Starka. Lady Mayrah and Wan Du were natural rivals, and who could say what went on in DaVille's mind? Not to mention they were only three; Starka did not include herself among the fighters.

She did not belong in this war or any war — especially not on the front line. All the same, she knew if she refused to wear the dagger DaVille would remind the girl of her inability to properly defend herself and subject her to yet another warmongering lecture. Starka found herself rolling her eyes at the mere thought of it.

After the girl donned her new linens, she tried sorting through her feelings. An unchecked flood of emotion seemed to overwhelm her and Starka wondered what being with a man would be like. A picture of DaVille entered her mind and she didn't resist. There was nothing more foreign to her than finding a man attractive — particularly this man — but sooner or later Starka knew she would betray some hint of arousal, despite how it went against her nature.

A soft knock at the door broke her from her reverie. She stood, wiped her eyes, took one last look in the dirty mirror, and pulled the door open only an inch to see none other than DaVille. She frowned at the coincidence and banished all thoughts of romance.

He leaned against one side of the jamb, nonchalant, but with a grim edge reminding her of a child who knew revealing the news he carried would surely bring him admonishment.

"We're passing Fort Sondergaarde," he said. "I thought you should come on deck and see it."

Without a word of explanation he turned to leave.

"I thought we were landing there," she called. "Why are we passing it?"

DaVille sighed, his shoulders and head dropped forward. Starka could not tell whether he was exasperated or truly sad.

"You'll find out when you come on deck."

STARKA RECALLED RHYMES AND LEGENDS OF FORT SONDERGAARDE recited to her as a little girl. Called an "invincible fortress," and other lofty names more recently, the fort city sat surrounded by tall cliffs that made an ocean assault impossible from three sides. An ancient strategist noted in a book she owned, *once you only need to guard one wall, defense becomes easy.* Fort Sondergaarde stood for centuries, if the legends were true, as a symbol of defiance.

The dead were everywhere, and the fort looked like it had exploded from the inside. Bodies and debris spread from the gates to the tip of the cliffs and even across the rocks to be washed by the waves. The remnants of the fort remained a smoldering pile of leftover timbers, mostly fallen in on itself. Starka refused to wipe the tears from her cheeks, saddened for all of the lost lives as well as the lost history.

As she stood on deck and stared across the water between her and the pile of burnt and mangled wood, she could see how many people formerly lived in the fort. All of the warriors, women, and even the children were now dead at the hands of the Carrion army. A knot welled up in her throat, but it prevented her from shouting curses and other un-ladylike phrases. Her eyes burned as she stifled sobs, and it was all she could do to keep from collapsing.

"Why?" she demanded. "Why would they do such a thing?"

She heard Lady Mayrah sigh next to her. "To show their strength," the woman said. "No one will stand against them now."

Starka looked toward DaVille and Wan Du, but both were engaged with the operations of the ship. She wondered about the truth of the prophecy and could not escape the feeling that she had failed to fulfill her part in it. She watched

CHAPTER 21 ~ The Ninth Avatar ~ 125

DaVille for a moment, remembering how he complimented the fit of her new attire. They were the first nice words from his mouth, and the girl still had no idea what to make of them.

Mayrah's words broke her concentration. "This makes four."

Starka turned to fully face her swarthy opposite. "Four what?"

"Cities," said Mayrah. "Four destroyed cities."

The girl nodded and wiped the tears from her cheeks. "So many lives. How could all of this have happened?"

Mayrah's eyes flashed with something that might have been anger or hatred. Starka felt the force of the bold words before hearing them. "Where I come from, we do not ask these questions. To doubt the cycle of life is to doubt your own existence."

Starka swallowed hard. Her own faith seemed to be failing every kind of test possible. As she looked at the debris of Fort Sondergaarde, Starka promised to try harder in the days to come.

"Where are we going?" Starka asked.

"The captain said he was going to take the Brong soldier wherever DaVille wished to go," replied Mayrah. "Will you follow him as well?"

Starka stood silent in resigned affirmation. The dark-skinned female nodded tightly and turned to lean her back and elbows against the ship. Her posture seemed flippant, but her next statement made Starka wonder if this was the same woman who took them captive in Rochelle days before.

"I don't have much of a choice at this point. Poor Mirrin took an arrow and won't live through the night. My other girls have opted to stay on ship until it reaches a port with commerce."

"What about your home?"

As soon as the words left her mouth Starka wished she could have taken them back.

"Home? Bathilde is dead and I have nothing to go back to." There was a long pause as the woman's demeanor calmed again. "No, I know where my future lies."

Starka thought she saw an extra pang of despair in Mayrah's eyes at the mention of the larger woman. As she watched the dark woman, Starka saw her fidget with an ornate bracelet.

"Was that a gift?" she asked.

"It is a symbol. In Rochelle, it was custom to join two lives together and wear a representation of that union. The bracelet is fit tightly so that it cannot be removed; it will stay on my wrist as long as I live as a reminder of my betrothal. It is only to be removed after the breath leaves my body."

"But you said your mate is ..."

"Dead," Mayrah finished for her. "I am doomed to be alone until I see him again on the distant shores. The bracelet discourages any other males from Rochelle from even propositioning me. Those who have relations with widows are put to the sword; it is considered the ultimate betrayal of the honored dead."

"I see," said Starka.

"This is why you kept hearing Bathilde refer to me as 'Lady' Mayrah so adamantly; it is an honorary title of sorts given to the abandoned widows of my people. She resigned herself to a life of singleness long ago, so it was more for solidarity than anything."

Mayrah's eyes visibly moistened at the mention of her friend, and never had Starka seen anyone look more defeated. She laid a hand gently on the older woman's armored shoulder and, as a sobbing face buried itself against her, DaVille's grim gaze shifted from the decimated landscape to make eye contact with Starka. Every muscle in his body looked tense, just as she remembered when hiding from the Carrion arrows.

"Are we not safe here?" she asked.

"Nowhere is safe, anymore. We're continuing north, to Flaem," he stated flatly before spinning on his heels and marching toward the rear of the ship.

CHAPTER 22 – *Wadam*

WADAM JUMPED FROM HIS THE BED WITH PLEAS FOR HIS LIFE still on his lips. The nightmare frightened him so badly the large priest nearly soiled himself in his sleep.

"Stupid dream," he muttered.

It took a moment for Wadam to regain his composure and remember where he was. Still on the ship, but, he hoped, nearly home. The portly priest sighed as he tried to remember the last time he wasn't on a boat, rocking back and forth with the waves and eating salted meat. Already annoyed with the ridiculous mission of escorting the girl south to ascertain this-or-that, her disappearing act gave him quite a few more negative things to say about her upon his return. At least they weren't still wasting time looking for her.

He did not want to spend any more time than necessary away from his warm, feather-stuffed bed and freshly-prepared meals. Wadam imagined his plants in dire need of water; the pages never took proper care of things while he was away! Half of his first day home would be spent ordering disciplinary actions against the young boys. They would learn eventually, he knew, but Wadam delighted in assisting them in their path to righteousness.

Casting the light blanket off of his sweaty bulk, the Cardinal moved to sit up on the small cot. Nothing in the room pleased him aesthetically, not even the eastern view out the small window.

The great priest donned his traveling robe and cinched the belt around his torso, as loose as he could possibly make it without leaving the possibility of the robe falling or blowing open. He opened the door and marched out through the hallway and up the stairs to the deck.

They were still at least a day out from reaching the Myst Cathedrals. His spirits perked up instantly as he noted land far off to the west. It could only be the southern tip of his coveted continent. The voyage would be over soon.

WADAM'S PRAISE TO GARVON FOR HIS SAFE TRAVELS WAS INTERrupted by a shout from the front of the ship. He hurried to see what the problem was and found the vessel's captain staring across the horizon at two large masses.

"What are those — land?" the priest asked.

The captain's customary scowl neither answered the question nor waylaid Wadam's discomfort. The ill-mannered man shouted up to the observer high on the mast.

"Oy! What do you see?"

"Black sails! They be ships, captain! Running low; can't tell if they're tacking or beating!" came the reply.

"What should we do?" Wadam asked aloud, to no one and everyone. With so little experience at seafaring, Wadam's goal immediately became to find the course of action with the highest possibility of survival and force it into action.

The first mate of the ship came near and spoke up first. "Not much we can do. We can either hope they're friendly or we can go around 'em."

"Can they see us?"

The first mate looked up and shouted into his hands, "Mickay! Which way they facin'?"

It took a few moments for Wadam to understand the terminology the observer used to answer the question. The "heading" of the black-sailed ships seemed to be the same as their own, which either meant they were simply bound the same direction or, the more ominous explanation, the exact same destination.

Wadam's heart began to pound. Again, he asked a question. "What if they're not friendly?"

The captain turned to the large priest and his chapped lips parted to speak. "The way I see it, we've got two choices."

Wadam awaited the rest with masked anxiety.

"We can either sail near to them and try and figure out who they are or we can try to outrun them. Only problem with that is they'll see us sooner or later, too. Seeing as we haven't passed a port in a while, I'm guessing we've caught up to them. If they're running low, like Mickay says, they're probably heavy, which means we could outrun them if we had to."

He chewed on his lip before continuing, "And if they're beating into the wind, sounds like they don't much know what they're doing."

Wadam had no idea which option to take, but believed with the entirety of his being that Garvon would protect him somehow. With war ravaging everywhere else, he began to fear the enemy's army may try to test his own country's defenses. A haunting suspicion crept up his spine from the dream that awakened him; if the ships held the enemy then he would have to alert Myst-Garvon. And he would have to put the ship and the crew in harm's way to do it.

"We seem to be able to do both," Wadam told the captain.

"Or neither," said the first mate under his breath. Wadam scowled at the young man who then retreated to the rear.

To the captain, Wadam commanded, "Sail as close as necessary to the ships until we can figure out who they are and what their intentions are. If haste becomes necessary, we'll just have to risk them chasing us."

With his instructions being carried out, Wadam slipped back into his cabin to put pen to paper once again. The dangers of the road were fresh in his mind and he had so much to say to his congregation if he were truly going to find his end.

"This war will bring nothing but more fear and death into the world," Wadam wrote, "and the evil that plagues the lands of the other faiths will destroy the people who embrace it." His pen worked furiously with a mission of condemnation; no more holding back his anger at the outsiders for bringing death to his doorstep. He wrote from his heart and allowed his true interpretation of the Divine Book to be shown in bold print on the page. All of his disdain and superiority poured forth onto the pages, his warning of woman's unpredictability, and the true inspiration of the Divine Force.

His manifesto would be his final and crowning achievement, Wadam knew, but he only hoped he could see it put into practice. He paused a moment from writing, absently chewing on his pen. One way or another, he decided, the priests would take back the reins of the country and the faith.

CHAPTER 23 – *Xymon*

HAT A COLOSSAL WASTE OF TIME, XYMON THOUGHT. Perched atop a cliff on the northwestern side of Flaem, he watched the army under Circulosa hurl itself against the walls of the city like an impromptu club. Even Drakkaram would have done better than this, the dark General concluded; it might have been bloody and lacking style, but it would have gotten the job done. Xymon saw things as his master would see them; pragmatic but focused. From this vantage, it became obvious the round General had no perception at all.

He reached his current position after abandoning his charges on the island east of the Myst Cathedrals. The narrow island, shaped much like a tooth, lay just across a narrow channel called the Baerow Strait. Named aptly for the jagged rocks of the shallow channel and the barbarians who lived there, the wild place would house his Carrion in secret until they were called forth again. The barbarians mostly stayed to the northern parts of the island, so Xymon heard, to keep away from the Mystians. The oddness of the northerners suggested they had created the Straits specifically to separate themselves from the zealots, and Xymon applauded the rumor.

Crossing from the subcontinent to the mainland was not difficult, but it took time to travel from the northern tip all the way to Flaem. Xymon bypassed the Northern Wastes as quickly as he could, as the snow-packed tundra held little safety for him. The camouflaged beasts that roamed it weren't exactly friendly, either. He stayed close to the coast and entered only a few small towns for sustenance under the cover of night. The great port city of Ince, sitting on its boot-shaped peninsula, held nothing of interest.

Further east Xymon navigated around a dense forest rather than enter the territory around Ferraut Castle, though he fought an urge to examine. He crossed Lake Flaem as the sun completed its descent and arrived at the city as night fell — just in time to watch the real spectacle.

The round General's siege weapons assailed the walls, but did little good. Stones and other projectiles exploded against the city's magical barriers and created a rainbow of color with each blast. Two days later, the Carrion were no better off than when they first landed. Circulosa's failure would ruin the reputation of the larger army if things continued in this way.

"One does expect more intelligence from a wizard," whispered Xymon as he pondered relaying the situation to Zion. He would already know, of course, but the dark General felt compelled to relay just how poorly the siege went.

In the meantime, Xymon penetrated the ranks of the Carrion soldiers undetected and ascertained every element of the round General's plan. He discovered that having given up completely on the siege, Circulosa merely used it to keep the city distracted and focused on its magical defenses while he brought forth four clusters of *scythorsont*, or doom-stone.

Scythorsont, one of the many tricks up a powerful wizard's sleeve, was a detonation crystal used for all kinds of tasks from mining to covering an army's tracks. Never before had Xymon seen it used to end a siege and certainly not with so much over-planning. At first, the dark General figured the Carrion soldiers were going to load the four clusters into catapults and fire them against the walls. This might have worked, but it was not what Circulosa had in mind for the doom-stones.

Circulosa used crews, not magic, to dig tunnels underneath the city's walls and place the crystals there. Upon initiating a blast the ground would shake and the foundations of the walls would be destroyed. They might fall, Xymon admitted, but the amount of time and effort required seemed more of an attempt at complexity than a viable strategy.

He knew Flaem kept its wards up because it did not want to become involved in the war. The Elders responded immediately to the emissaries Zion sent there and short of outright insult, consciously chose to maintain their well-known stance of neutrality. As a matter of principle it made sense to the General, but from a practical standpoint he didn't see the sanity of this plan. Whether or not the sorcerers desired to be left alone, a war could never ignore so powerful a potential ally — or enemy. Xymon cleared his head of all thoughts of the city and attempted again to focus on the instructions Zion gave to him.

Circulosa's plan remained flawed from the start. Whether the walls came down or the gates were willfully thrown open, an entire city of sorcerers unleashed against a third of the Carrion army would be a battle of folly. Until the soldiers could get close it wouldn't even be a battle of attrition; it would simply be a slaughter. From the range across the killing ground, the wizards would blast the army to ashes. The siege was doomed to failure, but it seemed the round General could even make a bad plan fail.

Surrender or defeat would be inevitable, regardless of his extensive plans to the contrary. Zion had been right to send Xymon here, the dark General decided, and quickly came up with the plan to dispose of the failure and his retreating soldiers.

Stealth came so naturally to Xymon he barely noticed anymore when blending in shadows. He wore the darkness as a cloak, just as Zion taught him. Because of Circulosa's inexperience and the untrained suspicions of his army, Xymon barely needed any of his innate talents to circumvent their efforts. It took only a few minutes to procure three of the four clusters of doom-stone and hide them inside Circulosa's ships. Two he placed in the main ship, where the General would reside.

He reached out to use the third cluster to locate the fourth, and Xymon relished the thought of completing his task. The General paused, weighing in his mind the difference between punishing Circulosa's failure and causing it. It would certainly be a spectacle to any eyes far away enough to perceive and survive it. Sadly, the dark General would not be able to see Circulosa's face at the moment of his death.

The wizard and his Carrion soldiers would be disintegrated by the explosion. Behind his mask a grin came to Xymon's dark lips. He repeated the words of Zion in his mind again like a mantra and continued his task.

They will be replaced.

CHAPTER 24 – *Cairos*

HE PAIR OF WIZARDS WALKED WEST ALONG THE ROAD toward Flaem. Cairos remained hopeful things would improve, but still could not gauge Gabumon's response. As an illusionist, the older man had to be deceitful by nature and therefore hard to read. He seemed genuine in their conversations about trivial wizard concerns, though Cairos remained unconvinced.

Landscape east of Flaem held little of interest; the forested lowland areas hosted the Trials when the northern deserts could not. Cairos judged, from the amount of time it took to reach the cave, it wouldn't be much longer until the city came in sight.

When he asked Gabumon why they didn't just fly, Cairos received a lecture on "retaining power rather than using it frivolously," followed up by a question of why he "was in such a hurry to return to Flaem." He ignored both.

Cairos glanced back to remind himself how far they already traveled. After Gabumon collected his varied and miscellaneous travel gear, he led Cairos out of the cave through a set of clean and peaceful passages. Amazingly, the old man seemed to have a map of the place memorized.

Their path west took them through a sparsely-wooded area and across two bridges, areas Cairos ignored during his aloof jaunt to the fortress. He took in the splendor of the eastern wilderness and saw the magic of nature all around. Its beauty reminded Cairos of an old goal to spend less time in the city in the future. If I *survive*, he thought distractedly.

While they walked, the older man told Cairos about the cave. Its depths were empty and abandoned but contained the remnants of a pillaged dragon inside — where Gabumon got the idea for his illusion. Typically hunters took the scales, teeth, claws, and a few choice bones, but left the remainder of the corpse behind to rot. Though a dragon's legendary ability to breathe fire was revered, no man — sorcerer or otherwise — could figure out a way to extract the essence of it. Therefore, the internal organs received the same treatment as the entrails from any other animal.

The beast, dead too long for Gabumon to do any research on, provided bone shafts long enough for staff halves. He assembled them by carving matched grooves and had the result coated in a silver alloy at a smithy in Flaem. The experimental staff resulted in an incredibly lightweight, yet hard-striking, weapon as tall as a partisan. While on that trip, he came across a tome with information on the cave and used the book to delve its secrets. As it happened, the Flaem curator did not take kindly to the volume being "borrowed" indefinitely.

"Of course," said Gabumon, "I left him a suitable illusion until I returned it. He must have discovered it before I intended him to."

Cairos grinned. Though the older wizard seemed shifty, he could really appreciate the man's logic and methods. The story also piqued his curiosity as to how many other dragon caves could be explored once the war ended.

∽

Upon seeing the detonations against the city's wards, both men broke out into a full sprint toward the eastern wall of Flaem. So many possibilities ran through Cairos' mind as he willed his feet to carry him faster. Flaem showed no sign of damage and disorder; the eastern gate stood firmly closed signaling the Elders and citizens refused to flee.

At the sight of movement, Cairos grasped the older man's shoulder and dove behind a small outcropping of stone. He peered quickly to make sure they had not been spotted, but the lurking figures — scouts, he guessed — fumbled about the perimeter wall and faced away from him. It took a moment for Cairos to find his breath enough to speak.

"I can't believe they're already here."

"It had to happen sooner or later," Gabumon said quietly. Cairos got the sense the old man's tone bordered on apologetic for not agreeing they should hurry.

Both men squinted and scanned the landscape. "The wards must be holding up," said Cairos. "It doesn't look like the Carrion are breaking through."

"So they're not. But that wouldn't stop you or me forever. And these beasts did overrun Illiadora," Gabumon responded.

Cairos turned to the older man. "They used different tactics then."

"What do you mean?"

"There was no siege at Illiadora; they simply invaded," answered Cairos. "How they got inside the city and opened the gates, I don't know, but that's what they did. They didn't waste their time and effort testing our wards."

"That would suggest someone different is leading them on this attack, or they ran into problems attempting to infiltrate Flaem."

"Probably the latter." Cairos nearly laughed at the difference in tactics. "When was the last time you ever heard of a city coming under siege?"

"Well, we're too far away to assume that it is even the Carrion army attacking Flaem," said Gabumon. "Let's take a closer look."

The younger wizard wanted to ask who else it could have been, but getting closer to the action would make the question moot. They hurried closer to the city, cutting southwest to stay hidden. Cairos brought a hand to his eyes and invoked a spell of "far sight" to take stock of the army.

"They're Carrion," he said.

"I can see that." Cairos looked to his partner and saw Gabumon's eyes glossed over with a similar spell.

They tentatively advanced, dashing from one spot of cover to the next, until they came close enough to see and hear the Carrion soldiers. A dozen large wooden catapults launched stones from the west with no success. Each siege weapon was attended by a team of grunts. Cairos watched the variety of fodder shot toward the city and could barely stifle a chuckle as each and every one dissipated harmlessly against the wards.Both sorcerers dropped low to the ground as a figure rose into the air above the soldiers.

"That's Circulosa," said Cairos, pointing to the floating man.

"Well, what are you waiting for? With him dead, his army will probably scatter. You know what happens when you cut the head off a serpent," Gabumon retorted, referring to an old adage.

Cairos found the old wizard's words less than encouraging.

"Sure, and what if I miss?" he asked. "We need more than just the two of us. Do you know of any way into the city?"

Gabumon laughed and gestured to the immense army of Carrion soldiers. "Don't you think they would have found it already?"

The question hung in the air between them as both men stood and listened to the repetitive splashing noises of the stones. After a moment, Gabumon snapped his fingers.

"The tombs! We can use the Tombs of the Burning Men. They look sealed from the outside, but there's not much to opening them."

Cairos nodded, familiar with the bloodline of the Burning Men. They were the ultimate decision-makers, the Elders of Flaem, and came from the long line of mages who laid the foundation stones centuries earlier. Their heads and hands, and any other uncovered part of their skin, seemed constantly bathed in flame, but they did not burn. It was impossible to calculate their ages — or even to touch them. The young wizard wondered how they procreated, but decided to save pondering that particular logistical challenge for another time.

"Look at him up there. He must fancy himself some kind of god." Gabumon scoffed at the round wizard.

"I will kill him," promised Cairos.

"You may get your chance today," said the older wizard. "Come; the tombs are this way."

✇

DEEP UNDER THE CITY LAY THE TOMBS OF THE BURNING MEN. JUST as in the east, the land beneath Flaem was nearly hollow from all of the mines and passageways. If the Carrion had not discovered a way to use them yet, thought Cairos, they soon would. To him, the entrance to the catacombs looked like a burial mound, complete with a large circular boulder to seal it. Burned into the face of the rock was the symbol of a candle flame, though it held no special significance among the Pillars.

"The stone is too heavy to push from its groove," said the older wizard, "and you'll find it resistant to any movement spells."

With a few gentle words, Gabumon invoked a small fire in the palm of his hand and placed it against the stone. The ground began to shake as the stone rolled away to reveal a gaping hole.

"I see you've done this before," Cairos jabbed, covering his mouth with a cloth to guard from the stench of stale air. He stared into the structured cavern, but only saw a wall of darkness. As soon as they crossed the threshold the ground shook again and the stone rolled sealed the entrance.

Gabumon seemed confident, but Cairos had a few concerns. He looked around the hollowed cavern and certainly felt closed in. Not even the slightest sliver of light shone through from where they entered. Low-blazing sconces adorned otherwise plain rock walls to illuminate a dusty and empty chamber. Cairos deemed the place devoid of life, absent even of spider webs and rodent corpses.

"How do we get back out?" he asked.

"Out?" chuckled Gabumon. "You don't know much about the death ceremony of the Burning Men, do you?"

Cairos shook his head, but Gabumon did not explain. When the older man moved further into the cavern, Cairos had no choice but to shrug and follow.

"Where will this put us in the city?" Cairos whispered.

"If we keep to the right path, we'll hit the sewers first," responded Gabumon, much to the younger wizard's dismay.

Cairos immediately noticed the cave's dank and warm air, even through the cloth against his face. The humidity threatened to choke him, along with a faint air of decay that floated on a breeze to indicate the place was, indeed, a tomb. The glassy black walls reflected light and hinted at an ancient volcano, but Cairos knew too little about them to be sure.

Wall sconces continued at intervals through the cavern, but they became more and more sparse as the men descended. Fearing it would become too dark to navigate, Cairos whispered to his *terasont* to create an impromptu torch. The stone let off an ethereal blue glow, awakening sets of glyphs and runes along both walls. Most were too old to be read, or nigh worn off, but he could feel the magic emanating from them.

As they walked, Cairos checked a few side passages and after a few quick explorations they found them all shallow and empty. Before long, Cairos' curiosity got the best of him and he asked to know what Gabumon meant before about the death ritual.

The old man returned a haunted look and the blue light gave his features even more solemn edges. "The wizard is led into the chamber and sealed in. This discourages robbery and is also a sacred part of their deaths. Odd as it sounds, their head and hands still burn even after their hearts stop beating."

Deeper in, the smooth walls gave way to lighter stone and packed dirt. Gabumon continued, "Their final spell nails their wrists and feet to the walls, where they hang burning until they expire."

The men turned a particularly sharp corner and came upon an unnatural intersection. The broken wall spread across the floor to create a digression in the tunnel, and crude digging tools lay discarded nearby. A dozen pairs of footprints in the fresh dirt led further down the smooth part of the passage.

Cairos knelt to examine the tracks. "Carrion," he whispered.

"Have to be." Gabumon answered, equally quiet. "We're not too deep yet and we have a ways to go before hitting the sewers."

"Why do you think they dug to an existing tunnel?" asked Cairos. "Are they trying to get past the walls?"

The old wizard nodded in the low light. "They kept going instead of running back to get their friends; must be trying to see how far it goes." The old wizard turned away from Cairos and peered down the passageway, presumably to gauge its length.

"Right. We should seal this up and go after them," said Cairos, determined to draw more Carrion blood.

"That, or we could just come out through their tunnel and surprise them," Gabumon returned with a grin.

Cairos shook his head, surprised at Gabumon reckless plan. "A dozen we can handle, but you saw how many of them were out there. If we can get inside the city and bring more wizards with us, a surprise might just work. Mark the wall and we can unseal it later."

They tossed the tools into the tunnel and both began to chant silent spells to Valesh to repair the wall. The rock reformed and repaired itself until it became impossible to tell where a breach had ever been made. The wall rang solid, not hollow, when tapped, and Cairos scratched a few marks on it with his fingernail.

Once finished, the men advanced further into the passage and came upon another sharp turn. A commotion made them pause, and Cairos saw a small group of Carrion solders in flight when he glanced past the bend. He snapped his staff up and the first few slammed into it while Gabumon cast a spell to dispatch the beasts. Dancing blades made short work of the Carrion bodies and sprayed black blood on the cavern floor. Cairos made a disgusted face, but had to admit the spell did its job well.

The pair dared a second glance around the corner and found the rest of the Carrion pinned behind rocks. Some strafed to dodge attacks from something further in, past where the passage opened to a much larger cavern. When the floor lit up with a blast of flame, both Cairos and Gabumon got a good look at what the Carrion fled from.

"By the Nine," Cairos rasped, "is this part of their death ritual as well? Play a game of 'get past the dragon and find your tomb'?"

"Go get him, youngun," said Gabumon.

"Me? You're the dragon expert!"

"Expert? Listen, just because I can make an illusion of one doesn't mean I ..."

It didn't take long for the bickering to catch the attention of the soldiers. After another blinding blast of fire, the sorcerers found themselves squaring off against six Carrion grunts in the small space. At the head of the six stood a hideous soldier with one good eye and sores all over its visible skin. In addition to its horrid appearance, this one seemed tougher to Cairos. The beast carried itself differently, as if it were a higher rank or an officer, and looked quite agitated.

With a pus-filled grin, the officer drew its serrated weapon and leapt toward Cairos.

∞

CHAPTER 25 – *Cairos*

AIROS PARRIED AND BLOCKED ATTACKS AS QUICKLY AS HE could with his staff and *terasont* in front of him. He recognized immediately these were not all grunts and it would take a bit of finesse to defeat the large — and particularly perturbed — Carrion officer. He narrowed his eyes at the ghastly humanoid form, but otherwise made no move to attack. His mind frantically tried to keep up with the speed of the officer's attacks, unable to formulate a spell. Gabumon, on the other hand, began tossing blue lightning forward with reckless abandon.

Unfortunately for Cairos the officer negated the spellcasters' advantages by unsheathing its weapon. The blue lightning became immediately swallowed up by the serrated metal blade, humming afterward, but otherwise dormant. The blade itself, half as tall as a man and notched along both edges, looked like it had seen many battles.

Cairos abandoned casting and focused on attacks with his staff. The officer laughed at the befuddled looks that appeared on the faces of Cairos and Gabumon. Using speech that nearly sounded human, the officer barked, "I am Rot, and I shall be the last thing you see before you die."

Dismayed by the prospect, Cairos leapt back as the point of the blade nearly made contact with his forehead. He brought his staff up just as quickly and sent the sword off to one side. Rot rolled with the momentum and spun its body to bring the sword around in a decapitating slash, but the young wizard bent forward in a lunge to anticipate the blow. As the sword sailed over his head, he brought the tip of his staff up underneath the chin of the carrion officer. The blow knocked it back as Cairos expected, but he found himself dragged forward by his cloak.

"Help!" Cairos shouted as he dove to the side.

"I'm busy!" Gabumon replied.

The younger sorcerer's dodge kept him from being sliced vertically in half. The expected downward swipe of the sword thumped against the cavern floor like a club and created a small fissure. Cairos leapt forward to counter, but the Carrion officer had already extricated the tip of its blade from the soft clay. After a quick parry of Cairos' staff the beast renewed its assault.

Gabumon employed his heavy longstaff to fend off the other Carrion. To negate the officer's power, Cairos positioned himself to retreat and draw his opponent's blade away from Gabumon. He hoped the old man would detect his plan, knowing the range of the blade's vacuuming magic was limited to close-range spells. Cairos had only seen similar powers in a few small artifacts, but they became much too heavy for use after absorbing magical energy.

From a considerable distance Cairos saw the flash of a flame burst. The attack shriveled one Carrion grunt's arm to the point where it simply fell off, but the beast kept attacking. Satisfied that Gabumon regained the advantage, the younger sorcerer shifted his focus back to his own fight.

Cairos knew he could not win without his spells. Though he wielded a staff — and believed all wizards should — the officer's melee training and proficiency dwarfed his own.

"A minor foe is no large feat, but an officer is an officer for a reason," he recalled from an old lesson. "Better to leave it to the swordsmen." Cairos growled in frustration, knowing that the instructor's death had been caused by his own flawed philosophy.

He concentrated on disarming the officer rather than defeating it. With each parry and counter he searched for ways to exploit openings on wrists, hands, and knuckles. Cairos used his hard staff to tap wherever he could and began to see the results quickly. His small attacks even brought a few snaps of bone and burst the putrid sores on the creature's forearm. With his teeth gritted, Cairos struck the area repeatedly and used his aversion to fuel his retribution.

Cairos' staff hit so hard the sinews began to become visible on the abomination's fingers, but it still held the blade and kept swinging. Even with all the damage he caused, the wizard knew there wasn't much time left before the officer overwhelmed him.

Each time Cairos parried, he tapped his *terasont* and whispered a quick spell to test the power of his enemy's blade. Again and again they were swallowed as quickly as he could get them out. His tactic was subtle, calling upon his knowledge of items imbued with a vacuum power. Every spell the item swallowed would increase its weight until something discharged or drained out the energy. Cairos watched patiently for the slowing of the officer's swings, but Rot seemed to feel no pain at all. After a strong downward swipe, Cairos saw the sword left a much larger fissure than before.

Calling upon the power of his *terasont* Cairos unleashed one of his more powerful spells. He phrased a command to Scythor, the Pillar of Death, and sent howling spirits at his opponent. The sword swallowed them all, much to the mirth of the officer, but when it attempted to counter, the beast found its sword would not budge.

Cairos dealt a shattering blow to the pommel of the sword and two of the beast's clawed fingers fell to the ground. The officer roared in response and swung the heavy sword with its weakened grip. The sorcerer quickly ducked the clumsy attack and heard an audible pop as the sword's momentum destroyed the officer's arm joint. The blade slammed against the cavern wall with half an arm still wrapped around it. Seizing the moment, Cairos slapped his rod against the chest of Rot, sending the officer to the floor on his back. He glanced quickly at Gabumon who clutched his side and defended using the reach of his long staff.

Cairos snapped his attention back just in time to see the officer stumbling down the tunnel with its sword in tow. He marveled at its strength and moved to follow without a second thought. Behind him, blue lightning lit up the cave giving his shadow a strange glow. Cairos allowed himself a satisfactory smile as he heard the older wizard's spell sizzle its way through the Carrion soldiers. His face turned back to one of determination as he heard the metal sword scraping the rock floor of the cave.

Confident that the fight would end soon, he increased the pace of his pursuit. He whispered a short prayer to Tera and a ball of light shot forward from inside his sleeve. Normally, the ball would have hung suspended, but within the confines of the cave it attempted to follow the call of the vacuum sword. The wizard ran as fast as he could to keep up with the glowing sphere, but knew it wouldn't take long to find the officer.

He turned at the familiar bend and found the point where he and Gabumon sealed the side tunnel. Rot palmed the wall, spreading black blood and pus from its wounded stumps. The officer seemed to be searching for some kind of illusion and cursing the very existence of dirt when the ball of light entered his field of vision. Rot spun and sliced at the intruder with its remaining claw, but the ball ducked the blow and entered the dropped sword.

From the bend in the tunnel, Cairos realized the best way to get rid of this menace — the spell that came to mind each time he saw the Carrion and remembered his escape from Illiadora. Underground, it would be dangerous, but his anger severely outweighed his judgment at the moment. He guessed the range would keep him safe from the effects, and the serrated blade would not interrupt him.

The wizard chanted to Valesh and the floor of the cave began to tremble. Cairos turned and dashed back down the passage as the ceiling brought the crushing force of dirt down on the head of Rot and the vacuum blade. Cairos expected the rumbling to stop as he got further away from where he summoned the spell, but to his dismay, it grew stronger. He saw the vague outline of Gabumon standing triumphantly in the cave.

"Run!"

As he approached, Cairos noticed that the older wizard stared at him, perplexed. He stumbled against Gabumon and pushed him toward the mouth of the larger cave. Cairos pumped his arms to carry him faster away from the collapsing ceiling.

The pair dove through the lair entrance and rolled to the side as the supporting dirt and stone dropped and sealed them in. Half-expecting chastisement, Cairos stayed on the ground and surveyed the cavern before halfheartedly attempting to dust his sleeves off. His head jerked to the side and his eyes grew in fear as he heard an unfamiliar growl. Cairos thought he heard a shout, but it was lost among the noise from the nearby dragon.

Bolts of bright blue lightning arced through the dark lair and struck wall and scale. Cairos heard the beast roar in response and felt the ground begin to quake for a new reason. A long red snout crept around a pillar of stone and its nostrils hinted at waiting jets of consuming fire. Cairos instinctively covered his head with his arms and screamed, expecting to be roasted in one last dramatic moment.

It took a few seconds for Cairos to realize that he was still alive. He looked up to see Gabumon in front of him.

"I tried to distract it. Why didn't you move?"

The older man's palms were up and his arms extended as if he cupped water. The spell created a shield in the shape of a bubble around both wizards, but Cairos couldn't focus on anything other than the beating of his heart. He wanted nothing more than to collapse back to the floor.

"Don't move," Gabumon commanded.

Cairos remained frozen, swallowing hard. "What?"

"This Fire Shield only protects us if we're still."

"I knew you were lying when you said you knew nothing of dragons!" The shock of fear ebbed away and he began to process the thought normally. A fleeting memory struck him about the terror that the true presence of a dragon could inspire.

The fire jets paused and Cairos saw steam and smoke rising from the transparent bubble around them. The giant head swayed back and forth as if agitated its foes were still alive. It turned and lowered to give them a sidelong glance with its murky yellow eyeball. A black slit of a pupil cut down the middle and it blinked vertically. The dragon's lip curled back in a snarl and a drop of saliva fell to the ground, sizzling on impact.

"We'll be safe from the fire, for now," said Gabumon.

"Great," replied Cairos. "What about the teeth?"

CHAPTER 26 – *Circulosa*

IRCULOSA GRINNED BEHIND HIS BULBOUS HELMET. HE couldn't deny his glee at the possibility that the tunnel collapsed on the head of Rot; the Lieutenant had been gone for so long there could be no other rational explanation. The other three officers he charged with the same task had long since retreated from their respective passages and prepared for the attack. Cave-ins were a risk he calculated into his plan, but Circulosa figured his officers would be intelligent enough to dig without killing themselves.

Apparently he placed too much confidence in Rot all around, but the General refused to believe bad luck would cause his downfall. The only good news was the two poorly-constructed ships of reinforcements; though it irked the round wizard to be reinforced by Drakkaram, more troops to bolster his siege were better than nothing.

Circulosa looked again toward his three worthy lieutenants. They carried out his plan perfectly; their *scythorsont* clusters were in place and they returned intact. His officers stood ready to lead the way for thousands of Carrion soldiers. All of the grunts paced, restless, poised to rush into the city once a breach appeared.

The round General ached to punish the unworthy; the blame for this could not be placed on his own shoulders.

After Circulosa's army trampled Flaem he knew no one would stand in the way of the Carrion. He swelled with pride at being given this assignment. With Fort Sondergaarde destroyed Flaem would be the last symbolic victory to crush the world's hope of defense or survival against the black flag of Zion. No other force could match their numbers — so said the oracle stones. Many had already died in the past month and it made Circulosa giddy to think how close they were to victory. The fall of the western wall of Flaem would be a signal to the rest of the world and Circulosa would be the one to send it. No one could resist the march of the Carrion army, especially with his power on their side.

How he longed to detonate the crystals now and leave the loose end of Rot in the hands of the explosive power the idiot carried. But the explosion would not be as impressive or devastating without the fourth cluster, Circulosa conceded. It was buried somewhere between his lines and the wall and would cause problems unless it exploded where it should. For all he knew, Rot had meandered in circles and left the crystal somewhere underneath his own army's feet. The cluster would detonate when the others were set off; all four were linked during their fabrication.

It took a great deal of power and time to forge the doom-stones, and each required the sacrifice of a hundred soldiers in their creation. Circulosa could not let his efforts be even partially wasted.

Again he cursed the failure of Rot. The General could delay no more, but also could not avoid the risks if he failed to seek out the missing cluster. Circulosa pointed himself in the direction of the fourth cavern and willed his levitating form into motion. He sailed through the volleys with no concern for the glowing projectiles still exploding harmlessly against the city's wards. Arriving at the cave entrance where he berated Rot hours earlier, the General entered the hole without even a pause for consideration.

CIRCULOSA QUICKLY REALIZED HE COULD NOT NEGOTIATE THE CAVern while floating; it became even more trouble than walking. His levitation kept him vertical rather than horizontal and more than once he had to dodge a stalactite aimed for his face. Flustered, the General dispelled his levitation and began to walk at a brisk pace instead. With the glowing tip of his staff leading, he traversed the carved tunnel searching for some sign of the soldiers. He avoided the smaller alcoves and passages that split off from the main tunnel, but from the waste materials and excrement in each of them, Circulosa surmised the cause for Rot's continued delays.

After his fruitless exploration of each digression he came to a dead end littered with digging tools. Perplexed and incensed, Circulosa was ready to retreat to find the correct passage, but chose to investigate the dead end first. He tapped on the wall a few times to check for an illusion, but the dirt and rock were indeed real. The rock did not sound hollow, but when his taps fell against the dirt they left distinct impressions, as if it had been assembled recently with no time to settle and press together.

With a great sweep of his staff and a command word, the dirt and rock parted to either side without upsetting the ceiling. The cleared earth revealed a clawed and decaying hand extended upward, and the General dared to hope it remained attached to the torso. Two of the lieutenant's fingers were missing, and this interested the wizard. Glad to be wearing gloves, Circulosa grasped the hand and pulled hard. The filthy form of Rot slid from the dirt, utterly lifeless.

With a smirk, the General tapped his staff against one of the Lieutenant's black horns. "Wake up," he whispered, his voice sounding even thinner in the closeness of the cavern.

The broken and filthy officer sprung back to life in a fit of expelling coughs. Rot's rasping echo sounded like hundreds of cats choking. Finally, to stop the noise and to get his attention, Circulosa grasped the Lieutenant's throat.

"Tell me what happened, Rot." His voice cracked, but Circulosa had no time to waste with formalities.

Between wheezes the reply came, "Dragon ... Sorcerer ..."

Circulosa released his grip on the subordinate's throat and grasped one of the black horns extending from its head. He pulled gently up so that he was looking into the hollow black eyes of Rot.

"Where is your detachment? Where is the crystal?"

"All ... dead ..." The lieutenant's head rolled when Circulosa removed his hand in shock. Rot did not make a motion except to breathe.

For a moment, Circulosa questioned why he even awakened the officer. A dozen soldiers were killed without one fleeing to report? The General decided he was not going to glean any useful information from this decaying carcass. His only choice was to find the sorcerer Rot spoke of.

"You know, I hear it really hurts when these get removed," said Circulosa, grinning behind his spherical helmet.

The Lieutenant could barely manage a protest before the General yanked the horn free from its home. Rot cried in agony, proving the rumor the General heard. He wondered if the Betrayer suffered this badly when Zion took his horns, and his lips twisted into an even bigger grin.

He quickly grew tired of the Lieutenant's wailing and decided to end its pain and move on. With a quick step backward, Circulosa brought his staff down against the top of Rot's head. A burst of light shot out of the tip in all directions, exploding the majority of its skull. The remaining horn fell to the cave floor and drained black fluid. With a satisfied smile, Circulosa hurried down the passage to find a challenge.

After a few steps, Circulosa found the hilt of Rot's broadsword protruding from a pile of earth. He could feel the unreleased magic emanating from the blade and pondered the possible strength of the sorcerer ahead. Though Circulosa would never have admitted being afraid of Rot, he knew others were — for good reason. The General quickly checked his staff to make sure it was in order and attempted to gauge his remaining magical strength. Despite the siege, he felt able to defeat another wizard before the end of the day. Concentrating on clearing the earth ahead, the General advanced down the tunnel.

Finding the crystal, Circulosa decided, would need to wait.

CHAPTER 27 – *Cairos*

AIROS KNEW FROM THE FIRST MOMENT THAT A BATTLE with the dragon was futile, but Gabumon would not give up, as if he had some kind of vendetta against the giant reptile. Fireball after fireball sailed through the chamber to explode against wall and floor. Soot and charred rock pelted the younger sorcerer, blackening all parts of Cairos' already threadbare tunic. With every spell a jet of flame was there to answer. Being unable to pause to cast anything himself, Cairos could not clear the dirt from the exit tunnel. It would take an immense amount of concentration to undo the cave-in he caused.

Not that it would make much difference in the end, he decided. Gabumon still stood defiant in the same place he had been when the dragon first attacked, and Cairos doubted he could convince the older man to run if they had the chance.

He grasped the older man's shoulder and shouted, "We have to get out of here!"

"Ha! Always ... running from something ... aren't you?" the older sorcerer didn't miss a beat with his defense, the words coming during short breaks between spells.

"What's that supposed to mean?"

The dragon reared back and let its roar fill the breadth of its den. Cairos fought against the shaking of his knees and squeezed Gabumon's shoulder even harder. Sensing the attack, Cairos pulled Gabumon and leapt toward the exit. The beast's teeth snapped together mere inches away from their feet.

Gabumon faced Cairos and shrugged off his arm. "What do you think it means?" he asked. "You abandoned your friends, our countrymen, and let them die at the hands of those Carrion monsters!"

Cairos shoved Gabumon to the floor, forgetting the dragon even existed. "Don't talk to me about abandoning my people, you old fool! You were not there; you can't imagine what I've witnessed. You did not have to watch your friends impaled, carved, and sliced open before your eyes! You did not watch Vortalus die with one stroke!"

Gabumon was visibly shocked at the mention of the Invincible's death. Anger flared in his eyes as bright as the dragon's flame. "I wish I had been there. I wouldn't have been afraid to die, standing next to my brothers! At least I wouldn't have turned about and run like a coward!"

"You old bastard," growled Cairos, "I'll kill you for that!"

A calm, high-pitched voice interrupted the spat. "You make my job far too easy."

Before either of them could react, a web of vines burst forth from the rocky soil and held Gabumon fast in place. Cairos leapt into the air, realizing only then that the exit had been cleared without him or Gabumon even noticing. His leap brought him away from the exit and away from Gabumon just as Circulosa stepped into the dim light. It was only then he processed the General's words.

"No!" Cairos shouted, but it did not distract the dragon. A wave of flames bathed the two figures even as his shout turned into an unintelligible scream of hatred. The fire incinerated his counterpart while Circulosa safely dodged a few paces back. When the flames ceased, Cairos saw the charred staff of Gabumon lying next to where he fell, but no remains of the body or vines that held him. The young sorcerer barely had time to process that he watched yet another of his brethren destroyed by Circulosa's actions.

Blinking away the tears in his eyes, Cairos shot an explosive dart toward the top lip of the exit tunnel. Circulosa leapt nimbly aside, carrying him deeper into the lair, but did not deflect the spell. With the blast, the ceiling of the smaller passage collapsed to trap both men inside the lair.

"Bravo," said the round General. He fired back with a burst of twisting yellow fire, but found he also had a dragon to worry about. Even in his anger, Cairos knew a duel would not last long, despite any talent of theirs.

Cairos easily dodged the General's spell — so easily he began to think his own tactic had been reversed. He looked up to see a sliver of daylight pouring through the ceiling of the cave. The blast weakened an area large enough for a man to fit through. Cairos dodged a sweep of the dragon's tail and fired a group of ice crystals at his opponent from the end of his staff.

Circulosa ignored the assault and leapt high above the snapping fangs of the beast. He fired the boring energy bolt again, past Cairos, and broke through to the surface. With a single command word, his levitating form sped through the falling dirt and rock and out the new exit.

BURSTING THROUGH THE HOLE, CAIROS SEARCHED FOR THE FLEEING General.

"Vexen curses you, coward!" he called. "Don't think you can escape me! Get back here you rounded traitor-to-your-race!"

Instead of responding to the taunts, the General spread his arms to the tips of his staff and began to pull them toward each other. A string of energy shot between the ends of the stick as it took on the shape and properties of a bow. Cairos' memory of Vortalus' defeat suddenly became clearer — the General used this secondary weapon to defeat the Invincible in one powerful shot.

Cursing again, Cairos realized he had emerged among the assaulting throng of Carrion soldiers. Strangely, there seemed to be more of them than he remembered before going underground and then he spotted two odd ships beached behind them. He grasped his *terasont* tightly to his chest and said a short praise to Urrel that if any amount of his good fortune remained, it would manifest itself.

As soon as he finished the last word, Cairos felt the ground beneath him shift. He launched into the air only a second before the dirt exploded under his feet. Two smoldering nostrils led the way as the head, neck, and both front legs of the magnificent red dragon burst into the open. The sorcerer steadied himself in mid-air and tried to regain his bearings.

He realized his fist was clenched so tightly around his *terasont* that his hand had gone numb; he had completely given in to his anger. One more had died — one more he would have to avenge — and it was his fault again.

The dragon's jaws opened in a tremendous roar as it dragged itself completely onto the surface. With its wings unfurled and its girth fully stretched, it nearly spanned the length of Flaem. Its body was so near to the wall that the Carrion's catapults began unwittingly barraging the beast with magic-infused exploding rocks. Cairos watched mesmerized for a moment as the large front claws dug into the ground and the neck craned back before it launched forward and spewed a mighty jet of flame. The nearest Carrion catapults became quickly engulfed and the soldiers themselves were even more quickly vaporized.

Unfortunately, to target its enemies the dragon spun to its side and sent its tail flying in the process. The corner battlement of Flaem's great wall suffered a huge amount of damage and was in danger of more if the beast didn't move away. Cairos grinned and praised Urrel again as he saw the dragon charge forward to consume the scattering Carrion soldiers. The city was safe, for the moment, which meant he could pursue his original goal: Circulosa.

Feeling a familiar twinge of warning, he immediately moved to dodge a blue energy arrow. The dart came so close that he felt the chill as it flew past his cheek. He spotted the source as the round General aimed his staff-bow again at Cairos' floating form. With the dragon advancing, though, he turned away and began to retreat with his soldiers. Cairos was in the middle of uttering another taunt when the twinge struck him again.

Taking the quickest action he could, Cairos simply allowed himself to fall toward the ground as if he were unenchanted. A huge pair of jaws snapped shut above him as he plummeted toward the ground, leveling off just before striking. He poured the momentum from the fall into propulsion and turned toward the fleeing Circulosa, who he could barely see through the crowding enemy troops behind their commander. Cairos halted to consider a different plan. Far in the distance, he saw the two large ships again and aimed for them.

The young wizard could not let the General get away after his actions in the cave. Cairos raised his staff and sent three fireballs sailing over the heads of the fleeing army, straight at their ships. The blasts glanced off without even a hint of damage.

Perplexed, he fired again, but to the same result. The researcher side of his brain took over for a moment as he wondered what kind of wood resisted spells so. Cairos had to recover quickly, though, as the fleeing Carrion turned back to the source of the spells.

Since he could not impede their retreat, the wizard focused again on their commander and rushed forward. He dodged one clumsy swipe of a blade without even looking at the attacker, but soon the swipes became more frequent and Cairos had to dive and roll to avoid being crushed by a huge hammer. He skidded to a stop, then, and found himself surrounded by Carrion soldiers.

Nothing would have pleased Cairos more than to call down the "Meteor" spell and destroy them all, but he could not take the risk, for he stood in the middle of his target zone. Melee would have to suffice. As Cairos tapped his *terasont* against his staff, he whispered one of a wizard's most dangerous phrases — the three words to invoke Vexen's direct attention.

"Bless my vengeance."

CHAPTER 28 – *Starka*

THE GARGOYLE'S HARROWING ASSAULT CAME PRACTICALLY out of nowhere. Starka huddled beneath a charred piece of wood that provided more comfort than protection while she tried to recall at what point it appeared. Hours passed since the first sighting, some time past the smoldering remnants of Fort Sondergaarde. With no other choice left open to them, the *Bloody Lady* continued up the coast toward Flaem.

"Arrows, loose!"

A cry renewed the attack against the flying creature as it passed. One of their major sails had already been shredded and dropped stones left holes in the deck, but they stayed afloat. The young girl whispered her thanks to Alsher for the blessing of survival and added a wish for safety from the frightening beast. Starka poked her head from underneath her makeshift shelter to see if this set of arrows affected the creature.

As the gargoyle came close, she saw it was the color of alabaster, a common white stone used to build statues of all kinds. It looked immense, nearly as tall as the ship itself and about as wide when its wings were cast wide in flight. Starka's first fear that the beast would pick up the entire boat passed; it did not seem to have enough intelligence for that.

Even from far away she could see its pronounced claws and spiked joints. The pair of long horns extended sideways from its head and curled up at the end. Everything about the gargoyle reminded her of the Carrion except its color.

She shuddered and hid as the gargoyle flew so near the ship that the beat of its wings sent the *Bloody Lady* leaning to the opposite side. No attempts by her or the crew to speak to the thing yielded any results; it seemed nothing more than an animal.

The latest dozen arrows bounced off the gargoyle's thick skin as had the previous attempts. Starka heard both DaVille and Satok curse at the same time and retracted her head to listen.

"Don't you have a sorcerer on board?" DaVille asked.

"Can't trust 'em. Always out for 'emselves," the captain replied. Satok's smooth answer showed his calm, though he already admitted no familiarity with this type of creature.

"What about your cannons?"

"Nah," said Satok, "they be for blastin' ships, not firin' in the air."

"Couldn't we just point them up?" Mayrah pressed.

"No, remember what happened back at the dock?" asked DaVille. "If we point the cannon up and fire, we'll be pushed down by the reaction and probably capsize." His tone held an edge of condescension, but Starka decided he must have felt warranted by his short past with the swarthy woman.

"Aye," the Captain groaned, then added, "Capsize."

Starka imagined some kind of elementary explanation of the ship tipping over via hand motions.

"Probably?" an incredulous Mayrah shouted. "Have you ever even tried it?"

An awkward silence followed.

Just as Starka decided to step out on deck, the ship rocked with a crash. She stumbled forward and fell, twisting so she wouldn't fall face first into a pile of debris. Wan Du came immediately to her side and guided the girl to her feet. She smiled warmly at him in gratitude, but he merely stared off into the distance as stone-faced as usual. Starka glanced over her shoulder to check if anyone else noticed her spill — or presence — but they remained engrossed in discussing the best course of action.

"You changed your clothes," said Wan Du. The large man spoke evenly, but for the first time, Starka noticed the words she heard didn't quite match the movement of his lips.

The girl looked at her new outfit and frowned, noticing that it was already wrinkled. "They were so dirty. I had to."

"Where I am from, our *Serené* priestesses would rather have been nude than don clothing other than their robes."

For a moment, Starka wasn't sure whether to take his comment as an admonishment or a solicitation. Her cheeks burned as she remembered the dagger sheathed at her hip. Everything she wore, from the scavenged armors at Bloodmir to this, seemed a far cry from the robe of her former Sisterhood station.

She opened her mouth to speak, but paused when she noticed a tear form at the corner of the large man's eye. Starka realized his home no longer existed; no priestesses lived to make the choice.

"Why do you believe what you believe?" Wan Du whispered.

The rest of the world and the danger in her mind seemed to fade away when the large man asked the question. The earnest question dazed Starka for a moment while she contemplated an answer. Her entire life up until leaving the Sisterhood was summed up by the common profession of faith she repeated thousands of times, but all of the events since her brother's disappearance forced Starka to reconsider whether things remained so simple.

Though she fervently wished to, Starka found herself unable to answer Wan Du's question. The comfortable phrases could not outweigh her visions of destruction. She kept silent and moved to put a comforting hand on Wan Du's shoulder, but he took a step away. Starka retracted her hand, a bit hurt, but realized he had not retreated — just pivoted into a defensive stance.

Past the large man, Starka saw the swooping form of the gargoyle renew its own attack. The beast's eyes and mouth were a deep crimson and a powerful light emitted from the latter orifice. As the beam crossed the surface of the ocean, it left churned water in its wake. She wondered whether it would set the ship ablaze or simply carve it in half.

DaVille crossed her field of vision as he dashed to the edge of the deck. He placed one hand on his other wrist, the wrist of the arm that carried the symbol of Vexen. He aimed his fist at the assailant beast and let forth a powerful shout. Starka noticed a distinctive red outline encase his arm before a beam of energy, similar to the one firing from the gargoyle, launched from the closed fist. The shot was true and slammed into the gargoyle's chest, knocking it off trajectory but not appearing to damage it otherwise. It flew past and careened up to circle back.

She rushed to DaVille's side as he fell to one knee. She grasped his arm afraid he might faint again. Instantly she pulled her hands away; her palms nearly seared. He waved her off and forced himself up again. Either he had not used as much energy as before or he became more resistant to the consequences of his mysterious power. Starka decided she couldn't care less, so long as he protected her from the intentions of the beast. As the girl watched it continue to curve around for another pass, she wondered how long they could keep up their defense.

The concept of defense gave her an idea, and Starka turned to face Satok. "Captain, we have to use the cannons!"

"I already told ye! Capsize!" He illustrated with a hand gesture similar to the one Starka imagined earlier.

"No, not to fire at the creature," she said. "We can to use them to dodge it!"

DaVille perked up at the girl's words. "That's a plan, alright. If we can effectively utilize all ten of them, we might be able to make it to Flaem. Otherwise ..." He let his voice trail off into something about "sinking or swimming."

Somehow, Starka knew they wouldn't be doing much swimming.

"Nine," Satok corrected. "They can't be recharged at sea."

Mayrah joined the conversation. "How close are we?"

Satok called up to the watchman who announced the city's towers in sight. After licking his finger and testing the wind, the captain counted on his hands and shrugged.

"Closer'n I thought. Keepin' course we make it in an hour." He indicated a mark on the horizon northeast very close to the land's edge and turned to a crewman to relay the plan. The sailor scurried below to ready the cannons.

"That's it, then," said DaVille, "we dodge until ..."

"Problem, Cap'n!" The lookout's shout from above interrupted. "That city be under siege!"

Satok removed a tube from his jacket and extended it, looking toward the city, then handing the device to DaVille. Starka's companion cursed at arcing flashes before all three of them nearly lost their balance.

The first cannon fired on the other side of the ship and the boat lurched to dodge as the pursuing gargoyle made a pass. Energy from its blast razed the water where they had been, but the lack of warning almost sent a few of the crew and a female passenger over the side.

"Oh, this is hopeless," Starka said after recovering her own footing. "How many cities are going to fall to them before someone does something?"

No one could speak to Starka's question; they simply stood aghast that someone put into words what they all felt. Or perhaps they contemplated throwing her negativity overboard to the potential glee of the gargoyle, Starka mused.

DaVille came close enough to whisper, "Tactless as well as naïve, girl. Just let me do the talking, okay?"

Her face reddened but she did not respond.

"THOSE CATAPULTS AREN'T DOING ANY DAMAGE AT ALL," SAID DaVille, still looking through the tube. "The city must have some kind of magical protection."

The ship shifted dangerously again in a dodge, possibly a moment or two premature.

"Aye," muttered Satok as he shook his head.

"But it can't last forever. The city will eventually be destroyed," Mayrah called from the opposite side of the ship.

"It's lasted this long," Starka countered, clinging onto the hope that there would be one place along her journey she didn't have to immediately flee from. Another cannon fired during the pause.

"She's right," said DaVille, "and if there were a place to make a stand, it'd be here, but it doesn't look like the city is even fighting back."

"They probably be avoidin' gettin' involved at all, after what happened to Illiadora," muttered Satok. "Indiff'rence won't save 'em this time."

"So they're just going to sit there and get destroyed?" Starka demanded. "Wizards are stronger than that, aren't they?"

"War is not just about strength," replied Wan Du. "And it isn't as if the city wishes to be attacked."

The ship lurched again as the fifth cannon fired. Everyone on deck seemed to be adjusted, as no one lost their footing this time.

DaVille continued, "There are only two sides in any war. If they choose to fight back they're choosing a side. If avoiding that means they don't actively protect themselves ..." He parted his hands and shrugged.

"Maybe they're just waiting for help," said Starka.

This brought a snort from Captain Satok, who obviously held no love for the city. "No one to help 'em," he said. "Let them wizards starve inside their walls. If they don't want to fight they be worthless and not worth helpin' anyhow."

Despite her travels, Starka refused to accept the captain's attitude. She sunk to her knees and grasped at the vertical posts holding up the rail like prison bars. With her eyes shut tight, she poured the contents of her heart into a silent prayer.

She held on as another blast took them out of harm's way. Starka paid respect to the Divine Female, Alsher, and thanked her for the life she had and for the protection of it thus far. The girl pleaded for the lives of the people of Flaem, calling into balance the four cities already destroyed by the inexorable Carrion. Her chest heaved as she sobbed internally and bit it back. Filled with sadness, her mind settled on what she knew of Wan Du's home and the image of decimated Fort Sondergaarde.

Starka begged with a final mantra that if there was still a just and loving protector, Flaem would be spared.

As her eyes opened, Starka realized she had just prayed for the salvation of people who did not even believe in her faith. Though it should have brought her shame, the girl felt a burden lift from her heart. A warm feeling in the back of her mind brought a smile to Starka's face as she wiped a tear away. Everything would be alright, she thought.

The sound of grating wood filled the air and she heard the captain shout a warning about being too close to shore. As she looked up, Starka noticed the city was much closer than before her prayer. Carrion soldiers were visible running about reloading catapults and performing other miscellaneous tasks.

To her surprise, two men shot up from a hole in the ground near the middle of the open field between the city and the army. Confused, she squinted and tried to make sense of the flying men just before the ground erupted.

Starka stood and stared in complete amazement as a huge red beast burst from the ground right behind the two men. First, the titan's head cleared the hole and roared. Its long, scaled neck came next as the beast clawed its way to the surface. In awe, the girl realized the only thing it could be.

Flaem was suddenly not far enough away. A few exclamations and curses came from the crew; the general consensus being that no one on the ship had seen a dragon before. The tremendous roar of the beast made Starka cover her ears and shiver.

Large rocks catapulted toward the red beast exploded on contact. This angered the dragon, though it did not seem to be hurt by the projectiles. The dragon turned to aim its fiery breath against the tiny Carrion, smashing a corner battlement of Flaem with its tail. Starka spun around and scanned the sky for the gargoyle, realizing the shock might have delayed a cannon and placed them in danger.

Before she could spot it, a shriek sounded above. Starka peered high to see the gargoyle paused in mid air and facing the dragon. Again she heard the immense roar of the red beast and the gargoyle darted toward it with mouth and eyes burning.

With the threat of the white monster gone, the ship became active again. Crewmen ran past her in all directions to repair the damage and ready for landfall. Starka turned and saw Captain Satok pointing to the front of the ship at two huge black-sailed vessels landed further north. The crew let out a muted cheer because, at the sight and initial action of the dragon, the Carrion army fled toward those ships.

"Fire the rear cannon! Get us ashore!" DaVille ordered. He unsheathed both longswords and stood at the front of the ship eyeing their blades for flaws. The girl looked past him toward the beach as the ship began to turn. From what Starka could see they would run aground quite easily with an added dash forward.

"Hold on ta somethin'!" Captain Satok called after he gave the order to the same scrambling crew member as before. The *Bloody Lady* dashed forward before Starka could follow the captain's order, but she kept her feet this time. Out of the corner of her eye, Starka saw Mayrah jump awkwardly from the side, caught a little off her guard by its sudden movement. As she looked forward again, Wan Du and DaVille leapt from the ship and the girl rushed forward to see where they landed.

Wan Du crashed amid a group of unsuspecting Carrion soldiers. Much to their detriment, none thought to put their weapons up in time. The large man felled one with his bare hands and took its enormous black halberd to dispatch the rest. Wan Du's angry battle shout resounded against the nearby hills.

DaVille landed on his feet, but rolled with the impact. Before Starka could blink the man had decapitated two enemies and moved on to a third. He batted a primitive sword aside with both of his blades and slammed into the beast with his hip to send it to the ground. Without losing momentum, DaVille slashed through its neck and kept running. He dodged a pair of arrows before leaping an embankment to attack their source. Starka heard two distinct screams before DaVille leapt into view again.

The girl marveled at these two warriors, unafraid to rush into the battle outnumbered and isolated. She could hardly believe the Carrion had been so victorious with so many killed by DaVille's blades alone. Outside the Cellto gate she had not watched him in as much detail, but her life was proof enough of his competence.

DaVille chose a path leading to one of the large siege weapons firing stones at the city's walls. She wondered, briefly, if DaVille planned to disable it to aid the city or to aim it at the gargoyle. DaVille sliced through soldier after hideous soldier, whether they faced him or not. After he decapitated three grunts with one stroke, the man paused as an immense Carrion stepped in his path. The beast, as big as Wan Du, wielded a pole with a chain connected to a spike-ridden human head. Even from a distance Starka could make out the distinct colors of flesh, hair, and blood. She wanted to retch but could not take her eyes off of DaVille.

His enemy swung its weapon with a rhythm that took planning to counteract. She noticed Wan Du headed toward DaVille; the large man attracted most of the attention of the Carrion army. The young girl winced for his sake every time she heard the thrum of a bow.

DaVille dodged to the side as the bladed head sailed through the space he previously occupied. The large soldier roared and yanked on the chain. As the ball returned, the soldier continued its swinging rhythm. DaVille stalked in a circle around the creature and waited for an opportunity to strike while Starka held her breath.

The beast pulled back and swung its mace in an arc, attempting to wrap it around DaVille rather than smash him with it. At the pause in its swing, DaVille leapt and thrust his two swords into the soldier's chest. Without even a pause to celebrate, he spread his arms and rebounded off the Carrion into a backward flip. Black blood sprayed as its limbs fell to the ground. DaVille left it for dead and engaged another pair of soldiers near the catapult.

She knew if DaVille fell in this battle, her choices were very slim as to where she would go next. The ship seemed like a haven for rescuing them from Cellto, but what payment would be required if she asked to stay on? Starka turned to find Satok standing close to her. He watched the battle, but his gaze seemed to look past it.

"Probably 'bout time ye got off, missy," he said, "afore the crew gets any ideas."

The words came as a bit of a shock, as the battlefield was not a safe place for her. Again, she felt her arm brush the cold metal of the weapon's pommel on her hip and shivered. It takes more than a weapon to fight, she thought wryly.

Starka gave a quick nod and turned back toward the city. She walked to front of the ship and lifted one leg over the side. Before dropping off, she looked back to thank the captain and found him in the same place, but with his gaze toward the two fighting beasts.

"I hope we see you again, Captain Satok."

"Aye. Might find me sailin' north after this battle be over. Might even find me some cargo." His lips raised in another dirty smile. "Ye go follow yer man."

Starka didn't ponder the meaning of his last statement until she was a ways away from the ship. She ran toward the city and tried to stay far from the battle as well as the shrieks and roars of the dragon and gargoyle. The beasts wrestled, oblivious to the smaller creatures likewise entangled across the field from her.

The wall of the city had been damaged in multiple places and Starka saw scratches and discolorations on both of the creatures. She stayed so intent on watching the clash of these titans that Starka failed to pay attention to where she stepped.

A dark breeze, like silk, rushed past her face so quickly she instinctively brought up a hand to protect herself. In her haste, she tripped and fell. The young girl immediately felt silly, but aside from her pride she remained unharmed. Looking past her feet, Starka marveled at what she stumbled against.

Entranced, she crawled back to take a close look at the stone — a mass of translucent black crystals clustered together that glowed with an incredible power. It looked like volcanic glass, but obsidian usually came in shards rather than clusters.

She dared to touch it with a fingertip and felt no ill effects. The cluster seemed to be about as big as a man's head. When she stood and lifted it, she realized its full weight. While light enough for her to lift, the odd-angled points of the crystals made it difficult to carry.

Holding the crystal, Starka began to feel suddenly strange, almost vulnerable. Though she didn't see any enemies close she began to wish for DaVille's presence. With an awkward hold on the stone, Starka abandoned heading for the city and rushed back toward the battlefield to find him.

CHAPTER 29 – *Circulosa*

IRCULOSA FAILED TO TAKE THE CITY AND NOW HE WAS even forced to run away. He wanted desperately to make a final attempt and call a charge, but Circulosa knew he would be sacrificing his entire army. With much of his power depleted from the long siege and the lack of rest, the appearance of the dragon made things all the more taxing. The reinforcements, such an advantage before, now seemed more of a hindrance; those not already dead now needed an escape.

That sorcerer is to blame for this, cursed Circulosa. The man and his dead colleague caused the creature's involvement in the first place. He took comfort that at least he killed one of them.

He signaled a retreat to the Carrion soldiers not already boarding the ships. The Carrion army's haphazard formations made him begin to question his normally steadfast subordinate officers. Their disorganization in the lines after the appearance of the dragon and gargoyle utterly maddened him. Normally erratic at best, the change made him realize the beasts were actually afraid. Though Circulosa couldn't deny its roar inspired a certain amount of terror in his own heart, his anger and shame quashed it just as quickly.

The arrival of the dragon onto the battlefield caused his defeat even more than Rot's poor performance with the explosive crystal. Circulosa snapped his fingers as the clusters returned to mind. Again, he considered making one last attempt to locate them. Though valuable, their threatening nature would prevent them from being disturbed if found. Citizens of Flaem would recognize the power of the *scythorsont* and give the crystals a wide berth — if they were smart.

"Circulosa!"

He cast aside all thoughts of the crystals when the General heard his name. Circulosa spun to face the source, but the cry came from two different directions.

The wizard faced three men, as all retreating Carrion soldiers already abandoned the area. Each man approached, unhindered and fully concentrated on him. Circulosa noted the face of the sorcerer who called the dragon forth, whether by accident or not. From a different direction came a large man he didn't recognize and a face Circulosa thought he would never see again.

"Impossible," he said, choking on the word. His heart beat in his throat as Circulosa made eye contact with the last man, and he gripped his staff tighter to keep his hands from trembling. "It can't be you! I saw you dead!"

Panicked, Circulosa drew his hand back and summoned a fireball. Pain stung his side as the magic drew upon his life force, but the General ignored it. While his mask guarded the expression on his face, accumulated sweat dripped into his eyes. He hurled the spell with a command word and aimed for the man's heart. The fireball missed widely and struck the ground somewhere beyond, but the man did not halt his advance.

As the three closed in on Circulosa, they seemed to realize their common target and all three paused. The General looked nervously from the wizard to the large man while the third man circled behind him. The round General spun to keep them all in sight, surrounded.

"I don't know who the two of you are," said the spurned sorcerer, "but stay out of this. I've got a score to settle." The anger in his voice normally would have made Circulosa cackle, but in his frightened and nearly exhausted state the General merely listened.

The large man ignored the sorcerer's words and spoke directly to Circulosa. "I am Wan Du of Brong," he stated. "Are you the one who poisoned my city?"

Circulosa could hear the accent in the man's voice, but understood him without the assistance of Acton, the Pillar of Speech. He sensed some sort of magic, but could not see it. A black polearm balanced on one of the man's massive shoulders, ready to swing.

As he blinked away the burning in his eyes, Circulosa focused on the third man. Unadorned, but with a mundane longsword in each hand, the man seemed a far cry from the warrior Circulosa remembered. His eyes clearly showed his intentions, as the man looked ready to dash forward at any time to show Circulosa the sharpness of his swords. Obviously, he had forgotten his first attempt against Circulosa's personal protection wards.

"Where's your master?" the longswordsman demanded, his final word spat as a curse.

The voice confirmed his suspicions, and Circulosa knew better than to pull his attention away. If the warrior lived, he was more dangerous than even Zion realized.

"Terrant the Betrayer! I saw you dead!" Circulosa's high-pitched voice cracked and betrayed his fear.

"Terrant?" the sorcerer asked, aiming his staff away from Circulosa and at the man. "I know that name, but you don't look much like a Carrion officer."

Circulosa nearly celebrated as the two men focused on each other rather than him. The General turned to Wan Du and spoke quickly, pointing his finger to indicate. "Your town was destroyed by General Xymon with the help of that man."

As Wan Du also turned toward the wielder of the longswords, Circulosa used a final burst of power to pull a layer of color around his body and project himself onto the deck of his ship. The last thing he heard before the teleport spell took effect was the angry clang of metal on metal.

CHAPTER 30 – *Starka*

WHAT IS HAPPENING HERE? WHAT ARE YOU TWO DOING?" she asked. Starka held the gleaming crystal with both hands, but struggled, as it seemed heavier than when she had first picked it up. After carrying it around the entire battlefield, the load sapped her strength. She shifted it to a comfortable position, against her hip, and stopped.

DaVille crouched on one knee with his swords together in a scissor to fend off the intense press of Wan Du's black halberd. Both men strained, but Starka could see this fight had barely started. Neither acknowledged the girl's questions.

"This is ridiculous," growled DaVille. "Why do you even believe what he said?"

Wan Du's response stayed calm, though his muscles flexed with determination. "Deny that it is true," he said, "and I shall spare your life."

"Wan Du! DaVille!" Starka cried. "Stop this!"

The larger man pulled his blade back and spun completely around while lowering the tip of the weapon and slashing parallel to the ground. DaVille leapt away and landed with both swords up in defense. He pointed one blade at Wan Du and held the other over his head, ready to strike or parry as necessary.

At this pause in the action a colorful, but well-worn man slid up next to Starka eyeing the cluster of crystal she carried.

"Do you know these two?" he asked.

Starka nodded without averting her eyes from the fight.

The man leaned close and whispered. "I'm rooting for the big guy. The other one made Circulosa run away."

Starka perked up at this. The Carrion army apparently retreated during her journey to avoid the dragon and gargoyle. She looked past the two men to see the two large ships with black sails turned northwest, away from Flaem. Her home lay in that direction, but she dismissed worries about it quickly — a retreating army does not go looking for a fresh fight.

The man continued the conversation with her even though she had not responded. "That's an interesting mass you've got there. Did you summon for it yourself?"

Confused, Starka turned to regard him. While looking directly at the man, she would never have been able to guess his actual age. He seemed young by a normal standard, but his clear complexion and other aspects of his look made some of his features difficult to decipher. He rested a staff against his shoulder in a relaxed posture and held a beautiful blue stone in his other hand the size of a chicken's egg.

Though an attractive man, the newcomer had a strange gleam in his eye. She identified him immediately as a wizard, and a chaotic one at that. His was just the kind of power that they needed as well as the kind they did not need.

She hefted the crystal to present it and said, "I found this on the other side of the field."

The girl began to gesture with her head, but stopped when she saw the man's eyes widen with astonishment and fear. "You found this? You didn't make it?"

Starka nodded.

"And you picked it up? Don't you know what this is?" he asked. Without giving her a chance to explain, he addressed the fighting pair. "Knock it off, you two! We're in danger here!"

The wizard held out his staff and whispered words Starka could not make out. Streams of color erupted from the weapon and halted between the two combatants. Wan Du tapped his blade against them, and while it created a beautiful chord of sound, the spell did not budge. DaVille turned to look in Starka's direction, but did not lower his guard.

"What kind of danger?" he asked.

"The most serious kind of danger," replied the wizard. "Do you know this girl?"

"This is Starka," said DaVille, also not giving her a chance to answer. "Who are you, anyway?"

"Cairos of Illiadora, at your service," he said with a curt-yet-concise bow and a flourish of his staff.

Starka winced at the mention of the destroyed city, but understood then why he asked her if she created the crystal. She also realized this Cairos knew much more about it than she did.

"What's wrong?" asked Starka, beginning to panic herself. "What is this thing? Should I drop it? Is it going to poison me?"

Cairos answered as if repeating a lecture from a classroom, though hurriedly. "It's *scythorsont*, or doom-stone. One of the most destructive substances in existence. Made of compressed magical energy and extremely volatile. A tool widely used in the Sorcerer's War to destroy large groups of soldiers and to literally move mountains. Common application for a powerful wizard was to make more than one cluster and synchronize them so they would explode at the same time."

"So this puts us in danger?" DaVille asked. "More or less danger than those two beasts fighting?"

Starka turned her head to see the razed battlefield still populated by the gargoyle and the dragon. Neither looked severely damaged, but Flaem's western wall looked in dire need of repair.

"The wall!" she cried.

DaVille waved off her worry. "They have wizards," he said. "Let them fix it."

Wan Du wiped a bead of sweat from his forehead, but kept silent otherwise.

DaVille sighed. "Look big man," he said, "I don't remember much but I know I was not there. The Carrion were responsible no matter who led them; they're the real enemy. Can we finish this another time?"

Wan Du scowled and nodded. "You are right," he concluded. "Not only are we in danger here, but the city is in danger as well."

DaVille furrowed his brow and turned back to Cairos. "The dragon may have chased off the army, but if we don't do anything about the fight our gargoyle brought, the city will still be destroyed. If we're going to say we won this battle, we've got to at least save the city. You said that crystal makes a big explosion?"

Starka had begun to think better of DaVille until his last sentiments. A typical soldier's way of thinking, she judged. *Who cares about saving lives? This is about winning.*

Cairos took a step back and shook his head slowly. "Yes, but you can't be thinking of …"

"That's exactly what I'm thinking," interrupted DaVille.

"What … what?" Starka demanded. "What is he thinking?"

"He wants to use the *scythorsont* to destroy the dragon and the gargoyle," said Cairos. "You can't do that."

Starka's heart sank further. Her hands began to moisten against the crystal, but feared dropping it would be catastrophic. She gripped it tightly to her stomach.

"Are you saying it wouldn't work?" DaVille challenged.

"That's not the point!"

"The city would be safe. It's got protective wards against magical attacks, doesn't it? What's the problem?"

Cairos narrowed his eyes at the man. "How do you know what kind of wards Flaem employs?" he asked.

"We saw everything the Carrion shot at it bounce off or disappear before it hit the city," replied DaVille casually.

"I told you before; usually there is more than one of these created at the same time. What if these were being used to end the siege and some are placed under the city? I ran into a group of soldiers underground who were trying to tunnel under the walls. There could be a dozen more of these for all we know!"

"Do you know a better way?" Starka intervened.

Cairos considered a moment before he spoke again. His fearful gaze toward the crystal made Starka feel incredibly uncomfortable.

"I only know of one spell that might be powerful enough to destroy those things and I refuse to use it here," said Cairos. "In fact, it should never be used again."

"One or the other, wizard. It's a risk we're going to have to take." DaVille took a menacing step toward Cairos, but both his arms hung idle at his sides.

"No, I won't let more innocents be killed," said Cairos. "There has to be another way."

"Another way?" DaVille exploded. "Can you kill a dragon? Didn't it chase you out of that hole in the first place? The gargoyle chased us practically all the way from Fort Sondergaarde and we couldn't even wound it!"

Cairos raised an eyebrow. "Fort Sondergaarde?"

"Yes," said Starka while she fought back a tear. "It came upon us while we were at sea."

"So what?" asked DaVille. "Who cares where it came from?"

"There's one old tale I can think of," Cairos replied. "More like a rumor than legend. Folk tales; you know how information gets lost."

"There are legends, too, where I come from," supplied Wan Du. "I have seen the Shinjou Dragon's resting place, but know nothing of gargoyles."

DaVille curled his upper lip and waited. Again, Cairos spoke like a lore instructor.

"Flaem is said to be the source of fire magic. Fort Sondergaarde was supposed to be invincible; a fortress that would stand forever and survive any assault. The two did battle during the Sorcerer's War because Flaem was the only nearby country that could attack the southern fortress. Perhaps the legends are mere allegory, but perhaps they speak about the sources of the cities' true power."

"Are you planning on providing any useful information or are we merely suffering a history lesson while in possession of an extremely destructive magic?" DaVille's tone bit hard, but Cairos shrugged it off.

"There must be a natural explanation for the creatures attacking each other," said Starka. She had nothing more to offer than that.

DaVille took another step toward Cairos. "We've got to use the crystal. You're not giving us any other option."

Starka heard the sorcerer let out a long sigh. "This dragon killed one of the only other remaining sorcerers of Illiadora, but it was Circulosa's distraction that made it possible. Even if it's to defend the city, it is forbidden to kill a dragon. You'll be hunted for the rest of your days with a price on your head. Circulosa was the real threat and he was moments away from seeing what his entrails looked like before you showed up."

DaVille's eyes narrowed at the accusation. "Don't you worry; I'll find that bastard and you can kill him as many times as you want. But before we can do that, we have to be done here. How do we detonate it?"

It took DaVille grasping the collar of Cairos' coat to get him to speak. "Forget it! I won't tell you. I'd rather die than put this entire city at further risk."

With that, Cairos brought his hands up and fired a blast of energy directly into DaVille's chest. Both men flew apart with DaVille landing flat on his back. Cairos whispered a command word and shot into the air, flying away from all of them at great speed. Starka barely had time to gasp and would have rushed to DaVille's side, but for the heavy crystal in her hands.

Forsaking all caution, she lifted and turned the device in all directions to try to further study its mechanics. She was startled when DaVille came up next to her, his chestplate in shambles, but the skin underneath completely untouched. Her eyes widened as she continued to look.

Another symbol appeared on his skin while Starka watched. It was another of the Nine Pillars, she believed, but could not recall which the sigil represented.

DaVille seemed not to notice. He sheathed his longswords and looked up at the fleeing wizard's form.

"Damned coward. I'll have to do this myself."

He placed one hand around his other wrist and aimed both toward the battling beasts. Starka closed her eyes and bit her lip in anticipation of the man's shout, but it did not come. When she turned back to him DaVille was staring right into her eyes.

"Hand the crystal to Wan Du," said DaVille, "and find a place to hide. This isn't going to be pretty."

The large man nodded before he took the crystal in one of his hands. "We will need to get closer," he said.

Starka crouched behind a rock enclosure and prayed softly. She thought of the people in the city and their safety. With her eyes shut tightly she heard nothing but the whispers from her lips. A slight breeze drifted down from the eastern mountains as a soft and pleasant reminder winter may soon come. After counting to one hundred, twice, the girl began to wonder what was taking so long and poked her head out for a moment to look for the men.

Wan Du and DaVille advanced dangerously close to the dragon. They took shelter in a rock formation not unlike the one Starka chose to hide behind. Neither beast spotted the two men, still completely engrossed in their own battle. Starka watched as Wan Du hurled the crystal into the air above the dragon. A red blast of energy shot from DaVille and the entire world went white.

Starka dove back into her shelter as the shockwave blew across the battlefield. Bodies and debris flew out to sea and, for a brief moment, Starka thought she saw a similar flash on the water. It was too quick and far away to tell for sure, but she said a quick prayer for the *Bloody Lady* and her crew.

"CAIROS SURE WASN'T LYING ABOUT THE EXPLOSION," DAVILLE SAID between laughs.

Starka did not dare to look at the result until she heard the man's voice. With hands still clasped, she stood and looked over the remains of the battlefield. Starka saw a tremendous valley had been carved into the plain stretching from the city halfway to the beach. The edge of the crater stopped an uncomfortable distance from her hiding place.

The hole where the dragon emerged from had widened considerably from the blast, creating an even more unsteady landscape outside the city. Starka followed as DaVille walked toward the middle of the crater. Neither bones nor flesh remained of the two beasts.

She tried to catch up to DaVille's long strides as he hurried down the slope of the expanse. Still a ways behind him, she saw the man stoop down and clear the dirt away. He extracted two small gemstones from the earth and held one up to his eye as she arrived.

"What are those?" she asked tentatively.

"The spoils of war," DaVille answered without shifting his gaze.

"Are they valuable?"

DaVille dismissed her hopes quickly. "Pretty, but not all that useful. See how they're opaque? Translucency is the sign of value in gemstones." He turned the stones over in his hand, but they remained too filthy for her to really see. "These I'll probably have put on my pommels as ornaments. I need to have these blades sharpened, anyway. Perhaps I will get them named as well."

His voice trailed off as he turned toward the city and walked away. She heard something about "being nearly up to one hundred;" Starka merely shook her head and ignored DaVille's boasting.

The girl turned back and waved at Wan Du, who opted not to climb into the crater. The huge black halberd he collected still leaned against his shoulder as he trudged slowly and calmly, meeting Starka as she climbed to the crest of the crater.

"Are you coming into the city?" she asked.

Wan Du shook his head. "Xymon is the one I seek, but I will need the weapon *Serené* gave to me before I can defeat him."

"Where will you go now? Cellto?"

Wan Du gave a silent nod in response.

"Isn't that dangerous? There could be more soldiers and ..."

He held up a hand to calm and silence her. She really was being unreasonable — and far too overprotective of a man she barely knew. Wan Du could obviously take care of himself, but Starka worried for the man. She pursed her lips at the possibility that she wanted him around simply so she wouldn't have to be alone with DaVille.

Recalling Elestia's command for *being of one mind* again, Starka realized that the brief alliance was over. Whatever hope she'd placed in it leaked away as she looked at the destruction — what DaVille might call their "victory." The addition of that sorcerer, Cairos, to their scattered cause might have helped, but he was nowhere in sight.

"Well," she said, "I shall pray for you, then."

The beginnings of a smile touched Wan Du's stoic scowl, but disappeared just as quickly. "I will pray for you as well," he replied. After a short pause, Wan Du added, "Be careful of the Carrion army. I have seen what they do. And be careful of DaVille — I do not think even he knows where his path lies."

"You've seen what they do?" she asked. "What does that mean?"

He left her with no answers, but waved as he walked away. As Wan Du made his way south, Starka said a sincere prayer for the man's safety. Though he worshipped something completely foreign to her, Starka felt comforted that he would do the same. She turned back toward the city and ran to catch up to DaVille before he reached the damaged western gate.

"What happened between you two? Why were you fighting?" she asked from behind. She couldn't see the expression on his face, but he halted and bowed his head.

"It's not important," DaVille replied. When he finally turned toward her, his face remained unreadable as ever. "Do you think saving the entire city merits us a free meal and a room for the night?"

STARKA SPENT THE ENTIRE AFTERNOON WANDERING AROUND THE city of Flaem. At first she felt unsafe in such a foreign place, but people seemed to completely ignore her so she explored further and further. By far, it was the most impressive place she had ever seen.

After her travels through the remains of Rochelle and the awful Cellto, the vitality of Flaem invigorated her. Just from being in such an active place for a day, Starka felt more alive than she had in years. Even all her time inside the picturesque Cathedrals of Myst could not compare to the dynamic city, so filled with magical power. She saw themes of the Nine Pillars everywhere she looked.

From time to time, she pondered the calm state of the city and was left confounded. Starka expected no official accolade, or anything resembling attention, but she wondered if anyone in the city really knew what had transpired just outside the wall. At first she looked for a raucous and triumphant celebration, but merchants and customers alike did business as usual. They seemed completely, and blissfully, aloof. Flashes and sparks of color distracted Starka from this train of thought until she decided to abandon it and enjoy the sights and sounds of Flaem.

Near the middle of the city recessed an immense well with coins of all shapes, sizes, and colors reflecting the sunlight from far underneath the water's surface. A local citizen informed her of the name of the place, "Urrel's Fount," and its purpose: throw a coin in and make a wish to the Pillar of Fate. She did not understand this, since she thought the Pillars were not worshipped as deities — just representative of traits of humanity.

When questioned, the citizen merely said, "It's the avatars that do the work," and sped off to resume his errand.

Still confused by what the term "avatar" meant, she came upon a structure that made her nearly blush. It seemed to be a temple, but shaped like the body of a reclining woman, completely nude. It was immense, taking up an entire city block, and the stairs leading up to its entrance were littered with both men and women. They were nearly nude themselves, offering pleasures of the body for a donation to the temple. Starka averted her eyes and hurried past, but did notice a sign labeling it as "Hemur's Tabernacle."

The shops of Flaem were structurally and aesthetically just as impressive as the drabbest house. Magic built this city, she knew, and it had done a beautiful job. Many buildings rose high into the air, even taller than she remembered the towers of Myst-Garvon. Tall poles brandished banners with wizard crests and glyph symbols.

In one district she saw nine poles arranged in a line, each with an encircled symbol. Recognizing the first one as matching what appeared on DaVille's chest, she asked another passerby about it.

"That is Tera, the Pillar of Life," the street urchin replied with a smile. She tried to ask the boy what all of the other ones were, but he hurried away from her as the last citizen had done. Life was, apparently, too busy in Flaem to stop and chat. With her, anyway, thought Starka.

No matter how impressive the gold-lined streets were, Starka longed for her simple abode on the other side of the world. The girl laughed at herself for even wasting time on the train of thought, but she wished none of this had happened. If she had never received the prophecy, Starka would have remained ignorant of the world's wondrous sights, though at the same time, out of danger.

She saw transient wizards of all shapes, sizes, and sexes, some performing small magic tricks in expectance of some kind of reward. Having no money, Starka rushed passed them and attempted to look as unimpressed as she possibly could — even while she marveled inside at their ability to summon and swallow fire or worse. The girl knew if she stayed to watch, she would become enthralled by their trickery — and possibly even interested in how to do it herself.

After an arduous journey through the entire western part of the city, she arrived back where she started. The Flaming Chariot, an inn DaVille chose completely at random, may not have been fancy or expensive, but it was comfortable. When the city's emissary had met them at the gate, DaVille told the man to find him there.

She passed beneath the hung horseshoes and into the common room. No musicians played since evening remained hours away, and Starka was far too exhausted to dance to their tunes. With her feet throbbing, she climbed the stairs and knocked on the door next to hers to let DaVille know she had returned. The door opened slightly and he directed her inside, motioning to the bed for her to sit. A new emissary stood in the room holding a scroll that seemed to be on fire, but was not burning.

DaVille reclined next to her while taking a large bite of fruit. Juice dripped across his chin and onto the blanket as he whispered, "You didn't miss anything. He just got here."

The emissary spoke clearly and without accent. "DaVille Dragonslayer," he began, "the Elders of Flaem recognize your heroism and acknowledge your assistance in routing the enemies of the free world. However, they request that once your business with the inn is concluded, you leave the city and continue in whatever direction you were heading before you arrived. You will not be allowed to return. They have sent a compensation of gold and ..."

"What? They want us to leave?" she protested. "But we haven't even told them about what has been happening!"

The messenger continued as if she had not spoken at all.

" ... silver. The title you have earned will not be declared publicly because the act of slaying was done in service and in ignorance. However, if you return to Flaem, they will lift this leniency and your life may be forfeited. Finally, they mandate that you do not share the details of your actions with anyone until you are outside the city. That is all."

Starka wanted to interrupt again, but a stern look from DaVille kept her silent. Cairos warned him what would come of destroying the dragon, but it seemed the Elders did not know of it.

DaVille nodded. "Please tell the Elders that we are grateful for their hospitality. We will honor their terms and leave as soon as arrangements can be made."

Starka could not tell if DaVille was sarcastic or sincere. He handed the man a coin from one of the sacks and closed the door behind him. After the messenger left, an awkward silence dominated for a few moments.

"Why don't they want the people in the city to know what happened?" she asked. "They could still be in danger."

Out of sheer audacity, it seemed, the man shrugged. "This is the first battle anyone has *won* against the Carrion, to my knowledge. The war isn't over, but we've got a far better chance of surviving with half their army gone. Who knows what the future might bring?"

DaVille moved toward the door, pulling his sword belts over his shoulder. "Flaem will not get involved regardless of what we say, so we'll just have to go somewhere that will. I'm going to find a blacksmith and have these sharpened. Get some rest; I'll arrange passage northwest toward Ferraut."

"Not another ship," she groaned. The words were out before Starka could stop them.

"I'll see what I can do," DaVille replied with a grin.

The country of Ferraut lay close to her home — at least when compared to Flaem. She wondered if they got close to the Mystian Continent, would she want to return? It depended on what DaVille thought, she supposed. Starka didn't feel of much use yet, but she believed a purpose to it all. Her fate was tied to this man, for good or ill. Whether or not DaVille was the catalyst in her prophecy, she had no choice but to stay by his side.

"More fighting, then?" the girl asked.

DaVille answered just before the door closed.

"Always more fighting."

CHAPTER 31 ∾ The Ninth Avatar ∾ 171

CHAPTER 31 – *Wadam*

THREE SAILORS LAY ON THE DECK, PIERCED IN MULTIPLE places by slim black arrows, while Wadam knelt over them. He prayed hurriedly for either their lives or their souls — his fear would not let him choose which. In one hand the Cardinal grasped a makeshift shield of wooden planks and the other he held open while he recited every prayer and blessing of Garvon that came to mind.

They needed to sail "dangerously close" to the other ships, in the first mate's opinion, before anything could be learned about their inhabitants. From afar, the ignorant watchmen believed they saw swarthy men headed up from the south; perhaps refugees from Rochelle. As they approached, the watch announced they weren't people at all — they had horns.

A panic took hold of the ship after the sighting and the captain ordered a hasty change of course, due east. The first attack caught Wadam and the crew completely off guard. Dozens of arrows pounded into the deck and the port side of the ship before anyone could protect themselves. The priest smirked at the first mate, quiet on his back with a pair of arrows in his torso, and thanked Garvon for small measures of justice.

"Don't we have any weapons on this thing?" asked Wadam.

The captain responded from underneath his own inadequate shelter. "This is a passenger vessel, not a warship. I told you before, our only real hope is to outrun them, but it takes time!"

An eruption of steam and a powerful wave hit the ship then, and Wadam's courage waned even further. "What was that?"

The captain dared a glance from his shelter to look at the other ship. "Cannon discharge," he answered. "They're trying to sink us."

"Why didn't they sink us before?"

"How should I know," the captain replied sourly. "I'm a sailor, not a soldier. They probably wanted to take us alive while we were in range, but now we're making distance on them."

This both excited him and worried Wadam, but he decided it must have been why the cannon missed. While they were close, arrows pelted the ship every few seconds, but those attacks dwindled. Without him noticing, the ship must have actually drifted completely out of range of their archers. The priest saw the captain come to the same conclusion and abandon his cover.

Wadam followed suit. "How many of those do you think they have?" he asked.

The captain shook his head with a grim face. "It only takes one to sink a ship."

Another shout came from the watchpost high above Wadam's head and he could only ask, "What now?"

He covered his mouth instantly because he hadn't meant to say the words aloud. The watchman called to look to the east, but Wadam couldn't understand any other details. Something seemed amiss, aside from their pursuers, but all he could see was water.

As he scanned the horizon further, the priest noticed the water didn't look the same as the multitudinous times he stared at it during the voyage — it looked taller, somehow. Through the din of renewed activity on the ship he could only catch one repeated phrase.

"Tidal wave."

Wadam retreated to his cabin as quickly as his stubby legs could carry him. He grasped armfuls of parchment, and in a rush, nearly left behind his latest essay. With his most valued possessions tucked close to his body, Wadam burst back onto the deck and rushed toward a handful of sailors lowering one of the smaller rowboats. The light craft looked more suited to surviving a huge wave, fitted with animal bladders on both sides.

It being his rightful priority, Wadam climbed inside the smaller boat first. Only half a dozen crew members could join him before the force of the water struck the front of the ship. They tipped vertically before the quick-thinking sailors sliced through the binding ropes. Wadam held on for his life as the tiny vessel struck the surface of the water and the wave washed over it. Through the tumult, he watched the larger ship continue to tilt backward. Wood snapped and men fell screaming until it capsized completely.

He shouted to the men to row fast away before the sinking ship pulled them down with it. They could not afford to look for survivors — if the undertow did not get them, some remnant of the enemy surely would. Besides, he thought, there was not much room on the small boat and only six oars with which to propel it.

The sailors before him were somehow blessed to have survived, he thought. Through the chaos, Wadam struggled to stay calm as half his new crew worked to keep water out of the craft. He whispered a small prayer for the departed, not the least of whom the captain, who went down with his ship in the face of the titanic wave. Wadam checked to the west, hoping to see their enemies similarly spilled into the sea. He did not see land or the black-sailed boats any longer. To the north, land seemed far away, but in sight. He bade the sailors to row toward it as quickly as they could.

Wadam sat against the rear of the small boat and hoped there would be a home left when he got there. The priest checked inside his robes for losses, but his papers had all survived. Though wet, the layers of parchment remained safe.

This had to be a sign, he decided. He needed to reach the cathedrals and announce the omen his ordeal inevitably meant; Wadam and the remainder of the crew were chosen by the Divine Male for some greater purpose, and he would make sure it included wrestling control away from the weak and merciful Sisterhood.

The rhythmic slapping of the oars against the waves eventually caused his eyelids to become heavy and he began to nod off. In his stupor, Wadam began to mutter his true thoughts about the followers of the Divine Female. Though the sailors may have noticed, they said nothing, even when he began to snore.

AS THEY APPROACHED THE COAST, WADAM STOOD – OR TRIED TO stand as the boat bucked beneath him — to survey a landscape he could only describe as "wet." Seaweed and pools dominated the beach no matter which direction he looked.

Last to step out of the boat, Wadam charged up the nearest hill to get his bearings. He should have been able to see the spire of Myst-Garvon from any-where on the continent, as it was the taller of the two structures and further south. No matter how much he squinted to the west, he could only make out small dales and more puddles.

The priest could not be sure whether they landed on the Mystian continent or the blade-shaped island east of the Baerow Straits. He made a protective hand signal and prayed that it was not the latter; the untamed peoples living on the narrow land were never kind to those who crossed the violent channel.

Wadam's heart leapt into his throat as the possibility hit him; the tidal wave struck the southeast coast of his home. Without a care as to which direction the sailors went, Wadam took off at a full run to the direction he gauged as close as he possibly could to be west. He prayed with each step that all of his possessions would be waiting for him — and not swept somewhere out to sea.

CHAPTER 32 – *Drakkaram*

ENERAL DRAKKARAM MADE HIS DISDAIN FOR HUMANITY obvious with the way he tapped his foot. The council of Cellto leaders took far too long to interrogate their guards and determine exactly what happened with the recent prisoners. Drakkaram, already sick of delays, simply wanted to know who escaped and why the Great Commander demanded so adamantly that they be caught.

With a slam of his heavy fist, Drakkaram demanded the attention of everyone in the room. "I know you understand that our relationship is tentative, at best," he stated with as much sarcasm as his lipless mouth could muster, "but know also that the longer I stay here the more I wish to lay waste to your measly city — regardless of the various services you provide."

A thick-robed and long-faced bald man finished up what he was whispering before responding to the infamous General. "Information is … scarce."

"And costly," another man muttered.

Before anyone could blink, Drakkaram had his clawed hands around the throat of the second man. A snap later, his limp body fell to the floor. Two Carrion attendants rushed forward quickly to retrieve the corpse, but Drakkaram waved them off. "This one's useless. Let the worms eat him."

The rest of the humans in the room swallowed noticeably, but otherwise made no gestures or sounds.

"Get me the information I need or you will see what the inside of your meat grinders look like while your hearts still beat," said Drakkaram. "The choice seems simple."

"Great General, we know that an interpreter offered some assistance to one captive, but he was killed before any information could be gleaned from him. Our guard Makson delivered the punishment personally and we await another report from him and his men. We also know the ship carrying some of those who fled headed north toward Fort Sondergaarde."

The General bared all his teeth in a grotesque grin. "If they hope to seek shelter there, they are in for quite a shock. Contact me when you have something useful to report."

As he stood to leave, the door slid open to reveal one of Drakkaram's lieutenants. "My General, we have captured a soldier who traveled with the escaped ones. Her armors bear the crest of Rochelle."

Drakkaram headed for the door with a dismissive wave toward the Cellto men. He pushed the Carrion soldier ahead of him to lead the way to what would inevitably be a wellspring of information and a torturous delight.

Drakkaram walked through the silent streets of Cellto and enjoyed the smells of fresh blood in the air. The unmistakable scent of animal blood never failed to excite him. As he followed his subordinate he pondered the apparition of Xymon from earlier that evening.

Circulosa will die soon.

The words nearly made the brutal General celebrate as if it were a declaration of victory. The round wizard weakling deserved to die for insulting him, no matter what rank he obtained. For a moment, Drakkaram wondered why he sent reinforcements north at all, but chose not to dwell on it. Zion knew a callous and callow human could never effectively command the forces of their army, but Drakkaram would not even attempt to understand the Great One's reasoning. If Circulosa was to die then it must have been Zion's will for it to happen.

FROM THE DOORWAY DRAKKARAM WATCHED THE LARGE WOMAN'S head roll from side to side. Her blood accumulated in pools on the floor of the chamber. He could see it pained her to even breathe, such as she was, suspended from the ceiling with her wrists bound together. Shards of metal protruded from her body in various places, both essential and non-essential, though every slash had been immediately sown up. She tested her bonds again in vain before the large woman slumped forward with closed eyes. Perhaps she is dreaming of redemption, Drakkaram mused.

She was a large specimen; he understood now why it took a score of his soldiers to subdue and capture her. He knew she would be weakened, especially after the beating she sustained, but her willpower could still resist normal means of interrogation. Still, the woman looked strong — she would make a fine Lieutenant.

His heavy boots dropped against the stone floor, echoing slow stomps against the walls. Her head twitched with each step, but it seemed she no longer had the strength to lift it. Drakkaram grasped her chin with a clawed hand and raised her eyes up to meet his black pools before speaking from his lipless maw. He spoke slowly to make sure she understood every word.

"Tell me your name," the General commanded.

For a moment the woman resisted. Drakkaram lifted his hand to one of the shards of metal protruding from her abdomen and began to press on it with his index finger. The woman screamed and groaned in pain until he stopped.

Between gasps for breath the woman answered, "Bathilde."

The General grinned again. She would not be as hard to break as he originally thought.

"You will not die today, woman," said Drakkaram. "No, your strength and prowess will be valued highly in my army. After we thrust the black horns into your head you will be naught, but a mindless wench to do my bidding."

He knew which words to choose to intimidate these people. Their pride and independence would always be a hindrance. He spoke to her as he would speak to a captured Circulosa, choosing the proper words to destroy her misplaced arrogance. Already he began to notice her eyes welling up with the physical manifestation of utter despair. *Perfect.*

"But it need not be that way."

"If this is the part," Bathilde rasped, "where you tell me you'll spare my life if I give you the information you want, you might as well kill me now and get it over with." With that, she spat at him.

Drakkaram, far from being impressed or deterred, let her head drop from his grip then spun his arm and back-handed her across the cheek. He struck her again and again, and the woman cried out. His palm pressed against her throat as he wrapped his large hand around it and raised her head up again.

"Tell me about those who you traveled with, or do you doubt that I can make you wish you'd never been born?" the general asked. Drakkaram lifted a long needle with a barbed tip and waved it across the woman's face as he added, "I will simply let you imagine where this can be placed."

Her eyes doubled in size and the large woman quickly spoke. "We were merely bringing prisoners here. I knew nothing about the pair of them. We caught them prowling around our encampment a few nights ago. There was a woman and a man."

"Yes, interesting. But who were they? Sorcerers?"

Drakkaram noticed something then, a little jerk in the woman's body, as if she were trying to laugh though mere inches from death. Even in defeat and despair, the woman had spirit.

"The girl was a fledgling priestess from the northwest. The man never said where he came from, but he seemed … a skilled warrior. Neither performed any kind of magic in my presence, but the man may have some kind of resistance to it."

The General delighted at the outpouring of information. Bathilde provided details she could have just as easily left out. Her obvious attempts at becoming useful were not lost on him, though she was already useful in Drakkaram's eyes.

She continued, "Lady Mayrah only fled here because we were being followed and assailed. Rochelle has already suffered enough at the hands of your army to resist any further."

He ignored her last comments. The dark folk of Rochelle were primitive and they already harvested all of the useful warriors who called it home. The woman's eyes glazed over as she approached unconsciousness brought on by her wounds. One last slap across her face regained her focus.

"Tell me more about this man," demanded Drakkaram. "You say he was a warrior?"

"He wielded two longswords against me." Her voice began to fade. More tears welled up in her eyes. "He … fought well enough."

Drakkaram took this to mean the man defeated her. It sounded similar to a report he heard about a single man terrorizing the small contingent left behind in Bloodmir, but the latter account mentioned nothing of a priestess girl. If one man could do all of that, the General would need a strong soldier to oppose and weaken him.

He turned to the doorway and spoke to the loitering Carrion grunt. "Bring me the largest pair of horns we have. After I am done here, I will speak to this Makson."

When he turned back to Bathilde he saw she had dropped into a sleep state. Very well, he thought, she would awaken when bestowed the horns—the pain was more than a sleeping mind could bear.

CHAPTER 33 – *DaVille*

HE CONSTANT, STEADY RING OF THE BLACKSMITH'S HAM-mer became a comforting noise to DaVille as he watched the man work. The bellows of the furnace operated by enchantment so the smithy didn't even need to leave his anvil to keep the fire hot. Though it took quite a bit of negotiating to get the man do to the job DaVille wanted, it would be worth every piece of gold. He had no qualms about spending the unexpected windfall, as it wasn't his money in the first place.

He became mesmerized by the white-hot glowing blade as the apron-clad man brought it from the fire and resumed his rhythmic pounding. Sparks flew from the tip of the hammer as it flattened the metal back into its familiar shape.

An addition of alloyed steel, a magically-enhanced and much harder metal, to the blade mixture incurred the additional cost. Augmented steel, though much harder to sculpt and more expensive to produce, showed its value with time. Per the smithy, anyway. Only use of creative bartering gained DaVille the deal in the end.

The blacksmith tried to run him off since it would be hours before he completed the work, but the owner of the swords and of the gems wanted to watch the process. He wanted to be present to see the power and effort poured into his weapons, though DaVille wasn't even completely sure why.

A reputable service provider of Flaem wouldn't cheat him, of course, but thieves were always a danger in a large city. He chose a smithy well off of the main streets for this very reason. Only a few weapons hung on display in the shop, and DaVille surmised from this the smith mostly worked on forges or altar pieces. Upon examining the craftsmanship of the display weapons, DaVille became convinced he found the right man — he needed the best weapons money could buy.

DaVille looked away from the sparks and toward the assembling northbound caravan he contracted to protect. Both men made out well from the deal, but he wondered how Starka would take the news. Even with the smith's renowned work in high demand, a trade route couldn't be secured without an escort through the dry plains.

The caravan would visit Travell, an immense temporary settlement, for the "city" purchased an inordinate amount of weaponry. The smith described Travell as a massive field of tents with no boundary to designate it, the City without Walls. In that way it remained more of a region than an actual township, lacking both a governing body and an organized defense. Apparently, enough of the "citizens" could agree on a need for weapons for — according to the squat man—it was quite a large order.

From there he and Starka would have to travel west on their own or find another caravan to reach their goal of Ferraut within the walled Five Points region. DaVille did not look forward to his return, but they had the only army large enough to stand against the Carrion.

In the end, the argument became circular; if the blacksmith did a good enough job on DaVille's blades he shouldn't have any problem protecting the shipment.

While weapon commerce always thrived in times of war, "land pirates" as the smithy referred to them also ran rampant. An army of bandits called the Amber Horde roamed the desert and routinely raided traders or anyone else who entered the territory unprepared.

DaVille agreed to hear the warning about them, wishing the entire time he could recount the day's exploits from outside Flaem's wall. One piece of information he did pick up was the Horde used mounts resembling large canines rather than horses. The interesting fact caught his attention, though he wasn't quite sure why at the time. Animals were troublesome in all shapes and sizes.

An incredible hissing noise caught DaVille's attention as the smithy dunked the blade in his cooling tank. It took nearly another hour before the new hilt and grip were set. Placing the opaque red jewel in the pommel came last. As the blacksmith handed the newly-crafted sword to DaVille, he took a few practice swings to gauge the balance and weight.

The sword moved perfectly in his left hand, as light as swinging a reed. He turned to the blacksmith to inquire about the diminished weight, but stopped when he noticed the weapon's crimson glow.

"I'll finish the other one, then I'll sharpen n' bless them," the blacksmith muttered, returning to his work. He either ignored the red halo or did not see it.

DaVille barely heard the man, transfixed that his arm shared the same glow as the blade. He looked from the sword to his arm, the arm the sword felt perfect in, and smiled.

CHAPTER 34 – *Mayrah*

ECOVERING FROM THE LEAP OFF THE SHIP TOOK MAYRAH a few hours. The warrior woman was violently awakened by a tremendous explosion shifting the wet and grainy sand she occupied. Mayrah began walking south away from the city as soon as she could stand

and find a weapon. The humble sword she used did not compare to Windsong, but she managed. Though sore, Mayrah ignored the pain and walked away from Flaem.

In a foreign land, and with no idea where to go, Mayrah only worried what to do when she reached Fort Sondergaarde. Perhaps she could swim across the bay beyond and reach Cellto. The waters held dangers, but the landscape made it impossible to travel around the bay without climbing icy peaks.

Mayrah considered going to Flaem, but knew it would not fix any of her current crises — especially if she stayed near DaVille any longer. His presence remained a thorn in her side since his capture. The girl, whoever she was, only complicated the situation further despite her sympathies. Mayrah cared little for either of them, but her heart ached when she thought about Bathilde and where she might be. In her mind, she imagined the mighty woman without her club, sitting silently inside a dark and moldy chamber in Cellto.

Bathilde had to be alive; she would have been aware of it if the mighty woman fell. There would have been a sign — the world would have wept at the loss of such a warrior.

NINE POINTS OF PAIN SNAPPED AGAINST HER BACK AND ELICITED a painful shout as she fell to the ground. Groaning, Mayrah turned to view her adversary. A dozen Carrion soldiers stalked like caged lions, led by a larger one twirling the whip that stung her. Mayrah stood and drew her mundane curved blade, again longing to hear her blue blade sing.

"If this be my last stand, fine," she said, "but I'll take as many of you with me as I can." Mayrah's noble threat was so sincere it even frightened her a bit.

The officer let out a guttural laugh and pounded his free hand against his chest. Small spikes burst out from his body to make him an even more formidable foe. His subordinates did likewise, to the same effect. Mayrah cursed — this was really going to hurt.

A tremendous shout split the air as three of the grunts separated into halves by the long, curving slice of a black halberd. Mayrah watched in amazement as a familiar soldier spun with the momentum of the heavy blade. He slashed through two beasts more he came to a halt, the weapon poised for another strike. The Carrion officer roared in protest and launched himself at the halberd-wielder while three of the soldiers came straight for her.

Mayrah parried and dispatched one of her opponents with a stab through the chest, but two more replaced it. She killed another even as rusty blades drew lines across her unarmored limbs. The flesh of her forearms dripped blood as she slashed wildly at the air. When her remaining assailants turned and fled, Mayrah did not pursue. They joined the rest in flight but the officer stayed, too caught up with the man she now recognized from the ship as Wan Du.

With each crack of the whip, she saw the officer's strength wane just a bit, but the large man did not falter. She sensed his strength came from somewhere other than just himself, and his roaring shouts only punctuated the effect. Despite this, Mayrah still wanted to spit as the name of his deity came to mind. *Serené* decreed mastery to its chosen people, and required sacrifice.

Mayrah wondered if they would both be better off if she ran him through — after he killed the Carrion officer, of course.

She shook her head and nearly admonished herself aloud; her world was no longer a place for such thoughts. Regardless of the rivalry before her mate died, Wan Du of Brong was her enemy no longer. Her mind clear, Mayrah sprang forward to assist.

With a vertical slash, she successfully severed the cords of the whip as the officer brought it back for a strike. The creature paused in confusion, and Wan Du stepped forward to drive the blade of his polearm into its shoulder. The weight of the blow drove it to the ground and Wan Du simply leaned on the pole of the weapon to keep the howling beast in place. Shrieks of pain filled the air as Wan Du crushed the shoulder joint with his sandaled foot.

At a pause in the screaming, Mayrah heard the question, "Where is Xymon?"

She wanted to ask why Wan Du spoke to the Carrion officer, but Mayrah went speechless when it answered. She couldn't understand the words, as they were merely guttural noises, but she saw in the large man's face he understood what it "said."

Mayrah stared, wide-eyed, at the creature writhing on the ground before her. How could this thing understand and speak?

Apparently, it refused to give the answer Wan Du wanted, for he leaned even more heavily against the halberd. The blade twisted, which brought more screams from the pinned officer. Black blood formed pools on the ground around them and it even coughed some up, spitting unceremoniously at Wan Du's feet.

Disgusted, Mayrah stepped forward and demanded answers. She drove her sword tip into the beast's other shoulder. It gnashed its teeth in agony and rage, baring fangs that dripped with pure hatred. She matched the look in its empty black eyes with a glare of her own.

"How is it that you can speak to the creature?" she asked.

The creature must have noticed her questioning look and began to chuckle, but she cut its mirth short with a twist of her own blade.

Wan Du answered, in his own stoic manner, "Because it used to be human."

She nearly lost the grip on her sword at precisely the wrong time. The officer detected her vulnerability and reached up to sink its bloody claws into her hand, but it was much too slow. Wan Du grasped the wrist of the humanoid beast and squeezed until Mayrah heard the sickening crunch of breaking bone. The arm went limp, but the creature lost none of its vigor.

"How do you know this?" she demanded, stepping back.

"I've seen them … transform men. My kin. Your kin," he said as tears streamed down his face. "They are taken alive as well as dead."

"How?" she asked, looking at the officer's black blood on her palms. "How is this possible?"

"The power comes from the horns. As soon as they are put into the head, the man changes into … this."

"All this time, we've been fighting … ourselves?" Mayrah felt her knees go weak but fought the urge to drop to the rocky ground. "Does anyone know about this?"

Wan Du reached for the officer's horns, but before pulling them out, he looked directly at her.

"DaVille knows."

CHAPTER 35 – *Xymon*

HE CAVE'S WALLS ECHOED WITH A CONSTANT DRIP OF water from somewhere deeper inside. A distinct yet intermittent popping and a few scratches were the only other noises to grace the deep cavern. A lone ray of sunshine filtered in through a hole nearly a mile above the floor of a chamber lined with stalagmites, but an unearthly green illuminated the walls nearly half the way up. The pungent smell of burnt flesh hung strong in the air, not quite masking the smells of sweat, dirt, and excrement.

A figure moved from shadow to shadow inside the passage, its presence not even noted by the small insects swallowed up by its veiled darkness.

Xymon explored the cavern systematically, exhausting one direction before he pursued his goal in the next, with the infinite patience of one confident in success. The gentle sounds masked his soft hiss, barely audible through one hand covering his mouth.

He found the prey squatting beside a tiny magical fire, the source of the sickly green that glowed against the smooth stone walls. Above the fire, the dark General saw a chunk of meat rotating — the prey's next meal. Xymon grinned and corrected himself: the prey's *last* meal. The wraith hovered in his place for a bit longer and watched, sensing something wrong about his prey.

The light of the fire showed the man to be completely naked and crouching, rocking back and forth on the balls of his feet. One arm turned the spit while the other wrapped tightly around his knees. He mumbled soft, indiscriminate words that Xymon dismissed as nothing more than insane rambling.

Grease from the meat dripped down into the fire with a sudden sizzle. The man leapt up with all four limbs spread, screaming a long and high-pitched note. By the wideness of his eyes, Xymon could tell the man was scared beyond words, but not of him; the General could not be seen blended in so well with his surroundings. The man was literally jumping at shadows, scared of any change he perceived inside the small environment.

All the same, Xymon held his breath and waited for the man to calm back down. The prey's chest heaved in panting sighs and all of his muscles remained tense, but he could not hold his stance for long. Eventually, the man slumped back into his previous position and began humming a low tune that sounded almost sad. Confident the man's attention was once again captured, the dark General darted through a few more shadows to find a place behind the man and then grasped the hilt of Nightwind.

Defenseless, the raving mad Circulosa could only gasp for his last breath as a black blade pierced his chest thrice in rapid succession. He fell to the ground on his stomach, convulsing, and then stared into the jade fire with blank eyes. The General supposedly died days before — when he chose to hide from the consequences of his failure — and the empty shell of a man lying nude and helpless on the cave floor testified to that fact.

Xymon threw his black cloak back from his shoulders and sheathed his blade. He knelt and waited for the symphony of finality to conclude. Circulosa coughed and choked out mouthfuls of blood, reluctant to die.

With infinite patience, the dark General watched the green fire gutter out while Circulosa's life force drained away. His eyes closed slowly and, just before the light expired, Xymon heard the wizard whisper a name he never expected to hear again.

"Terrant."

CHAPTER 36 – *Starka*

IT WAS THE HOTTEST DAY STARKA HAD EVER EXPERIENCED in all her twenty years. The special clothing they purchased for traveling across the unforgiving desert clung to her thin frame while sweat accumulated in every possible place. Her fair skin protested against the rays of the sun and the arid desert wind blasted her eyes as she looked across the northern horizon. Not even in her homeland on the subcontinent did the weather assail a person so, but that land was halfway across the world and nearly a distant memory.

Starka flashed a sidelong glance at the man sitting next to her. His weathered and battle-worn hands held tight to the reins of a pair of burdened oxen, two of the team that tugged their caravan slowly northward. The man she had come only to know as DaVille raised the leather thongs and snapped them against the rear flanks of the animals. DaVille also dressed in desert attire, but he seemed far more comfortable than Starka.

His shaded brown eyes gazed past the team, and into infinity, for all Starka knew. The same light cloth wrapped around his head shielded his face from the wind and sun, but left his vision clear.

Even after over a month of traveling with him Starka knew little about the man — save for his prowess in battle and arrogance outside it. He never left his newly-forged longswords out of his reach; those same swords saved her life more than once.

She already missed the comforts of Flaem and its opulent streets full of magic and wonders. The slow pace of the caravan gave her little else to do.

Even when she first sailed south from her homeland, Starka could pass the time by reading. Of all the sixty members of their group, only one brought along what passed for a book: a transaction ledger.

The cargo they transported was valuable, but it held no real interest for Starka. According to DaVille, the blacksmith commissioned the enterprise upon receiving a large order for his weaponry. Each wagon held an amount of swords, spearheads, and other implements the girl could not guess the names of. DaVille tried teaching her the names of each different weapon as a way to pass the time, but it failed to garner her interest.

Of course, she could not begrudge the purpose of their passage north; the folk who lived in the area called Travell had every right to defend themselves from the Carrion army. Starka just did not want it to be prophetic that they brought weapons. She had seen the grotesque black-horned creatures both up close and from afar. Given a choice, she preferred to see them not at all, but it seemed nothing less than her fate to be at the forefront of the conflict.

To shake her mind from worrying, Starka turned to survey the rest of the troop. She wiped the pooling sweat from her eyes and looked over the other wagons and their flanking riders. Most of them were sellswords like DaVille, paid to guard the rest on their passage north. Many of the others, those in the wagons, were representatives of the smithy or families who carried their own wares. Finally, there were passengers like her who, however uncomfortably, came along for the ride.

Nothing on her journey so far had helped to uncover truth about the prophecy, but Starka remained tied to DaVille — for better or worse.

Her eyes hovered over a nearby wagon for a moment to see one of the children of another such group of "passengers." The young girl's face was smooth and beautiful, dark in the manner of those from Rochelle. *Kisalarna-metangdaline* was her given name, but being an impetuous youth, the girl went by the nickname Kismet, or as she pronounced it, *Keez-met*. Starka wondered where the girl's accent came from, as Lady Mayrah and the other women she met from Rochelle spoke in a more common dialect.

Starka smiled behind her wrapped mask as she recalled Kismet's latest accusation about her and DaVille being lovers. "If you are not yet, you soon will be," the girl teased. Her creative attempts at humor refreshed Starka each time they stopped to rest. Risking a glance up at the sun, she tried to gauge when the next rest would come.

When she looked back, Starka saw Kismet's face drop in a scowl and her eyes narrowed. Shocked at the foreign expression on the girl's face, she raised a hand, but a wave of nausea overcame her. Starka's eyes slammed shut as she pitched back against the seat and saw, for a brief moment, the face of her lost twin brother, Fandur. It floated in the air similar to the time before, when it chased her off the relative safety of the ship she sailed south on. She wanted to scream, but her mouth felt full of bees.

A slap across her face jolted her back to reality just as her brother's mouth whispered a single word.

Raiders.

STARKA COUGHED AND SPAT AS SHE TRIED TO EXPEL THE SAND from her throat. DaVille stood over her, his hand recoiling from the vicious slap he delivered to bring her back to consciousness. She nearly railed him for the poor treatment, but realized her position first. Making her way to her feet, Starka avoided being trampled by the large, dumb beasts leading the next wagon. Still, her reddening cheek hurt, regardless of the good intentions.

"You alright?" DaVille offered as he helped her to her feet. The man didn't even apologize for the bruising blow.

"Yet again you save my life," she rasped, wiping more grains of sand from her revealed face.

DaVille's smirk was priceless. "Someday you'll pay me back all you owe me."

Starka's naïve mind could only grasp a portion of what he implied, but she caught it as a jest. Throughout all their time traveling together, he had not shown the slightest interest in her romantically. He might be simply cold or unfeeling, but she knew DaVille had much more important things on his mind. This war consumed his thoughts, though she did not understand why he took such personal responsibility with it.

As Kismet's wagon passed, she saw the girl staring at her with a face full of concern. The strange scowl disappeared entirely, but the memory of it haunted Starka as she raised her hand to wave at the youth. Kismet smiled and responded with a wave of her own.

"What happened?" asked DaVille, guiding her gently onto their vehicle. Starka still chose to withhold any confessions about her prophecies from DaVille, but it became much more difficult to lie with each one.

"It's just this heat," she said. "It's killing me."

With a sigh DaVille thrust his waterskin at her, which she took gratefully. Starka wasn't truly thirsty, but she sipped from it anyway, ignoring the warmth as the fluid rushed down her throat. As she swallowed and did her best to put on a smile, DaVille regarded her with suspicion.

The girl affixed her mask again across her nose and mouth and DaVille whipped the team into motion. With pursed lips, Starka tried to think of a way to alert DaVille to the possible danger her premonition revealed. After a few false starts, she resorted to looking around in a vain attempt to spot it herself.

To the east and west she saw nothing but bounding piles of sand and further away, mirages promising water. Her desert education had been swift in regard to the latter.

"Are you sure we're safe?" she asked, breaking the silence.

DaVille turned to her again, blinking, but not answering.

"I mean," she stammered, "I have read it is best to travel at night when crossing a desert."

He considered for a moment before answering, "Perhaps, but how would we see where we are going?"

Starka laughed nervously, admitting defeat. Her skill at manipulating a conversation remained woefully poor, but after another lengthy pause, she tried again.

"Aren't there raiders in this desert?"

"I'm not afraid of any raiders," DaVille said flatly, dismissing any allowance of fear on her part.

Then, as if on cue, the caravan ground to an awkward halt. DaVille pulled the reins up and reached behind the seat for his weapons. To Starka, he seemed overly eager to have them in his hands and usually did anytime the reins were not. The swords remained a complete mystery to Starka, but DaVille spent the better part of their pseudo-reward having the blades refined. So far, he only unsheathed them to practice after supper and before breakfast.

"They've got a broken wheel," came the relayed shout from Kismet's wagon.

Perfect, Starka thought, at least we can take a break.

"Not again," DaVille said under his breath. He stood and leapt from the wagon's seat. Looping his sheath's attachment through his belt, the man walked toward the front of the caravan. As soon as Starka moved to dismount she heard DaVille's command.

"Stay here," he said.

Exasperated, she simply sat back in the seat and threw up her hands. After a moment, though, she felt glad she had not followed.

"If that is not love then I do not know what love is," said Kismet in her usual dreamy voice. Every word had an abrupt end, and her timbre made every one seem like a note in a song.

"And how would you know love at your age?" Starka joked back. Kismet giggled and winked, but could not challenge the jibe about her youth. Starka invited the girl up to sit next to her and they watched as the men of the forward half began working on the wounded wagon.

"My father says you are pretty, but not prettier than me."

Starka blushed, not quite sure how to take the backhanded compliment. Kismet truly was breathtaking for her age.

"He flatters me," she replied. "What does your mother have to say, I wonder?"

Again the child laughed in her playful tones. "She is afraid of you, I think."

"Afraid?" asked Starka, sounding a bit more irritated than she intended. She forced the calm back into her voice and continued, "Why would she be afraid of me?"

"I cannot say. I think it is …" Kismet paused. Her eyes gazed upward and she pressed a finger to her lips as if searching for the proper word. "You are *Meestian*, no?"

"Oh," replied Starka. It took her a moment to decide how best to answer, as she didn't like lying to Kismet. "Sort of."

"What does this mean?"

"Well, I used to be priestess of Myst, but I am not anymore." Starka held her tongue from admitting anything further as her options became to lie or to make herself sound horrible. Kismet seemed to understand her reluctance and did not press further.

"Maybe that is for the best," said the young girl. "You would not be here otherwise, no?"

Starka let out a curt laugh of her own as she imagined life without DaVille. She would not have been in danger numerous times, pursued, imprisoned, or nearly disintegrated by the strange crystal cluster outside Flaem. The girl concluded she would probably be at home, alone in her one-room house, reciting prayers or knitting.

The world would have still seemed small, just as her knowledge of it was before the voyage began. In spite of herself, Starka smiled. An adage from the Holy Book popped into her head and she recited it without a second thought.

"You may amass a collection of as many fine linens as you like," she said, "but an unused cloak may as well be a stone."

Starka smiled again at the quizzical look from her young friend, but did not explain any further.

CHAPTER 37 – *Wan Du*

WAN DU STUDIED THE PROFILE OF THE WOMAN'S FACE FROM across the campfire. Though he tried his best not to stare for too long at a time, he was sure his stoic exterior masked his true intentions.

For some reason, Wan Du repeatedly found himself transfixed while alone in Lady Mayrah's presence. Unsure whether her flaxen hair or dark pallor made him more curious, the large man remained captivated. Her athletic yet curvaceous build strained the confines of her clothing and left very little to the imagination. At times, Wan Du had to force himself to keep his eyes on her face. Even after days of this routine, she did not seem to notice his attention.

As Lady Mayrah looked up from her task, her calm eyes danced with the flickering of the flames. He watched silently as she tended to her latest wound; little more than a scratch from a clumsily thrown axe. The ointment she spread smelled strongly of pine, but various roots, berries, and flowers made up the thick brown paste.

Carrion soldiers, though no less hardy, seemed to be quite varied in their skill and tactics. This latest attack, a long-distance ambush from a copse of trees, was sloppy and panicked at best. Wan Du decided neither their aim nor their looks improved when humans transformed to Carrion.

His companion took a wound when they rushed close enough to fight back, and even then, only because the Carrion outnumbered them seven to one. Even so, the man from Brong and the woman from Rochelle triumphed again to sit opposite their small fire.

Lady Mayrah adjusted her bracelet and the reflection on its surface caught Wan Du's eye. He wanted to inquire about its purpose and origin after noticing she never removed it, not even to bathe, but thought it disrespectful. Everything about the woman remained foreign to him, from her smooth dark skin to her cascading blond hair. The journey would have been less enjoyable without the woman, yet, he thought soberly, no less dangerous.

With a cough to clear her throat, Lady Mayrah broke the silence.

"How much further do you think it is to Fort Sondergaarde?"

Unbeknownst to her, Wan Du asked himself the same question for days since leaving the battlefield at Flaem. After meeting up with her shortly after, their course had been a vain attempt at due south. A few days in they abandoned the coastline route, as the sandy beaches gave way to impassable masses of cliffs and jagged rock formations. Heading inland they found a different barrier — a river far too wide to swim across. Lacking a better option, they turned south again.

Wan Du raised his hands and shrugged. "I hope no more than a few days."

Lady Mayrah's lips curled in what seemed to be a smile, but lacked the amusement that usually went along with one. She did not otherwise respond.

"I know, under normal circumstances, you would not have opted to travel with me, Lady Mayrah," he said. "I hope my words and actions have not offended you."

Her eyes widened a bit as she paused, nonplussed, before looking back at the fire. She spoke in a voice barely above a whisper.

"I know that, like you, I wish none of this had happened. You have given me no reason to fear you, Wan Du, and for that I am grateful. You will have to forgive me for any occasion where I did not show you what you thought I should, for I no longer allow myself to feel such things."

Lady Mayrah ended her sentence by turning to look out into the darkness, rubbing three parallel marks on her forearm. The marks of a widow, he thought.

Even so, Wan Du's heart lightened a little. It was the most the woman had said to him since the discovery that the Carrion were created from willing and fallen men. Her mind was no doubt filled with thoughts of soldiers and people she once knew — as his had been, back at Bloodmir — and whether she would find them "alive" as Carrion soldiers.

"Get some sleep," he said. "I will keep the watch tonight."

NEAR DUSK, THE PAIR HAPPENED UPON SOME OF THE LOCAL WILD-life. Two large beasts came charging from a thicket before Wan Du even heard their powerful hooves. He raised his weapon in a defensive stance, the long black-bladed halberd he took from a defeated foe, and waited to see if the animals would pass them by. Lady Mayrah, never one to back down from a fight, had her curved sword drawn and was behind him in a flash.

Their immense round horns made a loud cracking sound as the animals rammed their heads together. They seemed completely oblivious to the humans' presence, so Wan Du crept as quickly as he dared to avoid being caught in the fight.

"Magnificent," he heard Lady Mayrah whisper as the beasts continued to pound at each other. Both reared up on their back legs and came back down simultaneously with a resounding boom as their horns met again. Wan Du watched their powerful muscles cord again and again, but neither beast would give ground. The match seemed so even it could go on for hours with no clear victor.

It was a symbol so fitting that Wan Du could not help but speak.

"This reminds me of us."

"Us?" she asked. "You and I?"

The large man shook his head. "Brong and Rochelle."

Both of the animals were visibly strong, yet for some unknown reason, they seemed determined to fight for supremacy over each other. It occurred to Wan Du that anyone who stumbled upon a battle between the two previously-warring countries would have been as perplexed over their fight. The comparison, however, seemed lost on Lady Mayrah.

"We should go," she whispered.

Then, as if to accentuate the similarity, half a dozen black arrows leapt from the same thicket and plunged into the flesh of both animals. Both fell, crying madly with inhuman agony, as the hunters burst out to collect their trophy. He pulled Lady Mayrah with him further into the patch of trees they approached. He felt her anxious breath against his ear as he crouched low, and she pressed closer to him as they hid.

The Carrion were human in shape though their skin and appendages could no longer be categorized as such. The ones that hurriedly approached the dead beasts seemed ravenous with their long, grotesque tongues hanging from their sharp-toothed mouths. A pair of glossy obsidian horns extended from the head of each of the creatures and their empty black eyes were as lifeless as the animals they had slain. As the grunts descended upon their kill, the familiarity of it all tied Wan Du's stomach in a knot.

The Carrion made quick work of the felled animals. Using their claws, they tore away skin to pull at the raw meat just beneath. It reminded Wan Du of the first time he watched the transformation of a man into one of the misshapen soldiers. His grip tightened on the polearm in his fists — with their bows discarded, he knew the fight would not be a long one.

"I can take no more," he whispered. He sensed rather than saw Lady Mayrah's imperceptible nod before she stepped a pace away.

Sounding his familiar battle shout, Wan Du raised his weapon and sprinted for the feasting Carrion. His companion sounded her own charge a moment later and followed.

One of the creatures looked up from its meal in enough time to blink at Wan Du before the large man brought the blade of his halberd down through its head. Black blood erupted onto the ground as it fell forward across the dead animal and its comrades sprang into action. Even without weapons the Carrion were deadly foes, but Wan Du's strength and fury could not be matched. He batted one aside with the pole of his halberd into the slashing edge of his companion's sharp, curved sword and swung his leg up to kick the feet out from another. He allowed the momentum of his kick to carry his body forward, landing on the fallen grunt's back.

"*Retreat!*" he heard one of the beasts croak before Lady Mayrah sent its head spinning from its shoulders. Another picked up its bow and pulled back an arrow before he could get close enough to interrupt. Wan Du threw himself sideways and the arrow whizzed past his face a second before the tip of his halberd found the creature's abdomen; a cry of pain from behind him made his blood run cold.

After cutting down a few more of the fleeing Carrion grunts, Wan Du dropped his weapon and rushed back to Lady Mayrah's side. Half of the black arrow protruded from her chest just below her collarbone and her already dirtied traveling shirt was covered with blood. He hoped at least some of it was not her own.

True to their fallen leader's command, the Carrion fled back into the thicket and the sound of their footfalls died away. Wan Du heard none of it as he held the woman in his large arms.

"I'm not ... dead yet ..." Her breath and her words came in labored gasps.

"Don't speak. I am here. No further harm shall come to you."

Though knowing she never would have approved of his actions, Wan Du tightly shut his eyes and prayed to his deity, *Serené,* for assistance. The Master of the Winds and Waves had been silent for weeks — since Wan Du's imprisonment and escape — but if there was ever a time for prayer it would be now. He poured all of his rage and anguish into a desperate plea and felt Lady Mayrah begin to cough wildly. The shifting of her body brought the other half of the arrow close to his hand. With his knowledge of arrow wounds, Wan Du realized the shaft would need to come all the way through.

He opened his eyes and looked directly into hers. They were half-closed, now, but she remained conscious. Without even a word of warning Wan Du wrapped both hands around the arrow. As quickly as he dared — and before she had time to protest — he snapped the protruding portion of the arrow and pulled the rest through. Lady Mayrah's eyes shot open wide as her pain intensified tenfold, but her throat only let out a hoarse whisper to accompany it. Her head fell back and she passed out. Fresh blood streamed from the wound, but Wan Du checked her breathing before he continued.

"Kill the wizards …" she murmured, delirious with pain.

With no time to regard her modesty, Wan Du ripped the collar of her shirt away and pressed his hand directly against the wound. His other hand went against her back while he sat and cradled her body. Even smeared with her blood, the touch of her soft flesh aroused him, but Wan Du gritted his teeth and attempted to focus all of his energy on her survival.

An army of prayers spewed from his lips, both for distraction and in earnest plea for help. He held Lady Mayrah, settled in his arms as his wife or daughter would be in her place. He begged *Serené* repeatedly not to take another away from him.

For what seemed like hours Wan Du watched her face for any signs of life. Though she was breathing, Lady Mayrah did not so much as bat an eyelash. To keep his eyes from lighting on the wound — or her naked chest — for too long, he looked over the rest of her body.

His gaze locked on her bare wrist, though he was not immediately sure why. It took him a moment to process the band of slightly lighter skin before he realized something was missing. Either in the tumult of battle or the chaos afterward, the bracelet she never removed had broken. He knew it should have been the least of his worries — he held an unconscious and wounded Lady Mayrah to stop her from bleeding to death while the Carrion could return with reinforcements at any moment. But still, he felt the loss of her bracelet might be something ominous.

Slowly but certainly, Wan Du began to feel some kind of remorse for his rash actions. One part of him knew what he did might yet save her life, but something new and unfamiliar began to gnaw at him and he felt it had something to do with the bracelet.

Staving off any compulsion to move either of his hands, Wan Du closed his eyes and prayed once more that they would be safe until the morning.

CHAPTER 38 – *Starka*

TARKA BEAMED WITH THE ADMISSION THAT SHE ENJOYED the day much more sitting around with Kismet than she would have advancing toward their destination. Evening fell before the wheel could be fixed on the wagon. Bored with waiting, the girls opted to take a short walk around and stretch their legs.

"This wagon is owned by my uncle," said Kismet, indicating the vehicle as they passed. Starka smiled and nodded, astonished at how much of the caravan the girl's family owned. This particular uncle was the fourth she pointed out. Starka caught glimpses of spice sacks, malt barrels, and other consumable items underneath the tough covering tied to guard the cargo from the desert winds. She tried to pay her full attention to Kismet's normally interesting history, but it remained difficult as Starka couldn't get memories of the prophecy — and of her brother — out of her mind.

Without warning, Kismet abruptly stopped and held out her arm to bar Starka from going further.

"What's wrong?" Starka asked, straining to catch her balance and avoid pressing her chest into the girl's arm. "Who is this one owned by?"

Kismet shook her head and leaned in conspiratorially to whisper, "It is full of the unsavory characters."

Starka widened her eyes dramatically at the comment. If the youth didn't find DaVille unsavory, Starka did not wish to meet whoever inhabited the indicated wagon. Even so, the girl hadn't said whether she was related to its occupants or not.

Hunched down, they approached the rear of the wagon slowly and with open ears. Starka stifled a giggle at the frivolity of it all, but had to hold her breath entirely when she heard a parched but strong voice coming from the wagon.

"I tell you the truth, my friend. We are fighting a losing war when we should be trying to establish peace," said the man. "What do these Carrion want? Why can we not give it to them?"

Starka did not recognize the voice, but she was instantly glad DaVille was not around to hear him.

"Who is he talking to?" Starka mouthed. Kismet shook her head and shrugged.

The man continued, "You will see. This war is the worst thing for us all. Wait, come back! Where are you going?"

Before either of the girls could react, a hooded and cloaked figure hopped down from the wagon to face them. By the build Starka guessed it a man, but every inch of his skin was wrapped with a thick cloth dyed by soot. His eyes frightened her the most. Against the fading light of dusk, they glowed like blazing hot coals.

"Augh!" screamed Kismet. "Father, the leper nearly touched me!"

To Starka's horror the girl ran away in a panic. She stood alone before the man Kismet identified as not only unsavory, but also someone so diseased he could not even risk touching another human.

"Please excuse her," Starka began, "she's just a child."

The wrapped man remained stoic and unresponsive, breathing evenly but with a slight hiss. His body seemed rigid and solid, nothing like what Starka would imagine from someone afflicted with a deadly contagion. After a moment, he stepped past her and toward his destination. She turned to watch him go and jumped when the dissenter's voice started up suddenly from right behind her.

"You will not get a word out of him, my dear," the man said. "It is my suspicion that his tongue may be missing."

Starka's face twisted as she felt both revulsion and pity for the wrapped man. Without turning around she muttered some kind of dismissive thanks and began to walk away. Unfortunately, the man did not stop talking.

"As I am sure mine will be someday, should I keep on standing up for what I believe." His dry throat seemed to need a pause between each sentence, giving his manner a thespian flare. "Give peace a chance, I say! Yet the desert does not care. Flaem cared even less. Perhaps Ferraut will care."

Flustered, Starka walked hurriedly away and back across the length of caravan she traversed with Kismet. With her mind still on the wrapped man, she climbed into the seat of her wagon and took a few deep breaths before she even noticed DaVille standing among their tethered beasts. The set of his jaw and the decline of his brows signaled to her a lot going on in his mind, as well.

"What's wrong?" she asked.

"I told you to stay here," he replied flatly.

"Well, you were gone for hours!" Starka exploded. The girl instantly felt like apologizing, as DaVille had not caused her to be upset.

DaVille merely turned his head and faced her with the same grim expression. "There's food under the seat," he said. "Get some rest and I'll keep an eye out."

"Keep an eye out for what?" she asked.

"We're nearing the crossroads of Shargoth and the Northern Wall. If I were going to ambush a small party, that's where I'd do it."

Great, Starka thought, why did he have to tell me? She whispered a quick prayer that her sleep wouldn't be troubled with more visions about raiders.

"Once we reach the crossroads we'll only be a few days from Travell and we'll have an easier time of it," said DaVille. "The road's a bit rockier, but at least there are trees."

"Which means water," she deduced aloud.

DaVille shrugged. "At least the weather will change. This blasted heat is the reason no one lives here."

His gaze shifted past her to the wagon of the dissenting man back the way she came.

"They tell me he's against the war. What did he say to you?"

This is new, she thought, DaVille starting conversation. Starka staved off her hunger and nodded.

"He's scared someone will cut out his tongue for it sooner or later." The words tasted sour on her lips, almost like a betrayal.

"As well he should be if he's preaching coexistence with the Carrion. None of us will be safe until they're all dead." DaVille's conviction scared her a bit more, but also made her a bit bolder in questioning him.

"And what makes you think you're the one to kill them?" she demanded. "Why are you so effective at killing things?"

DaVille, in his own horrifying way, smiled before he answered. "There aren't many things I remember before I found you. Killing is one of them."

He paused for a moment, perhaps to prepare himself, before beginning another one of his war speeches. This one sounded so important that Starka was surprised she hadn't heard it already.

"A normal man trains to fight with a weapon, but I have trained to become a weapon. A normal man trains to master a single weapon, but I have trained to master them all. A normal man trains to defeat a single opponent, yet I have trained to engage hundreds. Surrender and death mean nothing to me. On the battlefield, there is only one goal and one thought."

After all of that, Starka was not sure how she felt having DaVille around. All of his adages and knowledge of battle made her think of the tactics of the Carrion. She shook the notion from her head, recalling that she was not only uneducated about war, but completely scared to death of it.

The mere possibility that she could identify a tactic or strategy made her want to laugh aloud. Her thoughts must have been plain on her face as DaVille scowled and finished, "You asked."

She attempted to stammer a response, not meaning to be condescending or aloof. DaVille's words proved quite poetic and beautiful, in their own way, but she could not tell him so. Instead, she sighed and surrendered. Without any further discussion, Starka reached for the food and began eating.

STARKA WOKE WITH A PRAYER OF THANKS ON HER LIPS FOR THE restful and dreamless sleep. As soon as her prayer concluded, though, a curse nearly followed it for the heat of the morning already coated her body in sweat. She hoped with all of her heart that there were impressive bathing facilities in Travell.

As the wagon lurched into motion, she sat next to DaVille and watched the northern horizon for any sign of what he had mentioned the previous night. During her sailing south from Myst-Alsher a month prior, Starka learned a bit of geography during her ship confinement. She remembered stories about the city of Shargoth and how it and the Great Northern Wall were devastated during the Sorcerer's War. The legendary destruction seemed somehow linked in her mind to what she saw when they passed through the remnants of Rochelle. The memory of the floating dead sent a chill up her spine in spite of the inexhaustible heat.

"How much further do you think until we reach the Wall?" she asked.

At first Starka thought he would be curt with her after their last exchange, but all seemed to be forgotten. "We should reach it by the end of the day," he replied, calm but serious. "You may not have noticed, but we can see it already."

"Really?" The girl placed her hand flat above her eyes and squinted. To her, it all looked the same — miles of sand into which their road trailed off.

With a sigh she sat back in the seat. From the back of her mind the same warning from the previous day echoed in her ears, and each time they crested a rise in the road she tried again to see the distant landmark.

Shortly after the caravan's mid-afternoon meal stop, Starka saw the great wall come into full view. She realized why, from further away, the immense structure blended into the horizon. By all accounts it extended to whatever boundary lay to the east, formerly creating a solid partition between Shargoth and Flaem. The closer the caravan came to the wall, though, the more apparent it was that the wall no longer protected anything. Dredging her memory, Starka compared what she knew against what she saw.

The once-great city of Shargoth, a place of great wealth and diversity. Queen Mordyra, governor of Shargoth and its outlying territories before the war, opted to join the coalition against Flaem rather than side with it. It proved a bold and dangerous move, since the desert city-state was the closest target for an initial strike.

Starka had not been able to extrapolate from any version of the story why the monarch turned against her neighbors, but the well-documented result of their response showed before her eyes.

A mile-long section of the Great Northern Wall had been completely blasted away in the first hours of the battle. The wall, heralded as the largest structure in the East, had stood as tall as fifty men. The stone bricks, each as tall as a man, had been excavated from a quarry somewhere to the south. Barely a brick in sight remained untouched by the destruction. Even after centuries, debris littered the area for hundreds of feet in all directions. The stone had been cleared from the road to create a long corridor between jagged stone piles. Any gate that once barred passage had either been destroyed or pillaged.

With effort, Starka removed her eyes from the destruction and looked past the Wall only to marvel at what lay beyond.

The city of Shargoth had given birth to an equally large ruin. Remains of buildings stood at their original height, their vacant windows giving them the appearance of tombstones with teeth. Even the toppled structures looked tall.

Streets once lined and paved with stone now looked like plowed fields. Lines and fissures scored the ground and carved through buildings as well. Scorched stone and earth had merely turned black, but Starka noticed in some places that fire had burned so hot it turned the sand to glass. It suddenly became clear to her why no one rebuilt over the ruins; the magic destroyed more than the people.

As the caravan rolled through the divide where the main road had been cleared and flattened, Starka noticed not one creature stirring amid the ruin. Turning to DaVille, she saw his gaze seemed more grim than usual.

"Are you alright?" Starka asked.

"We're not out of danger yet," he responded.

Dubious about his non-answer, Starka decided to press further. "Have you ever been here before?"

Her companion silently nodded and whipped the yoked beasts with the reins. Starka continued to watch him as the wagons moved through the city.

As they reached the first major intersection, a lone rider galloped alongside them and exchanged a few hurried words with DaVille before bolting forward again. The merchants in the rear, it seemed, were uncomfortable traversing through the ruins and requested all of the protectors to stay alert. DaVille scoffed.

After the messenger rode out of earshot, DaVille turned to her and said, "If a swordsman needs to be reminded to keep his eyes open, he's not worth his pay."

A somber mood seemed to overtake everyone as the wagons continued to roll through Shargoth. Little conversation could be heard, and Starka could not see Kismet anywhere. Though the silence seemed reverent for the ruined city, she began to get the feeling that everyone's nerves were taut. The warning of the rider and her premonition amounted to nothing so far, yet Starka could not shake her worries. An answer to her fears came in a form she dreaded since the previous day.

A different rider than the one before streaked back through the caravan shouting a warning. "The Amber Horde is approaching! Ready your weapons!"

Without a word, DaVille handed her the reins and extracted his swords from behind the seat. Again, she noticed the opaque jewels set in each hilt; the red and white reminding her of the dragon and gargoyle battling outside of Flaem. It seemed the stones were their remnants, but when Starka wondered whether their souls might be encased in the jewels she nearly laughed aloud. It was for the Pantheists in the south to believe in the souls of animals — not Mystians.

The wagon jolted to a halt and DaVille leapt to the ground. As the rider brought DaVille's horse, the warrior took the reins and swung onto its back. She wondered why another man had brought his mount, but assumed DaVille's reputation must have given him some status of leadership.

Dread instantly rose up in Starka's heart at the prospect of being left alone as the Horde approached. "Wait!" she cried. "Don't leave me back here, DaVille."

At the mention of his name DaVille turned back to look at her. When their eyes met she knew they were both thinking of how useless she would be in a fight, but also how likely she would be taken or killed if the raiders came.

"We don't know anything right now; they may not even want to fight," he said. "You'll be safe until I get back." DaVille's voice was less commanding than usual, but no more comforting.

"Come when you have sorted this out, but hurry," the rider said.

DaVille gave a curt nod before the man kicked his heels into his mount and rode off. Starka's companion turned back to her and his features seemed to soften, if only slightly.

"It would be easier for me if you stayed."

His imploring did little to calm Starka — it only gave her more mixed signals. Before she could ask him what he meant, though, her safety needed to be attended to.

"The only place I'm safe is next to you," she said, regretting every word. "I promise, I won't get in your way if you need to fight."

DaVille raised an eyebrow.

"I mean," Starka continued, "I will … I can look after myself."

One corner of his mouth raised in amusement as he shrugged his shoulders to signal acceptance. DaVille turned to one of the other wagons and waved over a boy Starka had seen before, but never spoken to. The youth came running over and nodded furiously when asked to watch the wagon and "keep near his father."

Starka held onto DaVille's powerful torso as they rode toward the front of the caravan. Though she had no idea what to expect, the girl could not help but smile in spite of her circumstances.

Now if I could only do something about this heat, she thought.

CHAPTER 39 – *Cairos*

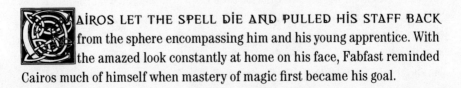

AIROS LET THE SPELL DIE AND PULLED HIS STAFF BACK from the sphere encompassing him and his young apprentice. With the amazed look constantly at home on his face, Fabfast reminded Cairos much of himself when mastery of magic first became his goal.

The nearby stump, formerly a vibrant and branching oak, let off a final puff of smoke as the years of concentric life ended their conversion to magical energy. Though the landscape's majesty diminished without the titanic tree, Cairos appreciated the grassy field for what it was and sighed in triumph as he let his muscles relax.

After a few deep breaths Cairos launched into yet another of his impromptu lectures.

"The problem with magic," he began, "is that it is too balanced."

Cairos allowed the apprentice a moment to take in the first few words before he continued. The lad showed promise from his first attempt at summoning simple spells, but for some reason, he doubted Fabfast's ability to assimilate the knowledge if imparted too quickly.

Or perhaps I am just a poor teacher, Cairos chided himself. Regardless, he needed an apprentice to carry on the traditions of Illiadora in the case of his own death. Though the ongoing war caused enough trouble, pursuing a staff of a dead sorcerer would present plenty of added danger.

"But isn't balance why magic exists, Master?" the youth interrupted, scratching his head.

Cairos scoffed. "Balance is a curse for us, Fabfast. Any spell that can be done can just as easily be undone. Every curse has an antidote and every attack a defense. Someday I will teach you of the Sorcerer's War and why neither side could win.

"For now, just know there is no true advantage down our path, save the overwhelming power that we strive to attain. Attack me and I shall show you."

Fabfast's eyebrows went wide and he began to shake his head. "Master, I can barely summon a flame in my hand!"

The boy spoke truth, but that was why Cairos employed the tree sacrifice. "You should be able to do more now," he assured. "Give it a try."

Though the apprentice raised his pliable sapling staff, he still looked unconvinced.

"Attack me," Cairos repeated, a bit more commanding. Fabfast hurriedly selected a spell from the small arsenal in his mind and uttered the words of a flame incantation. A ring of fire burst into existence around the tip of his staff and startled the boy. With a flourish of his own weapon, Cairos barked the phrasing of an ice spell. The two forces collided in mid-air and dissipated, their steam fading in the breeze. Fabfast quickly dropped to one knee as he felt the power of the magic drain from him. Cairos remembered the sensation well, and sympathized.

"Very good! But remember: it is not all attack-and-defense," the teacher said. "Do not think of magic simply as tricks and spells. True magic is a force much larger than that. Once you feel the grasp of power gnawing at your limbs and life, you will understand this."

He patted the boy's shoulder and continued, "Believe me, I am quite possibly the most unlikely of sorcerers to school you on controlling and limiting this power. Regardless, the *theory* must be understood — and understood well — before you can be allowed to unleash the *power*, and I'm all you've got.

"Learn first that to summon a column of flame on earth, as I have shown you, may look easy, but it is the principles and concepts behind those that you must master."

A silence stretched out between master and student and Cairos took the chance to admire their surroundings again. The landscape forced him to consider the devastation that the *scythorsont* would have left behind at Flaem. From the air, he'd seen two explosions — one outside the city, and a much larger blast out to sea. The first would have left a crater as well as collapsed many of the caverns beneath. If linked crystals detonated in the water, he realized, Circulosa was probably killed by his own device. The concept nearly made Cairos laugh out loud, but for the probable disruption it would cause. He decided it would bear more studying.

Since fleeing the battlefield at Flaem time passed quickly for the young wizard, and his instincts demanded his first priority be to pass on his talent. Only then could he pursue the great artifact that belonged to Circulosa with no reservations. While pondering the possibility of someone else finding the staff first Cairos lost track of time, but his mind quickly shifted at the sight of a nearby growth on the ground. He took one stride and then bent to examine the strange plant, speaking in a reverent whisper.

"My mother used to tell me that mushrooms were dreams of the departed that never came to fruition. She said that because the dreams were now useless, their energy manifested in a form that was useless, too."

Fabfast stepped cautiously toward Cairos, but kept silent. The wizard kept his eyes on the growth as he reached out to touch it.

"She didn't believe in magic, you know."

"Master?" the youth asked, the confusion in his tone nearly palpable. Cairos knew his choice of words baffled the young man and nearly laughed out loud.

To refuse to believe in magic was to deny the very world that one lived in — he imparted this knowledge to the boy when they first met. The master shook his head as he summoned the words to clarify.

"No, it wasn't that she didn't believe in the existence of magic. She didn't believe in its use," he said. "'There are herbal remedies and effort if you want to get things done,' she used to tell me. Sometimes I believe she meant to say magic caused more problems than it solved."

After verbalizing this, Cairos thought of the state of his world for the past weeks. Circumstances remained nearly the same as when he was born, when the Sorcerers War was in full swing. The war claimed his father, she always told him, and everyone else along with him. His mother had not lived to see it end.

Cairos lamented the accuracy of his mother's predictions by remembering the faces of those who fell at Illiadora. So many died the day he escaped — the same day the current war began. *I suppose they will call this the Carrion War*, he thought darkly, *unless the Carrion win it*.

Realizing Fabfast still waited for an end — or a purpose — to his story, Cairos stood and finished. "To a certain extent she was right, I think. But once you start a stone rolling down a hill you cannot simply turn your back and pretend the stone does not exist." With a flourish, Cairos turned his back on the reminder of his mother and began to walk away.

The spell he used to siphon the tree's power faded, but its results remained permanent. With the aid of the tree's sacrifice, Fabfast gained a year's worth of magic in an hour. Though Cairos regretted having to resort to anathema magic to train his disciple, he had too little time to operate and the staff of Circulosa constantly called his name. Pangs of guilt twisted his stomach remembering the one who taught him to siphon from plant life, but Cairos fought them down.

From one of his many deep pockets, he pulled a map to consult as he walked across the grassy plain. Far to the east of Flaem, near the Red River that flowed down from the Pillar Peaks, he had still not decided where to travel next. His finger traced a path north along the coast to the settlement of Travell, but he immediately dismissed this as a destination. They were not refugees, and Cairos still had fight left. Looking further at the map, he thought of returning to Flaem. Their goal, so far, remained to stay clear of all large cities, but this kept them dangerously unaware of the status of the war.

The pair traveled cross-country on foot, not even daring to take to the skies for fear of Fabfast's limited power. The ritual at the oak should have calmed a portion of Cairos' caution, but still he refused to test the boy.

Traveling to Flaem held its own dangers, for a specific taint accompanied the outlawed spells. Over time it would dissipate, but he had no desire to test its timeframe nor did he feel the need to explain its necessity to Flaem's adamant Council — anathema was anathema, plain and simple.

He waved this thought away casually as if he were shooing a bug, which coincidentally, he was, and paused to review the map more closely. A large "X" marked the area where he assumed the *scythorsont* on Circulosa's ships detonated, spreading his fleeing Carrion soldiers to the wind. Cairos would not let his hope die that the staff, a powerful weapon and artifact, survived the explosion and lay somewhere, only waiting for him to collect it. Perhaps the time had come for him and the boy to seek the treasure, Cairos thought. With a glance at the unarmed Fabfast, Cairos continued to weigh his options.

The apprentice's sparse beard, like everything else he wore or carried, looked completely foreign on the boy's face. His complexion, still tanned from countless days in the fields of his home, contrasted the apprentice tunic Cairos procured for him. The garment did not seem to fit Fabfast's muscular frame. He still wondered from time to time if the boy would have been better off training with the sword than the staff, but if his fate had not gone that direction already Cairos guessed it probably never would. All the same, at least Fabfast would enjoy practicing melee combat with a staff.

The boy might enjoy a staff like Gabumon's, he thought. It would get more use in Fabfast's hands than on a cave floor, and the older wizard no doubt would have wished some part of what he left behind to aid in defeating the Carrion. With that thought in mind, Cairos set off to lead the way north.

CAIROS WAS CONSTANTLY REMINDED WHY HE HATED FOOT TRAVEL. He would rather have floated, hovered, flown, or rolled but none of the mobility spells he knew were familiar enough to Fabfast to trust. The boy had flown once, for a brief moment, but took an immediate plunge. Luckily, he had been only a few feet from the ground. Cairos shrugged and continued his work around their small encampment.

They were nearing Flaem, but the currents he used to feel in a constant flow toward the city were abnormal. Since the explosion, something seemed to divert it, but the concept perplexed him. The wizard forced himself to be patient; he couldn't know more until they reached the city. Though powerful, *scythorsont* had not been used for decades, and no documents on it stated anything about disrupting magic currents. Of course, that didn't necessarily mean it couldn't happen, but it required further investigation to be sure.

"Studying the currents again, Master?" asked Fabfast.

Cairos started. His apprentice still seemed ill-fitted for magical talents, but had an uncanny knack for reading his thoughts.

"Indeed," he said without turning. "We're getting closer to the disruption and I believe it has something to do with the detonation. I just don't know what."

When Cairos did turn, he saw the boy stretching his own sore muscles. Not once had he complained about sleeping on the ground or being away from family or civilization. Fabfast seemed truly content with travel and sorcery training, so far.

Well, whatever keeps him away from slopping pigs and collecting eggs would make me happy as well, thought Cairos. He smiled at the thought of it until the memories of his own brutal apprenticeship stole the joy away.

WHILE THE BOY SLEPT, CAIROS STARED AT THE GRINNING MOON. IT was nearly full again; the second cycle since he left Illiadora like a rat from a sinking ship. Without warning, Gabumon's last words returned unbidden to his mind. *I wouldn't have been afraid to die next to my brothers! At least I would die standing rather than save my own skin!*

Cairos tried to push the memory away, but he could still feel the heat of the dragon's flames as they engulfed the old sorcerer. Guilt stabbed at him like a sword in the gut. If he, Cairos, had not entered Gabumon's cave to retrieve some trivial trinket then the old man would still be alive. He might well have been ignorant of the conflict outside his own demesne, but he would have been breathing. Instead, Cairos was breathing and torturing himself over another death he should have tried harder to prevent. One fewer sorcerer in the world. One fewer *Illiadora* sorcerer, he corrected.

With a deep breath, Cairos turned again to look upon the sleeping form of his apprentice. "Does passing on my knowledge to another help erase some of my cowardice?" he wondered.

The boy could never replace Gabumon, as the old man had been such an expert in illusion he even fooled Cairos into believing he fought a dragon.

"Sadly ironic that such a beast killed you, my friend," Cairos whispered. Instinctively his clenched fist found his open palm with force at the level of his chest. The sign of Vexen.

The symbol of *vengeance*.

A meaningless oath, now. He had vowed to avenge the deaths of his sorcerous brothers and failed so badly that he even caused the death of one more. Cairos was so frustrated with the direction of his own thoughts that he wanted to scream them out. Fabfast's steady breathing reminded him yet again his pain was to be borne silently and alone.

"Once we get to Flaem," Cairos reminded himself, "I can begin to set things right. Your staff will find clean hands, Gabumon, and then Circulosa's will be mine."

CHAPTER 40 – *Starka*

HE FRONT OF THE CARAVAN LOOKED NO DIFFERENT FROM the rear, but the view of the city certainly was. As Starka took in the northern quarter of the ruin even she could see a host of figures in the distance. Some members of the Horde stood on the tops of the ruined structures while some gathered in the rubble of the side streets. One stood in the middle of the main road with his arms crossed and his head high.

DaVille had her dismount before he dropped out of the saddle himself and walked the last twenty paces to the representative of the Amber Horde.

"Are we going to have a problem?" asked DaVille, his usual self.

Starka was shocked to hear DaVille speak first and merely looked on while the other man sized him up. The representative dressed differently than all of the desert dwellers she had seen. Strange animal pelts of red and gold wrapped his torso, forearms, and boots. Other than those, he wore very little clothing at all — mostly dirtied fabrics held to his body by thin leather straps. The hair covering his face and head matched the same highlighted color as his furs, and he wore a beaten and faded leather eye patch.

The man uncrossed his arms and spoke in a voice no less bestial than Starka expected. As he moved, she spotted the hilts of two long, curved daggers protruding from his belt, previously hidden from sight by his massive forearms.

"You would do well to show some respect, woman-worshipper," he growled. "You trespass here."

"Trespass?" asked DaVille. "You claim ownership here?"

The one-eyed man nodded once, unsettled by DaVille's mocking tone.

"You own a ruin," he continued. "How cute."

"State your business on the Red Dragon Road," the man demanded. "Or should I be asking her? Tell me, stranger, do you ask her permission to relieve yourself, as well?" His taunting finger pointed right at Starka, making her stiffen.

"Trade caravan on route to Travell," DaVille answered flatly, ignoring the jibes.

The representative appraised the wagons for an extra long moment even though they remained some distance away. Starka chanced a look behind her and noticed for the first time that men, soldiers of the Horde, stood in that direction as well. I knew the ambush was coming, she scolded herself, why didn't I say more?

"Goods?" the one-eyed man asked.

"Spices, grains, seeds, fabrics." DaVille counted on his fingers as he lied. "The usual."

The response was a scoff. "Well, I was only going to take a fifth of your cargo as my toll. Now I think I'll take a fourth. And possibly your tongue for your untruth."

Starka couldn't see it, but she was sure DaVille smiled. He always seemed to do that in the face of a challenge. His hand drifted across his body and casually placed itself against the pommel of his red-gemmed longsword. He spoke only two words.

"Please try."

The Amber Hordesman chewed on his bottom lip and narrowed his remaining eye, probably unused to such a challenge within his domain.

"Very well," he said, "but know you face the One-Eyed Dragon."

Her companion turned to the side and grinned. "In Flaem, they call me DaVille Dragonslayer."

Starka reflected they had not meant it as a compliment. Before she could blink, three blades were drawn. DaVille brandished one sword and deflected a stab toward his heart before backing up a pace. Starka did not have time to wonder why he did not draw his other sword before he leapt forward again.

The two men kicked up so much dust as they performed their blade dance that it became difficult to see. The One-Eyed Dragon was quick and powerful, but his range was limited. Anytime he got close enough to strike, DaVille's longer sword punished him for it. Steel rang against steel repeatedly; DaVille parried blows and a frightening grating sound split the air as the blades slid against each other. Yet even through all of this, neither man landed a blow to the other's skin. DaVille smiled throughout each exchange, and Starka shook her head in indignation. This was not the time for games!

"Are you ready to quit yet, one-eyed snake?"

The Dragon growled, but did not respond with words. His strikes became wilder and quicker, but still he could not land a blow. DaVille seemed to be toying with him the way he toyed with Bathilde the club-wielder.

Starka felt a strange shadow fall over her mind at the thought of the large woman. Though she was in the middle of the desert at midday, she became cold enough to see her breath. She fell to her knees as her vision shifted to a cold dark room in a tall black tower. A large silhouette, black on black, flexed its muscles in the darkness. Two eyes burned like coals and Starka felt them on her. They were so real she felt the heat from them. The eyes seemed right in front of her face. *The Carrion are coming*, she heard.

As she drew in breath to scream, Starka realized she was staring into the burning eyes of the wrapped man. The leper had his hands on her shoulders, shaking her gently. She blinked and tried to regain her bearings while the fight between DaVille and the Dragon continued.

"Are you alright?" came his faint whisper.

Starka fought back her fear and nodded, looking quickly toward the ground and away from those glowing eyes. Had the man broken her prophetic trance?

He stood and turned from her to face the two combatants. Starka watched as he made a familiar gesture, one the wizard Cairos made outside of Flaem, and a nearly-visible wall appeared between DaVille and the Dragon.

"Enough, Mendenha. I will pay your toll." The voice, still a whisper, carried loud enough for the intended parties to hear. With weapons lowered, the men turned in Starka's direction. Both panted from the fight and Mendenha seemed to be glad for the break.

"Show yourself," he said, "And tell me how you know my name."

The wrapped man simply turned and retreated without another word, but his spell hung in the air as DaVille tested it again. Starka continued to grow curious about the leper. Her companion shrugged and sheathed his sword while Mendenha followed suit. His lips curled in a smile as he spoke again.

"Fine, fine. You fight well, woman-worshipper, and are welcome at my fire this night. Your woman is, of course, welcome in my tent."

Starka jumped to her feet and balled a fist before realizing the man was merely taunting DaVille again. To her surprise, he waved it off and walked back toward her and the horse.

Mendenha raised his fingers to his lips and let out two high whistle blows. Starka moved to cover her ears against the shrill noise. All of the members of the Horde in the distance and in the city seemed to disappear at once, and a small party of men rode from behind a nearby set of structures mounted on large crimson dogs. Some of the beasts snarled and others dumbly looked on as they plodded toward Mendenha. All of the mounted men dressed similar to their leader but to a lesser degree, and nearly all looked like they had seen recent battle.

She jumped at DaVille's voice. "Come on, girl. Back to the wagon." Starka nodded, still a bit dazed from the vision, and let him help her onto his mount.

HOURS LATER, DARKNESS HAD FALLEN AND THE CARAVAN STILL had not moved. They accepted the Horde's invitation to camp, though Starka had not seen what the wrapped man offered for the toll. She hugged Kismet when the girl came running. The young girl's eyes grew wide as Starka relayed the events of the fight and they chatted the hours away until Starka realized she had lost track of DaVille. She sent Kismet to sup with her father and went off in search of her companion.

DaVille was standing close to the bonfire and staring at the wrapped man across it as Starka came upon them. She noticed that while the flames danced against the shine of DaVille's eyes, the wrapped man's dull coals kept their same glow.

"Tell me your name," DaVille said.

"You do not know me," came the whispered reply. Starka was surprised she could hear the voice over the roar of the fire.

"Stop being so mysterious," said DaVille, waving his arms. "Why do you not show your face?"

She wondered if DaVille even noticed her. Without thinking further, she knelt on a blanket a short distance away to listen.

"Tell me your name," he repeated. When the wrapped man neither moved nor spoke, DaVille continued, "You do know I can beat it out of you, don't you?"

The stoic mask of the wrap did not move, but something familiar about the situation made Starka think the man smiled.

"Please try," he hissed.

The conversation was interrupted with slurred laughter as Mendenha appeared. He slapped DaVille on the back, nearly to his detriment, before continuing to his own spot on the ground.

"Men, men. Let us drink and talk. Nothing loosens up the tongue better than desert ale." The man seemed as quick to festivity as he was to draw blades, one of which remained fixed to his waist though his fur armor had been removed. Angry scars and blackened bruises covered parts of his chest and arms.

"Not all of us need to drink away our pain, Mendenha." DaVille spoke without moving his eyes from the wrapped man. When he spoke the One-Eyed Dragon's name, he did so with a bit of disdain on each of the three syllables.

"What, these?" he asked, pointing to the scars. "Mere scratches. What brings a fighter like you to these parts?"

As their conversation continued, the wrapped man seemed to recess further and further away from it, though he did not move. DaVille finally turned his head to address the Dragon directly.

"I told you. Trade caravan headed for Travell."

This brought another hearty laugh from the Amber Hordesman. "A steel-tongued devil, you are. No, DaVille, I know men and I know this road. Skills like yours don't come from being an escort — they come from being a soldier."

"Believe what you like," said DaVille, shrugging.

"Come now, you and I both know escorting trade caravans is for green youths and hooded twops." Mendenha glanced sideways at the wrapped man, but Starka saw no reaction to the insult. By the firelight, it was tough to guess the Horde leader's age. His zeal suggested the man was young enough to still cause trouble and old enough to back it up.

It was DaVille's turn to laugh. "You do know men, I will give you that." Starka noticed he had addressed Mendenha's comment without answering him, yet the conversation continued. "Since when has the toll been a full fifth?"

The accusation stung Mendenha and Starka saw it in his lowered head. "Since the Carrion," he said shamefully. "Since you're one man and a caravan, I will tell you our story, but these words do not pass beyond this fire."

"I swear it," replied DaVille. Both looked to the wrapped man, but he made no promises.

Mendenha let out a long sigh before beginning his tale. "This is the tenth year that I have been the head of my clan. When the Wizards destroyed

Shargoth and the ownership of this land passed back to the followers of the Fire God, my father ruled a true Horde of nearly four thousand strong. It is only during my watch that our numbers have diminished so, as we are less than eight hundred now, including our women and young ones. It is the first time in over a hundred years that we are so few.

"It is the Carrion that have brought this blight upon us. They attack us ruthlessly and steal our animals in the night. My brother, Menkada, took a thousand men southeast in search of our lost dogs, but only twenty men returned and all were badly injured. The rest, I shudder to think of their fate. Some of our clan mothers have even taken to calling my reign *Sava Foire Destrack*; the Trial of the Fire God.

"It takes money and food to breed a man. And time, of course. But more than that, it takes a weapon in his hand to be more than a large moving target. We have been shadowing your venture for days and we know you carry the swords of the smithy Middel, the weapons kissed and blessed by the brightest fires in the world. It is these we seek so that we might fight back against those who steal our animals and murder our fighting men."

By the end, Starka found she had less sympathy than usual for bandits such as these. They caused her no harm, so far, and the passage north was a higher priority than the cargo in Starka's mind. Let them have it, she thought, but one glance at DaVille and she knew he would not part with it lightly. He already fought once for it and would fight again if the point was pressed. However misplaced, the man's sense of duty seemed at least to be solid.

Starka looked away from the flames and out into the desert night. Their goal was to reach the kingdom of Ferraut and form some kind of defense against the Carrion Army, but they were only a man and a woman. *It takes an army to fight a war*, she remembered hearing DaVille say. She wondered if they would find an army in Ferraut — or whether they suffered the same casualties as the Amber Horde clans.

In between pops from the firewood, Starka heard the baying of a dog. The One-Eyed Dragon's head perked up to hear the warning cry and his hand immediately went to his weapon. "Trouble," he hissed.

DaVille nodded. "Speak of the devil, and he shall come." When both his white and red swords flashed into view, a prayer leapt to Starka's lips.

∽

CHAPTER 41 – *Starka*

OW MANY MEN DO YOU HAVE WITH YOU?" DAVILLE CALLED to Mendenha as they ran in the direction of the alarm. Starka struggled to keep up, yet the fear of being left behind kept her on DaVille's heels.

"Thirty!" came the reply. The One-Eyed Dragon ran ten paces ahead and only briefly craned his neck to shout to his rear.

Calls came up from around the camp and the sound of drawn steel was nearly drowned out by the continual baying of hounds. Starka saw DaVille wielded his white longsword, but left his red sheathed against his hip.

"Don't lose me," she panted. "I can't see anything."

"That's the idea," responded DaVille. "Night raids work best at night."

Sounds of fighting came on quickly as Starka neared the wagons. Campfires illuminated the forms of several fur-clad men engaged with the dark shapes of Carrion soldiers. She nearly screamed at seeing the humanoid beasts again, and so close, but she throttled her fear and scanned the wagons in search of Kismet. Spotting the girl crouching underneath a wagon, Starka broke from DaVille and headed toward her.

"Find a safe place and stay there," he called to Starka's back.

She slid as deftly as she could to join Kismet beneath the wooden panels. Though quite uncomfortable, the thankful expression on the girl's face was enough to make Starka happy. Grasping her hand tightly, Starka turned back to see DaVille already in a melee with three grunts. She could barely make out his form amid the chaos and darkness, but each time she saw the white sword flash her heart stopped.

"My father," Kismet sobbed.

"What happened?"

"He is dead!" The girl broke down and buried her head against her sleeve. Starka wanted to comfort her, but her words would be empty; they were still in danger themselves.

Two pairs of feet stomped across Starka's field of vision as a hordesman battled one of the Carrion soldiers. The beast's guttural grunts sounded like wheezes and Starka hoped the battle would end quickly. Past the two, she saw DaVille coming closer, still slashing away. Strokes of white parted the veil of the night, drawing the dark blood of the Carrion.

A body hit the ground next to the wagon and Starka had to fight from retching. The Carrion soldier's neck had been almost cleanly severed and black blood drained into a pool on the glassy ground. It seemed an odd moment to notice, but Starka realized that patches of the sand had been turned to glass from the incineration of Shargoth. It was a dull, cloudy glass, but the heat from it made her imagination start to go wild. As she felt Kismet stirring next to her, she bade the girl to keep her eyes hidden. Better to spare her from having to see more horrors tonight.

"We have to move," she whispered. Crawling backwards with the young girl took more courage than Starka thought she had, but the far side of the wagon held no danger for the moment. Looking around, she kept herself and Kismet to a crouching position between the wheels.

A distance away she saw half a dozen hordesmen making a stand against twice as many Carrion grunts. Their hounds snarled and barked at the dark soldiers, threatening them to come closer to the dogs' waiting jaws. In a flash, Mendenha appeared at the Carrion's flank and began tearing through the shocked beasts. Seizing the moment, the hordesmen and their hounds dove into the surprised grunts and began carving their own way through.

Pain shot through Starka's head as she felt her hair being pulled upward by an unwelcome hand. She screamed in agony and terror as she saw the flash of a serrated blade glint in the Carrion soldier's other hand and then watched as the beast went tumbling forward. Her hair was released and the grunt hit the ground, its head collapsed in by a blow from above. Strange light blinded her for a moment and she brought her hand up to shield herself from it.

Kismet cried out in complete shock, "It is ... the *leper*?"

"There is no sense hiding it any longer," whispered the wrapped man. Wreathing his featureless head was a constantly twisting halo of flames that warmed her face, but did not seem to damage him. His eyes burned with the light of ten candles, like two stars inside a sun.

Her mouth fell open and before she gained enough composure to ask a question, the man jumped from the wagon and raised a staff in both hands. She looked past him and saw a charging throng of Carrion coming straight for them.

The whisper changed to an echoing shout as the word "Firestorm!" erupted from the wrapped man's throat. An oval of space behind him seemed to ripple and warp like a pond surface. The space belched smoke until huge gouts of flame shot forth to meet the advancing soldiers. The grunts fell in droves as the fire consumed their skin. Line upon line of the soldiers became incinerated by the spell he called forth, but the flames did not touch or hinder him in the slightest. The wind from the heat made his clothing billow, but it did not so much as singe.

Then as quickly as the spell began, the portal winked out of existence. Starka blinked once for amazement and again to clear the brightness from her vision before the man's flaming face turned back toward them. It took her another second to realize the entire battle had ended with that final blast.

DaVille rushed over and instinctively raised his blade against the wrapped man before taking in the situation, then lowered it a moment later. Kismet's arms found Starka's waist as the distraught girl begged for comfort.

"A Burning Man, I presume?" DaVille's tone was scathing.

The wrapped man gave a sweeping bow and a flourish with his arm before sliding the veil of his hood back over his head. His voice once again lowered to a whisper. "I am Adamis."

DaVille scoffed, sheathed his sword, then turned to walk away muttering something about tallying the casualties. Adamis walked back toward his wagon without another word. He paused as he passed Starka, flashing a glance with his glowing eyes, before leaving her alone with the sobbing Kismet.

CHAPTER 42 – *Starka*

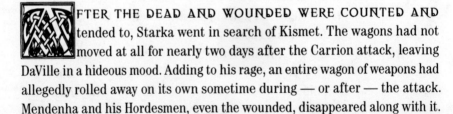

FTER THE DEAD AND WOUNDED WERE COUNTED AND tended to, Starka went in search of Kismet. The wagons had not moved at all for nearly two days after the Carrion attack, leaving DaVille in a hideous mood. Adding to his rage, an entire wagon of weapons had allegedly rolled away on its own sometime during — or after — the attack. Mendenha and his Hordesmen, even the wounded, disappeared along with it.

She had done her best to stay out of DaVille's way, as he constantly looked for targets to unleash his tirades on. He might not be angry with her, Starka knew, but it was still terrible to be in the path of his ire.

Worst of all, Starka had lost track of her young friend. Not even Kismet's family knew where the girl had gone. So distraught over the death of her father, she had rarely spoken since the night, according to one of the uncles.

"The only place she might be is near the grave," he had told her. Starka hurried off to find the copse of fig trees that became the man's resting place.

"Kismet?" she called out, hoping the girl would answer to her pleading voice. When no answer came, Starka edged closer to the dirt mound and stone marker within a nest of about twenty trees. She leaned her ear into the wind to listen for anything that would give away the girl's whereabouts, but heard only the whisper of the wind.

Finally, Starka sighed and turned to retreat back to the wagons. She jumped when she saw that Adamis had silently joined her.

"Why do you travel with him?" asked the wizard. The charcoal cloth covered his face, muting the flames that hid beneath. Likewise, his voice returned to a whisper.

"You mean DaVille?"

"I mean your man, whatever name he goes by," came the strange reply. "Why do you stay with him?"

"Why should I not travel with him?" she asked, indignant. "Not that it is any business of yours, but he saved my life and he seeks to end this war with the Carrion."

Starka felt good that she could summarize the purpose of their relationship just so. Her personal feelings toward DaVille, whatever they might be, should have been of no concern to Adamis.

Yet, oddly enough, he did seem concerned.

"Is that so?" he asked, the whisper mixing with a coughing sort of laugh. "What do you truly know of this man? Do you know what the symbols on his body mean? Do you know why he seeks to end this war?"

Starka pursed her lips, but could not retort. The dull glow of Adamis' eyes flashed brighter for a moment then dulled again.

"You do not even know where this man comes from," he surmised.

She shook her head in response to the continued accusations. Did she really know so little about the man she had placed so much trust in? If anything, Adamis was the deceptive one.

"I have no reason to believe he's been dishonest with me. He has protected me, though I can say that I do not know why. DaVille found me on a beach in Bloodmir after I had ..." Starka paused, unsure how to phrase the way she came ashore. She continued, "After I had been abandoned by my party from Myst-Garvon."

Adamis again shocked her with his response. "You went there based on a prophecy, didn't you? A prophecy about a man?"

"Who exactly are you?" she demanded. DaVille would have known he had gotten under her skin, but Adamis was different. The effect was the same, however, as the wrapped man merely stayed calm and ignored her question entirely.

"You are not the only one who deals in prophecies and visions," he replied. "The Mystian Continent holds no special ownership of this bailiwick."

Nothing he said made sense to Starka, and she found herself wishing he had never revealed himself at all. Life was simpler when he was a mute leper rather than another person who knew more than her about the events altering the course of her life.

"Next you'll be telling me about my brother," whispered Starka in despair.

"I know nothing of his whereabouts," Adamis admitted to her surprise. Starka no longer cared whether it was true or not.

"You go too far, wizard," she warned. "I appreciate your warnings, but they are worth nothing to me. I must continue traveling with DaVille until our task is done or until I am dead. I have nowhere else to go and no way to get there."

With that, she pushed past Adamis and returned to the wagon. He did not speak again as she left, but his questions remained in her mind nonetheless. She found her companion near a small pool of water and approached, tearing her head covering away.

"Tell me where you are from," Starka demanded.

DaVille turned his gaze from the small looking glass toward her and then back again, finishing the swipe of the blade down his cheek. He had neglected his hygiene since the trip began, and though Starka was glad to see him shaving again, she could not wait.

"Go away," he said simply.

"I am not going anywhere until I have some answers," she protested. "Just who are you, DaVille?"

Her companion growled and continued to ignore her questions. The majority of his face was covered in a smooth mud mixture and he wouldn't have much time to finish shaving before it hardened.

"Why do you only care now?" chided DaVille. "Did your little friend put you up to this?"

Nearly fuming, Starka stomped her foot and snatched the mirror from DaVille's view, hiding it behind her.

"Hey, what the …"

"Answer me, you barbarian! Who are you?" she repeated.

"Look, girl, if you're bored, I'm sure there are plenty of deaths around to pray for. That should be more important to you."

She moved as if to throw the mirror. "I'm sure it would be painful to peel off all that mud once it hardens."

DaVille's eyes narrowed. "Pain means nothing to me anymore."

"See?" Starka cried. "Where does that come from?"

"I'm a soldier," he shouted back. "That is all you need to know!"

Thankful the spot he had chosen to shave was well away from the encampment, Starka pressed him further. "No, it is not. I trust you with my life, yet I know nothing about you. I'm not traveling another step with you until that has changed."

She nearly added questions about his origins or the symbols on his body, as Adamis had raised to her, but she allowed his imagination and sense of privacy to vie for what information to share.

The man looked to the blade in his hand and frowned. He opened his mouth to speak, but Starka interrupted.

"I'm afraid of you, DaVille."

Her admission seemed to shock him for a moment. She tried to convey things in the shortest way possible; Starka couldn't have said aloud that she desperately needed him to just talk to her. She had trusted him with her life since the day they met, yet she could never shake the feeling that the fury of his blades would someday turn on her. Fear kept her silent, and until today, she had let it. But Adamis' words awakened a courage in her, along with a need to know that the man she traveled with was truly human.

DaVille's mouth opened, then closed again and Starka knew she had won, though she bit her bottom lip to avoid showing it.

"Fine," he said, "You starve for truth and honesty? I will answer a question for every one you do."

"Agreed." Only a moment later did she notice it had been too hasty — she had just agreed to answer the first question, not ask it. Handing the mirror back to DaVille, she held her breath waiting for his inquiry. He took a few quick swipes with his blade before pausing again to speak.

"Why were you near Bloodmir?" asked DaVille.

Relief spread over her that he avoided more lecherous topics, but it only lasted a moment. She wanted to choose her words carefully and nearly berated herself. Wasn't she the one seeking honesty?

"I received a prophecy," she said.

As DaVille finished shaving and washed the remnants from his face, Starka recounted the events that led her to Bloodmir. She carefully shared the words of the prophecy, Seeress Elestia's interpretation of it, Cardinal Wadam's reaction to it, and the vision of Fandur that forced her off the ship near the Blood Coast. Starka finished her story as DaVille pressed his face into a cloth.

"The rest you know, or were present for," she finished.

He stared into her face for a few moments before smiling.

"You did all of this because of a dream?"

"We take prophecy very seriously where I come from!" she protested. Seeing the furious look in her eyes, DaVille raised his hands in mock surrender. Fair enough, his shrug seemed to say — but it was not an apology.

"So you think I'm this catalyst?" he asked.

"You tell me who you are," Starka said through gritted teeth.

DaVille sighed and sat on a nearby ledge of stone. It looked to be the remainder of a wall long disassembled by wind and time. He contemplated his answer, but Starka could not tell whether the pause was good or bad.

"The only way to tell you who I am is to tell you who I was," he replied simply, as if the conversation held little more content than the weather. The man dropped onto the sand and indicated she do the same.

"Who you were?" she repeated.

In a flash, his tone changed serious. "But first you must promise, swear even, on your holy whatever-you-have, that you will not share what I tell you with anyone."

Starka sat close to DaVille so he did not have to speak any louder than necessary. "Why?"

"You'll see, but one question at a time."

With a nod, she waited for him to start. With a sigh, DaVille began his own tale.

"My name was DaVille Terrant, and I was a Carrion General ..." he paused as Starka's face filled with surprise, confusion and fear all at once ... "until I was killed."

CHAPTER 43 – *Drakkaram*

ENERAL DRAKKARAM WAS SICK OF WAITING. HE SURRENdered his will to the purpose of the Great Commander, but not even that could control his temperament. Slaughtering game animals with his bare hands in the forest east of Hakes grew tiresome, though the occasional pilgrim or merchant family broke up the monotony. Nothing could curb his appetite for death knowing that Terrant, the Betrayer, lived. As the General's gauntleted fist closed around his latest victim, he let the name spill from his lipless mouth.

"Terrant …"

Reports came from nearly every direction after the massive tidal wave decimated the northwest. The party he had pursued north followed a man of great power, one that the former General Circulosa identified as Terrant. Xymon extracted the knowledge from the wizard himself just before killing him. Drakkaram's sharp teeth met in a grin thinking of the round man's demise, though he was sorry he had not been there to do it himself.

Drakkaram could not believe the Betrayer still lived. Zion had said nothing in response to the reports; only the remaining Generals seemed to react, though it had been Zion who removed his horns personally. Drakkaram reached up and grasped one of his own three black horns, wondering how Terrant survived their removal. They had left him on the bloodstained beach of Bloodmir on the day the Carrion army destroyed Brong and Rochelle in a single blow and announced their mighty presence to the world.

The war, so far, went as Drakkaram had expected, save for Circulosa's failure to take Flaem. Illiadora fell so easily that even Drakkaram had confidence the wizard General could conquer Flaem. It did not sit right with the brutal General that Zion chose such a failure to lead a third of his army. To be destroyed by his own magical devices — it was too humorous!

The twitching beast in Drakkaram's hand brought his attention back to the moment. He tossed it aside and ignored the low growls as his Carrion grunts began tearing into the meat with tooth and claw. They were not much greater than animals themselves. Fodder, all of them, but not his creation that he had left behind in Fort Sondergaarde. No, she was something special.

Though her name had been Bathilde, it mattered little what comprised her past. She was Carrion now, and proud of it. How Drakkaram relished her turning ceremony and the days afterward! There were so few female Carrion and nearly all of them the worthless gray, capable of little more than drooling and killing.

But she had become so much more!

Drakkaram's lustful appetites had been sated over and over again as he made her belong to him. It was a glorious feeling to have such a willing and resilient slave to his brutal whims. She begged for more when he lashed her. She learned to love the needles. Most of all, she learned to crave him and the General grinned just thinking about it. Drakkaram left her in the south with the other projects and sailed for the country of Ferraut to get ahead of Terrant.

Spying movement in the distance, General Drakkaram focused his keen black eyes on it. A creature approached, becoming one of his own Carrion scouts.

"Look alive, underlings," he roared. "A scout."

Some Carrion, too stupid to understand the meaning of his words, reached for their weapons and suffered a jolt from their fellows. Drakkaram marveled at how dumb the grunts could be, even improved as they were. On the other hand, they had been human to begin with; what more could be expected of the puny creatures?

The scout bounded through the sparsely-forested area to come within reaching distance of Drakkaram. Only after coming so close did the scout kneel and touch its horns to the ground in respect.

"Great General, I bring news."

"Speak," he commanded.

"The party sent to Shargoth has been destroyed, My General."

Drakkaram stiffened. "And the Betrayer?"

"The Betrayer lives."

"How can this be?" Lieutenant Thistle demanded from the scout. Then to Drakkaram he said, "How could a handful of caravan guards fell nearly a hundred soldiers?"

Sensing the doubt in his lieutenant's tone, Drakkaram turned toward Thistle and narrowed his eyes. The officer was large, but no man or Carrion was larger than Drakkaram himself. His continued gaze caused the lieutenant to shrink back and retreat to another task.

The General turned back to the scout and requested it continue the report.

"The wildmen gave them assistance, My General. The Amber Horde remains unbeaten, but they are weakened considerably."

Drakkaram, having heard similar reports from many others, knew this last detail already, but did not let it detract from the scout's worth. At least it had a function among his armies — unlike many of his foot soldiers.

"And the caravan," he asked; "it will continue to Travell?"

"This news is days old already, My General. The caravan may have already begun to move again."

"Excellent," finished Drakkaram, waving the scout away. For a moment he considered sending it back after a rest, but his scouts were many and one more would make no difference. Sooner or later, Terrant the Betrayer would come and Drakkaram would be waiting for him.

CHAPTER 44 − *Wan Du*

THE SUN BURST GRUDGINGLY ABOVE THE EASTERN HORIZON and met Wan Du's wincing gaze. Pain and fear, unfamiliar emotions, turned his stomach in knots. His hands had gone numb hours before and still he saw no signs of life from Lady Mayrah other than her very shallow and labored breaths. From his whispered prayers throughout the night, Wan Du's tongue felt like he had swallowed seawater. But at least the sun was up — she had lived through the night.

Wan Du's mind remained solid; he knew the Creator made him for hardier nights than this. Kneeling before the poisoned well in Brong for days had tested both his body and his resolve, and there hadn't even been another dependent upon him for survival then. It was his companion that he feared for, though he knew her feelings would not have been the same if the situation were reversed.

More than anything else, he simply did not want to be left alone again with no one but *Serené* to talk to. Lady Mayrah did not know that feeling; she'd had compatriots when Wan Du first met her, few though they may have been.

Cautiously, Wan Du pulled the pressure of his hand away from Lady Mayrah's chest. As shameful as the act was, he had to look to verify whether the wound clotted. He saw no fresh blood on her skin. The pink hole stared back at him, and smelled foul, but it ceased to bleed for the time being. He decided, for the moment, not to wake her, but instead found some spare cloth to bandage her wound.

After wrapping the wound on both sides and tucking the cloth taut, Wan Du stood and stretched his legs for the first time in many hours. The sun had risen fully, then, and the pink and orange of dawn turned into the full blue of the clear eastern sky.

He celebrated the retreat of the stars, for each time they came out the stars reminded Wan Du how far away from home he was. He gazed back to the north, back toward Flaem's battlefield. Though far too serendipitous to be anything other than fate, the dragon and gargoyle's appearance facilitated the first win against the Carrion. He had no desire to return after seeing the destruction wrought by the sorcerous stone DaVille had used. He closed his eyes to shut out many of the memories from that day.

A soft groan split the silence of the morning as Lady Mayrah stirred. The Brong warrior turned and knelt as quickly as his sore body would allow. He tried not to let his concern for her wound show on his face, but to show his usual calm, stoic self.

"You live," he said, finding it better phrased as a statement than a question.

Lady Mayrah's face contorted into a grimace in response. Each breath cost her dearly, that much Wan Du could see. She needed healing and he knew precious little about the region to assist. They needed to reach Fort Sondergaarde, decimated or not.

"I had … a dream," she murmured. "A nightmare. I saw Rochelle being destroyed … by wizards."

Frowning, Wan Du tried to refocus the conversation. "The Carrion destroyed our homes, both yours and mine. They are the true enemy."

Lady Mayrah didn't respond, but neither did she look happy.

"Come," he continued. "I will carry you. We must head south." Wan Du tried to keep his sentences short as it did not look like she would remain conscious for long.

"Sleep. I will protect you."

With having to carry the woman, he realized he would not be able to keep his weapon. He retrieved hers instead, a curved sword shorter than his arm with a blade no wider than his hand. In a different situation Wan Du would have found humor in it; he could do more damage with his own bare hands. Regardless, he would need something to hunt, skin, and clean with. He sheathed the sword and moved to pick up Lady Mayrah. A movement of her hand stopped him.

"Your god would not think less of you if you left me," she whispered.

They were the least likely words he thought a dying woman might say. But this was a brave woman and too proud to become a burden in a time of survival. Wan Du smiled; he respected the offer but they both knew he would not leave her, regardless of what *Serené* might think.

"I will not abandon you," he said and lifted her easily.

THE FORESTED LOWLANDS PROVIDED MUCH TO LOOK AT DURING the warm season. Unlike the land near Flaem, where desert sucked all of the life and color from the region, the southern stretch Wan Du trudged through was fed by the Red River. He blessed and cursed it, alike, because the water altered their overland course more than once.

Wan Du fought to keep his bearings, but the sheer number of different trees and bushes amazed the man. Before long, the forest would fall away as the land they sailed past rose to high cliffs, so he enjoyed the foliage view while he could. No timber grew near Fort Sondergaarde. Nothing would grow there at all, anymore, without men and women to plant it.

Lady Mayrah slipped back into unconsciousness and Wan Du fought back pangs of sympathy. He could not imagine the pain her body must be going through. Throughout all his battles, an arrow never breached Wan Du's torso. Scratched by many an axe and sword, yes, and fingers smashed by hammers. Spears and whips smashed and slapped against every part of his body — even a collection of needle art to indicate his status. None of it truly hurt, he reflected, especially in the face of the tragedy. Still, they had both survived — so far.

For her sake he avoided any towns they came near, just in case the Carrion they fought off remained nearby or hunted their trail. Food became a challenge, but his stealth improved much over what it used to be. Stalking game with a sword was the most difficult part. Luckily, the pond fish were neither fast nor smart.

On the second day, he fed Lady Mayrah some meat which she chewed on lazily, still seeming in a daze from the pain. Wan Du could not allow her strength to wane as she fought against the wound and possible infection.

He did everything he could to keep her wound clean and keep it from festering. Each time he looked at it the hue of the wounded flesh changed, waffling between an intense pink and a nearly black, bruised shade. As often as he remembered, Wan Du said a prayer of thanks to his deity. Lady Mayrah survived because of the Master of the Winds — Wan Du believed this to be the case regardless of what befell them as he carried her further south.

They saw no other Carrion patrols, and for that the large man was again glad. Though he saw tracks and trails where they might have passed, Wan Du found no bodies, living or dead, of the soldiers or their prey.

On the fourth day the forest broke; they had finally arrived at the plateaus he remembered viewing from Captain Satok's ship. It had mostly rushed by in their attempted escape from the white gargoyle.

The path dipped down at the edge of the tree line and curved into a narrow canyon signaling the beginning of the plateaus. Looking to the west, he saw nothing but the vast expanse of the Inner Sea of Mana, looking as calm and tranquil as Lady Mayrah's resting form.

As he viewed the way south from the forested hilltop he saw the canyons weave in and out of each other as far as the eye could see. Jutting up from the horizon past it all was a shape which could only be Fort Sondergaarde. Or what is left of it, Wan Du corrected.

It would take more than two days to reach the remains of the fortress, so Wan Du decided to halt and rest for the night. He had no idea what awaited them there, but he did not want to meet it with sore feet. The large man's hand instinctively patted Lady Mayrah's sword sheathed on his hip. Each time he looked at his recovering companion, his resolve strengthened.

"We will reach the fallen fortress before the new moon." Though her eyelids remained closed, Wan Du knew Lady Mayrah heard his words.

"How we go from there, I do not know," he finished under his breath.

Chapter 45 – *Xymon*

YMON GAZED NORTHWEST FROM THE ROOF OF THE GREAT Watchtower, the tallest of all built structures. The darkness that enveloped him swept in all directions as the wind caressed the circular surface. The General's dark eyes narrowed as he gazed as far as he could, but could see nothing, not even the mainland. Frustrated, the dark figure turned back toward the open stairwell and descended into the laboratory below.

All manner of sights and smells assailed the dark General as he reentered the immense room. Half a dozen emaciated grunts scattered about the chamber, made busy by the scores of experiments the Great One assigned to them. At his appearance, the Carrion raised their heads and blinked mutely — ready to receive instruction. Their heads cocked this way and that in fast, short movements like animals while their fingers twitched. Xymon waved his hand dismissively and the thin workers returned to their tasks with fervor.

He reached another stairwell across the chamber and climbed lower in the immense tower. He bypassed the throne room entirely and entered the menagerie to find more of the strangely nervous Carrion at work. With his damaged vocal cords the dark General could no longer scream, but his whisper was more than enough to carry throughout the chamber.

"Feraldus?" he called.

It took longer than the General wanted for the former beast master of Illiadora to appear from its dark closet. Feraldus' bent form leaned heavily upon both upon a walking staff and a thick wooden appendage attached in place of a leg. The uneven horns in the creature's head marked it as unwilling, and therefore unworthy, but its empty eyes held no resistance. The darkness had completely taken over the man formerly known as Feraldus and only an empty husk remained to do Zion's bidding.

"Yes, Lord Xymon?" came the hollow reply. Feraldus shuffled around a pile of severed body parts to present itself.

"Show me what you have accomplished," the dark General commanded.

With a bow that would have been too humble for any self-respecting creature, the decrepit Carrion hobbled to a wall of large cages held closed by thick iron bars and brick. The long, clawed fingers of its left hand stroked the bars lovingly as the creature grinned at its creation.

"The mounting beasts you have already seen," Feraldus mumbled, pointing to the rather docile beast behind the bars.

"Indeed," replied Xymon. "What else have you wrought to please our Master?"

"Ahh," the bent Carrion grinned as if pleased with itself. "We have made these."

The creature Feraldus moved further along the row of iron cages, pausing only to point out the occasional anomaly in its experiments. Xymon noted the flying soldiers previously promised remained incomplete. Sprawled across the floor of three of the cages were dozens of winged creatures — half-rotted with body parts in complete disarray. Xymon could kill without a second thought, but the cruelty of these experiments displeased even him.

"Here, you see," came the tortured voice of the overseer. "This shall please the Master."

Dark power permeated from the cell Feraldus came to and turned. Xymon could feel the emanation, but could see nothing as he peered inside. From within came the stirring of metal on metal, like the links of a chain moving against each other. Two eyes like pools of blood opened and stared out from the rear of the cage, as far away as they could possibly get from the entrance.

"Is this another fusion?" Xymon asked.

In response, Feraldus' breath quickened and it began touching its fingertips together in a nervous rhythm. Its eyes blinked in rapid succession and it seemed to be less hindered by the wooden leg. A slow grin spread across its face, but the overseer said nothing.

Impatient, Xymon dragged one of his claws across the bars to startle the caged creation into a reaction. The crimson eyes did not flinch or blink, but merely stared back unperturbed.

"I order you to approach," the dark General commanded in a fierce hiss.

With the speed of an uncoiling snake the red eyes rose in the air until they were even with Xymon's. He felt the dark presence as it approached and his sword began to hum in response. The General inadvertently took a step back, placing a hand on the hilt of Nightwind, as the creature came into view and wrapped its brown fingers around the metal bars of its prison.

For a moment, Xymon could not believe his eyes. Though its visage seemed only vaguely familiar, the talismans of Illiadora's highest station on the creature's sleeves were unmistakable. The features of Vortalus lived again, transformed into something entirely new — and unmistakably sinister.

"What ... is it?" asked Xymon.

Feraldus hopped from one foot to the other, seemingly ready to come out of its skin. "Our great and powerful Master has bid me to replace the failure Circulosa, yes? This I have done!"

The declaration did little to calm Xymon, as it did not address what was different about the creature behind the bars. The General had seen thousands upon thousands of Carrion soldiers transformed, even overseen many of the applications himself, but never felt this before. Shining garnet eyes sat in place of empty onyx and the ripples of power signaled something both foreign and dangerous. Xymon clutched the hilt of his sword more tightly, but the Vortalus creature did not move.

"You were right to ask if this was another fuse! Feraldus has recycled Circulosa to remake Vortalus!"

At the mention of the two names the creature's eyes flashed brighter and time seemed to slow. A low growl in the back of its throat became a shouted command word, then a blinding explosion. Without a chance to draw or defend, Xymon flew back against the bricks opposite the cell and slumped to the floor.

THE RAW POWER OF THE GREAT ONE'S VOICE WAS ENOUGH TO awaken Xymon from his slumber.

"I am unsure what displeases me more, Feraldus," growled Zion. "The creation that has escaped, or the damage it dealt to my irreplaceable General."

Xymon's ego soared as his dark eyes opened to see the ceiling of the throne room. The mural of Zion's army razing the world's structures greeted him like a sunset — the familiarity and closeness of his Master dissipated any fear, doubt, or pain.

"I am unharmed," he hissed.

Paying no heed to Xymon's response, Zion continued to berate the overseer to the point of lifting the brittle creature and tossing it toward the exit.

"I did what you have asked," Feraldus rasped from the floor. It struggled to rise, but at least one of its limbs skewed at an odd angle.

"You have no idea what you have done by creating this thing, Feraldus," said the Great Commander. "Know that if your actions alter the outcome of my prophecy; your torment shall be unending."

A shudder passed through the overseer's body before its bones snapped back into place.

Zion added, "Now leave my sight until the flying soldiers you promised are complete. Your creations shall have no food until that time — save each other."

Xymon smiled, knowing it would be in Feraldus' nature to protest the last statement of the Great One. Another test, he thought. The dark General stood, the black form of his cloak sliding around his body like thick liquid. His torso screamed in agony as the sore muscles moved, but pain meant they were alive. The General fought back a wince — this was not the place to show weakness.

Xymon watched Feraldus limp from the chamber, then turned just as Zion's dark eyes settled on him.

"I hope that your displeasure does not extend to my own carelessness, Master," Xymon hissed.

After a moment of consideration, the three-horned demigod waved the comment away as if swatting at a fly. "Think no more on it," replied Zion.

"Shall I pursue this Vortalus creature?"

"No, my dark General, I have other plans for you," Zion said. "Let the leader of the fallen Illiadora be for now."

"What is your bidding, Great One?" Xymon knelt in supplication and raised his upturned hands.

"The force that you left behind in the Mystian Empire is being beaten back without your leadership. It is my wish that you collect your followers and return to them." Zion pondered for a moment, then continued. "It is also my wish for you to slay someone while you are there, as that is what you do best."

Xymon's face nearly glowed behind his smooth black visor. "It will be as you command. Show me who you wish to die."

Power erupted from Zion's fingertips and coalesced into a solid form in the air between the two Carrion. After a few moments, Xymon made out the features of a woman with dark, straight hair and pale skin. The face that stared back from the apparition was vaguely familiar to Xymon, though he could not quite place it.

The dark General inclined his head in assent. "It will be as you command," he repeated.

CHAPTER 46 – *Wadam*

UR STRENGTH IS WHAT UNITES US. OUR GOD IS WHAT PRO-
tects us. Listen well, all of you; we have been chosen for a purpose
and that purpose is to unite our brothers under the banner of power
and strike back against these dark oppressors!"

Cardinal Wadam's impromptu speech was enough to inspire confidence in the six sailors who guarded him. It took little convincing on his part and, indeed, that was as it should be. The Divine Male, Garvon, had saved the priest and his young compatriots from a deep, watery grave less than a month past only to deliver them into the hands of their extremely hostile enemies. Even so, the priest and sailors overpowered the wretched humanoids to fight on. Wadam attributed it to nothing less than the hand of Myst.

After responding with a shout to the speech, the sixth one that day, the sailors-turned-zealots unleashed a furious barrage of stones and swings of their cudgels. They tore Carrion flesh asunder and pushed their bodies past the point of exhaustion yet again. Wadam's defenders did not even pause until the last grunt was crushed to a black and brown pulp.

Wonderful, he thought. *What could be more of a sign from the heavens than our continued success attempting to reach home?*

"Pray that Myst-Garvon still stands," the large man answered aloud.

He rubbed his hands together and surveyed the latest skirmish. Ten more Carrion lay dead and his six warriors had naught but scratches and fatigue. A mere patrol squad, it seemed, watching the crossing near the Baerow Straits. Myst wished them to cleanse the continent — there could be no other explanation.

"We're nearly home," he declared. After a brief rest, the seven continued westward with Wadam confidently in the lead.

"Impossible," Wadam breathed. His knees slapped the still-moist foundation of Myst-Garvon and his palms reached into the rubble of his most sacred treasure. As Wadam wept, he felt a document shift inside his robe and he snatched at the parchment before it fell to the wet earth.

The wave must have changed how far the tide comes, he thought. One of the sailors hypothesized as such back when they landed their small boat, but Wadam still held faith he would arrive home and all would be intact. He closed his eyes as the tragic reality sunk in like a thousand needles against his flesh. The priest began to squeeze the parchment in his fists before he even realized what he was doing.

His curiosity piqued upon realizing the parchment he carried was not even one of his own. The small handwriting on the visible portion — now a bit crumpled — looked round and delicate. He searched his memory for recognition of the document and realized it could only be one thing.

The prophecy.

The founding words of the Orders echoed in his mind. *A woman's station is the Mouthpiece of God, the scion of communication* — and, in Wadam's opinion, the holder of all of the keys.

230 ~ *Todd Newton*

"No more," he murmured. In one swift motion, the priest tore the parchment in two. Wadam lifted one of the halves to eye level and paused to take a breath before he continued. "If usurpation is what it will take for this land to survive, so be it."

With his orator's intonation, Wadam announced, "From this day forth, Myst shall speak through me."

Then, without another thought, the priest shoved the end of the parchment into his mouth and bit down. It was the first time Wadam truly tasted power.

CHAPTER 47 – *Starka*

SLEEP ELUDED STARKA ALL THROUGH THE NIGHT, WHICH, she had learned, was not necessarily altogether bad. The length and breadth of DaVille's story was impressive, but his words had not been comforting. Nor were they meant to be, she admitted dryly.

As an officer of the Carrion army, he had killed. A soldier through and through, after donning the horns he became something more. Though his memory remained unsure, his past came alive in his dreams. Or rather, she thought, his nightmares.

He had told her all he remembered of himself in the long hours of their conversation. Villages she did not know, ones he said wouldn't have appeared on her maps, had been preyed upon in the dead of night. The men had all been transformed into the first Carrion soldiers.

DaVille knew and had been close to Zion, the Great Master of the black army, but could recall very little about the creature. In truth, the entirety of his story was so disjointed Starka was not sure if she believed it all. When he bowed his head and showed her the scars where the horns had been removed, Starka's heart nearly stopped.

"I should not have survived." Those were the words he used to discuss his death. Of all the things he could not remember, the circumstances and events leading up to the removal of his horns eluded him most. Pain was all he could remember. More pain than any words could describe.

Starka's heart and stomach tied each other in a knot during the recounting of his tale and this feeling continued to keep her awake. Frustrated, she left her bedcovers and dressed for the chill night. High above, the moon grinned at her predicament. At the end of his grisly account, DaVille offered her a choice.

"If you wish to continue with the caravan to Travell, I will not stop you."

Even now, hours later, she felt tested by his words. Her brain fought back and forth as to whether his tone implied that he wanted her to stay or the opposite. DaVille had made no gesture to touch her during or after his story; perhaps he knew he could provide no consolation for the truth of his past.

As she looked out over the dry darkness, Starka wondered where to find Adamis. After leaving DaVille, she thought to confront him again and question his motives. She would not betray DaVille's past, or her promise, but she wanted to know more about how Adamis accumulated his own information. Yet, he vanished much like Kismet. The wagons still had not moved since the assault and the Amber Hordsemen did not return. Starka doubted they would. As DaVille spitefully replied to those who inquired, "They got what they came for."

Still, Starka couldn't decide whether their actions were outright criminal or whether they were borne from their own need. Since the cargo of swords they carried away did not belong to her, the girl was removed from the responsibility for it. DaVille didn't have the luxury she did, having lost quite a bit already.

Stop it, she told herself, *he didn't tell you his story to inspire your sympathy for him.* Shivering, Starka pulled her wrap tighter against the night air and tried to redirect her thoughts.

Her worries for Kismet came creeping back. What would happen to the girl now, without her father? She had really latched onto Starka during their northern trek and it was going to be difficult parting, if that was what she ultimately decided.

If you wish to continue with the caravan to Travell, I will not stop you.

Could she really leave DaVille and stay with these friendly people? Trade danger for laughter?

Thoughts of endless sunny days spent braiding hair and sharing stories around the fire warmed Starka's heart for a moment, and she did not stop them. Her existence before the prophecy might have been a disgrace, but at the very least it made sense to her and was sustainable. Out here in the wilderness things became a mystery to be unraveled.

DaVille's past and her future seemed to be linked, somehow, and she knew the thread would not be easily broken. The consequences of abandoning her responsibility to her own visions would ultimately end in death when the Carrion trampled Travell, but couldn't she be happy until then?

᪣

"Starka?" a small voice ventured.

Turning to face the girl, Starka found she barely recognized her young friend. Kismet's face looked darkened and swollen with grief, her cheeks and eyes sunken from lack of food. She had dried blood trails from slashes on her arms and the moonlight made it difficult to tell how old the blood was or if it belonged to Kismet at all.

When words failed her, Starka merely knelt and opened her arms to embrace the girl. She willed all of her warmth and comfort to pass through the contact. After a moment, her memory produced a familiar prayer.

"I know you grieve," she repeated, "but the sun rises tomorrow. May the grace of the Divine bless you with peace."

Before long, the girl dropped to sleep in her arms. Starka lifted the diminished weight of her body and gently placed Kismet in her own abandoned bedroll. Standing and turning back to the empty night, she wiped a tear from her eye before noticing a second visitor.

"Your thoughts draw me, girl," came the rasping whisper. The hooded form of Adamis stood close to where Kismet appeared. Taken aback by the words, Starka could not reply right away. The sorcerer couldn't possibly read her mind, could he?

"Did you find your answers?" he asked, his tone derisive as if he already knew the answer.

Starka narrowed her eyes at the enigmatic man and folded her arms defensively, refusing to answer. Many retorts went through her mind, but the prayer she voiced moments before still hung on her lips. Peace, she reminded herself, otherwise Adamis' challenges would prompt her to open doors she could not close. Sorcerer or not, the man was dangerous, and Starka now realized that even men who saved your life were not always truthful.

"I know less of you than I do of him," she stated flatly, trying to mimic DaVille's confidence, "and I trust you none at all."

"It is ever our fate to be shunned," said the man. While Adamis spoke, his hands parted and he issued a slight bow. Starka wasn't sure if he described his heritage, profession, or prophetic seers in general with his statement. Before she could ask him to clarify, he spoke again.

"How will your friend feel when you abandon her?" asked Adamis. "You are her connection to the world now."

Every question he asked seemed planned to put Starka on her heels. After so many, she knew it to be intentional.

"I owe you nothing," she countered. "If you cared so much …"

"On the contrary," Adamis cut in, "have you forgotten that I saved your life? Doesn't that entitle me to your traveling company as it has with your man?"

Starka dropped her arms and stepped toward Adamis. Again he accused her of belonging to DaVille. Again he plucked her strings, and the girl could not take it for much longer. She had never met anyone so invasive; not even Wadam riled her this badly in all of their ill-tempered "discussions."

To her surprise, the sorcerer retreated a step and raised his arms again. Apparently, DaVille rubbed off on her more than Starka thought. The realization was not comforting.

"My apologies. I meant no disrespect," said the wizard. "I came only to talk briefly before I depart."

"Depart?" she echoed.

The hooded man nodded. "I seek to raise an army in Travell and strike back at the Carrion."

"What kind of army do you think you'll find there?" asked DaVille from the night. The sound of his voice brought a strange comfort to Starka, but his sudden appearance surprised her. Neither of them had heard the man approach, and the girl wondered if he intended it this way. Adamis paused, pointedly refusing to address the question directly.

"I once thought as you do, wizard. 'Rally the displaced and downtrodden'; is that your plan?" He scoffed. "There are no soldiers in Travell; only defeated men. The soldiers have all died already, or worse."

Starka walked further away from Kismet, hoping to take the conversation with her and allow the girl to sleep. The two men seemed born only to argue as of late.

"Soldiers are not what I seek," replied Adamis. "Sorcerers are."

This is a curious change, thought Starka; the hooded wizard is actually providing information.

"Save your effort …"

"And leave the fighting to you?" Adamis challenged. "Are you going to destroy the Carrion alone?"

When she saw DaVille's fists clench, Starka whispered his name and put a hand on his shoulder. He noticeably relaxed, but his words became no less frightening.

"If I must, I will," he said, "but I don't recall anyone asking for your assistance in the first place."

"The world cries for my assistance! This plague that you helped to unleash on us does not allow for survivors." His words dripped with venom, and Starka stifled a gasp. Had Adamis heard their conversation, or had he always known what DaVille was?

"None of our hands are clean," retorted DaVille. "Are they, wizard?"

"What do you mean, DaVille?" she asked.

"Ask him why he was cast out of Flaem," said the warrior. "Ask him why he is no longer welcome on the Council of Elders. Ask him if the stories are true."

"What stories? How do you know of this?" she asked. Starka could no longer keep the fear from her voice. Everyone around her seemed capable of more dishonesty and destruction than she thought possible. Her confidence in other human beings dwindled with each new person she met.

With a quick motion, Adamis removed his hood. His head blazed with flame and lit up the surrounding area of the camp. "Enough," he commanded. "Everything you have heard is true. I am the one who provided the means to destroy Rochelle. I am the one who unleashed Meteor. For breaking the neutrality, I am an outcast. How was I to know it would lead to this?"

Though his clear voice spoke with authority, Starka could not help the questions that came spewing from her lips. The memories of the devastated Lady Mayrah and her homeland were owed more than this.

"You seem to know everything else, though, don't you?" she cried. "How could you contribute to the deaths of so many innocent people?"

The fire engulfing Adamis seemed to falter for a moment as he felt the force of her words. All sympathy for the man drained away to nothing and the memories of floating, charred bodies and broken land replaced it.

"My reasons are my own. Rarely can one control what others do with their creation." At his last words Adamis' eyes shimmered brightly, then returned to their usual glow. For some reason, his words made Starka wonder about how things were faring back home, but she did not allow herself to dwell on it.

DaVille turned and met her eyes with a fierce look. It seemed Adamis' words had struck him also.

"I've made arrangements to leave in the morning," said her companion. "Make your choice and meet me at our wagon before dawn." At that, he turned and marched away.

When Starka looked around she found Adamis, too, had gone. She retreated to the sleeping form of Kismet and knelt beside the girl. "Do I truly have a choice?" she asked the night. A sad moan escaped Kismet's lips as the girl stirred.

"Can't sleep?" she asked.

"It is impossible with all this arguing," Kismet replied with a yawn. Again, the girl's accent brought a smile to Starka's lips. After a pause, Kismet asked, "Are you truly leaving me?"

Starka took her young friend's hand and whispered, "I must."

"Because of this prophecy? Is your man a part of this?"

"No," she replied, a bit too quickly. "Perhaps. I don't know. I don't know what to think of him anymore. I thought if I asked him for the truth I'd have fewer questions than before, not more of them."

Kismet yawned again and smiled. The girl couldn't understand how complicated — or dangerous — things really were.

"As my father used to say, 'love conquers all,' and I think it is rather romantic. How I wish I could come with you," she said.

"No, you don't," Starka insisted.

Her friend shrugged and adjusted the blankets, leaving only her head visible. "Enough of this. I must sleep and you must go, but tell me a story in parting. What do you think happened to my father after ..."

Kismet did not have to complete the sentence. Starka recalled the tale from the Holy Book and hoped it would comfort the girl enough to sleep.

"We believe that our Divine Male and Female, Garvon and Alsher, welcome the dead into their arms. To those who have lived valuable lives in service to others and the Great Cause, eternal happiness is granted in the Garden of Paradise.

"The sun never sets there, and its splendor cannot be matched by all the gold and jewels in the world. There the dead walk and tend to the growth while they look down fondly on their children and grandchildren, until those generations, too, join them to bask in the Creator's glory."

Before Starka finished her story Kismet had fallen into a deep sleep. Not wanting to leave her friend any sooner than she had to, Starka laid her head down next to the girl to catch some rest herself.

Starka's dreams were filled with the black horns and carnage of DaVille's memories, and she woke well before dawn's glow touched the horizon. With no desire to write any of it down, Starka collected her meager supplies and bid Kismet a silent and final kiss farewell.

Full of resolve, Starka marched to the wagon to join DaVille.

CHAPTER 48 – *Cairos*

WELL, THIS IS INTERESTING." CAIROS SPOKE MOSTLY TO HIM-self, but saw Fabfast nod along in astounded agreement. Upon seeing the change in the landscape, he realized the reason for the change in the magical currents.

As difficult as it was to believe, the fallout from the stone's blast created a null zone, a place of no magic. As he imagined it, the current of magic energy flowed around the blast radius rather than through it. Of course, he couldn't actually see the zone, but he felt it as he grew closer.

Null zones were mentioned in few of the scholarly tomes of Illiadora, but always written about with much fear and punctuated with the thought, *What if the whole of the world were like this?* Cairos shuddered at the prospect.

He pored over the possible causes in his mind. Historical study of the explosive stone clusters never yielded an aberration of this kind. Cairos considered the sword of the Carrion Lieutenant he had defeated in the now-exposed tunnels leading into the red dragon's cave. The magic swallowing blade had swallowed so much power that the beast could barely lift it, and to Cairos' knowledge, that power had not been safely discharged. He cringed, for if the sword had been destroyed then Gabumon's staff might have met the same fate.

Fabfast probed the border of the null zone with his finger as a child might poke his older sibling. Upon closer inspection, Cairos saw a visible boundary caused by the blast: the sandy soil within the radius darkened slightly in hue. This has to be fairly confusing to the boy, Cairos thought, as he's only just been newly-introduced to his own magical power.

"You can stay here and wait for me, if you like. There is no telling what strangeness has been drawn to this place."

The young protégé shook his head loyally. "I can fight," he stated simply.

"You certainly know how, as you have shown me, but you have no sword or shortstaff with which to do so," replied Cairos. "Besides, you're much too valuable."

Fabfast's expression lowered as he seemed to feel a bit ashamed. Cairos had dragged the boy through so much just to be his apprentice; the last thing he needed was to break the boy's heart.

"But I suppose a weapon is why were here, isn't it?"

The familiar smile returned as Fabfast nodded once with finality.

Cairos pondered their destination and their route for a moment. The lair of the dragon they found was half-exposed by the blast, but littered with piles of rock covered in the melted sheen of other, less hardy, stone. The *scythorsont* had really done a large amount of damage to the landscape and Cairos was saddened thinking it could not be repaired by magic. The snobbish Flaem Elders would probably leave it this way until it could, he thought darkly.

Trying to navigate the unpredictable slope of the crater and gain access to one of the many cave entrances pock-marking it seemed an unnecessary challenge. Aware the trip would welcome the return of more unpleasant memories, Cairos beckoned Fabfast to follow him to the entrance of the Tombs.

The simple stone doorway lay well outside the null zone, which brightened Cairos' spirits a bit. He recognized the gentle slope of the mound and recalled the same angle of descent shortly past the entrance. The master allowed Fabfast a few moments to study the tomb's entrance before imparting its secret.

"Tell no one of this," he said firmly. Speaking a command word to Tera, the Pillar of Life, Cairos breathed a flame into being in his hand. He held the flame out in offering and then placed his hand against the burned symbol on the stone door.

At first nothing happened and Cairos began to wonder if the blast had actually defeated the magic here as well. Finally, the large stone began to move. It was perfectly dark inside and Fabfast turned to him, perplexed, after gazing in.

"It's an effect of the magic. You won't be able to see anything until you enter. Let me go first, just in case."

Terasont in hand, Cairos stepped into the engulfing darkness of the Tombs of the Burning Men. Mere heartbeats after Fabfast followed, the stone drew itself closed at their backs. The somber silence of the chamber reminded Cairos of its purpose and its residents. Gabumon may not have found his final resting place inside one of the comfortable sarcophagi, but this was just as much his tomb as theirs. He bade Fabfast to practice his illumination magic to show the way through.

Familiar intersections and passageways slipped by as the pair of wizards descended into the Tombs. Cairos ignored the urge to touch the smooth walls and continued following his apprentice until they came to an unfamiliar patch. He remembered causing the cave-in to defeat the Carrion officer, but the dirt of the cave had been cleared by a magical hand. Must have been Circulosa, he thought.

The corpse of the officer was nowhere in sight for which Cairos gave thanks to Urrel, the Pillar of Fate, but neither was the Lieutenant's enchanted blade. As he walked through the passage, the wizard felt the currents pushing against him and halted.

"By the Nine," he cursed, "the zone extends even this deep."

"Should we proceed, Master?"

Cairos considered it for a moment before replying. "I'd rather we found a different way, if we could."

Turning back, they took a separate branch of the tunnel that led in a curving path parallel to the null zone. Soon, it became apparent the blast had not only shifted the rock aboveground, but it also altered the caverns in which they stood. Nowhere was this more apparent than where their small passage opened to a much wider cavern. Cairos knew without even glancing around that they reached what remained of the red dragon's lair.

A sound echoed from inside the large cave that sounded vaguely like a voice. Cairos pulled Fabfast to the side of the entrance and whispered a blessing of Acton, the Pillar of Speech. Carrion words filled his ears as his hand clenched around the blue stone.

"Let's get these eggs and get out of here," one said. "This place makes my skin crawl." These words brought jeering from at least two other beasts, as well as grunts of agreement.

"Stay here," Cairos whispered to his apprentice.

Rounding the corner of the lair's entrance, Cairos rushed forward and raised his battlestaff like a javelin. He shouted the words of a lightning spell and made to launch the weapon into the air. Just before he let go of the staff, Cairos attempted to halt and nearly tripped over his own feet. His spell chant went unanswered.

Nothing happened at all. Nothing, except the heads of half a dozen Carrion grunts turned his way.

CHAPTER 49 - CAIROS

LL SIX OF THE BEASTS WERE CONFUSED AND SURPRISED by Cairos' entrance, but did not have a chance to recover before his melee instincts took over. He had dealt with a loss of magical advantage in these very tunnels and was not going to let a few soldiers do him in. The wizard ran forward again, charging the nearest Carrion and burying his staff in its forehead with a quick overhead stroke. It fell, gurgling, as the other five retreated a step to regroup.

To Cairos, these Carrion did not seem as menacing as the usual ones. They were still the leather-skinned horrors with claws, teeth, and shiny black horns protruding from their heads, but not armed the same as the ones who had sacked Illiadora. Neither did they exhibit the fervor of the army outside Flaem.

None of the five still standing held any sort of weapon at all, just odd satchels. Cairos spun his staff in the air and drove it against the chest of one of the soldiers, knocking it flat to the ground, breaking its sternum. He turned just in time to deflect a clumsy swipe from a clawed hand while the final two Carrion ran for the exit passage.

He struck out with a kick to hit the closest soldier's knee and knock it backward with a pop. Cairos shouted to Fabfast that two of the beasts were coming his way, but the apprentice had already revealed himself. Wielding what looked to be shafts of lightning in each hand, Fabfast made quick work of the fleeing grunts.

Cairos beamed with pride; not only had the boy mastered a few spells, but mixed them well with his combat styles. An unexpected development, but not at all negative. As the older wizard finished off the two Carrion he had disabled, the apprentice came to his side.

"Are you out of your mind?" Cairos chastised the apprentice despite being impressed by his work.

"I just wanted to help," the teenager said. "They don't frighten me." Fabfast wiped his hands against his tunic as if filthy from the fight. His eyes remained downcast, but as Cairos placed a forgiving hand on the boy's shoulder, he smiled.

"You fought well," praised Cairos.

"Did I hear them talking about eggs, Master?"

Nodding, Cairos looked around the large chamber. "It's possible there are some dragonling eggs down here. We found a dragon here before."

The boy, uneducated as he was, did not show the slightest bit of fear at the mention of the large beast. Of course, Cairos thought, he had not seen its rampage on the battlefield.

"Pardon my ignorance, Master, but what is a dragonling?"

Cairos pondered the best way to explain it to the boy for a moment. "You have seen butterflies, correct?" he asked. "Did you know that they must cocoon and change their form from a worm to become so?"

The apprentice nodded.

"It is similar with dragons. Dragonlings hatch from the eggs and only some of them will survive the hibernation deep inside a cavern where they change into the much larger creatures called dragons. Studies say the process takes somewhere near one hundred years, hence why we don't see many dragons in our lifetime."

"Why would the Carrion be interested in their eggs?"

"Good question, my apprentice, but we're not going to find out just standing here." The older wizard spun away. "Come, let's find what we came for."

CAIROS STEPPED FURTHER INTO THE NULL ZONE AND SWEPT THE width of the lair with his eyes. The changes made by the explosion gave the entire place an unfamiliar feeling and the lack of an aura gave Cairos a sense of numbness every time he breathed in. He replayed the snippets of the Carrion's conversation in his mind and began to wonder whether these dispatched ones might have been sorcerers once. Their lack of weapons remained suspicious.

"Fabfast, let's not stick around any longer than we have to. Search for a longstaff encased in metal. If you find it, give a shout, but do not touch it."

The boy wandered away, scanning the floor intently. Cairos watched him for a moment and had to stifle a laugh when Fabfast blanched upon looking up toward the ceiling. The lair was immense; even larger than Cairos remembered from being trapped in it previously. A pity he hadn't had the chance to explore it fully before the blast of the *scythorsont* altered it. Hopes of treasure dwindled. Columns of volcanic rock had been toppled everywhere, still, more than enough moonlight filtered in through the holes above.

"The sky does not look any further away," he whispered.

Cairos quickly decided he didn't like being inside the null zone's border. He couldn't see the difference in the air, but every fiber of his being echoed with the silence of it. If the entire world were like this, he would certainly go mad. Unbidden, thoughts of what would happen to the world if the Carrion prevailed flooded his mind. He fought back the dismal possibilities, but found it a losing battle. Whatever happened, he would have to stop them — the wizard owed at least that much to Gabumon and the rest of his fallen comrades.

Wrapped in his mind's trappings, it took Cairos a moment to realize his feet had taken him much deeper into the null zone than he wanted to go. Turning back the way he came, or thought he came, Cairos found he could no longer see Fabfast. The thick darkness closed in around him.

He took a few deep breaths to calm himself, but stemming the paranoia proved difficult. This is silly, Cairos told himself, but the words did not carry as much weight as they should have. Still, he moved from one pile of stone rubble to another, nervously searching the cavern.

Unlike the lair where he happened upon Gabumon, this den seemed completely devoid of previous occupants. Aside from the Carrion they dispatched, Cairos saw no other signs of life. This was odd, even for a dragon's lair, but not if he and the deceased wizard had been the first ones to visit. Good, Cairos thought, keep your thoughts steady and focused.

In the dark, the remaining stones in the columns seemed to shimmer. The effect unsettled him, but Cairos wondered whether the null zone had eradicated magical force within its area or simply dispersed it like dust in the wind. He thought again of the libraries at Illiadora and their few volumes on the subject, wondering briefly if this particular zone would ever be researched. To his knowledge every wizard in the city had been killed by the invading Carrion, but wasn't it possible some escaped?

Cairos continued to sweep the lair while lost in thought. The Elders of Flaem denied all of his requests to utilize their oracle stones regardless of his intent. Cairos scoffed at the memory, as if he would have tainted their precious stones. The wizard lifted a balled fist to the ceiling and shook it in the only direction he knew the city to be. It was then he heard a shout echo through the enormous chamber.

"Master! Come quickly! I have found it!"

Bringing his fist down triumphantly, Cairos turned and rushed back toward the apprentice's voice. He had to call to Fabfast more than once to find the boy again, but ultimately he arrived in sight of the kneeling apprentice.

"Don't touch the staff," repeated Cairos.

"I have not touched it," said the boy without rising.

Cairos could barely believe his eyes. Embedded within the stone floor was the longstaff of Gabumon, just as he remembered it. The weapon jutted out at an odd angle and Fabfast's position made Cairos curious, just for a moment, whether he had found it by tripping over it. He smiled.

"How are we going to get it out, Master?" asked Fabfast.

The amusement on Cairos' face vanished. Embedded in solid stone and inside of the null zone, it wasn't likely they would be able to extricate the staff. After Cairos donned a pair of simple wool gloves, he knelt to give the weapon a gentle pull. As expected, the staff would not budge. With the length of the weapon being taller than him and the amount equal to his height buried, it would be impossible to remove without magic.

Cairos tapped the butt of his staff against the stone and whispered a few words to Valesh, but the null zone swallowed them upon leaving his lips — similar to the effect of the Carrion officer's blade.

"Damn damn damn!" He stomped away and back again, racking his brain for some method to dig through the stone. "I'm a wizard, not a blasted engineer!"

Fabfast stayed silent and contemplative, but the older wizard knew the boy could offer no solution to this puzzle. Cairos took another deep breath and removed his gloves. He couldn't help but see the humor in the situation.

"This would be our luck, wouldn't it, Fabfast?"

"Master?" the apprentice asked, raising an eyebrow.

"Come on," he replied, "let's get out of this cursed null zone and find an ale house. This one is too tough to solve with an empty stomach and a dry mind."

CHAPTER 50 – *Xymon*

VERY HALLWAY OF THE CATHEDRAL OF MYST-ALSHER looks the same, Xymon mused. How anything so legendary could be so plain on the inside seemed humorous to him, yet he had to admit its mazelike passages created a challenge to reaching his target. Sleepy page boys patrolled here and there holding single tapers, their feet still wrapped in bed slippers and useless daggers slung at their hips. The fact that they were not watching for him made it easier to slip past them, but the urge to stop their frightened hearts was almost too much to resist.

Since the dark General returned to the northwestern continent he learned of all of the changes that had taken place. The failure Circulosa left in his wake wiped out nearly all of the soldiers Xymon left in wait — in addition to most of the structures along the coastline. His eyes were glad they could no longer look upon the golden phallus of Myst-Garvon. The building had washed out to sea along with many of its worshippers. It cooled Xymon's heart to think of that portion — one moment to be kneeling in supplication and the next to have the roof collapse on your head in a torrential flood. Double-edged swords were bittersweet that way.

Focusing back on his task, Xymon slinked along another of the dim passageways. All residents of the Female Cathedral were on alert for the former residents of the Male Cathedral, and the civil war created the perfect conditions for his assignment. He even waited a few days for tensions to heat up because of the efforts of the portly Cardinal Wadam, now calling himself the Mouth of Myst. It was ludicrous, but the simple-minded zealots of the subcontinent swallowed every word he said. Amidst all of the rioting, Xymon slipped into the cathedral without taking even one life. Another double-edge, the General thought.

The sensation of familiarity still gnawed at Xymon upon his return, and it could no longer be ignored inside the cathedral. Hearing a murmur from nearby, he cast off the distraction and backed into a recessed side chamber. Two attendants carried silver trays with lidded foodstuffs smelling of fish and greens. Two lightly-armored zealot soldiers followed close behind as escorts. He slipped in close behind the escorts and followed.

The party spoke to each other in hushed tones and shared their worries about the conflict outside the doors of the cathedral, all agreeing that only prayer could save them now. One of the zealots uncharacteristically asked how their benevolent and loving deity could let this happen and the procession came to an abrupt halt.

"Waness, how could you possibly pose such a question? This must be a test of our faith in the Divine Female and we must bear it as we have borne such things for hundreds of years." A stout woman holding a tray of the food seemed ready to shove it in the zealot's face. Her eyes flared and she breathed hotly through her nostrils.

The man's hands parted in a sign of surrender, but the other zealot spoke up. "Show grace, Fordha. You know his father has sided with the Wadamites." He spat the last word as a curse.

"Why have they taken to calling themselves that?" the other tray carrier offered, a weak attempt to alter the course of the conversation.

"Because it gives glory to Wadam, should they prevail," said Waness.

"But glory belongs to Myst, for He alone is worthy."

Xymon quickly grew sick of their words, as he had heard nothing but such dissent since his arrival. The dark General briefly considered decapitating them all with a single swipe of Nightwind, but his patience won out. These fools would lead him to his goal as soon as they began walking again. Waness looked about suspiciously as if the zealot sensed his murderous intent, but did not raise an alarm.

"You know where my faith lies, Fordha, but these times are dark and the pieces of the prophecy that I have heard only herald darker days ahead. For us and the world."

"Oh, the world can die and be damned," responded Fordha. "Those unsaved wretches will perish and burn one way or another."

The other maiden shushed her lightly, as her tone had grown too loud for the time of night. Xymon fought the urge to tap his foot against the smooth marble floor.

Fordha cleared her throat to calm herself. "Please forgive me, O Alsher, for I spoke too hastily." The large woman closed her eyes for a moment and her lips moved in silence.

"Our shift at the wall begins at the next bell, ladies. We must get the evening meal to the Seeress before then or you will be navigating the darkness alone."

"That's all well and good, Waness, but from what I hear we can take as long as we like. The old woman's gone a bit batty since Wadam returned without Starka ..."

The mention of the name caused a shooting pain to ripple through Xymon's head. The memory of Flaem and the *scythorsont* flooded his vision and the light from the girl who interrupted his collection of the fourth stone chimed his recognition. *Starka.*

"Are we still meeting in the bell tower later?"

The unnamed zealot ran a lecherous hand down Fordha's arm and Xymon felt a shudder pass through his body at the implication.

"Not if we don't deliver this food, eh?" She muttered impatiently, shaking her head. The second tray bearer turned and continued down the hallway forcing her companions to follow.

♦♦

THEY ARRIVED AT A LARGE DOUBLE-DOORWAY THAT XYMON WAS surprised he had not noticed before. Its intricate engraving of two large eyes was disconcerting — even without the dancing gleam laid on them by nearby sconces.

It is interesting that these people do not believe in the magic of the Pillars, Xymon reflected, as they seem to take every effort to make things seem enchanted. He waited as the men and women entered the chamber and watched them exit, each in separate directions. For a moment he was curious as to why they required escorts only when they carried food. The Seeress must be afraid of poison, he mused. Pleasant memories of his poison taking the lives of every human in Brong brought a smile to the lips behind his mask.

As he approached the doorway, Xymon continued the smile. If this were any easier, she would already be dead, he thought. The assassin only needed to open the portal a crack to slip inside. He found the chamber just as dim on the inside as the halls. A stand of candles had been lit on a table across the room near the only large window, but half had burned down to nearly nothing. The bed stood unused in the corner furthest from the door and ornate carpets spanned the length of the large room.

Xymon sensed only one presence inside and edged his way around the perimeter to reach it. The Seeress sat reclined on a cushioned bench against the windowsill staring out into the darkness of the night. The shades and curtains were thrown aside and the chill northern breeze crept in unabated. It almost seemed as if she welcomed in the darkness. A glance at her untouched food confirmed what the attendants said earlier; a pile of nine trays stood on the floor next to untouched glass goblets full of dark wine.

The sound of Elestia's voice startled him.

"Have you come to kill me, then?" she asked, a note of sadness in her otherwise strong voice.

The General's eyes went wide behind his mask. His stalking footfalls made as little noise as usual sneaking into the chamber. He wondered how she noticed him while facing the window.

"I see many more things these days," she answered, as if reading his mind. The aged woman turned her head slightly to cast a voided glance on Xymon's shadowed form, but the Seeress had no eyes.

Caught but not defeated, Xymon slowly drew his blade. As he poised to strike, she stopped him with a word.

"Fandur?"

A screaming memory assaulted his mind. Warmth. Light. Love. Home. *Starka*. The General dropped his sword to the carpet and brought his hands to his head as his horns began to shake against his skull. He hissed through the pain and nearly dropped to a knee, but fought against the tide of agony. With effort, Xymon retreated a step and regained his balance.

"I know it is you," said Elestia. "Fitting, isn't it? That you would come to slay me." Xymon had no response. It took all his strength to fight against the floodtide of visions in his mind.

"I will not fight you, Fandur. Not that I could, in my state." Again, the sound of the name reverberated through him like a large bell had been rung inside the chamber. "Alsher has been kind, blinding me to the horror that the world has turned our faith into. I have seen enough to know my time has come, but give me just one last moment, for I must choose my successor."

She took his silence and inaction as assent and stood, groping for the nearby table. A pen stood in an inkpot and a piece of parchment lay unrolled next to it. Xymon was not close enough to read the words but watched the broad, calligraphic strokes of a name.

s — The dark General fought to regain his bearings.

t — He clenched and unclenched his hands.

a — He knelt, but only to retrieve Nightwind.

R — The sword hummed in his hand, anticipating the kill.

k — Xymon raised his arm for the decapitating strike.

a —

The blow landed, spilling the blood of the Seeress across the parchment just below the name she had written. The General stood victorious over his kill before turning back to the door of the chamber. As Xymon slipped out, he silently wished never to hear his former name again.

CHAPTER 51 – *Cairos*

FTER SIX ROUNDS OF STRONG, DARK ALE, FABFAST FINALLY seemed to loosen up. Cairos felt the tension in his shoulders lifting, but the uneasiness he'd acquired from the null zone had not yet abated. He could once again perform anything in his magical repertoire, yet things still did not feel quite right. No one in Flaem had noticed them as Cairos and the boy had walked the streets and found a quiet tavern. Of course, Cairos mused, *I just might be used to the disdain of the people of the city.*

As a local drinking song began to sound throughout the common room, Fabfast moved to join the handful of crooning drunkards. With a quick hand on his arm, Cairos pulled the boy back down into his chair, nearly upsetting the table in the process. In between hiccups, Fabfast inquired what had revived his master's sour mood.

"We don't need attention. We need a plan." Cairos couldn't state it any more plainly than that.

He knew what he wanted to do. If he had been alone the choice would have been simple: fly northwest and find the staff of Circulosa. Knowing now how easy it was to sense the proximity of the null zone, he should be able to find another even in the middle of the sea. If it sat underneath a null zone, the staff would be difficult to procure indeed. Cairos needed to know before looking for it in earnest and he needed to have the boy's help.

It had been weeks since he had last peered into an oracle stone, but Cairos hoped the good grace of Urrel still held. If he couldn't find the staff on his own, Urrel and a good oracle stone would be his only hopes. Which meant he and Fabfast would have to leave Flaem sooner or later.

Things seemed to have calmed down since he had met and trained the apprentice. The Carrion in the lair had been the first Cairos had seen since the explosion of the *scythorsont*. That almost bothered him, but the ale kept him from worrying too much for the moment. The wizard was still curious what they had been doing in the cavern, but he had to set that aside as well.

Sobering, Cairos knew the time had come for the boy to sink or swim. Fabfast's unwieldy aerodynamic abilities would need to be corrected or Cairos would simply have to leave him in the city until he returned. He grinned, knowing that the alcohol in the boy's stomach would give him the edge against fear that was all he should need. Of course, Cairos thought wryly, it could also prevent him from remembering in the morning.

Dropping a coin on the table, Cairos rose to leave the establishment and drew his stumbling charge with him. The street was nearly empty as the hour was late, but the enchanted torches along both sides gave enough light to walk by.

Navigating through Flaem at night was a greater task than Cairos remembered. At large intersections, groups of late night temple-goers congregated and chanted to their patron Pillar's Avatar, hoping for something special to happen. They paid no heed to two inebriated men shambling by, but sometimes the crowds were so large that Cairos had to step in between people and make sure Fabfast did not get distracted and lost. The wizard's hazy senses led them on a meandering route toward the eastern gate and through the guard station just inside it. With tired legs the pair ultimately arrived in the soft, sandy dunes in the east outskirts of the city.

Cairos turned to Fabfast and forced the boy to make eye contact with him.

"Tonight you will learn to fly."

"But Master," he stammered, "I fall."

Cairos shook his head. "Just try hovering a few feet. If you fall, it will not hurt like it did before."

Fabfast absently rubbed his left shoulder before shrugging and giving Cairos a gentle nudge backward. The apprentice slowly closed his eyes and searched his memory and power for the spell of flight that he needed. Cairos heard him whisper familiar words to Valesh before feeling a breeze disturb his robe. The current of air terminated just above Fabfast's knees, it seemed, for it held the boy aloft with his eyes still closed.

"Very good," praised Cairos. "Flight without wings can work just as well, but it can also be less trustworthy. The point is to keep your concentration."

With that, Cairos swept the tip of his staff through the air current and Fabfast faltered an inch. It was just enough to break the boy's focus and he fell the rest of the way, landing on all fours.

Cairos sighed, shaking his head. Why was it that the boy could not master this one thing? He seemed adept at everything else, particularly combat spells. Perhaps it was his battle-oriented mind, Cairos thought. Fabfast was a good fighter and he would make an even better battlemage, but it would be a sad fate if he could only leave the mainland by boat. Wizardry was nothing if not impressive.

How he wished he could simply cast the spell for the boy and be off, but casting enchantments on others usually had unforeseen — and undesirable — consequences. Cairos had used this fact to his advantage during his own training and also had it used against him.

"You must not let things break your concentration. Even drunk, drugged, exhausted, wounded, blind, and underwater you must be able to cast and sustain a spell."

"Why, Master?"

It was difficult to accept that he had changed the boy's life so much from his simple former existence. Unfortunately 'wisdom and power are never the same gift,' as the old Illiadora adage went.

"Because, sooner or later, you will need to. We're in a war, Fabfast, and being able to escape to the air where few can follow will save your life faster than those two short legs can carry you out of arrow range. I fear that if I don't prepare you for what may happen in the future then neither of us will survive to see the end of it all."

Fabfast nodded, though facing the ground it looked more like his head lolled as if unsure which way was up.

"You're going to try this as many times as it takes tonight for you to get it right. This time, use wings."

BY THE TIME THE SUN'S RAYS TOUCHED THE GOLDEN SAND, FABFAST had mastered the spells of flight. Because of Cairos' continual prodding and praise, the boy kept up his will and strength. Cairos also knew it had something to do with the boy's increased power; first year wizards barely managed to levitate with the amount of magical current they had learned to master.

To the master's delight, Fabfast's concentration barely waned all night even though Cairos knew the boy suffered from a worse headache than his own. The older wizard truly hoped the boy remembered his words; thoughts like those were what had saved him from dying alongside his friends and classmates when Illiadora was invaded.

Fabfast could employ the power of Valesh for flight by wind, wings with feathers and wings of flesh. The brown draconian skin that covered the latter type was thin and strong and gave the boy incredible maneuverability while in midair. Cairos always thought it was a wonderful thing to be able to summon wings and remembered the foreigners that disdained them. Apparently to some it looked foolish for a man to bear wings.

The sun rose quickly in the east as they ascended to the height of birds. North of Flaem stretched the absurdly brown mass of desert and Cairos steered their course to skirt its western boundary. The explosion from the *scythorsont* had come from out at sea, but Cairos had been too far away to determine exactly how far — or how far north of Flaem Circulosa's ships had fled before being destroyed. It would take some searching to find the staff and he could only hope it wasn't somehow held in place the same way Gabumon's weapon was.

His failure to procure the longstaff gnawed at Cairos as he flew alongside his apprentice. Their wings beat almost in unison and Cairos noticed the boy did a fantastic job reading and riding the wind's currents. Muscle power was usually required to move the wings up and down, but once a height was reached it was simple to hold them in place and glide for a bit. Satisfied with the knowledge that they would continue northwest until he spotted or felt a reason to stop, Cairos relaxed. He kept their path close to the coastline for as long as possible since venturing too far out into the open sea would keep them from finding a viable campsite. Even magical wings had their limits as Cairos well knew.

For days they searched the sea while heading constantly northward, but they could only head a few hours over the open water before swinging around and back toward land. Not once did Cairos feel the same interruption to the currents, but that didn't mean it wasn't there. He had no way of knowing how water affected a null zone. After hours in the air, Cairos began to wonder just how far the ships could have traveled before being destroyed. Surely it could not have been too far if he had seen the explosions simultaneously.

Perhaps his original theory had been correct about the destruction of Rot's vacuum blade causing the null zone and no other such weapon existed on Circulosa's ships. Or perhaps it had something to do with the beasts that DaVille had destroyed. It could even be a combination of everything, including the humidity in the air that day; without a lab and some time Cairos would not know. Still thoughts of the null gnawed at him.

As their course took them further north than the River Attagos, Cairos decided their only real option was to find an oracle stone. There was simply no other way to find what they were looking for. Hakes was the closest city, but who knew if the opulent bordertown had mages of caliber enough to need a seeing stone?

"We head to Hakes, Fabfast. If they don't have what we are looking for we will continue to Ferraut."

As they approached the thick forest of the mainland, past the coastal cliffs, Cairos both felt and saw that something was not right. The King's Forest was teeming with Carrion though they seemed to take no notice of him or his apprentice. Heeding the warning of his foresight, and feeling a bit mischievous, Cairos signaled and banked eastward. If the Carrion were in hiding, that meant they were waiting for something. Even as he wondered what that was, Cairos began thinking of a plan to deliver them something unexpected. Perhaps it would be another good test of his apprentice's power.

CHAPTER 52 – Wadam

RE YOU SURE SHE IS DEAD?" WADAM DID HIS BEST TO sound either shocked or sad, but could barely keep the elation from his voice. It was the best news he could have received after his morning bath. The day started out perfectly — right down to the honey and lime scents that clung to his nude body.

"Yes, the Seeress is dead," replied Parson. "Killed by some unknown assailant apparently mere moments after her evening meal arrived."

Wadam gave his valet a good, long look. Since Parson stood at nearly twice Wadam's height, he had no choice. The thin assistant had served him for many years and somehow survived the tidal wave that washed away Myst Garvon with even his wardrobe intact. Parson had been away, celebrating a foreign holiday, when Wadam left for the journey south with the troublesome girl. Upon his return from the horrible eastern shore, Wadam's attendant presented him with clean and pressed robes and a meal fit for a king. The thought of it still made the Cardinal smile.

Parson's lacy white cuffs accentuated a black coat that fitted his thin form from his shoulders to his knees. Equally tight, tapering slacks the color of charcoal ended in his well-shined boots — also tapered to a point. Of course, the style was not just a keen fashion maneuver, Wadam knew, for concealed in every possible fold and double layer hid a blade or point of some sort. The former Cardinal saw Parson's talents exhibited numerous times in the past few days, when sloppy female would-be assassins revealed themselves. It astonished him how quickly and easily Parson could kill, but he moved with the grace of a dancer. A dancer with no mercy.

"I suppose we should send over some condolence gifts for her attendants, should we not?" asked Wadam.

"Always the diplomat, sir." Parson flashed a grin showing perfectly straight teeth with pronounced canines.

"Well," the priest continued, "one must think of his people in these times of trial and hardship. A little wine and food would go a long way to let the resisters know how much Myst still loves them. And you have to admit, it is much like losing a monarch."

A thin smirk replaced Parson's grin.

"You didn't have anything to do with it, did you?"

"Certainly not!" replied Parson. The tall man seemed offended at the concept. "You never ordered it."

Wadam chuckled inwardly. He almost wished he and Parson had been responsible for Elestia's demise, but the Great Book said *when obstacles are removed it matters little how — once you are a mile past them.*

"So they are leaderless."

"Indeed, sir. The Seeress apparently named a successor, but the girl has not been found and no one has come forward with knowledge of her whereabouts."

"Interesting. Perhaps instead of sending spirits to the disloyal wretches we should send an army instead?" he asked. "How fare my new troops?"

Again Parson flashed his grin. "The recruits are being trained, as you requested, in the way of Wrath. Sixteen men are ready for battle."

"Only sixteen?" Wadam slammed his fist against a nearby table causing a ripple to pass through his bulk. Parson immediately made a surrendering gesture in response.

"Men are few here, as you know. Most of the zealots sided with the Seeress, but perhaps things will change now that she is dead. Besides, sixteen men who do not fear pain or death fight much harder than a hundred common zealots."

"What would I do without you, Parson?" asked Wadam.

"Let us be glad we did not have to find out, sir."

The people would expect his response to Elestia's death. This could be interpreted as nothing less than a sign from the Divine Female. Signs could be misinterpreted, though, and he knew well by now that one event could be seen a thousand different ways. Wadam would have to make an address, and soon. He pulled on a fresh robe and belted it at the smallest point of his waist. Then, as natural as a soldier with his sword, Wadam began to write.

A small cough from Parson reminded him that the attendant had not been dismissed. Wadam reached to put more ink on the tip of his pen and realized there was a small detail he would need to put in his address.

"One more thing before you go, Parson," he said.

"Whatever you wish, sir."

"What is the name of the girl Elestia chose as her successor?"

Parson's back stiffened even further and his eyes looked away from Wadam for a moment as if nervous. When the answer was not forthcoming, the Cardinal folded his arms and raised his eyebrows. He had to know the girl's name, even if he wouldn't recognize her — otherwise he would look foolish.

"Well, I'm not sure I heard it properly, sir," came the hesitant reply. "I could be wrong and may need to check again. I mean, it was a very unreliable source that I received this information from and ..."

"Just spit it out, Parson. I really do not have time for this."

The attendant visibly swallowed. "The successor's name is Starka."

Wadam felt the color drain from his face as his pen dropped noisily to the desk. The insignificant girl, the one who caused him nothing but trouble since her dark prophecy surfaced, would receive the torch from Elestia. How could the resistance end with a figurehead like that? No, the girl would need to be dealt with.

Forcing calm into his voice, Wadam responded, "And we are sure she is not in the Cathedral? Myst, is she even alive?"

"Reports say yes, sir, but she has not come forward to accept the nomination. Tradition states she has until the Rebirth Festival to do so, but many of my sources say she is not even on the continent."

"Ha! The Festival! Why would we even have it this year after all that has happened?" Wadam pondered, but then waved the thoughts away. "It does not matter. Listen to me, Parson. If I truly have favor with Myst-Garvon, the girl will never make it back here alive."

Catching the command in Wadam's tone, Parson's lips slowly spread again. "I understand, sir."

CHAPTER 53 – *Mayrah*

HE ENTIRE WORLD SPUN EVERY TIME LADY MAYRAH opened her eyes. The pain nearly drove her mad and it hurt to breathe, but she took respite in the reminder that she was still alive. Wan Du had certainly saved her from death, though she was still unsure whether survival was a good thing. Her feelings culminated when she realized the bracelet was missing.

The token of her betrothal, the only symbol she had left of her mate, must have fallen off in the fight. She mourned its loss every coherent moment since the discovery. Time blurred through the pain, but she remembered a bouncing trip across the land. The field had to be leagues away by now. She would never see her bracelet again. With a deep breath, Mayrah tried her best to push it out of her mind. Even if she survived to make it back to Rochelle, there was nothing more she could do.

Strength returned to her limbs at a snail's pace. As she lay on a blanket of moist grass, Mayrah saw the flames of a small campfire. To take stock of her surroundings, she attempted to prop herself up on her elbows. Though she begrudged thinking of him so, Mayrah asked her companion how long she slept.

"Nearly a week," he replied, the tone not indicative of approval or rejection.

"So long?" she whispered. Wan Du nodded.

The smell of roasting meat tickled her nostrils. She had to admit that for a soldier from Brong, the large man could cook a nice field meal. Though a little apprehensive about eating his food, at first, her watering mouth and the need to regain strength eventually won out. She wondered if his meal preparation was meant to impress her in some mocking affectionate way, but ignored her instincts. Lady Mayrah refused to let herself hate or be suspicious of the man who saved her life, regardless of motive or consequences.

Her heart pounded in her chest when she first awoke after passing out from the wound. With her breasts bared to the wind, and Wan Du's palm nearly pressed against one of them, she had to bite back her rage at the near violation of her body. The feelings returned upon finding her bracelet missing. She knew the magic behind it and she fought to stave off the shame eating away at her insides. He should have let me die, she thought, for I can no longer return home.

Finding Windsong and Wavesong, the twin blue scimitars that belonged to her and her dead betrothed, remained her only reason for existence now. And Mayrah would let no arrow wound or lost bracelet stop her.

"That smells good," she said. Wan Du nodded again, not looking up from the fire.

She fought to a sitting position on her blanket and looked from the stars to the man's face and then to the roasting kill. Gingerly, Mayrah reached to her chest and touched the spot of the wound. A finger's width closer to her heart and she would have surely been dead. Perhaps it was not meant to be just yet, she thought.

They ate across from each other in comfortable silence. The sound of the forest crickets filled the night. She listened to their chirping until the contentedness of a full stomach allowed her to slip back into a finally restful slumber.

MAYRAH WOKE AGAIN, WELL PAST DAWN, IN WAN DU'S ARMS. SHE was instantly thankful for the shadows cast by the canyon walls as her eyes hurt to take in even that much light. Brush and rock sped by as Wan Du's large form weaved through the passes. Mayrah saw caves and passes blocked by rockslides.

This was on purpose, she began to realize after noting their frequency. Anyone marching an army to Fort Sondergaarde would be required to do so on the same path, nearly single file. Mayrah wondered how in the world the Carrion could have taken it.

Around midday the sun poked over the canyon walls and its focused light began to sting her eyes. Mayrah raised a hand in defense, but soon found it unnecessary as Wan Du took shelter in the mouth of a large cavern.

"Can you stand?" he asked.

She nodded, but hoped his hands wouldn't simply fall out from beneath her. Mayrah resented herself for being such a burden — she was a soldier, not some helpless body to be carried.

As her feet lightly touched the ground, she pressed them down flat and forced the strength to her legs. Her knees shook as if unsure and she kept a hand on Wan Du's massive shoulder. Hoping to take some of his attention off of her infirmity, she pressed Wan Du with a question. Lady Mayrah did her best to sound dignified.

"How have you been finding the way through? These passes all look alike."

"Mazes are children's toys," he replied. Though his words seemed rude, his tone did not carry a shred of condescension. "Always turn the same direction and you will eventually come out the other side."

Not the answer she hoped for, but it would do.

As Mayrah took a few steps to test her legs again, she found it easier — and less painful — than she feared. The cave was dimly lit from holes in the high ceiling, but the glow did not provide much to look at. Rock in the canyon created a constant pattern of bland with only veins of sediment to break the monotony. Mayrah reached out to touch the smooth cave wall, running her fingers against the lines of history.

"You are strong." Wan Du spoke from behind her and Mayrah was glad he could not see her face. She gritted her teeth and choked back a sob before turning back to the mouth of the cavern.

"This place is old," she replied.

Wan Du nodded stoically. He turned from her to the outside again. "Check your wound. I will keep watch."

How odd of him to give me modesty now, she thought. She gently shrugged the tied cloth from her shoulder and examined the puckered hole in her chest. It seemed a miracle that the wound was not infected. After merely a week, the tender flesh seemed almost healed already. Moving her shoulder still hurt, but Mayrah believed she could fight if the need came. After the woman replaced her clothing, she took a deep breath and steadied herself for the long walk to the Fort.

Just as they were ready to leave their cover, a cry sounded out overhead. Wan Du put an arm up in warning, barring her from leaving the shelter. The cry sounded somewhere between avian and reptilian, foreign from anything Mayrah had ever heard before. She could not see the sky, but she watched three large shadows dim the path outside the cave in succession.

"What are those?" she whispered.

Wan Du did not respond; either he did not know or could not describe them. If the Carrion had some kind of flying patrol, the path through the canyons would only become increasingly dangerous. Mayrah turned to look deeper into the cavern and decided they only had one choice.

"We'll have to see how far this cave goes," she said. The large man turned his head toward her, still silent. Mayrah continued, "Surely a besieging army would have tried to come through tunnels before. Perhaps the Carrion themselves ..."

Another screech from above interrupted her, and the choice was made.

⬦

EXPLORING THE CAVE WAS SLOW GOING. AS NEITHER OF THEM carried the means to make a torch, they remained dependent upon their senses and the small amount of light from the holes above. Mayrah did not much like being underground — it made her think of the horrors of the Syllowaste region south of Rochelle. Men spoke of untold treasures to be found there, but at far too great a risk.

Twice they doubled back as the passages dead-ended. Small pairs of eyes appeared and disappeared in the distance. Cave rats, Mayrah realized. She instinctively reached for her sword and patted the void at her hip nearly in panic.

"Do you wish your sword back?"

It was such a simple question, but to Mayrah it meant too many things for a simple answer. She whispered an affirmative and Wan Du returned the mundane scimitar to her.

"What about you?" she asked.

Wan Du's lip twitched in a smile for a quick moment. Having watched him fight, she realized it a silly question. Even weaponless, the large man would be far from defenseless.

After hours of flat travel the cave path began a slow incline. Mayrah reckoned it grew sharper as she felt her legs begin to stiffen and cramp, but she forced her feet forward. As they rounded a corner, she saw an opening and the blue sky in the distance. Dodging the stones she could see, Mayrah rushed to the portal and looked out. She could not stop the sharp intake of a gasp.

From their vantage in a cave high above ground level, Mayrah could see a nearly sheer cliff face stretched downward and all of Fort Sondergaarde. The ruined fortress looked gutted and burned, but retained the semblance of four partial walls. Circling above it, she saw the screaming creatures. The grotesque, flying beasts had the fat bodies and long necks of ugly birds, but their bodies had no feathers. Their leathery flesh mimicked the skin of Carrion and small black horns protruded from the sides of their long-beaked heads.

Below, inside a makeshift corral within the fortress wandered even stranger things. Four-legged beasts of burden seemed to be warped in the same fashion. Small, curved horns stuck sideways above their empty black eyes and their large bodies rose in a high crest at the top of their backs before declining to the rump and tail. Mayrah used animals similar to these to pull wagons, but the resemblance was only fleeting. Carrion grunts carrying whips and prods moved about them grunting and crying out in their fierce language. Mayrah remembered the fight in the north and turned to Wan Du.

"Can you understand them?"

The large man joined her, and though he hadn't exhibited the same shocked reaction, she could see concern in his face. "The Carrion are training them."

"Training?"

He nodded an affirmative and waited to listen.

"They call the large ones 'bison.' The flying ones are 'dragonlings.' And there are more that you cannot see. Look there."

Her gaze followed his pointing hand outside of the Fort's boundaries to the remains of a rock quarry much closer to their position. Mayrah gasped again as she watched horned dogs run in a circular pit, snarling at each other and the Carrion around them.

"Hellhounds." He spoke the words of her fears come to life. Mayrah knew canine beasts were the chosen mounts and pets of the northern barbarians, the Amber Horde, but she could not imagine what they were doing in this place. If the northern men were also in league with the Carrion, the entire continent could be in danger.

"Hold." Wan Du's deep voice pierced her thoughts. "They call for one named Feraldus."

Mayrah watched as a short, bent Carrion overseer emerged from a tented structure inside the fortress. The creature named Feraldus walked only with the assistance of a stick nearly as bent as its body. A tattered brown coat lay upon its back and dragged the ground behind it. Climbing a set of stairs seemed to take minutes, but the Carrion took a position and began to address the grunts. Wan Du translated the speech, his voice completely devoid of inflection.

"My Dearest Experiments, we are nearing the end of our preparations. Our Great Master is pleased with our work."

A noise erupted from the grunts — a cheerless noise.

Wan Du continued, "When the ships come tomorrow we shall leave this place together. There are not many that could stand against you, My Children, but combined with the strength of the beasts we have made you will be utterly unstoppable."

Things seemed to pause for a moment as if the Carrion were waiting for something more. Even after the overseer spoke his last sentence and the assembled grunts erupted in another massive cheer, Wan Du did not speak.

She looked into his face expectantly, but saw that all of the color had drained from it.

"Our King of Darkness shall have his Crown," Wan Du whispered.

"Oh, Gods ..."

"I know," he cut her off.

"It is fate that we have arrived now, before they have left," she said. "We must stop them. We must kill them all."

"I know," he repeated.

Just as Mayrah was about to speak again, another Carrion figure emerged from the same tent as Feraldus. The new figure stood tall, with considerable girth for a Carrion soldier. Mayrah had seen enough of the enemy's officers to recognize the improved armor this one wore designated it as special. Its horns were thick and curved immediately skyward. The figure of its body struck Mayrah as strange because it seemed to be decidedly female, something she had not noticed on a carrion soldier before. As the officer climbed to the dais and came into better view the muscles in Mayrah's hands clenched in rage. She turned back to the cave and fell to her knees.

"Mercy," Mayrah whispered. "Not her. Not Bathilde."

"Kill them all," Wan Du echoed.

CHAPTER 54 – *Starka*

EAVING THE DESERT WINDS BEHIND GAVE STARKA ONE OF the most comforting feelings she'd had in days. Without thinking, her fingers closed around the small jewel suspended around her neck and she thought again of Kismet. The poor girl had lost nearly everything during what should have been an easy family business trip. Now, in charge of an entire wagon of goods, her welfare was wrapped up in their sale when the caravan reached Travell. If it reached Travell, Starka thought darkly.

The stubborn mounts she and DaVille had been provided with were not the same type of animal that pulled the wagons, but they certainly walked as if dragging a load. Camels, he called them, but she found the beasts even less comfortable than horseback.

Huge lumbering steps of each leg bounced Starka in the saddle, leaving her no choice but to grasp tightly to the horn placed embarrassingly close to her crotch to keep from falling off. Only after hours of experimentation was she able to grip with her legs and lead the animal using the leather straps provided for that purpose. Her animal dumbly followed DaVille's for miles without her guidance, but she hoped to have some semblance of control if it suddenly changed its mind.

DaVille rode with all of the confidence and bravado she now associated him with. The man kept one hand lightly grasping the reins and the other on the pommel of one of his swords strapped horizontally across his lower back. Even though on guard, he seemed somewhat lighter and more amiable away from the caravan and its miscellaneous troubles. He sacrificed their portion of the sale of the blacksmith's goods, but reconciled it with the fact that their animals were packed with enough supplies to reach Hakes on the southern border of Ferraut. The money mattered little, if at all.

The pair made little conversation as they rode. It seemed the previous day's confessions used up most of DaVille's will to speak to her. In her mind, she still had reason to fear DaVille, but at least now she understood why he was so distant and guarded. He had been killed once already, and she guessed a man does not trust easily after that. Even so, the girl opted to stay with him.

She had never met a resurrected man before and the concept unsettled her to no end. In her vast time studying at the Myst Cathedrals, she learned resurrection was a capacity saved only for the Divine — and they were incredibly unlikely to do so at that. Alsher and Garvon passed to the next world to make way for all of their descendants — herself included — and they had no reason to come back. Not to mention DaVille did not strike her as the Divine type.

As if to reinforce her conclusion, DaVille spat a wad of brown curd from his mouth. At least he spat it away from her this time, she thought.

"Can't that sorry nag keep up?" he asked over his shoulder.

Starka gritted her teeth, and as gently as she could, whipped her beast into motion. Once she came abreast of him she pulled on the reins to slow the beast up and match his pace. The animal, annoyed by her fickleness, spat into the dirt as well and groaned.

"I think it wants to rest," said Starka.

DaVille seemed to take this into consideration, and Starka wondered if he would have done the same if she suggested it herself.

"The more we rest the longer it will take us to leave the desert."

"But I thought we had left it already." Starka turned in her saddle to survey their trail across the last few dunes and over a flat, white plain dotted with stones. Brush attempted to grow here, and a few insects had buzzed her head just minutes before. Signs of life had to mean they were leaving the parched wasteland behind.

"This is borderland," he said. "A river cuts across not far north of here. Once we cross it, we'll be in Ferraut."

She could barely hide her surprise at how far north they had come with the caravan. "Hakes must be fairly close, then?"

Her companion opened a saddlebag and produced a worn map scrawled on animal skin. He passed it to her and she unfolded it, allowing her mount to stray to its own course and tempo in tandem with DaVille's.

"We're there," he answered, indicating a star-shaped region labeled as Five Points. "The southeast corner of the Ferraut territory. Once we pass the river we should start to see the King's Forest. If we turned straight north there, we'd head to Brindle; see?"

Starka followed his finger and nodded her assent. A path traced from the city of Brindle, situated on the northern coast of the mainland, south and bit west to Hakes, then southeast diagonally until she saw the meandering line of a river. Beautiful scripted letters marked the *Attagos River* where her finger intersected its path.

"If," he continued, accentuating the word, "we keep from resting too much and thereby slowing ourselves, we should be in Hakes in three days. Four at the most."

As she passed the map back to DaVille, Starka sighed. Her life had become nothing but traveling and after seeing the furthest corners of the known world, she longed to return home. Little remained for her there, but Elestia's attitude toward her had changed when she brought the prophecy forth. For a short time at least, Starka became necessary again. It made her feel like a person for the first time in a long time, and filled a void untouched since Fandur's disappearance.

Apparently spotting the longing look on her face, DaVille commented, "Don't worry. There'll be a lot more to look at once we get to the Attagos."

Starka smiled away the homesickness and nodded. With a bit of satisfaction, she grasped the reins and spurred her beast forward. Only once she passed DaVille did Starka allow the tears welling in her eyes to fall.

THE MAP DID NOT INDICATE A BRIDGE, AND FROM HER VANTAGE point on the southern bank of the Attagos, Starka quickly understood why. It looked hundreds of feet across and its width did not seem to dwindle with distance east or west. She knew from the map that if they turned west, they would reach the sea before finding a place to cross. Turning inland, however, would take them further away from their destination. The crossing must have been the extra day added on to DaVille's estimate, she realized.

Seeing him dismount, Starka quickly followed. The lower half of her body cried out in soreness, particularly all of the parts that had made contact with the saddle. DaVille began unpacking for the evening, though there still seemed to be a few hours of daylight left.

"Are we stopping?" she asked.

"There is a ferryman along this stretch, somewhere," came the sure answer. "It's the narrowest part for a hundred miles. Could be that the war's scared them off, but it's doubtful."

"So we're just going to wait and hope they show up?" Starka regretted the words immediately after she said them, but DaVille shrugged off her tone and continued to unpack.

She began to think that he must have lived in this territory, judging by his avoidance of looking at the map and extreme amount of confidence that the ferry would be nearby. Starka almost asked to verify her suspicion, but decided better of it.

From the larger saddlebag on DaVille's mount came forth a small caravan tent canvas and hollow poles for its erection. Starka let DaVille assemble it alone, choosing instead to fill their waterskins. Both animals followed her to the river's edge, not waiting for her permission before lowering their heads to drink. Starka wondered if the beasts could swim the massive span, but then sourly realized all of their meager belongings would get soaked during the trip. As would she, based on the sour temper of her animal.

Returning, Starka found that DaVille had not only put up the tent, but started a cooking fire as well. True to DaVille's word, there was more to look at nearer the river than the borderland. The swift water provided the means for greenery and the possibility of a fresh fish catch should DaVille find himself adventurous. Starka had never learned to fish, though she had watched, bored, as her twin Fandur baited hooks and sunk them into any nearby body of water. As she recalled, he even attempted to fish in a well once.

Thoughts of her brother and their youth made Starka chuckle and DaVille looked up from his task with suspicion. It seemed he did not think sharpening a knife so humorous.

"I wasn't laughing at you," she stammered.

He waited, staring quietly in her direction, poised for the knife's next stroke across the sharpening strip.

"I was merely thinking of something funny. Something from when I was a child."

As he resumed sharpening, she heard DaVille whisper, "Cherish the memories you have." The words became a cold reminder of the questions she still needed to ask. With a breath to steady herself and build a bit of courage, Starka began the conversation anew.

"Listen, DaVille, I know we haven't talked much since, well since yesterday ..."

"But you still have questions," he finished for her.

DaVille drew the knife across the strip a few more times idly, but his focus was not really on his task. The sun dipped below the horizon and he stared toward it as if to mark the day's passing. He sheathed the knife in his belt and set about preparing a meal of unwrapped meat and vegetables in a pot on the fire. The stewing food smelled amazing to Starka and she realized how famished she was. From time to time she found herself so wrapped up in her fears that the needs of her body went ignored for hours. Sometimes it felt like fasting — minus the devotional prayers.

"Yes," she replied. "Yes, I do."

"We've got nothing else to do," DaVille concluded.

"Tell me how it is that you are alive."

DaVille laughed joylessly. Starka nearly took it as a ridiculing response, but then realized he was laughing at himself.

"Truly, I do not know," he said. "I remember dying. Or rather, I remember the pain before death, and I remember the pain ending."

Starka pondered his responses for a moment. Her expression or lack of response must not have matched his expectations as he absently stirred the meal.

"You don't believe me?" he accused.

"I didn't say that," she put forth, evading the truth. Why did she feel a need in her heart to believe him? "It's just that the dead are dead. We don't believe that what you've told me is possible."

"Who is we?" DaVille retorted. "Your priests and priestesses, locked up in your cathedrals, cut off on your continent? You're seeing the world for yourself, Starka. Can you honestly say you still believe a single book has all the answers?"

The use of her name made Starka blanch. DaVille rarely called her by name and even more rarely admitted he knew anything other than battle lore. She was almost afraid to admit it, but with demanding the story of his past, Starka seemed to have opened DaVille's floodgates.

She couldn't answer his questions. None of the easily repeated mantras, quotes of scripture, prayers, or sermons seemed applicable to these circumstances. Folding her hands in her lap, Starka stared into the fire and said nothing.

"Sometimes," he said, "I have dreams of floating in darkness while voices speak to me, but those mean very little. Sometimes an old man is there talking with me."

She perked up, grateful for the subject change. "Do you know who speaks to you?"

"What difference does it make? They are just dreams."

Starka scowled back, knowing full well he intentionally discounted her own dream and the prophecy that came through it. "But you said before your dreams are your memories coming back."

"Yes, though I have little desire for any of them." DaVille seemed pensive, but she supposed he could also just be exhausted from their long day of riding. She surely was, but she wanted answers nonetheless.

"What do they say, these voices in your dreams of floating?"

"You really are interested in this, aren't you?" he asked. "Fine, I'll tell you what I remember.

"There I am, floating through a sea of darkness so black that even if there is something to look at I can't see it. I can't tell if my eyes are open or closed; that's how dark it is. There's no light and for a long time there is no sound."

It was strange, at first, when she began having waking visions of the dreams he described. Starka nodded as he continued to speak, but it became difficult to listen and watch at the same time. She wished she had more recent lessons of interpretation, but tried her best to take it all in without them.

"Then," DaVille continued, "like a thunderous roar, the first voice appears. 'Why is he here,' it asks. I want to answer but then another voice says, 'Send him back. More time is required to prepare.'"

Hesitant to interrupt him, Starka waited to see if there was more to the dream. When he didn't add, she asked about the old man he had mentioned.

"White hair exploding out of his head in every direction," DaVille described while separating the prepared stew into two shallow wooden bowls. "No mustache, no beard, but his face is gnarled like an old tree. He talks without moving his mouth, but I can hear him just the same and he can hear me. He asks, 'do you want to live?' and I answer 'only if life comes with vengeance.'"

"Ever the soldier," Starka muttered. He ignored her comment entirely, as usual, but this time she was glad for it.

"'If the word vengeance is more important to you than the word life,' he says, 'then perhaps you are not the one we are waiting for. Only time will tell.'"

"I wonder what he means." Starka tried earnestly to piece it together in her mind.

"It means nothing!" he exploded. "It's a dream! The only thing that matters is I'm here and I know what my goal needs to be. If this is a second chance for me, then it is to kill before I am killed."

DaVille seemed to ignore the old man's point. Perhaps that's why all his dreams are recurring, she thought. He never learns his lesson.

Blowing lightly on her portion of food to cool it, Starka allowed the conversation to cool as well. She still couldn't let herself fully believe him, which held back her ability to trust him. Every day she put off her questions, Starka knew they would gnaw at her as they did before Adamis challenged her to ask them. In a way, his unrelenting challenges benefitted her. The strange wizard had pushed her over an edge she desperately needed to pass. Perhaps it was the change in her that DaVille responded to with this new openness.

"DaVille, since we met I have tried not to expect or ask anything of you," she said. "You have kept me safe even though it was only by protecting yourself that you did so. I have traveled with you these weeks because I had no choice but to trust you after that first day we met, even though your attitude has been unbearable at times. I thought that you were the only safe way to get back home."

A flood of tears came again to Starka's eyes with the admissions and she wiped them away. DaVille ate slowly while listening and did not interrupt.

"I know it is selfish of me to want to go home with this duty that I keep talking about. You may make fun of my prophecy all you like, but I have no choice other than to take it seriously. I think you are a part of this prophecy, but like you, I don't think I care anymore. My selfishness has won out and more than anything now I just want to go home. I want to be back in my small house in my warm bed where there are no Carrion soldiers and no wizards. The closest I ever want to come to a sharp blade is preparing my evening meals."

DaVille took all of this in and nodded a few times when she finished. Starka felt accomplished; she had finally been honest in return and a huge weight lifted from her shoulders. Fear and duty still vied for supremacy, but at least the struggle was now out in the open and she no longer hid from it. Her companion stayed silent for a few moments more, intently watching the dancing flames with a hollow gaze. Starka began to follow his stare and when he spoke again it startled her.

In a soft, even voice DaVille began, "You cannot imagine what it is like to be turned into Carrion. I know you have been hungry, tired, imprisoned — these things are mild human struggles. They can teach lessons as well as remind us that we are alive. Carrion soldiers, though, are not 'alive.' Not in the sense that you feel it.

"From the first moment the horns are thrust in, 'life' becomes an endless sea of pain and desire. Hunger, exhaustion, wounds; these things no longer matter in the face of the constantly reinforced will of Zion. *Kill, kill, kill*; that is the only clear thought. Death is almost a comfort, since it brings an end to the torture of being trapped in a body and a mind that are no longer your own. Some of the man remains, but I was told it varies how much. Some have no memory of what they once were. For me, it felt like my true thoughts were wrapped in a tight cloth and stifled. Your willpower is chained up and locked deep within the prison of the mind as far away from the surface as possible. The effect is so complete that part of you soon believes it wants to go along with the urges implanted by the horns.

"This is what listening to you makes me think of: being completely unwilling to fight against the circumstances of fate. It's believing even that there is intention in your course when the truth is you are just a piece on the game board. You accept your orthodoxy and your prophecy without a second thought to the source or the purpose and agenda of that source. Make no mistake; you are a soldier just as much as I have been since I was taller than my sword."

"Wow," she said. "I never knew you thought so much about me."

One side of DaVille's mouth rose in a smile. "Something about you must be blessed to have stayed alive around me for this long, but that isn't the only thing that makes you interesting."

With those words he rose with the bowls and went to the river to clean them. Starka watched him from the fireside as DaVille tended the mounts and ultimately returned to renew the fire's supply of fuel. Feeling somewhat awkward, Starka rose and walked toward the tent.

"Take the tent," DaVille called after her. "I'll keep watch tonight."

Starka smiled and nodded once before slipping into the tent. She was glad for the solitude, as his words gave her much to think about. As Starka slipped under the fur blanket, she felt a prickle of confidence in the back of her mind. She smiled until she slept.

EARLY THE NEXT MORNING, STARKA HEARD VOICES NEARBY OUTside the tent and stirred to greet the day. She stood, recalling a fading dream of Flaem and the strange crystal. It could not have been another warning, she thought, but it seemed so vivid. She remembered meeting the wizard, Cairos, and Starka began to wonder where he was now. Donning her traveling clothes over her sleeping shift she then pushed the tent flap aside to spot DaVille. Despite multiple voices, no sense of danger had entered her mind.

Just beyond the boundary of their small camp DaVille stood talking to a hunched man a head shorter than him. The man's shoulders seemed to be the same height as his ears and the sagging expression on his face nearly made Starka chuckle. The wrinkles made him smile and frown at the same time, and she concluded the man could not be anything but harmless. Starka joined the two men, standing just behind DaVille.

"Ah, so here's your ladyfriend, eh?"

The man's voice — and breath — reminded Starka of sour milk. His accent was thick and strange, reminding her a bit of Captain Satok who had sailed them north from Cellto.

"Indeed," DaVille answered dismissively. Starka noticed with a bit of disappointment that he did not introduce her. "Ferryman Carino, all we request is passage across the Attagos and we will be on our way. Our mounts shouldn't be any trouble. We are prepared to pay."

Carino's gaze had strayed to Starka's figure but snapped back to DaVille's face at the mention of money. They quickly worked out terms with DaVille haggling the man down from a questionable amount of gold pieces. By the time for their midday meal the small party was well on their way across the river.

The skiff was so large Carino needed two assistants to keep it on the intended course. Even so, they were an efficient team and the ferry strolled gently through the massive river's current and toward the other side. As they traveled, Starka heard DaVille talk offhandedly with the ferryman about his business and what he saw on the riverbanks of late. Carino admitted to seeing no Carrion soldiers on either bank in his territory — not that he would have approached them if he did, he added — but there had been quite a few mercenary bands requesting passage.

"How do you know they are mercenaries?" Starka asked.

"It's all in the currency," the ferryman replied as he manipulated the boat's rudder. "You can tell a lot about folks by what's stamped on their coins, get me?"

Starka nodded, wondering where mercenaries could have come from in the midst of so many destroyed cities. Perhaps Adamis finding an army in Travell wasn't as out of the question as DaVille thought.

"Where were they heading?" asked DaVille.

"A few toward Travell, but gods know why. Most head toward Hakes and Ferraut. Some say they saw a decree from the Five Points King that any man who joins up with the defense of the kingdom is promised a healthy reward."

"Not enough to make you abandon your post here, eh?" DaVille jabbed. When Carino laughed gruffly in response, Starka realized that he had a real talent for reading people. It was another reminder that she would not have made it far alone, which made her think again of DaVille's impression and wariness of Adamis.

"Who knows what's going to happen, ya know?" the ferryman asked as he looked past the northern shoreline and wiped a hand across his balding head. "Me an' the boys have taken to anchoring in the middle of the river here at night just to feel safe. Heard the other day, though, that some o' these Carrion even fly now."

"Fly?" DaVille echoed, incredulous but interested.

"If you can believe that," replied Carino, shrugging. "Some mercs who come up from Fort Sondergaarde say they saw lots o' strange things there. 'Course I don't buy into believing everything I hear, but a year ago I didn't hear any o' this, ya know?"

Starka had no idea what to say. Just when she thought she was learning the truth of the world, more impossibilities appeared. She knew what her peers back home would say about it all; the southern world was a bad place and the presence of evil, darkness, and wizards would eventually bring destruction upon it. Having seen the ruthlessness of the Carrion and the innocents affected, Starka would fervently defend those who died.

Perhaps they had been right to cast her out of the Sisterhood, after all, or perhaps DaVille's influence on her thoughts made her doubt what she had been taught since birth.

Either way, the ferryman was right. A year before, none of these things were possible. Starka no longer lived a quiet, simple life and she could not ignore the danger at her heels. But the question still remained: could she simply return home?

"How did you know to pick us up?" she asked.

"Band o' men downriver, traded gold for news," he replied. "Said we might run into a pair o' you. Strange ones, them red folk."

AS THE FERRY REACHED THE SHORE AND THEY DISEMBARKED, Starka waved thanks to Carino and his boys. They were honest folk, and despite Carino's invocation of an unnamed multitude of false gods, she respected their plight. DaVille remained silent as they mounted and continued northwest from the riverbank. Soon she began to see the huge expanse of trees Starka remembered marked as the King's Forest on DaVille's map. Just as the girl noticed a teenage boy collecting firewood close to the forest's edge, DaVille raised a hand in warning and reached for one of his swords.

A familiar voice from above and behind startled and halted both her and DaVille.

"Well, look who it is."

CHAPTER 55 – *Cairos*

LLOWING TIME FOR HIS STARTLING TO SINK IN, CAIROS slowly floated to the ground behind the travelers. It had to be fate to find them so far north of where he saw them last. Fate, Cairos thought, or they're following me.

"DaVille Dragonslayer," he greeted. "Interesting to see you this far north."

The girl named Starka turned in her saddle to meet his eyes. Though her lustrous brown hair remained the same, the girl looked quite a bit more haggard than Cairos recalled. Now, dressed in the remnants of desert clothing that clung to her figure, Starka seemed even more lean and fragile. He realized they must have traveled the road from Flaem, and it was probably by chance he found them.

More probable was that the Carrion hiding in the trees were waiting for these two.

"Starka, right?" asked Cairos. "A pleasure to see you again."

"Peace, wizard," the man called, hands still raised. "Let's talk."

"I'm listening."

"I find it easier to talk over a fire and a drink," said DaVille. "If you can see fit to avoid trying to roast me, I'll keep from dismembering you and we can have a nice chat."

Cairos smiled at the man's unwitting plea to his merciful side. He had gotten the drop on them; a simple fireball spell probably would have been enough to leave them and their mounts in tatters and Cairos would have been no worse off. But it would be nice having the girl around, however briefly, and having someone more to talk to than Fabfast.

"Sort of like a you-trust-me-I-trust-you situation?" asked the wizard. "Must be important."

The warrior lowered his hands. "Right."

"Sure; sounds like fun. Follow my apprentice there to the camp and I'll do the pouring."

AFTER A FEW DRINKS AND AN HOUR BY THE FIRE, STARKA HAD relayed most of their tale to Cairos and Fabfast. The older wizard listened intently and nodded in places, particularly interested in the caravan's ambush and victory through a certain flame spell.

"You're sure that was the word he used?" Cairos asked.

"Definitely," replied Starka. "He said 'firestorm.'"

Fabfast turned to his master with a quizzical look. "What does this mean, master?"

"It means they met a Burning Man."

"Which we already knew," DaVille finished. "His name is Adamis. You know him?"

Cairos nodded at the warrior. "I know of him. It was his spell that destroyed Rochelle, though it was Illiadora's magic."

"He seemed out to redeem himself," said the girl. Starka's voice sounded hopeful, but it was obvious she knew little of wizardry.

"Adamis seeks to raise an army of the dispossessed in Travell." DaVille looked across the fire at Cairos with a mocking gaze. "Do you think he has any chance?"

"Who can say?" Cairos asked. Then, he laughed at himself for a moment. "What am I talking about; of course he has no chance. All of the proficient wizards I knew who would participate in such a daring scheme are quite dead now. We, ourselves, only seek an object to increase our strength to do a better job. In fact, you're quite involved in our mission which I'm afraid explains our hospitality."

"Do tell," said DaVille.

"Well, it seems that when you destroyed the *scythorsont* outside of Flaem — however it was you did it — things changed a bit." Cairos paused for a moment, contemplating which words to use to explain the effects. "My friend, Gabumon, had a very powerful and old staff when he was killed by the dragon. The staff had been lying on the cavern's floor when he died, but now it is embedded within the rock. A quandary, as I'm sure you realize."

"Why don't you just *magic* it out?" DaVille asked, smirking.

"Well, I was getting to that part. It seems the other effect of the crystal's explosion, aside from the death of two very rare beasts, was the creation of what we call a 'null zone.' No magic can be performed for quite a distance both inside and outside what is left of the cavern.

"So we gave up on that one," Cairos continued, "and began seeking the staff of Circulosa instead. So far we've come up with no results."

At the mention of the wizard General's name, DaVille noticeably stiffened. The man's responses to Cairos' statements were interesting to watch. Cairos could tell the warrior did not trust him, but he seemed to be actively trying to avoid a conflict or argument, however cynical his statements were. He sat on a large stone with his arms crossed at his chest rather than resting near his paired longswords. Perhaps he's simply confident there won't be any trouble, Cairos considered.

"Where will you go now?" Starka asked.

Eager to join the conversation, Fabfast piped up before Cairos could stop him. "We head to Hakes to see the oracle stone!"

The older wizard sighed and smiled, shaking his head. "There you have it, our goals laid bare. I suppose we can trust you two, unless you have some plan of returning to your previous vocation, DaVille."

A wolfish grin crossed the warrior's face but he did not respond.

"Well," said Starka, "we are heading that direction, too."

Cairos instantly read their intent. "Oh? Planning on raising an army of your own from within the Five Points?"

DaVille laughed. "Nothing gets past you, does it, sorcerer? We'll have to convince the king to take some action, but there are no guarantees we'll even get an audience."

"Interesting idea. In that case, I might have a proposition for you." Cairos leaned toward the fire conspiratorially. DaVille followed suit, holding hands out to warm them.

"There are only two ways to quickly see the king of Ferraut, especially in wartime. One is if you are a criminal to be sentenced to death, and the other is if you are royalty yourself. Or, at the very least, of noble blood."

"I don't understand," Starka put in. "We wouldn't want to be the first, and we're most certainly not the second."

Cairos flashed a grin of his own. "Not yet, we're not."

"We?" she asked. "You're coming with us all the way to the kingdom city?"

"Indeed." Cairos had made up his mind, already quite fond of the plan he was brewing.

"The king may be smart and very well informed," said Cairos, "but he can't possibly keep track of every city and country that claims to designate a royal line of their own. Outside of the boundaries of the Five Points, His Majesty's knowledge must be somewhat limited.

"One of us must play the part of the noble. With all of the raids lately, it's not out of the question for a royal to come and offer aid. If you convince the king to 'march' and retake Illiadora, I will help you get there."

"Besides reclaiming your home, why Illiadora?" asked DaVille. "Not to be rude, but the king's going to want some justification. What reasons will you give him?"

"Simple," Cairos replied. "You and I both know the heart of the Carrion army sits at the top of the Great Watchtower, the tallest structure on the face of the world. Illiadora is a mere hairsbreadth away."

DaVille agreed with a nod. "With the defeat of Circulosa, they don't have near the numbers they planned on at this phase. Zion will cling hard to what he's gained so far while he rebuilds."

The wizard scratched at his stubble, for the first time realizing how much thought DaVille had put into his plan of raising an army. If the Carrion army was not already on its heels, he would put them there if given the chance.

"It would be the next logical step to end this war and its proximity to the southlands might inspire some help from any remnants."

"Have you seen Brong or Rochelle lately?" DaVille asked. "Much like our Amber Horde friends, they don't seem to feel much like making war anymore."

"What he says is true," Starka added.

"Except possibly to steal," Cairos heard DaVille mutter under his breath. He thought to ask for details, but it seemed irrelevant.

"Regardless, the king's army should be at least enough to make an impact. With the Carrion forces spread out as they are, someone ought to be able to strike the final blow."

DaVille brought a fist to his chest. "That I claim as my right."

Cairos continued, "It's settled then. You may have to go it alone, though, in the end. There's no room for an army inside that tower. Do you think you can do all of this by yourself?"

The warrior seemed thoughtful for a moment, as if considering his options and finding them grim. With a frown, he shrugged.

"I'll help however I can," said Starka. "Perhaps I can call for help from the cathedrals. We have somewhat of an army, too."

"The Mystians?" Cairos coughed out. Starka looked hurt, as if ridiculed, and the wizard had to quickly recover. "I don't mean to be rude, miss, but they're not in much of a position to do anything at this point."

"You have news from the northwest?" DaVille's question seemed concerned, but Cairos wondered about the sincerity of it. "The party we headed north with didn't mention anything of it."

Cairos sat quietly, hesitating; the news was not encouraging.

"It's not my place to judge affairs from the Mystian continent, so I will tell it to you as I heard it and spare you my … commentary."

"Go on," Starka said, her tone walking a fine line between fear and impatience.

"After the stone exploded, a massive tidal wave swept through the northern Inner Sea. Here in the east, the port of Ince felt a bit of it with many wrecks, but the high cliffs kept the water at bay. The northwest, I'm afraid, was not so lucky. The wave flooded the Baerow Strait, and from what I heard, completely destroyed one of the cathedrals of Myst."

Starka gasped and brought her hands to her mouth. "Myst-Garvon sat right on the southern shoreline! Your magic destroyed my home!"

Cairos raised his hands in surrender, not wanting to lay the blame anywhere nearby, but knowing it was DaVille who had exploded the cluster. "Save your accusations, as you haven't heard the worst of it."

The girl wiped the tears from her face and bade him to continue.

"Many were killed, as you can imagine," he went on. "But the ones who lived began to split the faith and fight each other. A man named Wadam appeared, claiming to be the Mouth of Myst and calling for the men to rise up and take charge. To subjugate the women, really. The Seeress was assassinated, by whose hand no one knows, and her named successor has not turned up to replace her. Basically, there is no one to oppose Wadam."

"Oh Myst, no, not Elestia," the girl sobbed. "Whom did she name?"

"No one would say," Cairos admitted, "but whoever it is has already become somewhat of a legend. Rumors are spreading everywhere that the girl left on a pilgrimage to heal the sick and raise the dead and that she will return to deliver the Mystian faith back to glory."

DaVille made a sour face at this, but Cairos had to ignore him. "As I said, I can't speak to my own thoughts on the matter, but the Mystians are usually scornful, particularly toward us wizards. The rumor that one would leave the continent to heal the 'evil' world is hard for me to put any belief in."

"I've never heard of such a thing," Starka replied. "I wonder who Elestia named. There are many who vie to take her place and if she did not name one who was present in the cathedral, it sounds like quite a mystery."

DaVille shrugged. "Does it make a difference?"

"It is a very good reason for me to return home," she replied, drying her tears. "I know Wadam, and I know his ways. If he succeeds, I may not have a home to return to."

Cairos nodded. "From what I've heard, after he takes control of the country this Wadam may very well start a war of his own."

"Well," DaVille said while standing, "there isn't much we can do about it tonight. I suggest we get some sleep and head for Hakes in the morning, together."

"About that, there's one more thing I'll need to tell you." Cairos stood as well, ready to abandon the remnants of the fire. DaVille and Starka looked at him intently.

"I believe there's an ambush waiting for you in the forest."

CHAPTER 56 – *Xymon*

ENERAL XYMON SAT MEDITATING INSIDE AN ALCOVE HIGH in the Great Watchtower and waited to be summoned. His thoughts had been a plague on him since he returned from killing the Seeress. He fought every day to keep the memories out, but found no peace. Light flickered in his vision when his eyes opened, so he kept them closed as much as possible. And on top of everything else, his horns hurt — which they had not done since their implantation.

The room was as cold as he could possibly make it. He welcomed no fire in his chamber, and he chose one with no windows. Xymon wrapped his cloak more tightly about his body and finally stood. Drawing his weapon, he began to flow through the forms of swordplay to distract his mind. With each swing and thrust of the huge blade, he fought against his intangible opponent. Nightwind's near-sentience helped calm him with its constant call for blood.

Fandur.

The sound of the Seeress' voice invaded Xymon again and he fell to his knees on the chilled stone floor. As the sword bounced away, he stared into the dark marble. Even in the low light, it reflected an image of a face he refused to recognize.

Half a face. *Fandur's face.*

His rasping voice erupted in a roar as he balled a fist and punched at the tile to shatter it like glass.

"That is not me," Xymon whispered. Fandur was dead. His past was dead. He was a General in the Carrion army, a killing machine. The Seeress had merely been hallucinating in her near-death and blinded state. Xymon reached up and grasped his short horns, not to pull them out but to reassure himself of his identity. He was Carrion, he was changed.

I know it is you.

The voice seemed to echo in the chamber even though it was only in his head. Xymon grasped the blade and grip of Nightwind and attempted to concentrate. He focused on the darkness and the will of the weapon, fighting back the madness that the dead woman continued to bring him.

Did the Great Zion know of his conflicted mind? Is that why his master had not called on him since? Could this be another test? Xymon fought back the questions with the same willpower. Though there was nothing nearby to kill, comforting waves of surety flowed through his frame as he rocked gently back and forth.

It was surely a test by his master to reconcile his dead past. The belief reinforced his will — he would not fail in this because he had not failed in anything else.

Xymon had tracked down the traitor Circulosa and brought him back to the darkness, despite all his magical attempts to cloak himself. The wizard General said quite a bit after his transition, before Feraldus took hold of his ruined body. Drakkaram had been sent to destroy the reported traitor. Xymon could not fathom how Terrant had survived the removal of his horns, but it comforted him that the Great Zion foresaw it all. Nothing escaped his attention or his reach — it had to be so.

Just as Xymon's breath calmed and he relaxed his grip on the blade, a gentle rap came to the thick door of the chamber. The General rose and moved to open it. A Carrion servant, possessing only one horn to give testament to its servitude, knelt on the other side of the portal.

"The Great Master bids you to audience."

Feeling something like joy, Xymon pushed past the servant and began weaving the path through the labyrinthine corridors to the stairway. As his silent footsteps ascended, the General reasserted his will upon his memories that they should stay silent while in the presence of his master. He could only hope that they would listen.

THE KING OF DARKNESS SAT UPRIGHT ON A THRONE OF BLACK marble. His chair, carved with skulls and sigils, made Zion look more of a ruler than Xymon had ever seen before. Though he wore no crown, his three horns were the only necessary testament to his elite status. The black silk that loosely covered his massive and muscular frame looked soft and shined back the dark light like water. Effortlessly, Zion lifted his hand to be kissed by his General.

Xymon knelt at the feet of his lord and brought his lips gently to the knuckles before realizing that he had not replaced his smooth black mask. It hung at his belt and his visage was revealed to all who looked upon him. The servant would have to be killed.

"What is your bidding, my Master?"

"Do you doubt me, my Dark One?" asked Zion, his voice dark and potent.

"Never, Great One." Xymon felt a crushing sensation on his heart that he hoped was only his imagination.

"Your thoughts betray you. I have seen a great many things, but I did not believe you would lie to me."

"Never, Great One," the General repeated. "I have only ever sought to do your will."

Zion nodded in response and seemed to consider his subordinate for a moment. Did the Great One truly know of his struggle since returning? It seemed obvious now. Zion had given him time to stew with his thoughts, waiting to see if he would take any unbidden action. The crushing sensation continued in his chest.

"You lost much of yourself when you came to me, but we both know you did not lose all." Xymon searched desperately for any hint of disapproval in his master's voice but found none.

"The one whom you sent me to kill named me, Master. Tell me that she is full of lies and I will think on it no more."

"Do not think that I sent you to her without knowing the truth, my Dark One. I know every piece and every inch of you. I know your pains, your thoughts, and even your fears."

Xymon hung his head, waiting to be named a betrayer like Terrant and Circulosa before him. When Zion changed the subject entirely, the General was startled and perplexed.

"I have a new mission for you."

Celebration caught in Xymon's throat. Without thinking, he donned the mask that hid his features and raised his eyes to the Great Master proudly. He still served a purpose.

"I wish you to take a gift to He Who Lives," said Zion cryptically, quoting his own prophecy. "You will find Terrant the Betrayer southeast of Hakes, and deliver the gift before Drakkaram's sloppy ambush scares him off."

Xymon's eyes widened behind his mask, but he knew better than to question the wishes of his master. He waited patiently for an explanation, but when one did not come Xymon did not protest. Zion clapped twice and a servant shuffled forth from behind the throne, gaze cast downward. Xymon recognized it as the same one that summoned him to the throne room. He laid a hand on his sword hilt and waited for Zion to speak again.

"I foresee that Drakkaram's plan will fail, though by no fault of his own. I wish you to find the Betrayer and give him this." Zion took a long box from the servant and presented it to Xymon, lifting the hinged lid for him to view the contents.

A well-shined pair of black horns, laid gently on a bed of velvet, stared back at him. As Zion closed the box he spoke again.

"I can tell that you do not understand, my Dark One. It is possible that neither will the Betrayer, but offer him no explanation. Simply tell him that this is a gift from me and leave."

The General took the box and rose to exit the chamber. The servant from before knelt to one side of the doorway. As Xymon reached back for a killing stroke, Zion spoke one last time.

"Take care that you do not engage him in combat," said the Master. "Heed my words, or you will feel my wrath."

CHAPTER 57 – *Wan Du*

AN DU HAD TO ADMIT THAT LADY MAYRAH SHOWED MORE courage and fortitude than most of the men he had fought beside. After taking a few swipes with her sword to gauge the pain involved she confirmed her readiness. He nodded, but a thousand questions about her safety raced through his mind in that single moment. The next time she became wounded could be her last.

The hellhounds in the quarry looked ferocious and large. Their claws and teeth could not be well fought with a sword only as long as man's arm, and Wan Du knew jumping into the fray against so many quicker adversaries would be suicide anyway. An archer company would have been useful, he thought, but they were only two. He could dispatch many grunts even without a weapon, but the Carrion soldiers would not be the biggest challenge in this fight.

"We cannot rush in to the quarry or the fortress. They are too many and too quick." He heard defeat in his tone, but Lady Mayrah did not seem to pick up on it. Her blue eyes flashed in the last of the daylight as her gaze looked beyond the massive stone pit.

"Then we need a plan," said Lady Mayrah. "Where is their water supply?"

Wan Du's gut twisted so hard that he nearly cried out. Through gritted teeth he said, "We cannot poison them."

Her expression flashed apologetic in response, but only for a moment. Too soon it was replaced by the warlike demeanor and commanding tone. "That's not what I meant. Quarries are low, right? Made by digging down in the stone."

The large man nodded, finally seeing her point. "Water flows downhill."

His companion looked out again across the landscape before turning to him and pointing past the stone valley holding the hellhounds. He followed her gaze and saw the shimmer of water. High water.

"But trenches take days to build."

She silenced his skepticism with a raised hand. "We do not need trenches," said Lady Mayrah. "The cavern walls are smooth here. And back in the canyons, the walls were smooth there as well. A river carved all that we have traveled through.

"I do not know this place, but I know water has traveled here. The quarry is deep and steep; water rushing in would keep any of its occupants from escaping." Her words were full of a strange hope, the sense of accomplishment one can only feel from defending his life. Wan Du wished he could feel the same confidence.

They set off to find the dam. The plan was a difficult one, especially because of the distance they needed to travel around the quarry and still stay out of view of the fortress which had an amazing vantage to spot guests. The pair decided to stick to the tunnels and hoped the route would lead them further south and to the water Lady Mayrah spotted.

One of the caverns they passed through seemed to skirt the edge of the quarry itself. Wan Du ran his hand along the wall to touch the smooth white stone before something caught his eye. The low light was reflected well by the alabaster stone, revealing a shape he recognized. As he reached for the object, Wan Du felt a familiar whisper in his ear. Carved from the stone, somehow, was a weapon. At the head of a short pole sat a mass of uncarved rock. Though surprisingly light for solid stone, it still did not compare to his halberd.

The club would do nicely.

✐

Avoiding detection was easier than Wan Du expected, as the Carrion seemed either too busy or too afraid to patrol the caverns that honeycombed the region. The height of the plateau still dizzied him, and one of the tunnels even led them to a sea-facing exit of sheer rock. They traveled throughout the day until Wan Du noticed dusk quickly approaching. Their light source in the tunnel would diminish until subterranean travel became impossible.

"We must hurry," he said.

Lady Mayrah gave him a pleading look. Though she was not stalling, she no longer seemed the least bit eager to attack the Carrion-controlled fortress. Since coming up with the idea of attacking the dam, the woman seemed to retract into herself like a hiding crab. Not that she had been talking much lately anyway, Wan Du thought. Besides, they were not friends, just two people thrown into a situation. If the circumstances were different, they would have nothing to say to each other at all.

The pair broke into the open just in time to watch the last rays of the sun slip under the horizon. Echoes of throaty canine growls and the stomping of hooves made the darkening landscape all the more frightening, but Wan Du kept in mind they were high above the beasts. Looking further south, the shadow of the dam came into view. Beyond it, the cliffs and plateaus seemed to extend east and further south to where the sea finally swallowed them. The path this dammed river took might be a mystery, but it was one Wan Du would take for granted.

Blocking and re-routing the water had first been done many years before, when men first began to carve the metal and wood and fit them together using interlocking joints. No magic had been employed to create the structure, only expert craftsmanship. Wan Du marveled at how wide it spanned, forcing the entire river flow to the west rather than its intended northern path. Crouching on top of the dam itself, Wan Du could see the river's path until it dipped into caverns they had not traversed. Using the cover of darkness he watched and listened to the Carrion soldiers as Lady Mayrah explored the area on the other side of the dam.

The area, like the caves, was left completely undefended. Wan Du nearly said another prayer of thanks, but thought he should save it until after their plan succeeded. The grunts in the quarry still seemed to be training the hellhounds, with growling and stomping a product of multiple showdowns of the canines against the bison. Though too far to tell which won the "matches," he was glad so many of the Carrion experiments would be destroyed by their assault.

The rest he would have to deal with.

Lady Mayrah silently joined him atop the dam and stared at the meandering drop of the riverbed. He turned his head to watch as she went through the same motions he had, perusing the possible weak or rusted joints, but the masterpiece of engineering seemed as perfect as the day it had been built. Magic could undo it, yet after seeing the destruction the exploding stone caused near Flaem, he was more loath to trust eastern sorcery.

"How are we going to bring this down in time?" asked Lady Mayrah.

CHAPTER 58 – *Mayrah*

MAYRAH LOOKED TOWARD THE RUINED FORTRESS FROM THE top of the immense dam. The remnant of Bathilde was in there, somewhere. Her thoughts darkened further as Bathilde's changed form came to her mind. Would the creature that used to be her friend die from the flood or would Mayrah need to plunge a sword into her breast? Her hands began to tremble. She had dispatched many Carrion soldiers during their travels, but none she had identified and recognized. Damn them for forcing us to fight ourselves, she cursed inwardly.

Wan Du's voice shattered her thoughts like a mirror. "We must find a way south across the channel."

Mayrah recovered for a moment, wrapping her torn shirt closer about her body. The temperature rose as the night drew to its end, but the shiver she felt had nothing to do with the weather.

"We have no ship," she said. "Are there any villages along the bay?"

"I know not," he replied.

Their hope would have to do for now. She lifted her cold, mundane sword to eye level and squeezed her fist around the grip. Its curved blade, however sharp, was no use to them at the moment. The crude stone club Wan Du found in the caverns might be of some use, but the dam seemed to be made of stronger stuff.

"We don't have much time," she reminded him. The dark blooms on the eastern horizon were indicative of the impending dawn. Luckily, the Carrion and their beasts had not rested the night, but still battled within the quarry's confines just a stone's throw away.

Wan Du confirmed her assessment with a deep humming noise. What would happen if dawn came and they could do nothing to stop the Carrion? Would he charge down to fight them himself?

"I have found it," he proclaimed, surprising her again.

Fighting off the urge to ask what he found, Mayrah merely watched him climb into a structure on the water-side of the dam. The grim pre-dawn revealed somewhat of a weir, but the murky water hid much of the detail. Mayrah waited as her companion slipped in to investigate further.

Wan Du's hands probed the mechanism under the water, but she could see little in the low light. Before long, he resurfaced and drew in a deep breath. Still fighting the urge to pepper him with questions, Mayrah offered him a hand up which he gently waved off.

"The Carrion have been here." The words chilled her bones and made her heart begin to pump faster. With five words, he had dashed her hopes. Wan Du lifted himself back up onto the dam and made no effort to dry his scant clothing. As the water dripped from his tensed muscles, Mayrah found herself transfixed for a moment.

"Tell me," she replied.

"There is a relief valve that opens the flood gate, but they have fused the metal. I have not tried to move it and I fear that it may not budge. I will use the club as a lever, though I may not be able to escape if the gate opens too quickly."

Mayrah listened carefully to every word of his explanation, knowing he would not let her attempt the feat herself. Wan Du could die any number of ways if the flood gates opened and the pull caught him. None were ways he deserved to die, yet she felt powerless to help. Recovered though she was, Mayrah could not match half his brute strength and this seemed the only way to accomplish their goal. They had no rope with which to secure him to the solid parts of the dam and no time to make or find any.

She nodded her agreement and understanding, then retreated to solid ground. As the woman took one last look toward the quarry, she heard the same terrible sounds that echoed throughout night.

When she turned back to Wan Du, Mayrah reflected on their brief history together. She met the man in Cellto, the prison city south across the immense bay from where they stood now. Her first impression of the stoic warrior was mixed. While initially she felt no sympathy upon hearing that his family had been lost, her heart moved when she learned the entire city of Brong died with them.

For all of her life, Mayrah had been told how ruthless and bloodthirsty the men from Brong could be. Their century-long conflict over the rightful control of the Blood Coast seemed the only indicator of this, though the feud remained something her own country was half responsible for.

Her thoughts turned to the two horned beasts they saw fighting before her arrow wound. Brief glimpses of the red dragon and white gargoyle outside the wizard's city accompanied them. Animals did not need a good reason to fight each other; they could simply do it to judge who was stronger or better. Weren't humans supposed to be above such things? In all the years Rochelle had fought Brong over a stretch of land that capitalized on their battles, why hadn't anyone raised how illogical it all was?

Her inborn hatred and prejudice had ebbed away, and she could only look upon Wan Du with respect now. She admired his indomitable spirit, whether deity-inspired or not. If he lived — if they both lived — through this, perhaps she could tell him some of these things. Mayrah rubbed the patch of her arm where her betrothed's bracelet once held securely and fought against the regret. Her mate and child were dead, her best friend had been turned into the enemy, and her home and people lay destroyed. Whatever the consequences, Mayrah would take control of her own life.

Knowing full well the potential of both outcomes, Mayrah turned back to Wan Du and whispered, "Do it."

THE TORRENT OF WATER CAME SO QUICKLY THAT MAYRAH PAN-icked. She fought the urge to call out to him, sure that Wan Du would get caught up in it. It wasn't until she saw the man's arms reach over the top of the dam and pull that she let go of the breath she had been holding. Just as the first golden rays of sunlight erupted on the eastern horizon, the flood exploded forth from the structure and into the smooth rock paths below.

Mayrah listened intently at the cries of the Carrion, but without Wan Du's method of translation she had no idea what words they used. All she cared about was that the screams and howls became stifled gurgles even from as far away as they were. The plan worked, from what she could see, and as the morning lit the fortress she saw the officers likewise take notice.

Wan Du joined her on the solid ground, dripping again, but grim-faced. Everything about his manner seemed to say, "It is done."

With no method of escape, they watched and waited to see the Carrions' reaction. Mayrah wondered truly how many soldiers and creations they lost when the crushing force of the water invaded the quarry and tunnels beyond.

"They are coming," said Wan Du. Mayrah nodded in response, but did not move to leave.

"If they want their revenge, let them come and take it." She swept the sword around her body to focus and prepare her muscles for the fight. As she did so, her last moments with Bathilde played out in Mayrah's mind. The stout woman held the line for their 'escape' into Cellto without a second thought. She sacrificed her life for Mayrah's, but met a fate worse than death in the end herself. Did Lady Mayrah not owe it to her friend to end her suffering?

A scream went up and three grotesque silhouettes rose from the shadows of Fort Sondergaarde. All three clutched a grunt soldier in their talons, but the creatures themselves looked formidable enough on their own. As they flew closer to the dam, Mayrah got a much better look at them than she had the days before. Huge, leathery wings complemented a bulbous torso and only two limbs with long, black talons. Stretching from the body was a long neck and a proportionately long head, like a pickaxe, adorned by the same black horns as their cargo.

"Do you think you could control those beasts to fly us south?"

Wan Du's shoulders rose and fell. "This coin allows me to speak in the language of the listener and hear in the language of the speaker, but I know not what intelligence those have."

Mayrah cursed under her breath.

"If they speak," he continued, "I will try."

With that, they both went into action. As the dragonlings flew low enough to deposit their soldiers to the ground, Wan Du leapt to catch one by the limbs and brought it sinking back down to the earth with him. The grunt went sprawling away from a kick placed in mid-jump by the large man and Mayrah rushed to engage the other two. Both drew their common serrated blades, but she batted them aside and sliced quickly through the necks of each. There wasn't time to allow their reinforcements to arrive and Mayrah knew she couldn't press her still-recovering strength too long.

The two free dragonlings retreated toward the fortress but stayed aloft, seemingly to watch the fate of their third. Mayrah looked to Wan Du to see he still had a grip on both its limbs and held it to the ground with all his strength and weight. The beast did not have enough space to flap its long wings to create enough lift to escape, and she heard it screeching in protest.

"Can you communicate with it?" Mayrah called over the beast's racket. She kept one eye on the fortress as she cleaned her blade. Wan Du made screeching noises from the back of his throat and the creature calmed enough to stop struggling.

"It wishes only to be put out of its misery," he replied. The man's tone had no feeling. "It has agreed to fly us across if we will kill it upon arrival."

Mayrah looked upon the beast with a strange sense of fascination. What had the Carrion horns truly done to the creature? It was a sentient beast that could be communicated and bargained with, yet its only desire in the world was to die. With no time for discussion, Mayrah stepped forward and took a firm grip on the dragonling's leg. The beast's talons wrapped as gently around her shoulder as they could, she hoped, and as they rose into the sky Mayrah searched for a glance of Cellto. She prayed silently that it would come into view before the beast's strength failed.

CHAPTER 59 – *Wadam*

UTHLESSNESS IS ELEGANT, IN TIMES SUCH AS THESE. THE evils of war cannot be ignored and we, as the very limbs of god, will not ignore them. Darkness has invaded our land and we have prevailed so far, but 'darker times lie ahead' as the scribe Hakkis told us before leaping into the volcano! Would that we all met a quick and painless end such as this, but it is not to be!

"The time to be dominated by the humble, by the females, by the magicians and the liars is over! Our brothers and sisters, though misled, deserve your pity! But they cannot be forgiven until they accept the plain truth and unite under the saving strength of Myst! 'Myst hath not the patience to convince thee,' as Isakkarh the Pious tells us — it was true three hundred years ago and it rings just as true today!

"Let the events of this morning be a constant reminder in our hearts. Those who died ran onto our spears, not the other way around! Myst delivered them to hell because of their misplaced conviction! Twenty of your brothers have protected you; bless them for their courage and bless them for their steadfastness.

"Rest now, one and all, for soon we will be One People again, just as the scripture has told us. With our unity we will fulfill the holiest of prophecies for peace to the End of the Ages and Myst will grant us authority to the end of the world upon His return! The sorcerers will be as grains of sand beneath our feet and the non-believers shall feel the wrath of our god! Amen!"

Raucous applause and shouting followed Wadam as he retreated from the speaking platform into the candlelit antechamber. The large man, though somewhat diminished from food rationing, let out an immense breath of relief and then allowed his mouth to rise in a smile. Waiting with a full glass of sweet wine was his valet, and Parson bowed fluidly without spilling a drop. As the tall man straightened, he complimented Wadam on the speech.

"It is good," Wadam responded with a sigh, quoting the Holy Book again out of habit.

"Indeed," said Parson, "our well-placed rumors of the successor's demise have nearly destroyed the resistance."

Wadam's temper rose at the thought of the girl. "Yet even our zealots cannot enter Myst-Alsher. What is the cathedral made of, steel-covered granite?"

The priest watched as Parson stifled a response and merely shrugged. Wadam grasped the goblet of wine and brought it to his lips without a care of how much he spilled on his person.

Twenty more days, he reminded himself. If the girl did not show up — or if his agents could locate and dispatch her — then her claim to the Seat would be void. The resistance would fall within days after; the martyrs would sacrifice themselves and write their lamentations to be found in a century or two. The priest made a mental note to make sure all such documents burned; the last thing he wished for after achieving such a victory for his god was a revolution from a later generation.

As Wadam finished the last of the wine he replaced the cup on Parson's tray and the servant bowed again. Turning to leave, the valet halted at the door and waited to be dismissed.

"It was a good speech, wasn't it?" Wadam preened.

"The people seemed to respond well, sir," agreed Parson. "The retranslation may have caught on better than you thought it would."

"I wish it were that, Parson, I truly do." At the thought, Wadam deflated a bit. For days he wondered why his followers seemed overly fervent to destroy people who had been their neighbors and friends, and though he condoned the behavior as faith-driven compliance, it puzzled and infuriated him behind closed doors. He hadn't mentioned it to the valet so far, but the time for confession had come and Wadam could no longer hold it back.

"I believe the people have been touched by this world, Parson. I fear that, even after unification, Myst may not come because he will refuse to be in the presence of such evil. Neighbor against neighbor, man against man — our relishing of this war makes me think that we are mere animals."

The valet nodded with a grim expression. "Have you prayed about this, sir?"

Prayer was no longer necessary for Wadam. Since he had devoured the prophecy, he became linked directly with Myst. The deity's thoughts were his own, and that was what troubled him so. Did his god doubt the nature of his creation? Was he feeling the retraction of the deity's love?

Wadam shook his head to banish the fears. The Holy Book explained all of this — he was just in the center of the storm. It had to be that way; Myst would let it be no other.

"Never mind, Parson," he said. "I feel much better now. I believe I will have the lamb tonight and another glass of wine before bed."

"Yes, sir," replied the valet, bowing again. "As you wish."

More than anything, Wadam wished he could see where the girl was. Unfortunately, the oracle stone held in Myst-Garvon had washed out to sea with the tidal wave. The Cardinal rubbed his hands together as he realized the other cathedral held one as well.

It might take a focus of all his resources, but Wadam needed that stone. When Parson returned with his repast, Wadam would give him a new mission to undertake.

CHAPTER 60 – *Starka*

TARKA RETREATED FROM THE MEN TO SORT OUT WHAT the wizard told her. Surely it could not all be true, but she had no way to refute it.

The news of Elestia's murder was the hardest to take and Starka allowed the tears to flow freely. The Seeress believed in Starka and her prophecy; perhaps she foresaw enough of what was going to happen to send the girl away. Starka tried hard to believe that. What was not difficult to believe, however, was Wadam's rise to power and rebellion against female "rule." His history and misinterpretation of the faith's fundamental teachings made it possible, and Wadam's popularity made it certain.

She scolded herself for wishing the rotund man had been more affected by the tidal wave that destroyed his cathedral.

Each piece of information Cairos relayed felt like a blow to Starka's gut. Thoughts of returning home to a desolate, fear-infested place she no longer recognized made her head swim with doubts. Who had the Seeress named, and why hadn't she appeared yet? If she did, what would Starka do then?

A noise from behind made the girl turn just as the sorcerer Cairos approached with a metal cup full of steaming liquid. She recognized it as a special "tea" he had prepared before to aid in meditation and recuperation.

"You look restless," said the man. He presented the tea and waited for an invitation to join her.

Starka smiled through her tears and indicated a seat nearby. She blew gently at the steam rising from the cup for a moment before testing the beverage. It was bitter and reminded Starka of the incense burned during the many prophecy rituals she attended. Though she had no idea what to call it, the herb mixture relaxed her joints and muscles as soon as the steam touched her nose. Turning her attention to Cairos, Starka gave thanks for the tea.

"Anytime," the wizard replied.

"It's odd," she began, returning to the topic he raised upon arrival. "These past few weeks I've been in danger so many times that I'm no longer afraid of what might happen to me. When you told me how things were going back home, I got scared for an entirely different reason."

"Scared you won't have a home to go back to?" he asked.

When Starka hummed an agreement, Cairos nodded. "What are you going to do?"

"I don't know," she fought to stifle a helpless sob in her throat. "What can I do?"

"Sometimes a person has to fight," he said. "We're all soldiers, after a fashion. Soldiers or slaves."

Her expression hardened at the lack of options. "I believe that a person fights when he or she has no other choice, but war should always be a last resort and not a gleeful game."

Cairos seemed trustworthy; she had no reason to doubt his sincerity or intelligence. But he also seemed more intent on unsuccessful flirtation and truly random digressions. His appearance was attractive enough, but everything about the wizard suggested immaturity.

"What will you do when all of this is over?" she asked.

The question was out of her mouth before Starka could stop it. She opened her mouth to apologize, but Cairos' quiet gaze into the night stopped her.

"We wizards know what it's like to be lacking a home to return to, especially lately," he replied. "We're a mobile bunch, so I figure I might do some exploring and see what I can find."

"No settling down for you?"

At this question, Cairos laughed. "I'm still young, yet! But no, I haven't known a girl long enough to be able to settle down with her. My parents died when I was in school and I've been on my own as a wizard ever since. What about you?"

"Me? Oh no, I don't have anyone, either. My brother ... went missing, about a year ago and our parents died right after we were born. The Church raised us."

Again Cairos nodded as she spoke, taking it in. Starka enjoyed how he listened fully to what she had to say and then took time to formulate his reply. DaVille usually ached so much to get his own words out that they either overlapped hers or cut her off altogether. She found herself smiling at the wizard without really meaning to.

"So you like the Church?" he asked.

Starka shrugged, unsure how to answer. "I owe the people a lot for taking care of us, I suppose. The Seeress was my mentor until ... well, until my brother disappeared, so it was hard to hear that she had been killed. I know what kind of man Wadam is so news of him was not as much of a surprise. Someone needs to stop him."

"We're back to talking about fighting again," Cairos chided.

Laughing, Starka agreed. "But I don't know anything about fighting. DaVille seems to think it's some kind of innate trait I missed out on."

"Your faith is a peaceful one, or so I've heard. A lot of Pillar philosophy is based on fighting, but that's not really what magic is about either."

"Doesn't your Pillar of Vexen encourage fighting for vengeance?" asked Starka.

Cairos exhaled into an understanding smile. For some reason, the girl felt she had a lecture coming.

"The Pillars represent so much more than what one word can sum up in them. I know it is difficult for a Mystian to understand," he said, "but DaVille told me you had a prophecy about an Avatar so it would be important for you to know at least something about it."

He took a breath to steady himself and then continued. "Many people, whether they are of a faith or not, think of the world as a game board. The pieces move, some die, others appear, but the only universal force is one of motion. Religions and philosophies attempt to explain why things happen on this game board, but their answers don't address the existence of magic. No offense, but the northerners mostly want to ignore that it exists at all."

Starka nodded and wanted to apologize. Magic existed, but she knew what Wadam and the other clergymen said about people like Cairos. Meeting a wizard hadn't exactly put her in awe of the profession, but Starka now found their fears and discrimination borderline ridiculous. Wizards were just people. Before she could think too much on it, Cairos resumed his explanation.

"The forces of magic, the Nine Pillars more specifically, rather than trying to explain anything about the world, exist to balance it out. To talk about a singular aspect of a Pillar is to severely limit the scope of its importance. For your example, the answer is yes, Vexen does encourage revenge, but it is not that simple. Many cultures believe in the exacting of an eye for an eye punishment; Vexen's focus is merely that justice has been done. Just as it would be valid to avenge the murder of a loved one, so, too, would it be just as appropriate to forgive them and waylay further bloodshed. It is inaction, in that case, that keeps the universe out of balance."

"Very interesting," was all Starka could say in response. While the explanation of the Pillar fascinated her, she also felt its understanding was a bit beyond her grasp. Even so, she asked, "What about some of the others?"

Cairos responded confidently, as if the question was raised to him often. "My personal favorite, if I can be allowed to have one, is the Pillar of Valesh. Valesh represents change and one never has to look very far to see that in the world or one's life. If we are to use the same philosophical idea that we used for Vexen, we could assume that the world would be out of balance when things do not change. This is actually why some devotees of that sect have praised the Carrion Army."

"That's horrible!" Starka remembered the dissenting man in the caravan and DaVille's intensity on the subject.

Cairos parted his hands and shrugged in response to her outburst. "You have to remember that when looked at objectively, this war has been an instrument of change. Believe me when I say that I am seeking revenge for those who have died at my side and I would rather this entire mess have been averted, but I don't need to agree with the opinion to understand it."

The concept hit Starka like a hammer blow. It made perfect sense, but no one she had learned from ever said such a thing. "So you've heard about my prophecy, then. Tell me what you think."

Again, Cairos was eager to speak. "Well, since the Pillar of Darsch does not currently have an Avatar, very little is known about the concept. You know what darkness is, of course, but much like life and justice, it is not something you can touch or capture. Darkness thrives where light is lacking. Some people believe it represents the unknown, or fear of the unknown, but some believe it is much worse than that. Some interpretations of ancient documents discuss the Pillar of Darkness as a portal to the abyss, a bottomless hell that will be unleashed upon the world at the time of the ascension."

"Is that the truth?" she asked.

"Who is to say? Honestly, it has been so long since the last ascension that most of what is floating around is speculation. Not even wizards live that long compared to the age of the world."

"What if my prophecy is right and the leader of the Carrion army becomes the Ninth Avatar?"

"If he has discovered some means to facilitate the ascension ..." his voice trailed off for a moment, then Cairos shook his head. "Whatever his goal, we have to stop him."

THE SOUNDS OF CONFLICT WOKE STARKA FROM A NIGHTMARE OF
her brother being tortured. She struggled for breath, as she always did after
the violent dreams, and tried to stand. With bleary eyes she peered beyond
the opening of her small tent to see DaVille engaged in combat with a shadow.
The moonlight provided no details already revealed by the noise.

She wanted to cry out, to ask what was happening, but with the fight less
than ten feet away Starka feared calling attention to herself. Rooted to the spot
and unable to tear her eyes away, Starka watched DaVille punish the stranger.

Blow after blow from DaVille's bare fists sent the shadow to the ground. He
did not seem to be fighting back, which was very odd to Starka, but it was difficult to tell if he was the worse for it. The dark form continued to pull itself from
the ground each time and stiffly rose to full height before being laid low again.

Sent onto his back, the dark man halted in standing for a moment. DaVille
straddled the man's torso and clutched one hand against his throat with the
other raised in malice.

"Now that we have gotten properly reacquainted, Xymon, you can tell me
why you're here."

The name Xymon seemed familiar to Starka, but she didn't have enough
time to recall the detail before the man spoke.

"I came only to bring the gift." The voice was barely audible, like the whisper
of a snake's tongue in the dark. Starka couldn't tell if the man had trouble
speaking because of the hand at his throat or if this was his voice's natural
state.

"Ah, yes, the gift," said DaVille. "Why did your master send it?"

"I know nothing; I was merely to bring it." After a moment, Xymon's voice
turned darker and he added, "Be glad I was not sent to kill you."

DaVille seemed to shrug off the threat. Suddenly a gentle light source burst
nearby and Starka realized Cairos had also awakened. DaVille looked up and
opened his fist in a halting gesture.

"Everything's under control, wizard."

Cairos crossed into Starka's field of vision and she had to stifle a chuckle.
His clothing was in complete disarray and he looked much like he had just
fallen out of a tree.

"I was on watch. How did he get past me?"

Leaning closer to Xymon's lying form, DaVille responded, "This one is like
a snake's shadow. Even when you know it's there, it's hard to see."

Believing the situation to be under control, Starka wrapped her travel-ing coat around her sleeping clothes and stepped out to join the men. Again, DaVille gestured to halt; he did not want anyone else to come close.

"What happened?" she heard herself ask, still a bit in shock at the situation. Starka noticed strangely that Xymon seemed to begin to struggle more as she came closer.

"Doesn't matter," DaVille snapped. Turning back to the dark form, he reas-serted his grip. "Hold still, damn you."

Starka felt her stomach sink. The shadowy presence she felt in the air was similar to the fleeting feeling she had outside Flaem — just before she found the crystal cluster. Then it felt like a sheet of silk dragged gently across her mind and she had forgotten about it shortly after as the crystal had entranced her. Now, though, it became much more intense. The silk was wool and there were layers of it closing in on her from all sides. She reached up to wipe a drop of sweat from her temple, though the night was cold.

"DaVille," she said softly, "take off his mask."

CHAPTER 61 – *Drakkaram*

MAZING," DRAKKARAM ROARED. "YOU WERE IN THE PRES-ence of the Betrayer and did not kill him. I should brand you as a traitor, as well."

Xymon, stoic as ever, did not respond. His shoulders didn't hunch and he didn't flinch at the threat as a subordinate would have. It was well known what happened to infighters, but even that prospect didn't faze the brutal General.

"But, as you said, you were told not to."

Drakkaram had to recant; he could not question Zion's orders to another General no more than he could question his own. If, indeed, they were genuine.

It was then that Xymon spoke, his voice uncurling like a viper. "You lie in ambush for Terrant now, but he is not alone. You should retreat while you still can."

"Ha!" Drakkaram pounded his fist against his chest plate and stood. His imposing height towered over Xymon, but the dark General neither looked up nor cowered. Taking a deep breath to steady himself, Drakkaram again prepared for what his peer had to say. "All of my scout reports state that he is with a woman. I have five hundred grunts here, but it shouldn't take more than ten to carve the pair of them into small, bloody chunks."

The smooth mask of Xymon's exterior did not move or change.

"They are not alone. A wizard travels among them. I know not what else."

"What is one wizard?" Drakkaram bellowed. "Circulosa, too, was a wizard and it did not protect him from his own folly."

A hollow rasping laughter eased from Xymon's lips. "He was blind to danger from any side. We must all remember that the dagger aimed at our back is the sharpest."

This piqued Drakkaram's attention. "You don't mean ..."

Xymon waved off the question. "I have seen only a portion of their camp and, I tell you the truth, it was difficult for me to escape alive."

The dark General gestured to his shoulder where Drakkaram noticed an earlier wound. Instead of knitting itself back together, as was normal, the wound festered and continued to leak the black lifeblood of Xymon. At Drakkaram's nod of understanding the dark General produced a long object in cloth. Upon unwrapping the parcel, the brutal General found a mundane looking longsword with an opaque white jewel set into the pommel. He noticed Xymon refused to touch the blade or the grip with his hands and grew wary.

"What trickery is this? You wish me to take a blade that you yourself will not touch?"

"You must feel the power contained within. Only by this will you know to abandon this ambush."

It was a challenge. Drakkaram could see it no other way. If he did not take the sword then his troops would look to Xymon as the dominant General and would look lower upon him. All of his instincts told Drakkaram he should grasp the sword and remove Xymon's head with it, but no matter how many times he fantasized about seizing sole control of the armies, the hierarchy prevented him from doing so. Besides, Drakkaram respected Xymon's uses.

He raised a hand to take the blade by the grip and white-hot power lanced up his arm. Drakkaram felt invigorated. His insides churned as if they wanted to leap from his chest and his eyes grew wide in response. At the same time, a pain he could never have imagined assaulted his head, responding to the dark power from his three horns. With effort, Drakkaram released his grip on the weapon and took a step back. The brutal General steadfastly fought the urge to collapse into unconsciousness.

Panting to recover from the pain for a moment, he waited for Xymon to speak again.

"I cannot tell you what that is, but I felt it, too, when the blade pierced me. If the traitor has more of these, or something worse, we may need to plan something different for him."

Drakkaram made a sneer and agreed to consider it. He had no other options after touching the reality of such power. What kind of magic could create such a thing that made his horns respond in so much protest?

"Can't you just slit his throat while he sleeps?"

The thought of drawing Terrant's blood made Drakkaram's lipless mouth rise in a smile.

Xymon slowly shook his head from side to side. "The traitor knew I was close to him even before I truly was. He is changed, though I do not know how. I believe this is why Circulosa chose to flee from him."

"Fair enough," Drakkaram allowed, "but I fear no one, not even one who should be dead and yet walks."

To prove his point, the brutal General once again reached for the sword and took it in both hands. He lifted his arms high, feeling the pain intensify as the sword drew closer to his horns, then pulled it down swiftly and lifted a knee to meet it. The flat of the blade struck against his greaves and snapped in half, ending the tide of pain from the weapon. Staring at the white jewel, Drakkaram saw that the hue of the stone looked vaguely familiar, but shrugged it off, tossing the hilt away and the blade in another direction.

He would have to muster his troops to return to the Watchtower and then east to see how his Bathilde's mission was coming along. He hoped she returned already and saved him the trip.

Grateful parts of the General's body stiffened in anticipation.

CHAPTER 62 – *Cairos*

FTER MUCH EARLY MORNING SCOUTING VIA AIR, CAIROS was shocked and wary that the Carrion disappeared from their ambush position in the forest. While remaining carefully aware of his surroundings and his dependable senses, the wizard dropped to the remains of their camp. He saw the refuse here and there of the small detachment of humanoids; discarded animal parts and offal mingled in piles poorly concealed by bushes and other uprooted wildlife. They left an obvious trail, but the wizard had no desire to follow where it led.

Cairos was ready to return when a glint of steel caught the light in the edge of his vision. He instantly went into a crouch, bringing his staff to bear and clutching his *terasont*. When nothing moved, he crept toward the shine and found a broken sword. Curious, the wizard took a closer look. The blade had been snapped in two, but the hilt was the same as one wielded by DaVille. Only a few inches of the mundane metal blade were still present past the guard, but the opaque white jewel encased in the hilt remained intact — though subdued. Leaving the blade portion behind to rust, Cairos slipped the sword hilt in his pack for further analysis and continued to peruse the abandoned encampment.

As the morning began to warm, Cairos realized they were in no more danger of ambush. Though the Carrion made no practical attempts to cover their former presence, it seemed obvious that they had vacated the spot permanently.

Upon returning to Starka and DaVille he found them both still recovering from the events of the previous night. DaVille spent the remainder of the dark hours alone, poring over a box. Its contents were a mystery to Cairos, but he thought better of asking the warrior about it. Starka, seeking solitude as well, retreated to her tent. The only evidence of her continued existence was the frequent sound of sobs. Crying seemed all the girl knew how to do, but she deserved time to sort it out. It was always staggering to find someone you knew had been transformed into one of the Carrion monsters, but Starka's twin went a step further. The wizard wondered if her views of DaVille's past had changed, but let his thoughts lie — the girl had been through enough without his questions assaulting her.

Finding Fabfast near the tree line, Cairos hailed the boy. "I have a mission for you, my apprentice."

His face lit up, but he had a moment of hesitation. "Me? ... Not us?" he asked. "I'm to go alone?"

Cairos nodded and slipped the sword hilt into his palm. The early morning light made the white stone on the pommel shine like a white mirror.

"I need to know more about this jewel. I need you to take it to Flaem and give it to a friend of mine to be studied and stay until he gives you an answer."

As discreetly as he could, without alerting DaVille or Starka, the wizard gave his apprentice the details he would need to find the suitable sorcerer in Flaem that Cairos could trust. After seeing what the sword had done to General Xymon, he needed to know if this jewel held any secret to defeating the Carrion. Soon, it became obvious Fabfast would not be excited to return to Flaem by himself.

"You know the spells necessary to contact me if you must. Our bond is strong. You will be fine." His reassurances didn't seem to waylay the boy's worries in the slightest.

"Listen, Fabfast. The research that I need done may be essential to ending this war. Besides that, the null zone is a much undocumented phenomenon; this is why my friend will jump at the chance that this stone is somehow related. You will be doing something very great in my stead, as I must travel with these two."

Finally, the boy's expression broke into a smile. He awkwardly hugged Cairos before packing the sword remains away and launching into the air. Cairos watched him go and wished the boy good luck before he returned to Starka and DaVille.

THE REMAINING THREE BROKE CAMP SHORTLY AFTER A SMALL MEAL and followed the nearby road north toward the forest. Refusing a mount, Cairos walked easily alongside Starka. The girl wore a tired, bleak expression and stared unwaveringly downward. No one seemed eager to break the tense silence, which Cairos took as a bad sign for Fabfast's popularity, but as they approached the looming wooden giants their mounts grew restless.

"What's wrong?" the girl asked. Starka's throat was so raw that her voice was barely audible.

"The mounts are afraid of the trees," said the wizard. "The forest grows so close together here that it is very dark and they can't see well. They're used to open fields, open grazing."

DaVille grunted and dismounted, moving to lead his beast forward by the reins if necessary. Cairos motioned for Starka to stay put and took her mount's lead. Her eyes said something of gratitude, but the dark circles blending from down to her cheeks suggested she was too tired even for that.

As they came alongside the warrior, Cairos noticed his remaining sheathed longsword was adorned with a red jewel on the pommel. "What exactly happened last night?" Cairos asked.

DaVille reached up to rub his temple, clearly a sore spot from attempting to defend the girl. "If you heard of me before we met then you must know who General Xymon is. He came to deliver something to me and left a bit sore for it, that's all."

Cairos noticed that he conveniently left out the portion identifying the General as Starka's brother. He decided it was for her good and steered the conversation elsewhere.

"I've been meaning to ask you, how did you detonate the crystal outside Flaem? Was there another wizard traveling with you?"

Shrugging, DaVille produced his arm in the low light of the forest. Cairos saw the symbol of Vexen on the skin, but it was not obvious how the mark got there. Ink sinks into the skin and burns a scar, but this was something different. It looked much like the skin was pressed outward into the symbol, and colored crimson. With a shudder, Cairos remembered the symbol appearing in air between him and Gabumon.

"I see," he said. "And this grants you some power?"

"You're the wizard; you tell me," DaVille retorted, dropping his sleeve back in place. "All I've been able to do so far is blast a few things — soldiers, walls, gargoyles, and that crystal. Why so curious?"

Cairos allowed a few moments to pass before answering. He didn't want to press DaVille into defensiveness, but after speaking to Starka about her prophecy he needed to know more about this man she had become attached to.

"Usually symbols don't do anything on their own. Any belief to the contrary is purely superstitious." The wizard tried to stop before saying too much; he thought it best to avoid a complete lesson in what was obnoxiously labeled as *pillar worship*.

"It's not the only one." Pausing, DaVille pulled his coat aside to reveal a similar raised symbol from the skin over his heart. It seemed to blend into his skin better, but it was unmistakable: Tera, the Pillar of Life. Cairos hid his intrigue by nodding once and looking away, but it was difficult not to ask if there were more than the two.

The forest thickened considerably and though the hour neared midday, the light remained scarce. Northern trees produced broad leaves that mingled together in their quest for sunlight and allowed little to filter to the ground below. The muddy loam was awash with ferns and a strange mixture of moss and stubborn grass, none of which were well-liked by the mounts. Cairos noticed that their steps were careful and decided that his should be as well.

Coming across a stream the three decided to water the animals and get their bearings. Cairos took the chance to consult the map with DaVille while Starka remained engrossed in her own thoughts. He decided the few hours of travel so far into the forest merited them nearly a third of the distance they needed. With much of his energy depleted, the wizard politely declined the request to scout ahead via air to gauge their real distance from Hakes. At least until the next morning, he promised.

The party continued roughly northward hoping the lack of light had not affected their sense of direction. Cairos kept a fairly decent gauge of it with only a small amount of magical power, the only amount he could spare, and checked occasionally to ensure they stayed on the correct heading. As they made their way, he attempted to point out some of the wildlife to Starka to pull her attention away from whatever gloomy introspection she could not escape. Cairos was successful once or twice when he pointed out a prancing doe or feline, but largely she seemed to ignore him.

They made camp when the meager sunlight dwindled enough to indicate the day's end. Leaving the watch duty to DaVille, Cairos found a quiet spot between two particularly large trees and collapsed. Late the next day they would reach the wall of Ferraut's boundary and follow it north to Hakes to attempt entry. He slept fearing that not another word would be spoken between the three until they arrived.

CHAPTER 63 – *Wan Du*

MELLTO LOOKED MUCH TO WAN DU LIKE THE PRISON HE remembered it to be. Even from the air, it was not a pleasant place to look upon. The beast that made their escape possible did not falter during the flight across the bay, and for that he gave thanks. *Serené* blessed him yet again, though Lady Mayrah shook nervously through the entire trip. The dragonling could have killed them a dozen ways but it had not, so Wan Du believed it a fear of heights that shook her. Having stared over a sheer edge of the Thousand Steps, the large man conquered that terror as a child.

After the beast gently laid them onto the sandy earth, it dropped its neck to the ground, but did not speak. The dragonling was eager to die, and Wan Du did not make the beast wait.

Their walk to the great prison-city had thankfully not been a long one. Displaced citizens had built impromptu structures outside the walls, mostly because there was no other place to go in the south, but they could not suffer illusions of safety. One large, black-sailed ship bounced gently with the waves, anchored in the bay. Though the city's walls were thrown open to all travelers, they knew not what faced them inside.

"We are only here to find the weapons," he said.

Lady Mayrah agreed with a curt nod. He did not want to seem like he was giving orders, especially to her, but Wan Du knew neither of them could afford to get mixed up in the struggle against the Carrion until properly armed. He was again weaponless after being forced to utilize the stone club as a lever, but at least it worked. Wan Du earnestly hoped they foiled the Carrion army's current and future plans at husbandry.

Hope of success in Cellto seemed a bit bleak as they entered the eastern gate. The stone facades of shop fronts were mostly bare of both customers and merchants. People milled about the roadway aimlessly, but always cringed when a member of the city guard came near. Wan Du kept a sharp eye and ear out for those who might recognize him or Lady Mayrah, but after venturing past a half dozen guards it seemed unlikely. Escaped prisoners though they were, Cellto seemed largely not to notice their presence at all.

It made sense, as the guardsmen had more dangerous forces to contend with — allies or not.

At Lady Mayrah's suggestion, they entered what seemed to be a prominent weapon shop on the main street. The building was immense both inside and out with various colors of steel reflecting torchlight from every corner of the interior. Wan Du marveled at the quality and variety of the blades and showed the true desire of a man interested in a purchase until a lively man appeared by his side.

"Do you like our wares?" he asked. The man spoke in a perfect Brong accent which comforted Wan Du a small bit. At least the question of his magical ability to speak other tongues would not come up.

"I am looking for something special," he replied.

"Ah, we have nothing but special weapons here! I am Malagor, and I am at your service." The salesman swept into a bow that encompassed both Wan Du and Lady Mayrah. "May I show you something in particular? A large mace, perhaps?"

Lady Mayrah blanched, but did not speak. She laid a hand on Wan Du's shoulder before turning to look at a distant rack of blades.

"I seek a halberd. It is this tall," he gestured, "and the color of pure snow. Do you sell one like this?"

Malagor pinched his chin in thought. Only after the words had come out did Wan Du realize that his query might seem suspicious. The man that took his halberd might have a better reputation than one of Malagor's customers.

"White steel? That is rare, indeed!" he proclaimed. "Unfortunately I do not have what you seek, though I can show you a very comparable alternative!"

The merchant's hand swept in front of him as he walked, regaling Wan Du with all of the names of smiths that supply his store. There were quite a few, but Wan Du did not recognize any of them. He wouldn't, of course, since all the blacksmiths he knew were deceased.

"Here we are!" Malagor led them to a long rack of nothing but polearms. A few of the longer weapons nearly touched the high ceiling of the shop with long, straight blades of spears. Beside these partisans, one such weapon had a double-blade like a serpent's tongue, but Wan Du's eyes swept over it without a pause.

There were many halberds, each with a single-edged blade or outward-facing crescent. Some had bronze tips and the lightweight poles of wood and bamboo, but the majority were counterweighted steel. None, as Malagor stated, shined with the white Wan Du sought.

"These are all very nice," he said in his usual stoic manner.

Malagor nearly danced as his arms flailed to indicate one weapon after another. A few of those he indicated had names like "Dovesquatter" and "Rangersbane," but most were untested and unadorned. Wan Du wondered if the named ones were taken from captured men like him or if their previous owners had been killed for their weapon; a bad omen for the new buyer.

"I will look for a suitable substitute," the large man said to wave off the energetic merchant. Malagor smiled from ear to ear and nodded before sauntering away to find another customer. As Wan Du stood admiring the collection, Lady Mayrah rejoined him.

"Quite an array they have, but my blade does not rest here," she told him in a low voice.

"Nor mine," Wan Du agreed. He wondered how much further they should wander into the city without a weapon of his own. As Lady Mayrah browsed, the large man watched her fingertips run across the metal. The torchlight played off of her dark features and light hair, and the dirt and bloodstains did nothing to mar the woman's strong beauty.

"Do we even have the means to pay for any of these?" he asked.

Having been on the road for so long, their concerns of money had been nearly nil. Wan Du could not remember the last time he possessed a purse; possibly before his capture. Lady Mayrah shrugged in response to his question, reaching to feel for coins inside a pouch hanging from her waist. The expression on her face was not encouraging.

"Perhaps we should collect some funds before we continue our search," he concluded.

Just as Lady Mayrah seemed about to agree, Malagor came bouncing to her side. "Why the long face, my Rochelle beauty? Are our wares not pleasing to your discriminating eye?"

Knowing full well how difficult it would be to manipulate a salesman, Wan Du decided a version of the truth would have to suffice. "At the moment, we cannot afford even the worst of your great collection. Do you have any work?"

Instead of ruining the man's mood, as Wan Du feared, his words actually seemed to improve it tenfold.

"Absolutely! For a big, strong man like you there is always much to do!" Malagor cackled at his own rhyme and beckoned them toward the rear of the shop. He lifted a curtain and allowed Wan Du and Lady Mayrah to pass beyond it into a small, dusty room before dropping the partition back into place.

Suddenly, the merchant's demeanor changed. His mood seemed to darken and the smile disappeared from his face. Malagor lowered his voice to speak to the travelers.

"You have the look of a pair that I can trust, eh?" he asked. "Here is the truth. Impressive though my collection may be, I have not received a new shipment since the occupation. The Carrion blockade the bay and my storehouse is nearly empty as business continues to do well. What a problem to have!"

"Surely you would not like to involve us in anything illegal," Lady Mayrah stated more than questioned.

"Gods, no!" the man laughed. "It's just that my usual man, Targo, is off visiting family in the southern reaches! He's a Guild member and if they get wind of me 'replacing' him they might have a thing or two to say about it. Not illegal, no, I just need for you to collect for me what is mine and bring it back here. I will take the inquiries of the Merchant's Guild when they ask, but they well know my shop is my livelihood and it can't suffer just because of a vacation!"

Wan du nodded, taking in the fullness of the situation. It would be a bit demeaning to play courier, but if Malagor would be indebted to him then so be it. He turned to Lady Mayrah.

"You can have a better look around while I carry out this task." She nodded and turned to leave the back room of the shop.

THE TASK OF COURIER TURNED OUT TO BE EVEN A BIT MORE demeaning than Wan Du originally thought. Waiting for him at the dock was a wagon with no beast to lead it, and the intention was that he become the beast. After presenting his written credentials to the cargo master and being led to the correct load, Wan Du stared at it for a moment with some hesitancy. The covered two-wheel cart sat tipped forward with its lead poles resting on the wood of the wharf.

Looking around, Wan Du spotted the area damaged by Captain Satok's ship during their escape. He wondered where the salty man was now, and wished him well for saving their lives twice over. Sniffing the wind, Wan Du decided dragging a cart halfway across Cellto wasn't nearly as bad as rotting in the prison. It took so much effort to lift the front of the cart to set it into motion, Wan Du realized that Targo must be a large man as well.

As he wheeled his way through the streets, backtracking through the city, Wan Du continued to watch for the notice of city guards and the Guild that Malagor spoke of. The shopkeeper made it seem like there would be cutthroats watching his every move from every street corner, and indeed there were, but none stopped Wan Du to ask his business. People mostly parted the way in front of the cart and he paused for those who did not so they could maneuver past him. Trampling a citizen would not garner him any positive attention.

The trek back took nearly twice as long as his walk to the harbor, but Malagor greeted him warmly upon his return. "You are wonderful!" the merchant cried. "I could nearly kiss you, my friend! I assume you did not run into any trouble?"

Wan Du shook his head and began to assist Malagor with unloading the cart. Wrapped stacks of mundane stock weapons reminded him of bundles of firewood, although there were a few choice items among the piles. He grasped a large broadsword and actually marveled at the weight of the metal blade, wondering what sane soldier would wield such a heavy weapon.

Lady Mayrah returned during the unloading, but merely watched and waited until all was done before she approached. As usual, the expression on her face was telling enough that she did not have to speak. She found nothing in the other nearby shops matching his weapon or hers.

"And now, my friend, comes the reward you seek," said Malagor. "Please feel free to choose anything in my shop to bear with you on your journey, and on top of that, I will even pay you one hundred marks!"

Lady Mayrah raised an eyebrow. "Why so generous?"

The shopkeeper tut-tutted at the protest and handed a pouch containing the money to her. "You have done me a great service! Why should I not be grateful?"

Wan Du watched the expression on the man's face change as a handful of leather-clad cutthroats approached them. Lady Mayrah seemed to sense their intent and her hand moved to the pommel of her curved sword. The large man rested his hand on the large broadsword he touched earlier, as it was the only weapon in reach.

Ever the salesman, Malagor immediately attempted to intervene. "My friends from the Guild!" he greeted. "What brings you here on this lovely day, Roark?"

"Don't play dumb with us, Malagor," replied the leader. The man had a deep scar across one cheek and carried his weapon in its sheath rather than strapping it to his belt. "You know the rules of the Guild and you know we don't allow outsiders to do our jobs. Iblis said to send his thanks for giving him a reason to eliminate the competition."

Wan Du didn't allow the speaker any more time. Grasping the broadsword in both hands he issued a shout and brought it to bear with a great sweeping swing parallel to the ground. The nearest Guildsman attempted his best to block the stroke, but the weight of the blade split his meager sword — and the man — in half. Lady Mayrah leapt upon the one closest to her, batting away his shortsword and impaling the man through the gut.

"Oh Gods!" cried Malagor, ducking for cover.

The remaining two men charged in with their blades high, but faltered when Wan Du planted his feet and held the immense sword pointing in their direction.

"Figs, go back and tell Iblis about this. And hurry!" called Roark.

"Stop him!" Malagor cried, clasping his hands together. The man's eyes were wide with fear. As Wan Du moved to engage the speaking man he spotted Lady Mayrah picking up an all-metal throwing dagger from the load of weapons.

Wan Du swung the broadsword again and the flat of the blade struck the hard housing of Roark's ribs. Crying out in a gurgle of pain and spitting blood, the man dropped his weapon and slumped to the ground. Wan Du heard a cry from down the alley and saw Figs with Lady Mayrah's borrowed blade protruding from his buttocks.

"Oh Gods," Malagor cursed, "I've done it this time."

Looking over the dead and wounded in the alley, Wan Du could only silently agree.

CHAPTER 64 – *Wadam*

AMNED REBELS," THE LARGE PRIEST WHISPERED, MOSTLY to himself. Wadam could not find it in his heart to find any more respect for the resilience of the female gender, only disdain. The women and all who followed them were making his life more difficult every day.

Parson and his new soldiers were less helpful than he had hoped. Killing a few of the resisters as examples only strengthened their resolve. Now, holed up as they were in Myst-Alsher as if it were some kind of fortress, they merely waited him out. If they wished a siege, though, a siege they would get.

Wadam wondered if the fools had sent for aid from Ferraut, but quickly dismissed it. No one wanted anything to do with the Mystians with a war on. That, at least, worked in his favor.

There had been one success in the past few days of their siege. One of the zealots broke through a rear chamber and acquired the oracle stone last used by the blinded Elestia. Though Parson advised against its use because of the ill omen of Elestia's wounding, the Cardinal could not help but be tempted. He needed to know where the girl was, if alive.

Wadam did not understand why the Seeress lost her eyesight, but he believed it divine punishment — same with her death. Thorns in his side were being removed, and that meant divine action.

Except those damned rebels, he thought.

The compound's bells rang out and Wadam counted along. He studied again the written "Interpretation of the Prophecy of the Ninth Avatar," attempting to extrapolate some relation to his own actions or success. Again he found nothing, and Wadam cursed the girl who immortalized the words. The poetic language of the visions remained too difficult to understand.

He wished to think of himself as the catalyst, but wielded no swords. At Parson's suggestion, Wadam thought of having a pair fashioned as in the story, but he decided against it.

Mostly, it sounded like doom was knocking at every door and the world only had one chance for survival. It was the concept of survival — not redemption — that gnawed at his mind as he read and re-read the lines. The eighth bell tolled and Wadam tore himself away from the desk to seek out the evening meal.

Waiting in his dining chamber were two familiar persons and as Wadam entered they both bowed low.

"Pleasant evening, sir," spoke Parson smoothly.

The other figure, a poison-taster named Nello, said nothing, averting his young eyes as if studying the design on the carpet. Nello had been the luckiest so far, lasting a full three days of ingesting bites of Wadam's meals.

Looking at the adequate repast set before him, Wadam smiled. Freshly sliced apples and enormous grapes flanked a perfectly roasted slab of meat, itself doused in a creamy orange sauce. Tart bread wedges were stacked at all angles inside a basket. Some peeked out from under a thin cloth, attempting to become prematurely stale. A bowl of leek soup steamed nearby, as well, and a goblet of mulled wine was so close to his hand that Wadam almost grasped it before the boy could do his sworn duty.

The priest wondered if Nello took some perverse pleasure in consuming the wine, but it mattered little. Wadam's life was more important than the boy's sobriety.

"Carry on, Nello." Wadam waved the boy forward and bade him to partake.

Slicing a middle chunk from the roast, Nello slipped it warily into his mouth and began to chew. Wadam saw his eyes close in pleasure as he tasted the morsel, but waited in anticipation just the same. Next, the boy bit heartily into one of the breads and washed it down with a swig of the wine.

Nello's hand reached halfway to one of the enticing red grapes when his legs gave out and he hit the floor. Wincing, Parson sighed and pushed the food away from his master.

"Why on earth would they possibly try a fifth time, Parson?" he asked, incredulous. "They are killing their own people."

After apologizing and bowing profusely, the valet had another pair of servants drag the corpse from the room. He then left to find some untainted food and a new taster while Wadam wondered which part of the meal had killed the boy. It was a morbid thought, but he remained curious as to what kind of poisons they had attempted.

Had Nello suffered before he died? Had his eyes closed in an acceptance of his fate rather than pleasure at the taste of the food? It didn't matter, of course, but Wadam had little else to occupy his mind. Or his stomach, come to think of it.

When Parson returned with only honeyed cakes and a pitcher of well water, the priest waved off his evening meal and moved to retire for the night.

"Shall you be needing me any more tonight, sir?" asked the valet.

Facing the tall servant, Wadam set his jaw and pointed back to the table. "This has got to stop, Parson. I don't care what you have to do. You can start with killing the cooks if you think it necessary, but I tire of this game they play. If they will not respect the authority that Myst has bestowed upon me then they are not worthy to be ruled by it. The new moon will come soon and with it all of their hopes will be dashed. If they continue to resist after that, they will starve."

"As you command," replied the valet. It was the only response Wadam would have tolerated.

DESPERATE FOR CERTAINTY, ESPECIALLY AFTER HIS LATEST BRUSH with death, Wadam had no qualms about removing the heavy cloth from atop the oracle stone and gazing into it. It took all his will to make the rock come to life and obey him, but with the assistance of his prayers to Myst-Garvon, he began to see through it. Jumbled images of people and places miles away formed together like floating pieces of stained glass, breaking apart before changing again.

Wadam saw himself as if from outside his body. In his dressing gown he felt naked, and saw yet again that the garment did not flatter his girth. The vision reddened and his perspective carried to the Cathedral of Myst-Alsher's barred doorway. Desperate resisters near the end of their guard shifts looked dehydrated and downtrodden, as if the morale had been sucked from them.

Perfect, Wadam thought.

He tried to shift his focus to the past and pictured the girl Starka as he remembered her. Brown hair, light skin, pretty in the fleeting way of young females; the girl's visage came into focus while huddled against a rock wall. A sudden flash of light enveloped Wadam's vision and he felt the force that had created the tidal wave to destroy his home. Was Starka somehow involved in this? Would anyone believe him if he said it was so?

The thread of Starka's travels was difficult to keep a grasp on, much like trying to hold a bar of soap, Wadam thought. His focus would slip away to a random passerby in the caravan she seemed to be traveling with or someone else. More often than not, the warrior she traveled with seemed to be a magnet for his vision, though nothing at all looked special about him.

Giving in to the dominating flow, Wadam attempted to focus on the man. Instantly, he felt the presence of something else nearby, prowling around his mind. The priest never felt anything similar when using the oracle stone, so he ignored it at first. Soon it became more insistent; the presence rubbed against his mind and caressed his thoughts as if trying to glean something from the contact. Shifting his focus from Starka's companion, Wadam attempted in vain to track the source of this strange probe.

Instantly, the Cardinal regretted his decision.

The field of his vision swam with crimson and black. Pain lanced through his head and stretched all the way to his fingertips. His jaw snapped shut and his teeth gnashed as his fist balled in an attempt to endure the agony. His dreams, his nightmares, sped before his eyes as if he were falling through them.

Wadam tried to cry out, but his mind was too separated from his body for either to manipulate the other. When his own nightmares were exhausted, Wadam began to see things even worse. Corpses infested with maggots reached for him through a haze of smoke. Carrion grunts with truncheons attacked so viciously that they dismembered a man and then proceeded to eat the parts. Disemboweled and crucified humans screamed in unison, their entrails holding them fast to the instruments of their destruction. He tried desperately to shut his eyes and cover his ears, but he had no control over the vision. Ultimately he decided that his only chance was to sever the connection to the stone.

Ripping his mind away from the presence took more fortitude than the priest thought he had. When the back of his head struck the carpet of his bedchamber Wadam lay still for a few moments remembering how to breathe.

CHAPTER 65 ∽ The Ninth Avatar ∽ 309

Horrified, Wadam saw that blood soaked the front of his gown from his neck to his feet. He wiped the sticky fluid from his lips and chin and stared at it, trembling.

In a panic, Wadam realized he could not move. The oracle stone, he saw from the floor, sat in its place also bathed in his blood. When the Cardinal tried to speak, no sound came out. Stuck in the prison behind his eyes, Wadam could only wait and stare at his blood until someone thought to search for him.

CHAPTER 65 – *Mayrah*

FIGS WRITHED IN PAIN AS MAYRAH'S KNEE GROUND INTO his back. With his face shoved into the dirt of the alley, he unsuccessfully called for assistance. After she removed the knife from his rear and placed it against his neck, the young man quieted and just focused on breathing. His eyes burned with hate, but Mayrah was a female soldier — not just a female. The thought brought a smirk of satisfaction to her face. Wan Du joined her in hauling Figs to the enclosed area of the shop's back room while Malagor disappeared into the store proper, presumably to usher out any curious customers.

Cleaning up the bodies of the three dead Guild members proved difficult, but Malagor purchased a slaughter lamb and obscured the scene with its entrails. It was only in case any city guards came asking, according to the merchant, but Mayrah was not deceived. Guild members no doubt accounted for at least a tenth of the population of Cellto — someone would miss these four when they did not return.

Malagor did not dally long before he closed the shop for the day and rejoined the travelers in the rear chamber. Between profuse amounts of apologies he offered them anything he could to set aright this blot on their travels and to help them get out of the city as quickly as possible. Mayrah bit her tongue against refusing his "help," as she blamed him for thrusting this predicament on them in the first place. Fortunately both she and Wan Du had experience being in danger.

After binding the prisoner's limbs and patching his wounds, the questioning began in the dusty storage room. While Wan Du spoke to Figs, Mayrah stood back and spoke quietly to Malagor. The line of questions quickly became similar so the shopkeeper and the Guildsman defended their actions.

"Who is Iblis?" Wan Du avoided outright violence, but used his size and manner to intimidate Figs. Mayrah looked on, impressed that the man contained his rage so well; she had aimed for Figs' buttocks on purpose. If he lived, he would remember the pain of the wound for weeks to come.

"He is the local Guild head, the boss of the eighth district!" Figs answered. Not satisfied with this answer, Wan Du turned to Malagor for more information.

"What do you want to know about the man?" the merchant asked. "I have met him on more than one occasion and I dislike him, as you heard from the dead man, Roark."

"Go on," prompted Mayrah at his pause.

"Iblis is old and well-established here," said Malagor. "His store is larger and better than mine and those are the things I care about. Quite a bit of his business comes from Bloodmir; you both should know well how the stores work there. I am proud that I deal fairly with my customers — be they buyers or sellers — and I do not accept the weapons of the dead, save family heirlooms. All men need money at some point."

She did not interrupt the shopkeeper though his self-righteous tirade did not help them. Iblis might be looking for them even now and it did not help her or Wan Du to know of the man's politics. The mention of Bloodmir seemed to bother Wan Du, as he perked up at the name.

"Tell me what this man looks like," the large man demanded.

"He is tall, aged. Keeps his hair groomed well and his clothes are always fancy. His mustache is how everyone identifies him."

Mayrah watched her companion's face harden at the mention of the mustache. "Wan Du, what is it?"

The large man took a deep breath. "I believe this Iblis is he who captured me and took my weapon. I must find this man."

"Find him?" scoffed Figs. "You're not likely to get away from him after what you've done!"

Lady Mayrah crossed the small room and placed a foot against the young man's neck. "Enough out of you, boy." Then, turning to the merchant, she asked, "Where do we find Iblis?"

CELLTO WAS NOT AN ATTRACTIVE PLACE AND MAYRAH VOWED TO herself that once she left she would never return. The stench of raw animal meat and offal saturated every street and path they followed through the city. She still felt a pang of mistrust for the humble and lively shopkeeper, in spite of his assistance. He had knowingly pulled the pair into this predicament, though the consequences became more than he calculated. Mayrah fought the temptation to drag Malagor with them to prove their innocence to the Guild — cutthroats like these rarely listened to excuses.

Strangely, the House of the Guild was not hard to find. The edifice was the cleanest building on the street and seemed to advertise its clandestine doings to all but the city guard. The occasional armored soldier walked by as she watched, but they avoided even a gaze at the building. Mayrah wondered about the political pull of such an underground organization, but cut off her thoughts. It was not her problem.

Her femininity garnered some lecherous glances from the sellswords outside the Guildhouse, but Mayrah knew well enough not to respond. Wan Du stayed quiet as ever with a grim set to his jaw. His long strides carried a determination that Mayrah had to fight to keep up with. The main door of the building sat closed but unguarded.

Inside, Mayrah took a moment to allow her eyes to adjust. In the minimal torchlight they were greeted by an attendant. Wrapped in a lavish tan robe and with hair cut close, he looked like a dignified gentleman compared to Figs. The man studied them and furrowed his brow before speaking. His voice reminded Mayrah of wine turned to vinegar from being stored too long.

"May I help you?" the attendant asked.

Wan Du responded before Mayrah could speak.

"We must see Iblis."

The attendant screwed up his face at the large man's request. "A moment," he said.

After the man retreated out of earshot, Mayrah leaned toward her companion to voice her discomfort of the situation.

"They don't know who we are," he whispered back.

A few moments later the robed man shuffled back into the foyer and bowed deeply. "My humblest apologies, travelers, but Iblis is currently away. If you can return in two weeks I will be happy to setup a meeting. May I have your names?"

Wan Du ignored the question. "We must see Iblis. Where is he?"

Mayrah held her breath for a moment as she waited for the attendant to answer. Every second they stayed in Cellto, the pair pressed their luck, but demanding information inside a Guildhouse was stretching it even further. Strangely, the man did not seem put off by Wan Du's approach in the slightest. He must be used to demands, she thought.

"He is currently managing quite a boom at our Bloodmir store. He travels back and forth, you see? If you would like, I can tell him to call on you when he returns."

"No," said Wan Du. "We will go there to speak with him."

This elicited a gentle laugh from the attendant. "Do as you like, but it may take some time. The City Council just mandated a shutdown of the port district. Something about warships being spotted, blockades, you know how it is."

"We certainly do," Mayrah put in. She smiled gently, knowing the city would have some ulterior motive for doing so—they were already in league with the Carrion army. "Thank you for your time," she finished and wrapped her arm around Wan Du's larger one to pull him from the building.

ONCE OUTSIDE, HE TURNED TO HER WITH HIS USUAL STOIC EXPRESsion. "We will have to travel by land," he said. Mayrah nodded, knowing well the route they would need to take to reach Bloodmir, but said nothing.

For a moment, neither moved and Mayrah even forgot that their arms were locked until a familiar voice called out from nearby.

"Lady Mayrah?"

Her heart skipped a beat and the air in her lungs turned to ice, as the voice sounded just like her dead mate. Its owner could only be one person, and she had no choice, but to turn to greet him.

"Pelhadar," she feigned elation and quickly removed her arm from Wan Du's. "My brother."

The man she remembered smiled back and raised his one good arm, his empty sleeve hanging limply at his side. Left lame for years, his dark skin surrounded yellow teeth and eyes. The filthy covering he wore screamed more than suggested his profession. Mayrah knew well the reason his expression faltered; the hand she raised in greeting was missing her betrothed's token. That, and he had happened upon her with a man from Brong.

"I would ask you how you have fared, but I can see that you have taken care of yourself well," he spat. "How did you go from commanding a garrison of survivors to becoming the whore of a slant-eyed bastard like this?"

Wan Du turned toward Pelhadar and his expression changed from one of calm to a look of pure hate. Mayrah raised a hand to stay, him but Wan Du spoke anyway.

"She is no whore," he said evenly.

While Mayrah appreciated the defense of her honor, nothing Wan Du said would help her now. Mustering up her own disgust for the man who was her betrothed's brother, she grasped Pelhadar by his sweat-soaked collar and pulled him toward her, feeling the familiar bump of a sword hilt press into her hip.

"Are you angry I didn't come to you, Pelhadar? Is that it?" she whispered. "You were always jealous of him because he had everything you did not. Did you think to steal his sword when he died, as well?"

The man's eyes widened at the mention of her mate's blade. "Don't change the subject, slut," he growled. "I name you Mayrah Vowbreaker, and I will make sure our people spit on your grave long after you die."

Again, Mayrah held Wan Du back with an upraised hand.

"I will bear my shame because I must," she said venomously, "but I will not see his blade in the hands of a lame coward." With that, Mayrah reached and pulled the blue blade from its sheath at Pelhadar's side. The metal caught the light and glowed all the more brightly in her hand. Grinning, she held it to Pelhadar's cheek.

"Even if I do not die in this war, I am dead to you."

"It is lucky that you found one of your weapons so soon," said Wan Du.

"Right," she replied tonelessly. "Lucky."

Only later, long after they had purchased horses with Malagor's money and struck out west from Cellto, did Mayrah allow herself the mourning tears that her words deserved.

CHAPTER 66 – *Starka*

iFE HAD SUDDENLY BECOME MUCH HEAViER FOR STARKA. Every mile they rode brought her closer to truths she was still not willing to face, and nothing she believed to be true seemed real anymore. Nothing could have prepared her for the sight that had assaulted her eyes the night before.

Whether from his current Carrion state or from DaVille's beating, she could not be sure, but what Starka saw, without a doubt, was once her brother. Half of his face was all but missing, twisted into a gnarled grimace and nearly black. Veins and pus appeared where his beautiful eye and cheek used to be, the skin rotted into death long before. The other side of his face was stricken and pale and seemed well on its way to joining the corrupted side. Even so, the empty black eye held something that Starka could only hope was memory. Or humanity.

"By the Nine," Cairos had whispered, "he looks just like you."

Starka collapsed to her knees without the strength to even cry. After the news of the state of her home, this was too much to bear. *Not you, too, Fandur. It can't be.*

Her brother's lying form turned from mildly struggling into a raging cornered animal. With what seemed like little effort, Fandur's remnant cast DaVille off and through the air. The warrior slammed against a tree trunk and collapsed to the ground. Starka, too distraught to be afraid, watched Cairos meet a similar fate when he attempted to intervene. The loss of light made Starka's heart nearly leap from her chest.

She stared, horrified, as the shadow of Fandur stood and hobbled closer to her, reaching out a hand to touch her. The painful cry that erupted earlier turned into a beastly whine.

"I killed the Seeress," he whispered as he drew close, "but she named you as her successor."

Starka collapsed forward and placed one palm on the ground to try to stay somewhat upright. Could he be lying? Why would he tell her this?

Before she could respond, the white tip of a blazing sword erupted from his shoulder to elicit another howl of pain.

"No!" she had cried. A vision of her nightmare pressed its way back into her mind, but she fought it down. "Please!"

Reaching up with the hand from his opposite side, Fandur grasped the blade and pulled while spinning to land an elbow against DaVille's head. It was not a lethal blow, but it sent her companion to the ground. With her eyes closed to the images of Fandur's transformation, Starka heard the words, "I'm sorry," before the darkness had swallowed her entirely.

DaVille remained a resurrected enigma, her brother was a Carrion officer, and the source of all her faith suffered from the greatest schism in its history. A house divided cannot stand, she recalled from the Great Book, but her mind remained likewise divided.

Cairos became a pleasurable traveling companion, but she could not bear to pay him any attention. The wizard was a fascination to her almost as much as DaVille, but for completely different reasons. Every thought or possibility she attempted to focus on led her to a dead end and every question brought only more uncertainty. There were no answers on the frontier and the imposing press of the forest only forced Starka deeper into her thoughts.

"Sasia, that's what we should call you." Cairos spoke as if he had discovered gold. It took a moment for Starka to register the wizard was speaking to her.

"Pardon me?" she asked.

"Well, when we reach Hakes we have to start acting the part of our farce. It will be even more credible if we can convince the authority there that we are who we say we are. You," Cairos flourished a hand to create a sparkling flash of color, "shall be Duchess Sasia of Melnoch, chosen emissary to aid the cause against the Carrion Army."

Starka nearly laughed out loud. She thought the plan foolish, at the least, but with as much flamboyance as Cairos exhibited it was absolutely doomed. She looked toward DaVille who ignored the conversation entirely. Looking back at Cairos' expectant face, she could not hold back a smile.

"And who will you be?"

The wizard pondered it for a moment and Starka realized he had been thinking only about her the entire time. It was quite flattering.

"I am a court wizard, of course. And they shall call me Brocatus Quezacotl Vamstillus." Another wave of his hand brought forth dancing sparks and intertwining streams of colorful light.

"Quite a mouthful, but it certainly sounds official. And DaVille?" The warrior turned upon hearing his name.

"I am your bodyguard and servant," he muttered, obviously unhappy with the role. "My name will be irrelevant at court, and don't expect me to speak much."

"Ah, the plan is coming together nicely." The wizard rubbed his hands together conspiratorially.

"Do you really think it will work?" asked Starka.

"Why wouldn't it," said DaVille, "you're pretty enough to be royalty." From his mouth, it didn't sound like a compliment.

THE SOUTHEAST WALL ENCASING THE FIVE POINTS OF FERRAUT stood taller than any Starka had ever seen. As they neared the base, she looked up and guessed its height, easily twice what surrounded Flaem — possibly more. It reminded her of the Great Northern Wall near Shargoth. Bricks flowed together so closely even a scrap of parchment could not be slipped between them and the face was covered in a dull tan sheen. Any army facing an obstacle of this size would be tempted to turn back, she thought.

Coming close to the wall, they turned parallel to it and rode northeast. DaVille, after consulting the map one last time, concluded that they should reach the Hakes gate before sundown. Starka, still struggling with her thoughts, decided it would be best to press on regardless of her uncertain future. The homecoming she desired would be difficult, and probably violent, but it remained a ways off and there were important tasks to be completed before then. She looked to DaVille for strength and watched him for a moment as she rode at his side.

The man was dressed simply as always with a well-traveled tunic and similar breeches. His booted feet slipped gently into the stirrups of his mount and he led the beast with what seemed like willpower alone. His remaining longsword was strapped across his back and always at the ready as his gaze scanned the horizon for threats. Day after day they traveled and he showed no sign of fatigue or weakness, even to the point of disdaining each. At night, she knew his dreams still plagued him; memories of the two lives he had lived.

Her gaze traveled to the simple oblong box that hung, strapped shut, on his mount's rear. What kind of gift would the commander of the Carrion offer this former officer?

Stretching her legs in the saddle, Starka turned to her other side to watch Cairos amble next to her. They rode at a pace he could easily match, whether by magic or endurance alone she wasn't sure, to save the energy of their beasts.

None of the three dressed extravagantly, but Starka figured that might play to their favor if questioned. Wealthy foreign duchesses had nothing to gain from highwaymen except attention and danger, while three travelers seeming as paupers were likely to go unnoticed. The problem would be somehow proving the plausibility of their origins.

Starka felt only a small amount of shame at how excited she was over-pretending to be royalty. Every new part of her quest seemed to assault her faith anew, this most recent being a complete lack of honesty necessary for survival. One of the questions that plagued her mind more and more was how her faith could have a place here in the "real" world.

Day to day life at home was simple. People were simple and their dealings were the same. Wars were fought elsewhere, places where greed and deception ruled men's hearts — or so the Great Book told. But could it be truly evil to bend rules, to survive, if one's cause was just? It had to be, though she wondered how those thoughts would affect life when she returned to the Mystian Continent. Was she just as much of an outsider now as Cairos would be?

Forgoing a rest for an afternoon meal, the group continued until the gate through the wall came into view. Or rather, the pair of gates. A larger gate of wood reinforced with strips of metal stood shut next to a smaller archway, barred by a simple portcullis. As the three approached, an armored and hel-meted guard greeted them from the other side. He bore a huge partisan, thin enough to slide through the metal gate Starka noticed, and a shield embla-zoned with an empty star. Five Points, she concluded.

"Greetings, good sir!" Cairos called joyously, overplaying his part just a bit. "We request passage."

The soldier nodded but did not move. Metal gears shrieked to life as the portcullis rose to accommodate the height of a man. A dozen armored soldiers similar to the one standing guard dashed out to flank the group, but held their spears upright and did not threaten the travelers.

"All those who would pass through the gate are subject to inspection. State your names and business." The guard's voice was commanding, yet not angry.

Starka spoke up, trying with all her might to sound confident in her role. "I am the Duchess Sasia of Melnoch. I am on a diplomatic mission to the King of Ferraut," she said, "to offer aid in the war."

Looking quickly to Cairos, Starka received a grin and a nod to confirm her perfect delivery. It took effort not to let her expression and posture waver when the soldier frowned and replied, "Never heard of you."

The wizard was there to pick up the conversation. "Doubtless you enjoy the products of our spice colonies, though! Come, my good man, let us share a drink as friends and I can regale you with many stories of our good duchy."

Shrugging, the guard called his soldiers back and gestured for the three to come through. Apparently they were not a threat. After breaching the portcullis, though, a pair of unarmed soldiers walked over to meet their mounts as others took an interest in their provisions. Starka turned in her seat to watch the inspection of DaVille's packs, mostly to see if the mysterious box would be opened.

"What's in here?" One of the soldiers tapped the wooden box with a finger. DaVille, true to his role as well, deferred to Starka without a word.

"Nothing of consequence, I assure you." She turned to address the leader again. "My bodyguard worships gods unknown to me and his methods are tolerated in my houses. Please allow him some privacy."

"Very well," he said. "The toll is fifty silver for crossing the Hakes Gate."

Suddenly taken aback, Starka became defensive. The words poured forth effortlessly at paying such a horrendous toll. "My dear sir, are all diplomats treated so poorly in Ferraut? Write me a note to show this 'toll' and I shall take it up with your king."

The officer seemed unsure of how to react. Starka searched her thoughts for something else that could convince him. "And please make sure your name is included."

"Ah, of course, milady." The lead guardsman surrendered the path for them and the team investigating returned to a barracks nearby. "Please excuse our boldness, miss. Regulation requires a toll, you understand."

Starka waved him off and bade her mount forward. Only after a safe distance did she let out the breath she had been holding. Cairos flashed a smile again.

"You were amazing," he praised. She blushed and looked to DaVille who merely shrugged. Starka looked back at the immense wall one last time before they entered the city of Hakes, saying goodbye to the safety of anonymity.

CHAPTER 67 – *Cairos*

OMESICK AS EVER, CAIROS AVOIDED THE EYES OF OTHER wizards he passed along the streets of Hakes. They could be easily identified by their ostentatious clothing and accompaniment of a staff or gnarled walking stick. Some even invoked clouds of power to follow them around, but only for display.

Though the population of wizards in the kingdom was small, their presence was a constant reminder of his mission and the friends he had lost in the initial attack at Illiadora. With every step, Cairos reminded himself of his promises; if his plan went well here in Ferraut then he would be well on his way to winning Illiadora back.

The three passed merchant booths and street musicians without any interest; their goal had already been discussed at great length and it was not hard to view even from the outskirts of Hakes. The monolithic town hall, the source of authority, towered singularly above the flat-topped houses and shops.

Just as Cairos noticed the sun beginning to touch the horizon to the west, he heard DaVille suggest a stop at an inn for the night. The wizard shrugged, assenting that the functions of the local governance would only be available during daylight hours. The only remaining thing was deciding how to spend the rest of the evening and night while the warrior and the woman rested. He barely focused any attention while DaVille procured rooms, but made a note of the name of the inn before stepping back out onto the paved street and stretching his travel-weary muscles. Possibilities lay in both directions on the north-south street and torches brought them to life.

Arbitrarily, Cairos turned to his right and began a leisurely stroll. He had only taken a few steps when a twinge of warning forced him to stop and turn.

"Hello," Starka said sheepishly, obviously a bit unsure of what she was doing.

Cairos smiled at the girl and invited her to walk beside him. "My Lady Sasia, are you not tired from the journey?"

"Not tired enough, it seems," she answered, mirroring his smile. "What brings you out instead of resting?"

The wizard shrugged. "It would be nice to see what's going on, if I can find an oracle stone. Otherwise, I've heard the northern kingdom grows some interesting vegetables. Is that why you're out as well?"

Starka laughed, a delightful but obviously nervous noise.

"DaVille seemed to be satisfied getting everything in order with the mounts and then laying down for the night," the girl answered. "I'm not sure what helps him stay so calm, but I've had far too much to think about lately to keep it all to myself. Since you were the one that told me about it, I figured I could talk to you some more."

"You mean about what is going on back at your home? I'm afraid I've told you everything already."

The girl waved off his statement. "There's a difference between information and reaction. Lately I have been getting too much of the former and I have been too afraid for the latter."

"You did seem quite sad on the road," said Cairos.

She sighed. "Overwhelmed would be a better word."

"I see. But you don't know me well; why speak to me and not DaVille?"

"DaVille?" This time Starka laughed with genuine humor. "One might as well ask an infant to write a symphony."

Cairos raised an eyebrow. "Is he that bad?"

"Well, no," she replied, "and it's not so much that he doesn't care, I think, but just that he loathes emotion altogether. I used to find that frightening about him, but the more miles we travel together the more I think it's what he uses to cope with his reality."

As they continued walking, they headed into a prominent mercantile district of the city. Wares were on display every few feet and even imposed on the road in some places. Racks of dresses and robes clogged the way forward. Discreetly, Cairos turned them back toward the main street.

"He's a very complex man," said Cairos offhandedly. "I would hate to still be on his bad side."

The girl looked pensive for a moment, then forced out an admission. "I'm sorry about what happened with the crystal."

He turned to regard the girl and gauge her sincerity. Regardless of her having only indirect responsibility for what happened, it seemed she truly regretted the damage the explosion caused. Again he smiled.

"Why is that on your mind?"

"I have been having more dreams lately and some have been about what happened outside Flaem," the girl confessed. "I know the loss of the dragon grieves you."

"Don't think on it. Something had to happen, right?" Even as Cairos said the words, his thoughts drifted back to the battle.

He remembered chasing General Circulosa through the hole and the dragon following. Cairos pursued Circulosa even through his throng of reinforcements. The thought bothered him then, but he hadn't had time to consider it.

Where had the additional forces come from? The wizard recalled the two odd vessels beached behind the Carrion army; the very ships they escaped onto that then apparently detonated at sea with the *scythorsont* aboard. If a null zone was created at sea, could the ships be the key?

There was only one place he knew where enchanted wood was widely utilized. *Fort Sondergaarde.* The enchantments didn't seem to take on large structures — it was only when each plank or post was spelled did the process work best. It took an exorbitant amount of time and magical power to accomplish. But a structure centuries old, he thought, and one that withstood the Sorcerer's War ...

"Sometimes I wish I could stay as calm as you do about things."

Cairos laughed, but did not comment. He was a bit embarrassed that his thoughts had completely distracted him from the conversation.

"That day was only one in a series of very strange days for me," Starka continued. "I'm not quite sure how it is I'm still alive, but after hearing the news from you it seems my fate is not becoming easier. Then there's the matter of my brother."

She looked to be fighting back tears and bravely succeeding. Cairos was caught for a moment between trying not to pry and wondering whether Starka truly wanted to talk about things. His limited experience with women had not taught him much, but foremost in his mind was that more than anything, women needed someone to listen and not try to fix things. Shrugging off his desire to stay aloof, Cairos inquired further about her brother.

"It has been so long since I last saw Fandur that I thought he was dead. Now it's apparent that his situation is much worse than that and I am unable to help him. When DaVille attacked him part of me was already begging him to stop, but another part pleaded for my brother's death. Does that make me a horrible person?"

Cairos shook his head somberly. "Wishing death on someone to end their pain is an act of mercy and should not make you ashamed. Death is strange to many people because they do not understand it, not that I am above a limited understanding myself, but what's interesting is that if you change your perception of death it does not seem so menacing."

"What perception do you mean?" she asked.

"Well, I'm not sure if this applies to where you come from, but many people I have met believe strongly that death is something that should not happen. As if people would be happier with infinite lives. Wizards, I think, have a bit of a different perspective, because we tend to live a bit longer and grow bored when there are no longer new things to do and learn. Death does not become a looming specter then to bring an end to a life of enjoyment and happiness; it becomes a merciful conclusion to a long life well lived."

"I see what you are saying. But what if our lives are not well lived? If we were to let go of our fear of death, we would be able to view it as something less threatening. But isn't that a sort of malaise? Why fight this war if our deaths our inevitable?"

As they paused to peruse a storefront of northerner beverages, Cairos considered Starka's response for a moment. He selected a cream-based sweet drink and offered Starka her choice. She respectfully declined.

"Everything you have said relies upon perception. What do you suppose the purpose of this war is to begin with? Are the Carrion merely out to exterminate all of us and then take our place as the new inhabitants of our land?"

"It certainly looks that way," replied Starka hesitantly.

"So we have no choice but to fight back, of course."

"That's what DaVille would say."

Cairos took a seat on a simple bench and offered the other side to Starka. She smiled and sat facing him with her hands in her lap. The flaming street lamps danced in her eyes and shadowed her pale skin. Her eyes looked infinitely gentle, but her expression held a fierceness that Cairos caught; she was forcing her life forward one painful step at a time.

"What happened, in Flaem, when you entered?" he asked.

Starka chewed on her lip, remembering. "An emissary met us, told us not to speak of what happened, and titled DaVille as Dragonslayer. Then he gave us a reward and asked us to leave the city and not return."

"Neutral to the end." Cairos sighed and shook his head.

"Why won't they fight?"

"Wizards are neutral, Flaem most of all. I'm here because it has turned personal for me."

"Is that neutrality why people don't trust you?" she asked, still a bit hesitant, as if she would offend him.

He smiled again. "Well, our neutrality comes from our relativism. That's actually why people don't trust us, not because we won't fight."

Starka cocked her head as if she had never heard the word before. "Relativism?"

Cairos mentally prepared for a short lecture. "The belief that truth is relative; what is true for me may not be true for you. It is the reason we do not join in the causes of others. Don't ask me to comment on what Illiadora did to Rochelle — we have paid our debt for that."

"Surely you don't believe that relativism will save the world, especially now."

"No," said Cairos, "that's precisely why we allow the rest of you to exist."

For a moment Starka wore a horrified expression until she realized he was jesting. All nervousness gone, her honest laughter seemed to make the lamps burn brighter. A few passersby even smiled at the couple on the bench. While Cairos appreciated the sentiment, he did not the attention. Finishing his drink, the wizard moved to stand.

"Cairos, what do you know about the Avatar of Darsch?"

"The Pillar of Darkness?" asked Cairos, pausing to consider the question. "It's currently the only Pillar without an Avatar. Mystics have been talking about it for decades. The Burning Men are even supposed to have a document predicting the time of the ascension, but it's not something they'd let someone like me see. Why do you ask? Did you hear it has something to do with the war?"

"My prophecy has something to do with it," she said. "DaVille doesn't believe in it, but he has been having dreams of his own. I can't tell you of those, but I can tell you about what I've seen."

While walking further, Starka shared the contents of her vision with him. Cairos listened intently, but the wording was poetic and too difficult to understand in parts.

"Do you believe DaVille is this catalyst?" asked Cairos.

"I don't know what to believe anymore," she replied. "You could be the catalyst at this point and it would not surprise me."

That brought a grin to Cairos' mouth. "I'm just a simple wizard out for vengeance. Do you want my advice on this prophecy?"

Starka nodded, listening intently.

"Stop worrying so much about it." She flashed a confused expression. "What I mean is, whatever will be, will be. The more you think about something so vague, the more you're going to tie yourself up in knots about it. Look, let's head back and we can speak some more after I use the stone to see a few things."

The girl nodded again. Steering them back toward the inn, Cairos dropped Starka off to get some rest before he set out on his own to find a temple.

ONLY A FEW HUNDRED PACES FROM THE INN, CAIROS HEARD THE
echo of Fabfast's voice in his head. The boy sounded so excited to speak with
his master that Cairos thought it best to retreat into an alley for the duration
of the conversation.

"Master, we have discovered the origin of the stone!"

"Well done, Fabfast. Let's have it."

The connection wavered for a moment, but Cairos whispered a spell to Acton,
the Pillar of Speech, and the boy's voice came through louder than before.

"… from a stone quarry near Fort Sondergaarde. It has some interesting
enchantments, but they seem dormant. The stone doesn't usually have these."

Cairos hummed in deep thought. If the gargoyle fighting outside of Flaem
was an enchanted statue made of the white stone, it would explain the stone
remnant DaVille found in the *scythorsont* crater. If he presented the same
components outside Flaem that day, could he recreate the null zone?

"Fabfast, do you remember the dragonling eggs in the catacombs?"

"Yes, Master. I collected a beautiful red one yesterday to study."

Great, he thought; best not tell the boy what he planned to do with it.

"Excellent. I need you to continue your mission for me, Fabfast, can you do
that?"

"Yes, Master," the boy replied, "whatever you need!"

Cairos smiled at his apprentice's excitement. The boy was actually having
fun collecting components and doing research. It reminded Cairos so much of
himself at that age, all the more reason they must defeat the Carrion.

"Find me more of that stone," said Cairos. "Get me a chunk about as large
as your egg; can you do that?"

"Of course, Master. Is there anything else you need?"

Taking a deep breath, Cairos asked for what he believed the final piece of
the puzzle to be. "I will also need a piece of Fort Sondergaarde."

"A piece?"

"Yes, the fortress has been destroyed, but there should still be some wood
from the walls left. Any size of portion you can carry would be fine. Contact
me immediately when you have collected these things."

Despite everything he told the boy at the edge of the King's Forest, Cairos
began to worry.

"One last thing, Fabfast."

"Yes, Master?"

"Be careful."

∽

IT WAS ALWAYS DISCONCERTING TO SEE A TEMPLE TO THE HEMUR cult. Shaped like a human woman's body and anatomically correct — to the point of having the entrance between the legs.

Cairos ignored it as he climbed the steps. He waved off all advances from the ecstatic worshippers, scantily clad and attractive though some of them were. Inside the temple the freshly lit incense and long-burning wax candles assaulted his senses and made the air feel heavier. As an attendant approached him, Cairos wrapped his hands in his sleeves and attempted to look calm.

"What may I do for you, Master?"

Using the most familiar expression for the action he desired, Cairos responded, "I seek your oracle stone to commune with Urrel."

An expression spread across the acolyte's face that could only be described as horrified. The young man looked around as if Cairos had just told an incredible secret and crouched as if preparing to jump. Cairos raised an eyebrow and waited for the attendant to explain his odd behavior.

"No one may see the stone, Master. Judge Filius has declared it tainted by some evil. I have been told it is the same across the city. Balach attempted to use it two days ago and all of the blood was drained from his body."

Cairos didn't recognize the names, but nodded just the same. The wizard reached out gently and placed a hand on the boy's shoulder in comfort as he wiped away fresh tears.

"I understand, but I must use it. I can donate a large sum to Hemur if it will help." Or I could just render you unconscious, Cairos added under his breath.

The young man wiped his eyes again and nodded. "Your fate is in your hands," he whispered before turning and leading further into the temple. Cairos followed on the acolyte's heels, hoping not to meet the same fate as Balach.

When they reached the room containing the stone, the attendant remained outside and sealed the door behind Cairos. The small dais that supported the oracle stone stood covered in a heavy velvet drape and dried crimson stains dotted the floor in pools. Cairos did his best to ignore the bloodstains as he reached for the cloth and removed it.

The stone itself looked not at all menacing, but it remained covered in a thin red sheen similar in theme to the rest of the room. The cloudy globe sat immobile within a carved bowl section of the dais and the symbols of the Nine Pillars were etched in a ring around it. Cairos absently rubbed the grooves of Tera and Hemur with each hand and gave Vexen a passing glance as he steeled himself with deep breaths. Whatever presence the local mystics feared certainly deserved some caution on his part, but his need for knowledge outweighed his fears.

Cairos placed his hand palm-down against the oracle stone and closed his eyes, reaching out with his consciousness. Though a dull red haze seemed to filter his vision slightly, he felt no pain or ill effect as he connected with the magic of the stone. Testing the waters, Cairos attempted to view himself and the room he stood in and found it the same way he remembered. In the poor light he could barely make out his body and the stone dais, but the stone worked predictably.

Launching boldly from the room, Cairos bade the stone to show him the room where Starka stood or slept. His vision blurred as the surroundings changed and he immediately felt the energy of something nearby. The viewing remained true, though, and Cairos was pleased to see Starka making ready for a night's sleep on a cot similar and close to DaVille's. The image of the young woman in naught but a dressing gown interested him, but Cairos' attention immediately diverted when he saw a third presence in the room.

It looked more like a shadow than a person. When the wizard attempted to focus more on it, the presence became elusive and even more difficult to make out — but it lingered. Cairos pushed his own presence toward it and instantly cried out in pain as a rush of red washed across his vision. Whatever it was, the presence was hostile.

He forced more strength into the stone, calling upon Tera with a whisper of his bodily lips. The image of Scythor appeared in the air ahead of him, much like he remembered Vexen doing with Gabumon. Scythor's image looked black like branded flesh, and as it became more clear, Cairos felt a constriction around his heart.

The other presence seemed to project a feeling of pleasure, as if it smiled, but Cairos did not allow himself to be deterred. If the creature could perform magic against him through the stone, it was likely he wouldn't be able to escape it merely by attempting to break the connection. Instead, Cairos fought back.

Fueled by his anger and desire, he once again called upon Tera and poured his raw emotion against the stone. A spark in the center of the room quickly erupted into a burst of light that consumed the vision entirely. Against a sterile white backdrop, Cairos saw only the shadowy figure; the Scythor symbol disappeared with the room.

Words echoed like cymbal crashes in Cairos' mind. "You will die today, neophyte."

"On the contrary," Cairos responded, "I believe that if you haven't killed me already, you'll find that very difficult indeed."

The muted colors of the figure solidified, though it remained mostly black. Blackened robes that had once seemed of many colors covered a tall and wide figure wielding half of a staff in each hand. From its head sprouted two grotesque horns and its face was unmistakably Carrion. As Cairos looked closer, the figure seemed to have two faces. Both fought each other as the visage rearranged itself constantly. Even worse, Cairos recognized one of the faces to be the old master of Illiadora, Vortalus.

"What are you?" he demanded.

Wishing to answer with weapons rather than words, the beast rushed forward with its half-staves waving. With a quick thought, Cairos pulled his presence back a few steps and pressed forward a spell of shielding. Rainbow colors burst forth and chords chimed as the Carrion beat against the spell wall. Cairos had only a few moments before his attempt faltered and the rush continued so decided his course quickly. He had to force the creature out of the spectral realm of the oracle stones, and then find it and destroy it later. Cairos prepared himself for another spell and called in as much energy as he could, screaming the words to extricate the presence of Vortalus from the stone's world.

A shockwave exploded from him and seemed to pick up the creature with it, but Cairos was pulled away from the stone before he could see the spell truly resolve. The grating voice followed his consciousness, impressing a few last words upon Cairos.

The Darkness rises, the Ninth Avatar is coming.

Hitting the wall with some force, the wizard collapsed to the floor. The acolyte entered the room and hurriedly threw the cloth over the dais. Cairos barely had a chance to tell the young man he was fine before he blacked out.

CHAPTER 68 – *Starka*

"WHERE IS THAT WRETCHED WIZARD?" ASKED DAVILLE. "WE don't have time to wait."

As the man paced the room, night came and went. By morning, Cairos had still not returned to the inn. This was the day they were supposed to gain an audience with the local governor and secure a means to the capitol — including a reference. Any hope of credibility would be shattered if the wizard mysteriously disappeared. Either way, the excitement helped keep Starka's mind off how unbearable her life had become.

She jumped up with a start when the door thudded open and two scantily-clad teenagers stumbled through it supporting the weight of the wizard. Cairos' head lolled, though he looked to be in one piece. Starka opened her mouth to ask what happened but DaVille preempted her.

"Where the hell have you been?" he demanded. "Too busy taking in the local sights?"

The girl wondered what he meant by that, but Cairos waved him off. "I had to talk to Fabfast," he said, "then I had to find an oracle stone, and I did, and things just get more complicated after that."

The wizard pressed a golden coin into the palm of each assistant before shuffling them out the door with words similar to, "you haven't been here; you never saw me." Shutting the door, Cairos pressed his back against the wood and closed his eyes to take a steadying breath before speaking again.

"Something had ... corrupted the stone," he added. "And it was watching you."

"Me?" Starka asked, growing more anxious by the second.

"It could have been either, or both, of you," said Cairos. "But it was here. I saw it in this room. We battled and I banished it, but ... well, I'm not sure exactly what happened."

"You're saying some kind of creature was here in the room and I didn't know about it?"

Cairos turned to look DaVille directly in the eyes before responding. "Have you ever heard the name Vortalus?"

DaVille nodded and the wizard continued, "It was him. But I saw him die in Illiadora. And, I know you might not believe me when I say this, but it was also Circulosa."

"What do you mean?" asked Starka. "They both attacked you?"

"No," Cairos replied. "They were both there, but they were sort of trapped in the same being."

"That's ridiculous," DaVille added, "and Circulosa is dead anyway. How could they be the same being?"

Cairos shrugged. "I'm telling you what I saw, what I heard, and what attacked me. Something is out there and if it is some kind of Carrion resurrection of Circulosa and Vortalus combined, this whole war may have just become impossible to win."

Strangely, Cairos didn't seem to be devoid of hope the way his words were. He seemed almost happy, like he knew something no one else did.

"What do you mean?" Starka asked again. "You said you defeated this thing, right?"

The wizard shook his head. "I banished it from the oracle stone realm as it was trying to kill me. Priests and other wizards have been killed by this thing, according to the acolytes, so there's no way to know how long it's been active. Or how long its been watching us."

"It couldn't attack us?"

"No, but it knew where we were. It could have found us or brought the entire Carrion army down on our heads while we slept."

"Maybe it's a Carrion creation that is rebelling." DaVille grinned and added, "It has been known to happen."

"Perhaps," said Cairos, "but rebels don't usually do their master's bidding. Doesn't Zion want you dead again?"

The warrior didn't respond and his gaze turned to the oblong wooden box across the room. Starka watched as his brow furrowed and his gaze intensified, but the man still did not speak.

"He also mentioned something about the Ninth Avatar," added the wizard.

"My prophecy?"

"Not more dreamy nonsense," muttered DaVille.

"This may not be nonsense. If the Carrion leader has discovered how to ascend ..."

"Look, either way it doesn't matter, right?" Starka concluded, eager to be done with the topic and DaVille's derision. "Like you said, we have to carry on with our plan whether something new is trying to kill us or not."

"True enough," Cairos admitted.

Nodding, DaVille began donning his bodyguard costume elements. It seemed he was getting a head start on playing silent.

IN THE EARLY AFTERNOON, DUCHESS SASIA OF MELNOCH AND HER entourage sat in the shade of a beautiful olive orchard outside the mansion of Governor Ghandaros. The regional leader of the Hakes state was a tall, well-built man and took every available opportunity to woo Starka with a charm and wit that she could barely appreciate. DaVille and Cairos took turns making a grimace behind the man's back each time the governor turned to her, and Starka did everything she could to keep her composure. Luckily, acting like a foreigner in Hakes was not a stretch of her imagination.

"It is so lovely here, Governor. I will have to return this way after I meet with your king."

Ghandaros gestured to the blossoms of a nearby tree and spewed forth a contrived verse about Starka's beauty. Poetry had never truly impressed her, and with this man's graying temples showing off an age at least double her own, Starka almost wanted to retch. The governor was not bad looking; actually quite average in nearly every regard, but his pseudo-confidence made her want to giggle more than anything. Starka did not allow him to change the subject, however, and again reminded him of her diplomatic mission. The opulent orchard distracted the man, and she could only give in to his delaying demands if they ultimately paid off.

"Of course, of course," replied the governor. "What is it exactly that you need from me, my sweet?"

Starka looked away to hide her annoyed eye-rolling. Chiming in for the first time in minutes, Cairos supplied, "We seek a recommendation from Your Lordship. The world is at war and no borders are safe; we come to offer assistance yet an audience with a monarch is so difficult a thing to achieve."

"Don't I know that!" Ghandaros spouted, slamming a fist on the leg of his chair. "We may like beautiful things here, sir, but that does not mean we are cowards!"

Starka quickly moved to put a hand on the governor's shoulder. "My Lord, I understand you are lacking men and resources to protect your border. My companion merely meant to share our own plight within that context. Can you help us meet with the king?"

"Unfortunately, my dear, I am unable to leave my post. I could send a letter with you or ahead of you, or both, but only the king himself can say whether or not he'll see you. Actually, to be completely honest, his daughter is closer to the throne than the king himself. I've seen her do strange things with those jewels of hers."

Cairos perked up, curious, at the mention of the princess and her jewels, but didn't say anything.

After Starka returned a quizzical look, the governor attempted to mask his comments. "Even so," he added, "you may need to do something more to grab the king's attention."

Glancing first at DaVille and then at Cairos, Starka smiled. "I'm sure we will figure something out."

"That's good to hear," he said. "You are in the Kingdom of Coups now, Duchess. Being creative will merit you much in the coming days. Now, if you'll excuse me …"

⁂

THE TRIO LEFT HAKES AT THE SAME PACE AS THEY ARRIVED, BUT the orchards and buildings were a full day behind them before discussion began about the governor and his musings.

"What did he mean when he called this the Kingdom of Coups?" Starka asked.

Cairos laughed. "That's what a lot of those in power call Ferraut, though it's not a well-liked nickname by any current administration, so it isn't likely to be published."

"The Five Points of Ferraut each supply a ruler in turn after one dies," DaVille supplied. "It's common practice for the next in line to 'secretly' have the king poisoned or otherwise dispatched to speed up the progression."

"Right, which means the kings don't usually stay on the throne for long," said Cairos. "Each king has loyalty to his own state, usually raising or lowering taxes to demonstrate this. Commerce is spread out enough because of geographic placement that it nearly evens out when the kings only rule for short terms. Wars don't scare Ferraut much, usually, since death is almost a way of life for them already."

Starka quickly became fascinated and wanted to hear more. "So this murderous government actually functions?"

"It takes a brave man to become king of Ferraut knowing what might lie in his very near future. The people respect that and all of the politics are very above-board because few men have time for secrecy. The kings don't have much time, anyway, but the governors, advisors, and committees play quite a role in running things as well."

She lost track of how long they discussed the strange government of the kingdom when the walled capitol finally came into view. Their mounts had been comfortably ascending grassy hills, but halted in reverence upon seeing the monument of stone across the field ahead.

Starka swallowed as she looked from one end to the other, taking in that the castle itself was a city. Towers both great and small jutted up from the outer walls and at irregular intervals from the interior, most ending in conical spires and waving immense banners in the afternoon breeze. Awed by the structure, Starka fully realized the reason a man would willingly become king of Ferraut.

"I wonder how long it took to build," she gasped.

"The outer wall took sixty years," DaVille responded, "And the rest another three hundred." Taken aback, Starka was convinced DaVille came from here.

"So," Cairos began, "what is your plan to garner the king's attention?"

A slow, lecherous smile spread across DaVille's face. "Do you remember Ghandaros talking about the king's daughter?"

Starka scowled at his humor and turned away. For a moment, she actually felt another pang of jealousy, but ignored it. She slapped her mount's rump and rode ahead of the men to avoid listening to the next plan — it clearly didn't involve her.

Evening fell quickly inside the high walls of Ferraut Castle. The courtyard, which was really the city portion, extended in all directions to buffer between the inner wall and the castle keep. The keep was a more manageable size for a castle proper, but towering above the surrounding city as it did, Ferraut Keep looked almost divine. The majesty of the structure reminded her of the Cathedrals of Myst, and she had to fight the pains of loss and homesickness before the impressive vista forced her to turn away.

DaVille told her to wait outside a saloon. An odd place for people of their false station to be, Starka thought. Of course, she now regretted passing up listening to DaVille's plan, but his moods toward her were becoming ever more unpredictable. With a sigh, Starka continued to take in the city's sights and people.

While studying a nearby man, Starka noted that all mounted soldiers in Ferraut were referred to as "knights." Their mixture of armor and clothing hovered between functional and elegant, but in all cases was undeniably impressive. Each knight carried a long sword sheathed on his hip and a huge spear with his mount, though some also had axes within reaching distance on their backs. Some owned triangular kite shields painted with everything from dragons to inviting naked women, though some were adorned simply with symbols like the crowned Five Point Star of Ferraut.

One such a knight flew through the doors of the saloon to land in a heap in the street. With visible effort, the armored man rolled onto his stomach and rose, fuming, his reddened face full of rage. Starka watched with mouth agape as DaVille came striding out from the doors. He stood in front of the tossed knight and crossed his arms, calm as usual.

"So, you're the man who says he single-handedly killed a thousand Carrion at the Battle of Kamran Wall?" DaVille challenged. "You certainly fly as if you're full of hot air."

Roaring like a musical horn, the knight immediately drew his blade and pointed it in DaVille's direction. The warrior simply laughed and shook his head. Raising his arms in mock surrender, DaVille pointed one finger past the man's head at the patrol who even Starka had not noticed.

An older officer rose in his stirrups and doffed his plumed helmet to survey the situation. Starka cringed, waiting to hear a seize-and-imprison order for DaVille. What she heard instead was even more surprising.

"Sir Fahldegrahf," said the guard, "I sincerely hope you have a good reason for drawing steel against this unarmed man."

CHAPTER 69 – *Cairos*

ELL, I GOT US IN THE AUDIENCE CHAMBER, DIDN'T I?"
Cairos smiled at DaVille's question. "You certainly did."
The warrior seemed proud of himself as he examined the wall hangings inside the large room. At one end sat a squat throne on a two-step dais, and the door they entered was across the chamber from it. Six immense columns were evenly spaced throughout the area. They reached from the

floor to the high ceiling, draped in purple cloth. It impressed him, and Cairos wondered what the true throne room looked like.

A lightly-clad page stepped from the shadowed corner of the room and announced the king's arrival.

"Presenting His Majesty, King Ettubruté of Ferraut, and Her Royal Highness, Princess Sineya of the Crowning Jewel."

As the young man finished speaking, an immense power swept into the chamber and nearly made Cairos fall to his knees. Wrapped in dyed animal hide, the king looked every bit like he had gained the throne by force of arms. Puncture scars highlighted one cheek and he seemed to be missing a portion of an ear, though all four limbs were intact. Though wrapped in the softest furs in the northern territories, Cairos knew the king was more than met the eye.

By contrast, the princess seemed years into the act of portraying a host of qualities that were least true. Dressed as richly as her royal father, Sineya bathed in mismatched layers of purple and pink that seemed bent on hiding the true mass of her figure. Her face could not lie, however, and a dollop of fiery orange hair reined in by her circlet was a mere distraction from everything below.

Cairos hid his surprise behind a smile and dropped to a knee in obeisance to the royal family. When he looked up again, the wizard watched the princess grasp a strange wand and slide a brilliant pink sapphire into the claw-shaped setting at one end. With a wave and a whisper, her entire appearance shifted to one that pleased Cairos in every possible way.

There is magic at work here, he thought. Cairos wondered if Starka and DaVille even noticed the woman's arrival before the change, so engrossing was the visage of the king. He made a note to bring it up to them later, as well as inquire more about the seemingly magical princess.

"Your Majesty," Cairos greeted the king by touching a hand to the thick carpet and bowing as low as necessary, "may I present Duchess Sasia of Melnoch." With his free hand, Cairos gestured to Starka and turned his head to take her in.

In the few hours after DaVille's incident with the knight, Starka transformed even further than she had in Hakes. A long bath, hair trim, facial coloring, and wardrobe purchase truly changed her into the striking beauty she was no doubt always meant to be. Her straight, brown hair had been pulled back and up into a modern northern style that left her pale neck and ears in plain view. Jewels glistened on those surfaces, accenting her eyes and painted lips.

Cairos looked away before he became enamored with her appearance again, but was glad to see the king had a similar experience. DaVille knelt in the rear of the chamber and kept his eyes only on Starka, noticeably avoiding eye contact with the royals.

"It is truly an honor, Your Majesty." The girl spoke without any hint of fear and Cairos was impressed. She must have practiced.

"We are honored to receive you, Duchess." After the formalities, the king eased onto the stone chair and reclined a bit. "My daughter tells me you are here on a diplomatic mission, yet your man insulted one of my knights in the street earlier today."

Starka worked quickly to apologize. "Please allow me to take the blame, Your Majesty. We are but foreigners here and my bodyguard can be a bit coarse to those he thinks may try to be his peers. I have relayed his behavior to my father on numerous occasions but …"

"Oh, on the contrary," the king interrupted, "the man was apparently spreading lies about his own reputation. This is of special interest to us because that particular knight had been chosen to sire an heir with our daughter and was poised to receive a large sum from our own vaults! If, indeed, his claims of heroism are as exaggerated as he says, then perhaps Sir Fahldegrahf would be more useful as cannon fodder."

Cairos waited for the king to laugh at his own jest before joining in. The wizard noticed the princess' eyes were practically glued to DaVille, though he did not return the stare. It seemed strange, and Cairos got the impression somehow that the girl was in heat.

"This is irrelevant to us, however, in view of your diplomatic mission. We would be more than happy to accept your assistance in this war as it seems we have common goals of survival, of course, but we have no plans to leave these walls and chase the Carrion across the map. All of our military advisors have suggested we wait this out, as we usually do, and the threat will eventually vanish."

The king's flippant attitude toward the Carrion was unimaginable, but for the context of the Kingdom of Coups. With daggers pointed at him from every direction, Cairos thought, why would he seek to die by the sword?

"With respect, Your Majesty, since your mind is made up, then hearing our proposal will not cause any harm." DaVille's confident voice filled the chamber as he stood and advanced to kneel again even with Starka.

"Very well, out with it then."

Cairos cast DaVille an unsure glance, but the warrior merely winked back and continued. "Our goal is to utilize a nominal force of Ferraut Knights to distract the Carrion army and lead them out of their base so that it can be crushed by the strength of our army."

"A nominal force, you say?" asked Ettubruté.

Locking eyes with a worried Starka, Cairos didn't dare shrug, but also could not speak.

"Indeed," said DaVille. "Between Ince and Illiadora lies the island of Kasar, the home of the Great Watchtower. It is here that the Carrion leader hatches his plans. Any other congregation of them is a forward base or temporary haven. Even a small fleet of Ferraut ships sailing past Kasar would imply such a threat to a very strategic city; they would move to defend it with such a great force that the Watchtower might be nearly abandoned."

The king hummed thoughtfully. "We agree this is an intriguing plan, and certainly not something our advisors have proposed. Personally, we do believe it would be better to eradicate the Carrion than wait them out, but could not find a way to do so without risking something similar to what you've proposed happening to us. Strange, don't you think, that we had not thought of this?"

"Yes, Your Majesty."

Cairos was floored. Ettubruté all but agreed to take back Illiadora, and while the wizard hadn't expected to be captured and executed, he had been expecting a little more resistance from the king. The charming voice of the princess cut through the silence of the moment and threatened to undo it all.

"What do you offer us in return?" she asked.

Even with the world torn apart by war, Cairos realized, there was still room for humanity's petty ambitions. When DaVille offered nothing immediately, the princess spoke again with a suggestion.

"Your Majesty, let us have this obviously capable man kill Senator Hakkark. If he can do this, he is welcome to sire an heir with me and he will more than deserve as many ships as he asks for."

The princess finished her sentence with a wink and a pantomimed kiss. Remembering her original appearance, Cairos stared at the floor to mask his disgust. He thought he heard Starka gasp, but when he looked to his side she seemed to be masking some emotion as well.

"You look like healthy breeding stock to us, warrior," said the king. "Can you vouch for his health, Duchess?"

Starka looked appalled. "I ... I cannot say ... That is ..."

The princess laughed heartily. "Oh dear, that came out wrong, didn't it? No, Duchess, I just mean is he healthy or has he had any blood illnesses?"

Swallowing visibly, Starka replied, "I'm aware of no diseases."

"Wonderful," said the princess, clasping her hands together. "Then, will you agree to these terms?"

A long silence stretched. Cairos readied a response, but was cut off by DaVille. "Tell me more about Senator Hakkark."

CHAPTER 70 – *Starka*

FTER THEY RETIRED TO A LARGE, SHARED PALACE ROOM granted by Ettubruté, Starka could no longer stay silent and turned on DaVille and

"How can you even consider this?" she demanded.

DaVille waved her concerns away with his usual air of nonchalance about killing. "This man is in our way. If I don't kill him, someone else will later. That's how things work around here."

Looking to Cairos for support, Starka saw that the wizard was not even listening. He sat, wrapped in his thoughts, on one of the opulent sofas inside the large main chamber.

"There has to be another way," she pleaded. "You need to tell him you won't do this and there must be some other way."

"You must not speak to royalty very often," retorted the man.

"What is that supposed to mean?"

DaVille smiled, mocking her slightly. "You never tell a king he is wrong. That is, unless you're fond of losing limbs. If this is what he wants, this is what he will get."

"But you can't just kill an innocent man." Starka folded her arms across her chest in defiance. "If you do, I'll … I'll …"

"You'll what — leave?" he scoffed. "We're almost close enough you could swim home. Our ruse has done its job well enough. Take off if you like."

Narrowing her eyes, Starka considered how to refute him.

"Besides," he continued, "how do you know this man is innocent? Maybe he slays children and drinks their blood in his spare time."

"I just meant he hasn't done anything you know of that he deserves to die for."

Shrugging, DaVille repeated, "The man is in our way."

Starka retreated into one of the bedchambers and slammed the wooden door behind her. She leaned back against the barrier, wishing there were a way to convince DaVille. The entire situation was ludicrous; murdering an innocent man would be too high a price for what the king offered. It was too high a price for anything.

She realized it might be the rest of the offer that had piqued DaVille's interest. Though the princess' appearance seemed a bit shifty when she first entered, Starka remembered only the beautiful face she put on when making the offer to bear his child. Starka spared a quick thought for Sir Fahldegrahf, most likely rotting away in a cell deep below her feet, and what his future might have been like if she had not shown up.

But wasn't this all to save humanity from death at the hands of the Carrion? Starka's thoughts remained their own battlefield ever since she left the caravan so many days before.

The tears came forth before Starka even realized it. She put her face in her hands and collapsed under the weight of it all. Her brother, her people, and now even the lives of strangers were all in jeopardy because of her prophecy. As she sobbed wordlessly on the cold stone floor, Starka felt the blame of the world press her down into despair. Feeling completely hopeless, she turned to the last bastion of hope she had left. Starka prayed from the depths of her heart and soul, beseeching the Divine Female to have mercy on her and to guide her.

As the whispers dripped from her lips, Starka's tears began to recede. If justice and mercy could only be served with her death, then she would stand in front of DaVille before he could kill the Senator. Starka would put herself in his way and accept the punishment her place and actions prepared for her.

Finishing her prayer, Starka uttered gratitude for a way out.

"Tomorrow," she whispered, "I die."

HOURS LATER, ONCE SHE HAD COMPOSED HERSELF, STARKA OPENED the door to continue her conversation with Cairos. She was interested to hear more about wizards and he hadn't spoken of the young apprentice in days.

She found the sitting chamber empty and dark but for a single window to the stars. Gentle light bathed the soft rugs in the various grays of midnight.

"Cairos?" she ventured.

Silence greeted her for a moment, an eerie lack of noise that made Starka's heart begin to pound inside her chest. She took a step backwards and felt for the door handle, but grasped cloth. The shock of the presence destroyed her previous will to die and Starka let loose a scream of sheer terror until a gloved hand closed over her mouth and sharp steel pressed against her back.

Soft lips caressed her earlobe and a voice like honey whispered, "Now I have you, girl. You won't be causing us any more trouble."

Her eyes widened as she felt the point in her back press harder and puncture her skin. Closing her eyes, Starka whimpered, but the blade tip receded before it pierced her all the way. The hand flew from her mouth and she heard a crash of furniture. Light from a crimson blade blazed to life to make the room look bathed in blood.

"Are you alright?" she heard a familiar voice ask. Starka tried to nod before collapsing toward the floor.

"Coward!" Cried DaVille, swiping his blade in an arc and down on the prostrate form of a black-clad man. The assassin was ready for this, though, and spun up with a curved dagger in each hand. He poised to throw one her direction, but DaVille moved into the path and batted the missile away easily.

"Oh, please," the man taunted, producing another blade. "You're only delaying the inevitable. The girl will die tonight."

Settling into an offensive stance, DaVille raised his sword to eye level, parallel to the ground. "You'll have to kill me first."

"Ha, gladly!"

Red flashed each time their blades met and Starka did her best to retreat behind some cover while still watching the fight. DaVille slashed at his opponent's midsection, but the man dodged backwards, pushing his arms out wide to avoid the blow. Allowing his momentum to carry forward, DaVille landed a well-placed punch across the man's jaw and sent him spinning to the floor. As he waited for the assailant to rise, he taunted back.

"Novice. Do they only send you to kill helpless girls?"

Starka was not sure whether she should be offended or appreciative. Why did he still protect her?

In her moment of distraction Starka missed how the tables turned, but the man was back up again, pressing DaVille with stabs and slashes of his own. DaVille parried most, taking a few scratches to his arms with corresponding grunts. His casual smile strained and soon transformed into a look of determination.

With two quick swipes of the red sword DaVille opened long cuts on his opponent's chest and forced the man to retreat a few steps. They stood facing off until the chamber suddenly awakened with a flood of candlelight. King's

guards ran into the room in full armor, swords and axes ready. They surrounded the two combatants and waited as the king himself entered the room.

"My Lord, you are in danger here," one of the knights called.

King Ettubruté seemed unimpressed by the attacker. "We thought it might
be a member of the Hooden Phage. Now we see it is merely Parson."

"You know him?" DaVille asked, sword still poised to strike.

"He was an assassin in our employ, but saw a better opportunity out west."

"Out west," breathed Starka, "You mean he went to the Mystian Continent?"

The man's face awakened in her memory — Wadam used an assassin as
his personal valet.

"Enough of this," muttered Parson. He moved with one dagger low to disem-
bowel DaVille and lobbed the other high into the air toward Starka. She dove
beneath a nearby table, hearing the sickening crunch of wood as the dagger
hit home just above her head and the death knell of her attacker at the exact
same time. When she recovered, Starka saw DaVille wiping his bloodied blade
on Parson's black bodysuit.

"Is this how you treat all of your guests?" he asked. The threat in DaVille's
tone was palpable, and the king looked none too comfortable with it. The surrounding soldiers looked at each other, perplexed.

"We did not authorize his entry here," replied the king.

"No, but you sure as hell didn't bar it, either," DaVille accused. "Not only are
we in a time of war, but you have daggers pointed at your back daily and an
assassin is able to waltz right in?"

DaVille's eyes flashed red in anger and he plowed through the two nearest
guards before the king was able to retreat out the door. Starka almost cried
out when the point of his blade tapped the king's shoulder.

"Sineya!" The king cried out in panic.

The princess burst through the door with her wand in hand, reaching into
a pouch with her free hand to produce a stone of some kind. Starka saw her
features changed somewhat from earlier, and her girth had grown considerably.
DaVille moved behind the king and kept his blade poised while the guardsmen
stood stock-still, afraid to breathe.

"Unhand him," the princess ordered. She placed the stone into the claw of
her wand and aimed it in DaVille's direction.

"Won't you just kill them both and say it was an accident?" Cairos chimed
in from the doorway. He hefted a stone in his palm about the size of the one
Sineya employed in her wand. The princess gave an exasperated growl and
flicked the wand in the king's direction. Her expression changed to surprise as

the wand stayed silent and mundane as a piece of wood. A smile from Cairos let Starka know he had been a few steps ahead of her, and the wizard gripped the true stone in his own hand.

The princess screamed as she was launched from the floor, hitting the ceiling with so much force that it rendered her unconscious. Cairos then plucked a different stone from his pocket and the eyes of the king and his guards all glazed over immediately. Starka realized they were in some kind of trance.

"The girl's no expert, but it seems she has some talent," remarked Cairos, seemingly to himself. "This telekinesis stone may be just the thing we need."

Then, evidently realizing everyone in the room was staring at him, the wizard snapped out of his musings and addressed the king.

"New deal, Your Majesty. There's only one way this is going to work and it is non-negotiable. You're accustomed to being a puppet-king to your daughter. Now, though, you're mine."

Cairos was no longer smiling as he walked to stand face to face with Ettubruté. "You will agree to launch a fleet to retake Illiadora from the Carrion under my command. They will sail past Kasar as planned. We leave first thing in the morning, as soon as your already-mustered troops can, and you will remember nothing of tonight's events, save these orders."

The king gave a weak nod of assent, but otherwise did not move. Cairos continued, "This assassin was sent to kill you, but DaVille here dispatched him so you owe the man greatly. This is your explanation to whoever asks about the fleet. The same goes for your guards. Understood?"

Again, mute nods were the only response.

Only after entranced servants cleaned up the chamber and a signed, sealed declaration of Cairos' military endeavor had been delivered did the smile return to the wizard's face. A bandage was placed against Starka's back after DaVille examined it and ruled it no more than a flesh wound. She wanted to tell him how grateful she was, even how sorry she was, but she let the words go unspoken between them. The look in his eyes told her that somehow he knew, and he also knew they would part soon. His tirade might have been an easier way to get rid of her — one without having to say goodbye.

Cairos packed the stones he collected into the pockets of a newly-delivered coat and turned to DaVille ready to leave for the docks. Flashing a smirk the wizard jibed, "Nice job forcing my hand. What ever happened to 'not talking to the king that way?'"

CHAPTER 71 – *Wan Du*

HE MILD WARMTH AND DESERT SANDS, FADING FROM brown to white and back again, only served as a reminder that the pair would soon reach the ruins of Rochelle.

After seeing the altercation between Lady Mayrah and the man who recognized her, he realized a lot more about his feelings for her. The large man wanted instantly to jump to her defense, no matter the cost and no matter the cultural boundary. His companion was being assaulted — whether verbal or physical made no difference.

But it was even more than that, he admitted.

The woman he rode next to in silence was attractive, brave, bold, and loyal to a fault. She was a fighter and treated him as her equal, something completely unheard of before the Carrion came. Months ago, they would not have occupied the same room without disdain and violence.

He accepted the loss of his family as divine action — not punishment — but it was in the hands of *Serené*. This attraction for Lady Mayrah, though, was strangely alien to him. Now more than ever, he found himself staring at her profile as they rode in silence. Wan Du honestly began to wonder how she felt about him after what had happened in Cellto.

They made camp on the sandy plains a day's ride west of Cellto and a light supper was thrown together by his companion. He thanked her heartily for the meal, a simple stew made with familiar ingredients packed for their journey. Tasting the vegetables local to the southern region made Wan Du think of home all over again.

As if reading his thoughts, Lady Mayrah took that moment to ask, "Do you think you will return to Brong after the war?"

Wan Du sighed, momentarily relaxing his stoic exterior. He avoided thinking about it since he had left in a rage seeking revenge so many weeks prior. He looked toward the blue scimitar Mayrah held lovingly as she sharpened the blade and got lost in the motion, forgetting even that she asked him a question until the woman met his eyes.

"I do not know," he said. It hurt to put his uncertainty into words, but he could not lie.

"Perhaps it won't matter in the end," she responded.

"What do you mean?"

Lifting the blade above her head, Lady Mayrah swept it in a downward arc as if splitting an imaginary log. She nodded satisfactorily before sheathing the weapon in the scabbard her mundane scimitar used to inhabit. It took an adjustment to make the blue blade fit, but she said she didn't foresee it occupying the sheath for much longer.

"If we die," she clarified, "it won't matter what we intended to do after the war."

For a moment, the woman shone through the warrior's façade and a tear crept down her cheek. Absently, she wiped it away and then rubbed at her wrist. Wan Du remembered the bracelet that used to cover it.

"I'm sorry about your bracelet," he said. "That is why he attacked you, isn't it?"

Lady Mayrah began to nod, then shook her head and laughed. "It doesn't matter. I have been traveling with you for weeks and it probably shows by how comfortably we speak to each other. He saw what you were and made the judgment in an instant."

"So it is doubly my fault," Wan Du stated flatly.

"No," she corrected, "there is no fault. If I still carried the prejudices of my people, I could also cling to the belief that I had a home to go back to. I let go of both the day I was wounded, when we saw the rams fighting."

Wan Du froze as she moved from across the fire to sit next to him. He dared not even breathe as her head leaned against his arm.

"It is a bleak existence we resign ourselves to when our mates die before us, Wan Du. We see the future in an instant; a long, lonely walk through life with no one to share our triumphs and failures. There are no more battles, no more struggles, save the internal ones with grief. The bracelet is not just a reminder of our loss; it is the curse that binds us to this world in perpetual mourning. There is no joy to be found in weaving every day until we die, so I chose the sword and I chose you. I regret neither."

Listening to her soft voice, such a contrast from her usual commanding tone, Wan Du calmed. He searched deep inside himself for the courage to ask the deciding question and uttered it before any second thoughts could quell his desire.

"If we survive, would you return with me?"

He could no longer see her face so he could not tell if she smiled, but Lady Mayrah did not speak. A long, uncomfortable moment was spent staring at the fire before she sat upright, stretching a hand up to his shoulder. Her other hand came up behind his neck and, before he could prepare himself, Wan Du's lips were pressed against hers in the most exciting and forbidden kiss of his life.

They made love with a passion brought on by weeks of tension and pressure. Abandoning all caution, their naked bodies intertwined under the stars, which contrasted so much with their travels and heightened the experience for Wan Du all the more. Miles from civilization, neither cared in the slightest if anyone could hear. Both surrendered completely to the moment and exhausted each other only to wake up still nude and embracing when the dawn broke.

As Wan Du dressed and moved to clear the camp trail, he noticed that Mayrah did not have the inkling to move much herself. She watched him go about the tasks with an expression of relief. When his companion did finally rise, she did so slowly and allowed him the opportunity to admire her form in various stages of dress.

Though Wan Du tried only discreetly to watch her, Mayrah seemed to know she held his attention; an unspoken agreement to savor the moment one last time before resuming their warlike ways. He smiled inwardly at the chance outcome of their survival, silently promising to enjoy her taste and touch at every available opportunity until he no longer could.

WHILE SHE CLAIMED TO HAVE SOME GUIDING SENSE TO THE SECOND blade while holding the first, Mayrah only had a general sense of direction to travel. Wan Du accepted that their course was due west until they reached Bloodmir, but as they grew closer to it his companion admitted she felt no more inkling than that.

The pair rode south far enough to avoid sight of Rochelle; it was a pain that Mayrah preferred to elude and word of her presence might have traveled there faster than she did. Wan Du said nothing of the subject of her destroyed home, but continued to scan the horizon for any sign of their enemies. The flatlands of the south provided a decent view in all directions, but at the same time, nothing to look at.

Their camp the next night was uneventful, with no repeat of the previous night's passions because of their proximity to Bloodmir's border. Wan Du took the first watch, but found himself glancing back constantly on Mayrah's sleeping form. As he lay down later, he wondered if the same habit plagued her.

Shortly after dawn the next day they passed from territory held by Rochelle into Bloodmir. Further north, the narrow channel provided a faster route to reaching the battlefield, but at the base of the peninsula a wide road led the way to the city.

It was obvious from the trade caravans and mercenary bands that the province was very much alive and doing more business than ever before. War was good for this centrally-located coastal region, and scavengers picked battles far and wide to peddle their wares here. Wan Du kept his eyes open for any Carrion soldiers, but it seemed there was no mingling of the forces — regardless of how friendly or symbiotic Bloodmir's relationship was with the army.

Bloodmir, the city, had grown since he had last seen it. Peddlers of all kinds loitered even the outskirts, stacking their items on the small retaining wall that marked the boundary. Mayrah scowled as Wan Du led them past the shouting merchants and their unscrupulous clientele. Once inside the city, they dismounted and hobbled their beasts in a public corral. Relying on Mayrah to point the way, Wan Du followed the path she wove through the city toward Iblis and their weapons. All the while, the large man hoped things would continue to be this easy.

In Bloodmir, though, he knew things were rarely so simple.

CHAPTER 72 —- *Drakkaram*

RAKKARAM STARED FROM A HIGH WINDOW IN THE GREAT Watchtower alongside his greatest creation and waited. The brutal General decided that he hated to wait; he would much rather have been stomping skulls anywhere else than standing idle inside Zion's fortress. Ever since he had abandoned the ambush for Terrant, the General felt a sense of wrongness with the entire situation. Turning to where he imprisoned Xymon, Drakkaram's lipless maw rose into a victorious grin.

"Release me," the dark General commanded. The slick bars of his prison were an interesting device, similar to the ones that housed the hybrid Vortalus before his escape. Drakkaram had been assured they would hold this time and had reason to trust this information. Threats of death went far to cement a deal after all other beings in the room were slaughtered.

"Silence, you traitorous scum," said Drakkaram. "Don't you think I know why you halted our ambush? Your sweet tart sister travels with the betrayer and you didn't want me mounting her before beheading her. Isn't that right?"

Drakkaram watched with sadistic glee as Xymon struggled against his bonds. Seething, the dark General reminded Drakkaram of a caged wolf just after the horns were thrust in. Hungry for blood.

"I have a cure for your kind of treachery." Drakkaram snapped his fingers and Bathilde leapt into action. Her immense club crushed the bars of Xymon's cage and counter-swung quicker than the dark General could react. The club connected with Xymon's forehead and decimated his skull, leaving his small horns intact but disembodied.

Drakkaram clapped for the performance, grinning all the while. He remained the last original Carrion General, and it was obvious why he lasted so long. Even the grunts cowered from him, and with the unheard of audacity to kill a peer officer he would be nigh untouchable.

Of course, his thoughts reminded gently, Xymon had been responsible for Circulosa's demise, but no one had been there to witness it. From his account to Zion, the dark General's act had been borne more of mercy than mission. Drakkaram spat on the still-twitching form of his former peer, then pointed to the two nearest grunts to clean up the mess.

Walking back to the window, Drakkaram smiled again when Bathilde came to stand at his side. "You have a place at my right hand," he told her. "I am pleased with you."

Though she didn't speak, Drakkaram knew she would show appreciation later. One who was not pleased with his actions, however, swept into the room and completely robbed Drakkaram of is budding grandeur.

"By Darsch," cursed Zion, "what have you done, Drakkaram?"

Keeping his back to his master, Drakkaram merely replied, "I took care of a traitor."

He heard Zion step across the chamber and kneel next to the corpse of Xymon. Amid the silence Drakkaram did not move, but merely admired the island landscape far below and the sea stretching out toward Ferraut well past his vision.

Suddenly an icy hand grasped his neck and the General froze mid-breath. Cowed by Zion's awesome presence, Bathilde collapsed to both knees and kissed the floor.

"You are fortunate this will be over soon." Before Drakkaram could even begin to ponder the meaning of Zion's words, the master continued, "Soon the fleet from Ferraut will pass us on their way to the southwest. I have already dispatched our troops to Illiadora in advance of them."

"Whatever force they can muster," said Drakkaram, "it will not be enough ..."

The grip constricted, cutting off the air through his throat. "Do not dare assume I need confirmation from you. All that is required of you is obedience in defending this place; do you understand?"

Drakkaram tried to nod, but couldn't move. He managed a grunt.

"You must personally make sure that the betrayer does not enter my chambers. Kill him any possible way you can, and do it yourself. Your underlings may handle anyone else that shows up. Am I clear?"

The General swallowed and grunted again. Immediately after Zion released his grip and exited the chamber the brutal General began barking orders. He stationed all remaining squads on the lower floors and increased garrisons at the walls.

After a trip to the top of the tower, Drakkaram decided to stay near the entrance with Bathilde — just in case the horde of grunts was not enough to stop all comers. Zion had not made clear how many assailants would be invading, but for Drakkaram's ambitions to ultimately succeed, his defense plans would have to first.

CHAPTER 73 – *Mayrah*

AYRAH JOINED WAN DU AS HER COMPANION STARED AT an armor post. The dummy wore a familiar sight; a suit of Brong warrior armor, now forgotten by its owners and besieged by the elements. The chest and shoulder plates already showed signs of rust and abandonment. She could almost see the tears of anger welling up in the large man, but turned away to give him some privacy.

"This is the spot where I was captured," he growled.

She nodded in response, but said nothing. He told her the story before; the events leading up to their serendipitous meeting in Cellto. Mayrah had been afraid of Wan Du then and what she might do to protect herself from him.

As discreetly as she could, Mayrah slid a hand across her abdomen, wondering if a life would grow inside of her again. With the other hand she grasped the handle of the blue scimitar at her side. Each, in its own way, represented the past and the future, and as Mayrah turned to face Wan Du again she found nothing but determination in his eyes — all grief was gone.

"Let's get this over with," she whispered.

Drawing her hand back up Mayrah placed her open palm near the surface of the metal. Feeling a strange press of air, she detected the enchantment that caught Wan Du before. With a silent nod she drew her blade and took a step back, ready to sever the wooden post on his command.

Wan Du took an extra moment to let out a long breath, as if wanting to say something, but also trying to avoid it. Mayrah smiled; they were both aware of the mortal danger they were in, but wouldn't speak of it, not even to comfort each other.

"Do it," said Mayrah.

It took mere seconds for the magic to take hold on Wan Du's body. His jaw clenched and his eyes widened as soon as he grasped the chestplate, but Mayrah did not move to rescue him. Acting her part, she merely waited for the security force to show up.

Sixteen feet tapped the dirt path and the noise of metal shaking multiplied by eight came roaring only a few moments later. Short, stocky merchant guardsmen wore oversized vests of interlocking armor plates over thin padding. Their donned helmets were all plumed with beast hair or feathers and each carried a long spear and large round shield. Mayrah grinned inwardly; they had been fighting the Carrion for so long, she almost wanted to give these men a chance to surrender.

The guardsmen descended upon Wan Du and fanned out in a semi-circle to encompass Mayrah as well. Their spears came down in unison, reinforcing the leader's command of "don't move."

Mayrah did not give the men a chance to advance, however, but dropped to one knee and swept her blue blade through the wooden post as easily as butter. Wan Du hurled the remains of the armor dummy at the nearest soldier, who still had a confused look on his face when it was crushed. Not to be outdone, Mayrah leapt forward and between the points of two clumsily held spears to swipe her blade through the necks of both men.

To their credit the remaining five, one of them the leader, regrouped. As calm as ever, Wan Du continued to use large objects as weapons rather than the puny spears of their adversaries. Two men flew through the air and crashed into their comrades to disable all four. Mayrah dashed past the leader's guard and settled in behind him with a blade on his neck. The man began shaking almost immediately, and Mayrah had to pull his helmet off to get his attention.

"What is your name?" she asked, not for the first time.

"H ... Hajim," the man stammered, "I am called Hajim."

Mayrah leaned closer to the man's ear, tightening her grip on his neck. "Hajim, tell us where we can find Iblis, and you may live."

The name of his master inspired obvious fear in the guardsman. "Don't kill me; I'll tell you whatever you want to know."

Wan Du walked to where the post and armor had landed and retrieved the plate. He rubbed it with his hand and paused as if coming to a realization. Mayrah watched him intently, but kept a firm grip on Hajim.

Looking from her to their captive, Wan Du said, "I have a plan."

HAJIM NERVOUSLY LED THE WAY AHEAD OF MAYRAH AND WAN DU, playing the part of their captor. Mayrah laughed a bit upon hearing of the simple plan, but she had to admit, it worked. Despite all logic, they passed regiments of other guardsmen — similarly equipped — who failed to raise an eyebrow to the man from Brong and Rochellian woman following behind their fellow. Mayrah attempted to look a bit downtrodden and with the state of her clothing, found it easier than she expected.

The city of Bloodmir became more fortress-like as they followed Hajim. Where a large inlet of water allowed, a pier and quay stood to accommodate all importing and exporting. At the center of it all was a tower large enough for half a dozen overseeing men. Mayrah spotted two archers, two men carrying ledgers, and a tall man with a mustache.

Iblis. Wan Du's tense muscles meant her companion noticed him as well. Like a coiled spring, the large man looked ready to snap when the moment came. She watched his taut muscles as they followed Hajim down the planks of the pier and toward the tower.

Leaning over the side railing, Iblis called down to the trio. "Ho there, Hajim! Are these the criminals who ..."

The mustached man did not get a chance to finish his sentence. Pushing Hajim out of the way, Wan Du launched his shoulder at the nearest leg of the tower.

Mayrah barely had time to lift her scimitar from Hajim's belt before the guardsman fell screaming into the water. Her companion's body assaulted one leg and another like a rampaging beast. The sound of snapping wood alerted all of the nearby soldiers and dock workers of something awry. Over a hundred men turned and watched in shock as the overseeing tower fell.

She spryly leapt through the guts of the downed structure, all the while watching for archers. The only struggling body she could see was Iblis himself, weighed down as he was by thick robes and various kinds of gaudy metal jewelry.

"Why must you come to ruin us further?" he screamed. "Your war is over, and that fact has cost me enough already!"

Hearing Wan Du call from behind her, Mayrah turned in time to see the large man throw a bundle of rope to her. She nodded and sheathed her scimitar to catch it. Immediately after heaving the coil, Wan Du turned to meet an onslaught of workers and guards. Mayrah watched for a moment as Wan Du fought them back; he took up the majority of the path width so none could get past him, but she worried how long he could remain an obstacle.

Forming a knotted loop Mayrah cast the rope around the struggling Iblis and cried out success to her companion.

"Get to the nearest ship," he responded. Feeding the rope through the strange angles of the tower was simple, but dragging the large Iblis proved to make the journey challenging. Mayrah resolved to pulling him in until the rope was short and then clubbing him once across the head with a nearby plank.

Mayrah reached a schooner at the end of the pier and tossed the mooring ropes away before dragging the limp Iblis into the low-decked boat. Realizing she should call Wan Du to join her, Mayrah looked back just as the large man's leap carried him to the railing. Out of breath, and bleeding from two serious spear wounds, Wan Du pulled himself into the ship.

"Are you alright?" she asked.

With closed eyes Wan Du nodded, sitting back against the railing and catching his breath. Mayrah looked beyond him to see the pier still a flurry of activity. Two boats were filling with crew and making ready to launch.

"We don't have much time."

"No," the large man agreed, "but we do have a hostage."

Taking up the two large oars, Wan Du got the ship in motion toward the far end of the inlet. Mayrah immobilized Iblis further before moving to attend to

Wan Du's wounds. She drew some healing herbs from a belt pouch and smiled again.

"Was that all part of your plan?" asked the woman.

He shrugged, but she thought she may have caught another glimmer of a smile on his lips.

CHAPTER 74 – *Wan Du*

HE RETRIEVAL OF THE HALBERD AND THE SECOND SCIMITAR went far better than Wan Du had expected. Iblis turned out to be little more than a bumbling fool. Once separated from his power base and commanding position, he led them to view his "private collection"; the cache of weapons rivaled anything Wan Du or Mayrah had ever seen.

And all of it, he knew, was lifted from either prisoners or looted from the dead; many, he saw, from his own comrades. Wan Du fought with all his resolve to keep from looking for other weapons he might recognize and wondered if his companion did the same.

In truth, he was half-tempted to take a few extra pieces from the collection, but all thought faded once his eyes set upon the glowing white blade. Wan Du had tested the familiar weight of his halberd and checked the blade for nicks of use.

After regaining what was rightfully theirs, the pair threw Iblis into the sea to swim home before sailing north. Mayrah's spirits lifted after she held both blue scimitars. They fascinated Wan Du, but he had no use for them himself.

Now, as they passed a fleet of full-laden warships bound for the opposite direction, their crew of two tried very hard to be ignored by the regiments of bowmen standing vigilant on the decks. Wan Du hailed them with a wave, but the ships did not respond, even to the point of not changing course to avoid the smaller boat.

As the waves made by the cruisers lashed against the hull of their smaller craft, Wan Du looked up at the pennants waving above the sails. Each ship bore a white flag with a five-pointed star — the mark of Ferraut, according to Mayrah — as well as a solid red flag signifying they were headed to war.

The Ferraut ships continued southwest and Mayrah shouted something over the churning water about them heading for Illiadora. As they watched, a flying object hurtled toward the ships from the east and slowed down enough to land.

"What is that?" she asked.

Wan Du narrowed his eyes and placed a hand against his forehead for a better look. "It is a man. A wizard."

As he and Mayrah continued to watch, the flying man moved from ship to ship to ship. Wan Du lost interest and instead focused on getting their boat back in motion. His eyes turned direct north, for the Great Watchtower of Kasar loomed on the horizon.

The island of Kasar looked quite flat and not very large. Stone walls surrounded the cylindrical tower, said to be the tallest building in the known world, and its base took up most of the island that the walls did not.

Beaching the craft was not as difficult as it could have been, Wan Du realized, since the Carrion guarding the area were all dead. He glanced from one body to the next to see if arrows from the ships they passed had killed the grunts, but the slash wounds discredited the possibility. Looking past the beach, Wan Du gripped his halberd tighter when he saw a familiar man standing at the large metal gate. For his part, the man simply looked back.

"Is that who I think it is?" Mayrah whispered.

As they approached, the answer to her question lifted a hand in greeting. DaVille Terrant, named a former Carrion officer in the battle outside Flaem, stood before them wielding a red longsword. He offered his free hand open in a gesture of peace and both Mayrah and Wan Du grasped it in turn — though a bit hesitantly.

"I did not think to see you again," said the large man.

DaVille shrugged in response. "Still looking to kill me?"

Shaking his head, Wan Du replied, "The Carrion are our real enemy, just as you said."

"It looks like you didn't leave any work for us," said Mayrah. The comment served to calm the tension, but the three remained grim. "Any idea how to get inside?"

The warrior surveyed the wall from one direction to the other and then up and down. "Too high to climb."

"Can you blast it like the wall in Cellto?" Wan Du asked.

"I thought of that, but I need my strength," replied DaVille. "You know who's in there, don't you?"

"That is why we have come."

"Where is that girl who was with you?" asked Mayrah. "Starka, wasn't it?" She seemed genuinely interested in the girl's well-being.

"Home with her people by now, I expect. Our travels are a long story best told over a fire and a mug, if we survive this." Wan Du nodded his agreement with the man, then moved to the wall and threaded his fingers together to form a sling.

DaVille shrugged again before moving to get a running start. He sheathed his blade and then charged directly at Wan Du, placing a foot in the makeshift stirrup. The large man lifted with all his might, propelling DaVille as high up as he could, and grunting with the effort. He let out his breath when the DaVille's hands gripped the top of the wall. He lifted himself up and over before calling down sardonically, "Are you sure you want to come in?"

"I think he enjoys this too much," said Mayrah.

The walls reverberated with clicking and grinding before the gate moaned open to reveal an empty courtyard. Wan Du expected more grunts to be guarding the tower's outer door, but saw only an open portal, shadowed on the inside. As DaVille rejoined them past the gate, he noted the open door was an obvious trap.

"They know we are coming," Wan Du agreed.

DaVille craned his neck, looking where the tower had stood before disappearing into the clouds. "From that height, they probably watched us leave."

"No more jokes," Mayrah said as she drew her scimitars. "How are we going to do this?"

Producing his blade as well, DaVille set his jaw and stretched his neck from side to side. "I'm entering through the front. If you two want to wait until I give the all-clear, be my guest."

"You're the same headstrong fool I captured in my camp, DaVille. What's to stop them from filling you with arrows the second your toes touch the ..."

Mayrah's words were cut short as a large figure strode out from the tower doorway. Wan Du recognized the figure vaguely, and guessed by the words dying on Mayrah's lips it was someone she knew. DaVille had the audacity to laugh.

"Well, if it isn't the mace wielder," he shouted. "The horns don't really suit you, woman."

"Silence, worm!" The huge mace she wielded shook the ground as she dropped the business end from her shoulder. "It is true. I was Bathilde, but now I am something more."

"No ... Bathilde ..." Mayrah sobbed silently in a hand placed over her mouth. Wan Du moved forward to keep the woman from coming closer and noticed the Carrion grunts filing quickly out of the tower door behind her. DaVille moved to intercept them and left Mayrah and Wan Du alone with the large Carrion woman.

"I see you have taken a new mate, *Lady* Mayrah." Bathilde's accusatory tone was scathing, and Wan Du took it as a direct insult to them both.

"How is it that I understand her speech?" Mayrah asked.

"I know that you do not fear death," he responded to the beast that was Bathilde, "but insult her again and I shall give you something far worse."

Bathilde merely laughed. "Neither of you can best what I have become. Perhaps the betrayer might have a chance, once I have killed you, but my former commander is in no condition to fight."

As she finished speaking, Wan Du heard Mayrah begin to choke and vomit onto the ground behind him.

"Isn't it so fitting," the beast woman continued, "that I shall take this child from you as well?"

Wan Du's thoughts immediately spun. Child? What did she mean? Taking no chances, he launched toward Bathilde and spun his halberd. She deflected the blow, but it halted her forward motion nonetheless.

The large man ignored everything else; the sounds of DaVille dispatching the grunts as they funneled out the doorway, Mayrah's shallow breathing, even the soreness of his muscles faded away in the face of the fight. If Mayrah was truly with child, *his* child, then he would give his life to protect them.

"If what you say is true," he said, "then I am no longer the last of my people."

"No, you Brong dog, you have soiled my countrywoman with your seed." Bathilde spat the words, seeming to have a few troubles with her fangs against her large lips. "It is too early to hear a wretched half-breed's heartbeat, but I can smell fear in her womb."

Wan Du growled from deep in his throat and moved to an offensive stance. His opponent grinned and threw her head back, tossing her matted mess of hair back from her shoulders. "Come then, big man. After I kill you, my master shall feast on your flesh."

Though he was much too tall to duck and maneuver around the huge swings of Bathilde's club, the halberd parried them without breaking. Her sweeps of the spike-headed weapon were quick, however, and her jabs even quicker. Bathilde pressed forward and Wan Du jumped back. The woman's momentum carried into a roundhouse swing.

Seeking to avoid the brunt of the assault, Wan Du stepped in close rather than retreating further and raised his weapon vertically to block. His arms shook from the impact as he released his lower hand's grip and landed an uppercut across Bathilde's jaw. The Carrion woman staggered back and roared, bringing her weapon up for another swing.

She could not be worn down, as he originally hoped. The horns in her head granted the woman inhuman strength and stamina, and he knew it would only take one blow from her weapon to end the fight. His attacks, on the other hand, seemed only to anger and frustrate her, for he could not connect with the shining white blade.

"*Serené,* help me," Wan Du prayed under his breath. "Guide my strikes."

After a flurry of traded and dodged blows, Wan Du and Bathilde separated. The large man retreated an extra few paces to stand next to Mayrah and spared her a quick glance. She recovered from her fit of sickness, but remained distraught over the battle with her friend.

"Why, Bathilde?" Mayrah suddenly screamed. "How could you join them?"

"How dare you ask me why," the Carrion woman fired back. "You left me outside Cellto to die!"

"That is not true!" Mayrah sobbed. "I tried to wait for you. I looked for you. I believed you were dead and I mourned for you!"

She even lifted a forearm to show a reddened line underneath two others. The creature's eyes narrowed as she looked from the scars to Wan Du.

"I see how you mourn," she accused.

"Would you kill her please?" DaVille piped up from near the doorway. Wan Du looked past his opponent to see the man fending off four grunts with pikes, unable to get close enough to retaliate.

Bathilde laughed heartily and waved Wan Du on. The large man nodded, gripping the pole of his weapon tightly. "Be ready," he told Mayrah, but did not wait for an assent.

Wan Du launched himself forward, cutting across diagonally with the blade of his weapon. Bathilde deflected the cut, but was forced to retreat a step and prepare to riposte with a backhand swing. She did not get a chance, however, as Wan Du continued forward and barreled into the woman. They fell to the ground, both disarmed. The large man held one of Bathilde's hands and placed the other on her throat. Her fangs lashed toward him, but his grip was strong.

Even when the claws at the end of her fingers stabbed into his chest, Wan Du held fast, gritting his teeth through the blinding pain. Only a few more seconds, he thought. His patience was rewarded when Mayrah appeared.

Without ceremony or words, she knelt and grasped the horns protruding from Bathilde's head and yanked with visible effort. With a scream that pierced Wan Du's eardrums, Bathilde pushed her claws forward as she died, spraying black ichor from her temples and mouth to coat the surrounding ground.

"Very nice," DaVille called, finally finding an opening and slicing through the quartet of Carrion assailants. The man hurried over with a concerned look, and Wan Du realized the claws remained buried in the flesh of his chest. His lungs protested and the large man coughed up blood, a contrasting dark red to the dead Carrion's pooling black. He heard Mayrah crying again and saw her kneel next to him to help pull his body away from her dead friend.

He collapsed onto his back and closed his eyes, listening to the waves break against the nearby shore. The words of *Serené* came back to him clearly, then. *Though you will not see the end, I was here with you in the beginning. Fear nothing; seek and find your revenge.*

Wan Du caressed Mayrah's face one last time as he pushed out his final breath.

CHAPTER 75 – *Cairos*

AIROS HELD THE STAFF OF CIRCULOSA ALOFT AND STUDIED the carved runes on its surface. In the sunlight of the afternoon, the lacquered wood glowed with power. Princess Sineya's stones made this possible, though the origin of the perplexing bits of magic remained a mystery. All that mattered to him was the telekinesis stone had been able to extract Circulosa's staff from a null zone deep beneath the Inner Sea of Mana, as well as Gabumon's staff from the solid stone. Just another thing to study once this is all over, he thought.

He looked from the staff to the horizon in an attempt to spot his occupied home, Illiadora. No longer, he promised silently; today your liberation is at hand.

Ferraut's war cruisers were fast ships and the twenty he had been "lent" by the king were the best available. Each held a working crew, a regiment of men-at-arms as well as fifty crack archers with strung longbows. The attack would begin even before they reached the shore. In the meantime, Cairos practiced with the intricacies of Circulosa's staff, forcing it to contort into its bow shape and back again. The weapon fascinated him.

By his side again was Fabfast, his apprentice. The boy had done a remarkable job acquiring the objects Cairos asked for. Fabfast paused from studying the chunk of white stone and grinned at his master.

"Fabfast, this is going to be a dangerous experiment and we'll only get one chance at it," said Cairos. "Be ready, if we see Vortalus."

The apprentice nodded. At a call from one of the lookouts, Cairos looked to the horizon again. Bright flashes of light burst across the sky in the exact direction of their heading and the captains called alerts for all hands. The knights donned their battle armors and shields creating a cacophony of metal and buckles. As the oars carried the ships quickly nearer the tip of the peninsula, Cairos saw he was not the only one with the idea to retake the city.

The wizard counted at least twenty levitating bodies hurling arcs of fire and lightning down past the city's defensive walls. Ballista-sized bolts responded and catapulted stones harrowed them in response. A Ferraut officer approached Cairos' side to likewise examine the situation.

"Who the hell are they?" asked the man.

Cairos tried to find a leader of the throng of somewhat-soldiers led forward against the Carrion and spotted a man engulfed in flame. Grinning from ear to ear, Cairos uttered the name of his new best friend. "Adamis."

"Begging your pardon?"

"Allies," he clarified, "now get us there!"

SHOUTS OF "MAN THE OARS!" AND "BEACH THE SHIPS IF NECESsary!" went up, but Cairos could wait no longer. He closed his eyes to take one last calm breath before speaking words to Valesh and launching himself into the air to join the attack. Fabfast followed closely behind.

Painful memories began to gnaw at him when Cairos saw the earthy debris outside the southern gate, now mostly cleared away by Carrion sappers. In place of the pillar of dirt he summoned fought a column of Carrion soldiers, doing their best to hold the city against the assault of refugees led by the Burning Man, Adamis.

"Looks like he found his army," muttered Cairos.

He sought the man out and landed as near to him as possible. "Adamis?" shouted Cairos.

The flames died down as Adamis heard his name. He retreated and turned to see Cairos waving from nearby. With caution, Adamis approached. "I am Adamis," he said.

"Cairos and my apprentice, Fabfast. I also brought some friends," Cairos replied as he indicated the Ferraut ships just beginning to unload their store of men and arrows toward Illiadora's eastern wall.

"Reinforcements, then." The flames around the man's face hid his smile, but Cairos was sure it was there. "Excellent."

As if in direct response to Adamis' comment, a large explosion rocked the ground outside the southern wall of the city. Bodies of men and Carrion flew through the air away from the small crater created by what seemed to be another wizard.

All fighting paused as every eye turned to see the creature that was Vortalus rise from the smoke. Waves of fiery power flew through the air as the creature swept his half-staffs forward, hurling away the invading soldiers without even being close enough to touch.

The Burning Man rushed back into the battle, attempting to force his way to the front, and Cairos followed with Fabfast. Gripping his *terasont* tightly, he made ready for a sacrifice.

"Clear a path!"

Men and women haphazardly dressed in bought and borrowed armor moved aside to create a trench allowing Cairos a clear view of the beast that Vortalus had become. The sight of the actual creature sent shivers up his spine worse than they had within the oracle stone. Vortalus and Circulosa had merged into something hideous; a creation borne of two dead sorcerers and a pair of dark, twisted horns.

Cairos invoked a spell to Scythor, the Pillar of Death, and directed all of the energy provided by his *terasont* back in on itself. The resulting effect was immediate; the blue glow of the smooth stone pulsed brightly and then extinguished. The beautiful sky hue turned to a translucent black crystal only hinting at the power it now contained. He carefully handed the crystal to Fabfast, who put it together with the egg and stone while holding the telekinesis jewel in his other hand.

"Now, Fabfast!"

The conglomeration of the *scythorsont*, alabaster, and dragonling egg hurtled toward the Vortalus creature. Cairos brought the bent staff to eye level and pulled back the energy to fire a bolt. He narrowed his eyes, remembering the invasion of the Carrion in this same place, the death of his friends, and the death of Gabumon because of Circulosa's actions.

"Bless my vengeance," Cairos whispered, and the line of energy connecting the ends of the bow-staff turned a deep crimson. The symbol of Vexen again appeared in the air before him, between Cairos and Vortalus, and the wizard aimed through its center.

Confident or confused, the Vortalus creature waited in a guarded stance for a while staring at the three stones Fabfast moved toward him. When Cairos' red blast struck the *scythorsont*, the resulting explosion hurled away everything within twenty feet. The light blinded Cairos, and Fabfast cried out and covered his head.

Cairos knew this would not be enough to kill the beast. He had seen the deaths of both the wizards that made up the creature, and yet here it was. As he approached to view the corpse of Vortalus for a strange second time, he held back the bile in his throat. With his power and influence gone from the Carrion army's confidence, the invaders renewed their assault and swept over them ruthlessly.

The wizard allowed one last moment of silence for the twice-dead thing at his feet, for Gabumon, and for all of his friends before he heard Fabfast approaching.

"The stone, Master?" asked the boy. "Are you going to complete the plan?"

Using the telekinesis stone, Cairos hollowed out a large chunk of earth from the battleground. It took a huge amount of energy, especially without his *terasont* to bear some of the load, but he was able to deposit the dirt and stone on top of the crater that he had made with Vortalus underneath. The null zone would be his resting place, beneath many tons of earth — a place he could not escape. It looked like just another mound outside the city, complete with a couple of newly-sprouted mushrooms.

"Master, the Carrion! They are fainting!" Fabfast hopped from foot to foot with glee. Cairos realized he had lost track of the battle while burying Vortalus.

Feeling another odd shudder across the magical currents, Cairos bade his apprentice find a safe place and rushed with all haste to the city's oracle stone.

Even after all the time the city spent occupied, the divining chamber remained untouched. It looked the same as the day he fled from it. Steeling himself against all the possibilities in his mind, Cairos placed his hand over the globe and concentrated on DaVille.

CHAPTER 76 – *DaVille*

O, HE CAN'T BE DEAD. NOT HIM, TOO," MAYRAH SOBBED and pressed her fists against Wan Du's chest. DaVille stood close by, looking on the spectacle with something that he hoped resembled pity.

"He was a brave man," was all he could say. He didn't feel the situation could bear the "war is difficult, people die" attitude. Both of them had lost enough in this war, and it only fueled his anger as he looked back to the Watchtower.

"Kill me," he heard Mayrah whisper. "Please, DaVille, I can't bear this any longer."

He nearly laughed at the sentimentality of it all, but thought the better of it. "You're with child, aren't you?"

"None of that matters now," she said between sobs. "I am alone again and I cannot go on without him. Please, just kill me."

"Do you think Wan Du would want that?" he asked. The words were out before DaVille could stop them and brought a new onslaught of despair from Mayrah's lips.

He knelt beside the woman and put a hand on her shoulder. "I'm no good at this," he began, "but listen. You are the only person here that has a chance of making it out alive. Get your revenge by surviving. Have children and grand-children and tell them what a legend he was and how he died for justice. You have life in you, yet."

Mayrah allowed herself to be led back to the beached ship. DaVille set her in it before pushing the boat back out to sea and wondered only afterward if he should have loaded Wan Du's body with her. Then again, he thought, looking at the corpse until she reached land might make things worse.

He watched to make sure she took up the oars, and though her face remained flooded with tears, she seemed determined to heed his advice. Satisfied his last distraction was out of the way, he turned again toward the tower to see Drakkaram standing under the gate.

"A moving speech, betrayer," the General shouted. "She will suffer for what she did to my creation. I think I will revive her lover and send him after her. Once I've dealt with you, of course."

The brutal General stood tall and held his massive black blade in one hand. "Come inside whenever you feel ready."

DAVILLE SMILED AT THE CHALLENGE. STRANGE WHISPERS assaulted his mind as he reached for the long wooden box. A gift, Xymon had called it. He opened the lid gently and ran his fingertips over the horns.

Zion had unknowingly given him the greatest means to defeat his forces. DaVille almost wanted to laugh — did he truly think DaVille would rejoin the ranks after so much had happened?

It took bold strength to take up the horns and plunge them into his head, but the transformation began before he could reconsider. All of the bones in his body seemed to break at once and he fell face down onto the sand screaming in agonized ecstasy. The whispers in his brain intensified, even becoming coherent for a moment, as he lay motionless on the beach.

Eight voices, some male and some female, commanded him to rise. The Carrion DaVille opened his eyes to reddened vision and lifted himself from the ground. His arms felt light and strong and the sword he grasped was like holding air. A familiar longing made his other hand grasp into a fist, but there was no weapon to place in it.

Memories washed over DaVille of two triangular blades — his *katar* — extending from his fists and tearing through the bodies of his victims. The human side of his mind recoiled from the bloodlust and attempted to reassert control. He stood, but the Carrion side forced him toward a nearby corpse to collect its bladed weapon. Anything would do, his instinct whispered.

Kill, kill, kill.

The halves of his brain vied for control as DaVille approached the tower. His red blade led the way, a clearly discernable symbol glowing brightly on his forearm. He saw a different symbol on his other arm, but the memory of Drakkaram's challenge distracted him from caring. The Carrion DaVille approached the doorway to the tower and marched inside.

In the low light of few windows and with the redness of his vision the chamber seemed to be covered in blood. Past the wide expanse, a metal stairway spiraled upward to the next floor over a hundred feet in the air. A twang snapped DaVille's attention from staring upward as an arrow shaft embedded in his shoulder. Growling in response, DaVille charged a small contingent of live bodies and slashed three times to separate limbs and heads from them. He felt invincible and climbed the staircase with a gleeful readiness for the fight that he knew lay ahead.

Nearing the top of the staircase, DaVille deflected the falling form of a body as it hurtled in his direction. It took only a passing glance to identify the corpse as Xymon. The Carrion side of him grinned inwardly as it noted one less obstacle to be in his path, but the human side grieved for Starka's sake. Xymon would have had to die anyway, but DaVille felt better for not ending his life.

As he entered the second chamber of the tower, the light improved and DaVille saw the challenger he sought. Drakkaram stood with his sword tip penetrating the floor and both his hands on the pommel. The greatsword gleamed like black glass and the General's sharpened teeth ground together as he glared at DaVille.

Kill, kill, kill.

"So, you were rejected by the darkness when my father killed you," the General taunted, "and now you reject the light to seek your revenge. You truly are a betrayer, and now you are worthless to everyone. Even if you do manage to best me and kill the Great Zion, your life will be forfeited as well."

Neither side of DaVille's mind wished to respond except with blows. He charged forward from the staircase and swept horizontally with both blades, but the attack was easily deflected by the huge black sword. The punch that came after it connected squarely on DaVille's jaw and sent him reeling to the floor.

He leapt up immediately and did not allow Drakkaram a chance to gain the advantage. His human side forced caution, but his Carrion mind cried for another impulsive strike.

"Even with horns, you cannot kill me, Terrant," said Drakkaram. "Never could. You were only ever effective against the helpless. Our Master needn't have bothered worrying about your return."

With that, Drakkaram began a charge of his own. The black blade sailed through the air making a strange musical whirr. DaVille deflected it with the mundane sword in his left hand, but bringing up the red sword to stab proved too slow. Drakkaram stepped forward and elbowed the attack away to send DaVille to the floor again.

Kill, kill, kill. KILL KILL KILL!

The whispers returned with a vengeance, plaguing DaVille to dispatch his enemy with all haste. An angry female voice bolstered his resolve by ensuring him that nothing could stand in his way as the symbol on his right arm burned brighter. With a roar that would make a dragon envious, DaVille called upon his destructive power and slashed a downward strike with the red blade. Drakkaram brought his own sword up to block with the flat end and held the guard with such force that the blade snapped with an explosion of light. DaVille's sword continued down and through the General's forehead, separating his body somewhere near his navel.

A shocked expression was the only response from Drakkaram as he fell to his knees. DaVille allowed his Carrion side to take hold, bringing both blades to bear like a scissor to decapitate his opponent. As Drakkaram's head dropped to the floor, his three horns shattered.

The whispers rescinded from a triumphant cry and DaVille continued to the next set of stairs.

DAVILLE RUSHED TOWARD THE UPPER FLOORS OF THE TOWER, ULTI-mately coming to the throne room. With nary a cautionary glance he strode in holding his blades ahead of his body. Two steps onto the carpeted floor, a burning brand slammed into DaVille's back and forced to him the ground as his swords clattered away.

Paralysis took hold of his limbs and he fought to keep his face from being buried in the carpet's fibers. The smell of blood and waste was thick, and the Carrion DaVille roared at the indignity.

A dark laughter echoed from the walls as Zion stepped into his field of vision.

"Fool! Did you think you could challenge me?"

DaVille could only growl in response as the numerous voices in his head also screamed their protestations.

"Everything you have done has been part of my plan," said Zion. "You have brought the power of the Pillars back from death with you with a mission to kill me. But you have failed, betrayer, and now the ninth symbol is upon you."

Zion paused, lifting his hands to the ceiling. "The Darkness rises," he continued, "and I shall be its king."

The pain on DaVille's back let out sickly popping as the burning intensified. His human side registered the brand's location while his Carrion mind roared and fought. Unable to move, DaVille sputtered wordless cries of agony and rage, but the heat and pain did not let up. Zion lifted the iron away from his skin and stepped to the center of the chamber.

The tall three-horned creature, dressed in layers of black silk, lifted his great clawed hands again in triumph.

"Darsch, Pillar of Darkness," he summoned, "I have mastered your means and call you now to accept me as your Avatar!"

Thunder boomed from outside the tower's walls, shaking the floor. Lightning flashed through the tall window and a howling wind began shifting the objects inside the throne room. Parchments and candles whirled around and past him. Zion's clothing billowed and snapped as the gale force buffeted DaVille's newly-cooked skin.

Amid the storm, he heard the voices again. Eight other places on his body began to warm, though nowhere near the heat from the center of his back. With the warmth came an awakening of his limbs, and then strength. Both sides of DaVille's mind agreed he had only one option.

On all fours he charged like a bull, thrusting his horns into Zion's abdomen and carrying them both out the large window. Zion's death scream was cut short amid the tempest, and as they fell time scattered in DaVille's mind's eye.

All at once, he saw his brief history on the planet; images of battles, mostly, then of narrowly escaping death in a prisoner camp and befriending the man he'd just killed. His time spent as a Carrion sped by in a red wash, sparing him from the gazes of those he'd brutalized: the pain from his horn removal; meeting the girl Starka for the first time. The naïve girl reminded him of sacrificing for the sake of others; what it was like to be warm even when others were cold.

He saw Xymon, Drakkaram, and Circulosa assembled. Cities razed — the goals of the one whom he killed. Cities in ruin, their peoples fleeing with their faith likewise in ruin. More Carrion generals rose to take their place, and the killing continued without end.

DaVille suddenly became aware he was glimpsing the future.

"Choose," said a voice. A strong female, distantly familiar.

"Choose what?" DaVille struggled out.

"You have very little time for questions," hissed another voice.

Storm clouds parted as he fell. Death was coming.

"Will you become an agent for balance, or will you continue to destroy?"

The images hurtled by, but one stuck out among them as DaVille focused on the girl: Starka, as he left her, on the prow of a ship. Addressing a rapt congregation. A message of hope.

He owed her more than this future.

"Choose!" eight voices urged as one.

"Balance," he answered.

Before he struck the ground, DaVille heard one final whisper.

"He has done it," said the old man in his dry tone. "The prophecy has been fulfilled."

CHAPTER 77 – *Starka*

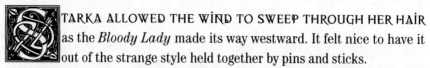TARKA ALLOWED THE WIND TO SWEEP THROUGH HER HAIR as the *Bloody Lady* made its way westward. It felt nice to have it out of the strange style held together by pins and sticks.

Absently, she wiped a tear from her eye as she recalled her last words to DaVille before he set sail with Cairos in a different direction. In the end, DaVille simply waved. The wizard lingered longer, wishing her good fortune though somehow doing absolutely nothing to bolster her confidence.

As usual with both of them, Starka mused. Still, she thought of DaVille as a pillar of strength in her otherwise flight-filled life. If someone so strong with no reason to gain could stand up for a girl like her then her people deserved someone strong to stand up for them. Starka examined the parcel that contained one of Parson's wicked daggers and again considered heaving it over the side to rest at the bottom of the sea. It wasn't that she planned to do anything dangerous with it; she just didn't wish to handle something that had undoubtedly been the instrument of many deaths.

Watching the horizon, Starka began to count the number of waves the ship surmounted until the sun began its last slip beneath the waves.

"We be gettin' there tomorrow," called Captain Satok from behind her. Turning, she took another look at the handsome sailor and slipped the package beneath her arm.

"I know, but that doesn't make it any easier."

The captain nodded and left Starka to her thoughts. She sighed, realizing that — ready or not — she would have to face how different things had become. Would she be attacked upon arrival? No, the captain and crew would not allow for that. The fully-charged cannons would protect Starka — as long as she stayed on ship, of course.

Starka couldn't decide whether she was more worried about speaking to the people who knew her or those who did not. From all the information Cairos relayed, she would be treated as kind of a legend; a healer of the sick, raiser of the dead, and a deliverer. She would have to hold back from screaming out she wasn't any of those things — just a girl coming home from a journey.

As she reflected upon all the things she learned, the faces of her companions came to mind over all else: the way DaVille's smirk hinted at something deeper; Wan Du's perpetual scowl hid his gentle nature; and how Cairos' smile seemed to be the only genuine thing about the wizard. She stayed on deck with her thoughts until long past sunset, a fixture among the busy sailors.

STARKA GUESSED THE CROWD GATHERED SHORTLY AFTER HER SHIP had been spotted with the dawn's early rays. A throng of Mystians, both male and female, lined the beach as far as she could see. Some had come even though they could not walk, and some were obviously blind or crippled in other ways. Still, this was the moment she had prepared for.

Going over her last conversations with Cairos again in her mind, her thoughts solidified. Her heart seemed to swell with pride that she had known so many brave people on her journey and wished the wizard well, wherever he was.

Toward the front of the crowd, feet resting in the playful tide waters, sat a wasting-away Wadam. The man's large body looked like it had been drained of all substance, and even from the deck of the ship, Starka could see he was not the tyrant she remembered. His eyes didn't even rise from the water as a dainty young nursemaid wheeled him forward.

With a steadying breath, Starka climbed on a crate to give the people a better view. Some stared at her dubiously, but she saw no overt malice in their eyes. Elestia's death left a void in her heart as well as theirs, and Wadam's attempt to fill that void had damaged their trust in leadership. To heal the wounds of her people, Starka would have to address both of these things at once.

"Behold, I return to you, people of the Mystian Continent, and I am not what I once was." After her first planned words came out as she intended, Starka paused to look from one end of the crowd to the other before she continued.

"When I left my home some time ago it was to fulfill a prophecy that I had received even as an outcast member of the Sisterhood. An outcast! Thrown away because of assumptions and implications! I have come to tell you that accusations and deflations are worth less than actions and motivations! What I did or did not do did not change the people of this continent.

"But I am not here to talk to you about my past. The prophecy I received contained information on the ascension of the Ninth Pillar, a magical force that we do not even believe in, yet the prophecy came to me. This was my first indicator that there is one world, and we all live in it.

"Even now, our neighbors in this world combat the legions of darkness to halt the completion of the prophecy I received. And what have we done? By all accounts, you have splintered and fought among yourselves while the world has suffered. You have sat here, safe and insulated, while the Carrion hordes laid siege and waste to the cities of our fellow human beings. I have seen these cities, and I mourn for them as well.

"But most of all, I mourn for the death of our faith as I knew it, the merciful and loving body of souls that kept us bound together toward a common goal. When all my hope was lost in my travels, I still believed that the Divine Male and Female would somehow reveal their plan and snatch us from the jaws of death. Yet at every turn, the war seemed to worsen, and still we were too frightened to move.

"The catalyst mentioned in my prophecy was indeed a man, it was all of us! We can be pushed or pulled to aid or impede the progress and success of this world. Some are willing to make the sacrifices necessary while many of us on the Mystian Continent view the mainland as a world apart!

"Many people accuse wizards of being untrustworthy and elitist, but if anyone can be accused of elitism it is us! We can no longer think of ourselves as better than everyone — we all have the potential to do great and brave things. This does not marginalize or discount our faith — or theirs — but it should strengthen our solidarity. No longer can a person be declared evil for where they were born. No longer should anyone be looked down upon for being different than us.

"My friends, my people, today is the beginning of a new age for us. Our faith and our mission may have become blurred, but you know as well as I do that we still have a chance in this world. Out of the debris of Myst-Garvon can rise something new, something even greater than before. For too long have we been a distant, intolerant people, and if it is anything that my travels have taught me it is that the rest of the world has merit.

"I have seen wizards ready to lay down their lives to maintain their principles of neutrality, showing me that sometimes it is braver not to fight back. I have seen the poor, downtrodden and displaced souls that this war has affected, traveling to places like Travell because they had nowhere else to go. Our benevolent continent will not take them in! I have seen a man and a woman from two feuding nations reconcile their differences to fight together against a common foe. I have seen a man selflessly pursue justice and protecting the meek at the same time as a matter of duty, forsaking all personal gain. We have much to learn, but we have many sources to learn from!

"Elestia once told me that we must be of one mind to save our world, and I have held those words close to my heart ever since. But never were they more true! This is why I believe there is still hope for us. Our future begins now, today, and it will not wait until tomorrow. We will let the world know of our love for it and our acceptance of its differences while still maintaining our own beliefs and mission. Should those of the world choose to worship next to us then so be it! And if not, then we will allow them their freedom and love them anyway. Whether people are born in a certain place or not, whether they believe in a certain thing or not, they are all our brothers and sisters and they live just as hard lives as we do. The people of this world deserve our respect, and they shall have it.

"Henceforth I shall be Seeress Starka, and today shall be the first day of the Age of Acceptance!"

A riotous cheer rose up from the crowd as if it had been holding back since her first word. Starka turned to glance at the crew of the *Bloody Lady* and saw them all tearful. Turning back to the people she had accepted to rule, Starka realized the hope she talked about was alive in her.

Her journey killed the scared girl of her youth, and gave birth to the brave woman she never knew she could be. Whether it happened that night in Ferraut or sometime after, for the first time Starka felt her rebirth was complete. She mouthed a prayer of thanks to the Divine Female before she went to disembark and join her people.

EPILOGUE

THE NINTH AVATAR HAS ASCENDED.

The words carried as much reason for celebration as they did woe as he wrote them on a parchment bound for Flaem. Cairos figured they might already be aware of the events that brought about the Ascension, but they had not witnessed it. Save Adamis, of course, who rapped at the chamber door just as Cairos thought of him.

"Enter," he called.

The hood and gloves masked the man's features, but Cairos was used to his presence. "Elder Cairos," came the whispered greeting. "The students are ready in the quad for the null zone demonstration. Fabfast has asked me to remind you that you promised to attend."

"Very well," he replied, "I'll be along shortly."

Adamis nodded and turned to leave.

"Professor?" The word seemed both strange and fitting at the same time. Perhaps the whole business of being in charge was the same, Cairos thought. "Will you be attending?"

"Ah, no," said Adamis. "I have sixteen students presenting on Light Deprivation this morning. I hear the things they have discovered bear direct interest to keep things from getting out of hand with the exchange students."

"I see." Cairos smiled at the exchange program — his idea to unite Flaem and Illiadora in the new world. "Well, perhaps we can swap results over a mug of ale later on."

"Perhaps." With that, Adamis left.

Cairos wetted the tip of his quill and continued the letter to the Elders of Flaem. Operations at the school picked up considerably since the end of the war, and even the Elders could not deny the value in their students studying under the man who *knew* the Avatar before his ascension. Their questions never ceased about the nature of the man himself, but Cairos' answers never changed.

DaVille remained an unknown; Starka was the only person to ever peer inside of his soul, but far be it from Flaem's Elders to write to her. Cairos realized that he owed the new Seeress a letter, as well, and moved to pull another parchment from a nearby shelf.

Things were going well, he mused, and he had enough work and research to keep all the wizards in two cities busy. At least until the next war.

SEERESS STARKA PRAYED OVER THE ENTOMBED REMAINS OF HER brother as the first brick was laid over the top of his resting place. She wiped a tear away and waved off an attendant holding a handkerchief.

"Regardless of our differences," she declared to the congregated mass, "the people of this world are owed our attention in this new age. I have known them, and I have known their hearts. May my brother rest in peace knowing he contributed to bringing us all together in a world of peace, however tentative it might prove to be."

She thought again of DaVille and his sacrifice, remembering where they had found his body tangled up with the creature Zion. While the Carrion commander had wasted away to no more than a blackened skeleton, the body of DaVille remained intact — though wounded and marked in ways that gave her nightmares even days later.

His suffering was complete, she thought while sighing, and the rest of ours continues. DaVille's name garnered a gross amount of popularity after his death and apparent ascension, but Starka would take the location of his buried body with her to the grave.

King Ettubruté and his daughter died a scant week after her visit to Ferraut, and Starka felt it only fitting she form some kind of communication with King Hakkark. Establishing a worldwide church would be more difficult than she thought, but Starka prayed for strength and resolve from Garvon as well as patience from Alsher. With the memories of Fandur and DaVille always fresh in her mind, Starka settled into her chambers with a heap of parchment and began to add her own volume to the new Holy Book.

The new Church of Myst could still not endorse use of the powers of the Nine Pillars, but they could not afford to be ignorant of it either. As Starka penned her tale, she wondered what the future might bring.

IN THE FINAL WEEKS OF HER PREGNANCY, MAYRAH SUFFERED greatly from the effect on her body. By some miracle, a group of Mystian missionaries had taken up residence outside Brong. They were more kind than she remembered of their ilk, and attributed that to Starka's influence as their new leader. After hours and hours of painful labor, the priest she had befriended announced her addition to the world.

"Twins! A boy and a girl!"

Her joyful tears were thanks enough to Wan Du's deity and her own; she believed they had replaced the child she gave up months before and also had given her another. As she lay awkwardly on her side in the birthing chamber, Mayrah smiled despite the exhaustion.

In Brong she had started a new family, a new people, and a new future. Mayrah said a quiet prayer of thanks to DaVille before sleep overtook her.

ABOUT THE AUTHOR

Author Photo by Stephanie Romine

TODD NEWTON HAS BEEN READING SCIENCE FICTION AND FANTASY
and writing habitually since childhood. *The Ninth Avatar* is his debut epic
fantasy novel. Todd holds a Computer Science degree, works in technology and
lives in Colorado with his wife, Micah, and their two dogs, Leonidas and Suki.
He is currently completing his third novel.

LaVergne, TN USA
13 January 2011
212285LV00003B/86/P